COURTING EMILY

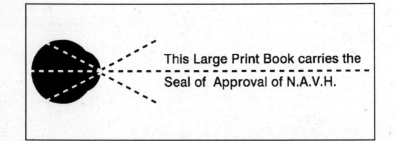

This Large Print Book carries the
Seal of Approval of N.A.V.H.

COURTING EMILY

AMY LILLARD

THORNDIKE PRESS

A part of Gale, Cengage Learning

GALE
CENGAGE Learning·

Farmington Hills, Mich • San Francisco • New York • Waterville, Maine
Meriden, Conn • Mason, Ohio • Chicago

GALE
CENGAGE Learning·

Lillard,
Amy

LIBRARY OF CONGRESS CATALOGING-IN-PUBLICATION DATA

Lillard, Amy.
    Courting Emily / by Amy Lillard. — Large print edition.
      pages cm. — (Thorndike Press large print clean reads) (Wells Landing ; #2)
    ISBN 978-1-4104-7762-0 (hardcover) — ISBN 1-4104-7762-2 (hardcover)
    1. Amish—Fiction. 2. Large type books. I. Title.
PS3612.I4C68 2015
813'.6—dc23   2014047730

Published in 2015 by arrangement with Zebra Books, an imprint of Kensington Publishing Corp.

Printed in Mexico
1 2 3 4 5 6 7 19 18 17 16 15

*To all my newfound friends in
Lancaster County.
Thank you for answering my
many questions,
for reading,
and sharing your stories with me.
I'm eternally grateful.*

*To Emily,
for lending your name to this character,
and to Stacey,
for always being there whenever
I need help.
You mean more to me than you will
ever know.*

ACKNOWLEDGMENTS

I have so many people I need to thank for helping me with this book. So many that I'm sure to forget to add someone. Please forgive me if I do.

My thanks go out to Stacey Barbalace, for always reading even when you've already read it time and time again. To Amy Clipston and family, for continually answering my questions about stock car racing. They are the true champions and any mistakes are mine.

I owe a special gratitude to my editor John Scognamiglio, for loving this story (almost) as much as I do. To Team Kensington, thanks for making my books look so fabulous. And many thanks to the editorial staff for making this country girl look like a pro. That is not an easy feat! I appreciate all that you do.

And of course to my family, for suffering through first writes and rewrites, edits, and

all the late nights when the deadline looms.
My "boys" are the best.

PROLOGUE

"Come with me." Luke Lambright took her hands in his, warm and calloused. Emily's skin tingled where he touched her. Oh, how she wanted to tell him yes.

Bright sunlight spilled all around them. How could she tell him *nay*? She had loved him as long as she could remember. She loved everything about him, from his dancing blue eyes to his unruly hair that was as dark as a raven's wing. He was the handsomest boy she had ever seen. Since they were no more than ten or twelve, they had talked about getting married, the children they would have, their house, their farm.

But now he was leaving. In broad daylight. Boldly walking away from the Plain life they had always known. Walking away from their shared dreams of a simple life in Wells Landing.

Luke wanted to experience the *Englisch* world, go to see movies, dance, and drive a race car for money. Even as much as she loved him she couldn't understand what spurred his dreams in such a different direction.

"Luke, I —" She stopped short of giving him an answer. Her heart wanted to tell him one thing, but every other part of her knew she had to stay. Tears sprang into her eyes. She blinked them back. "I —"

As if he knew she was about to tell him no, he pulled her into the circle of his arms. He held her close. Pressed against his warmth, she felt like she was home. His heart pounded under her ear, his breathing steady and true.

"How can I leave?" She managed to keep her voice from cracking, the building sob from escaping.

"How can I stay?"

She pulled away to look into his blue eyes. Normally they sparkled with a mischief to rival any *Englisch* troublemaker, but today they were cloudy with longing and hurt.

"You can't ask me to choose, Emily. I can't."

"I know," she whispered. "Nor can I."

Leaving with Luke, leaving Wells Landing would mean saying good-bye to her family, her *mudder* and *vatter* and all of her *shveshtah.* And because she had already joined the church, a *meidung* for sure. A shunning.

"Ich liebe dich," he said, cupping her face in his hands and pressing a kiss to her forehead.

"I love you, too."

How could she leave? How could she ask him to stay? Why, oh why, did love have to hurt so bad?

He trailed his fingers down the snowy white linen of her prayer *kapp,* tracing an errant tear that had somehow managed to escape.

"I'll call you, you know."

She nodded.

"And I'll come back for visits. I'm not a member of the church. They won't shun me."

She tried to smile at his hopeful words. But would her father let her visit with the wayward son of the community? She knew he wouldn't. *Dat* would barely let her see Luke a'tall now as it was. They had been sneaking around so much, they didn't even ask for courting visits any longer. And once he left the community —

"Are you afraid I'm going to forget you?"

Emily swallowed hard and gave a small nod. It was her worst fear of all: he would forget her and find some *Englisch* girl who understood things like race car driving.

11

"I could never forget you, Em. You're my best girl."

She closed her eyes as he traced the outline of her brow, the curve of her jaw. *Lord, please protect him; let him see the error of his ways. Let him come back to me.*

A car horn honked. Emily started at the noise, her nerves and emotions raw from the pain.

"I've got to go." He gave her a small kiss, just a brief touch of his lips against hers, and then he was gone.

Emily watched, tears running unheeded down her face as he hoisted his suitcase and placed it in the trunk of the car. He still wore his Amish clothes, though his shirt was untucked and his hat had been shucked long ago. Already he looked different. Already he was apart from her.

He looked back at her once as the *Englisch* driver revved the engine. Luke smiled and waved, then opened the door and disappeared inside.

She pressed the back of one hand to her mouth to stifle her sobs as the blue car pulled away taking with it the only boy she had ever loved.

How was she ever going to live the rest of her days and be happy without Luke?

CHAPTER ONE

"Emily? What are you doing out here all by yourself?"

Emily Ebersol jumped as the voice sounded behind her. She whirled away from the sight of the beautiful Thoroughbred horses that Abe Fitch and his nephew kept and turned to face Becky Riehl. "W-what? I mean, *jah*. I'm fine."

Becky's gaze followed the line of sight and watched as the horses frolicked and played. Twin dimples dented her cheeks as she turned her attention back to Emily. "I didn't ask how you were. I asked what you were doing out here alone. There is a wedding celebration going on at the house." She gestured behind her toward the rambling farmhouse Andrew Fitch shared with his *onkle* Abe.

"*Jah*. Right." Had she been so deep in thought that she hadn't even heard the teen's words correctly? "I just —" Needed a

13

break? Had to get away? Wanted some time alone? She dipped her chin toward the pasture. "You know."

Becky stepped up to the fence and folded her arms across the top wooden slat. "They are *schee.*"

Emily allowed her gaze to wander back to the beautiful horses dotting the lush green field. The scene was pastoral and peaceful yet it brought her no comfort. "Why aren't you with the others at the singing?"

Caroline and Andrew's wedding was over, but the celebration had just started. There would be a singing in the afternoon and another in the evening with more food and cake in between.

Becky made a face, somewhere between a smile and a grimace. "They're still getting everything ready, but I don't think I'm staying."

"Is Billy Beiler sitting with someone else?"

The young girl sighed. She'd had a crush on Billy as long as Emily could remember. Even when they were both in the schoolhouse and Emily was their teacher.

"You know tradition," Emily said. "He'll sit with a different girl at each singing. All the *buwe* will."

Becky sighed again. "That still doesn't mean he'll sit with me."

14

As true as the statement was, Emily could offer no rebuttal. What sort of advice could she give? The one man she wanted had left the Amish entirely. She hadn't heard from Luke in months, even with all of his promises to call. And she worried that by now he had forgotten all about her. She pushed the thought away and concentrated on the girl before her. "He surely can't sit with you if you are out here with me."

"Will you go in with me?"

"Of course." Despite the differences in their ages, Emily had always gotten along well with Becky. She supposed it was the other things they had in common that bonded them together. Like the fact that both of their families relied on dairy animals for their primary living and the number of girls in each house. Both Emily and Becky had four other sisters to share the burdens of cooking and cleaning.

Emily linked her arm with Becky's and turned them back toward the house where the wedding celebration was in a small lull. The first round of dinner had been served and the next wave was waiting.

The last thing Emily wanted was to go back into the house and watch her friend Caroline with all her wedding-day happiness. It was petty of her, she knew, but see-

15

ing her friends and their pleasure together was almost more than she could take in such a large quantity. She'd have to pray about it tonight. Maybe again in the morning.

If only Luke hadn't left.

"The twins were sad when you didn't return to teaching this year," Becky said as they made their way up the drive toward the house. "Little Norma, too."

"*Jah.* I miss teaching them and seeing them each day." She was sad as well, but her father had decided she needed to be at home helping with her mother's cheese-making business. Maybe one day she could convince *Dat* to let her go back to teaching. Until then, she was doing all she could to make the best of the situation.

Normally the singing would be held in the barn, but it was a beautiful, early fall day, and the benches had been set up around back. The weather in Oklahoma was typical: the sun shone bright and the wind ruffled the leaves in the trees. It was far too nice of a day to sit indoors.

"*Dat* thought it would be best for me to help with the girls and with *Mamm*'s business."

Becky nodded as if she understood, but the young girl would never truly know how

Emily felt. Teaching had been the one thing that had been hers and hers alone. To have to give that up mere weeks after Luke had left . . . Well, she had prayed and prayed. Maybe she would understand one day herself.

They had just rounded the corner when Elam Riehl, Becky's older brother, approached, the brim of his hat pulled low over his eyes. "There you are, Becky. It's time to go."

Becky bit her lip and cast her glance to where the young people were starting to settle themselves in their seats. "Can't we stay just a little while longer? The singings are just about to begin."

Elam shook his head. "*Ach,* no. The cows have to be milked whether there are singings or not." Then he added, "*Goedemiddag,* Emily," as if he had only then realized his sister wasn't alone. He tipped his hat toward her, settling it a little higher up on his forehead.

"*Goedemiddag,*" she returned.

Why had she never noticed before how big Elam was? Maybe she only noticed now because his bulk seemed to block the sun. Or perhaps that was the fault of his serious green eyes and stern mouth.

His demeanor brooked no argument and

something in Emily hated the disappointment on Becky's sweet face. It wasn't her fault the cows needed to be milked. "If it's okay with your *bruder,* I can take you home if you want to stay for the singing."

"You will?" Becky gushed, then she sobered slightly as she turned back to Elam. "Is that *allrecht?*"

He seemed to weigh her words, against what Emily didn't know. Had he always been this serious? "*Jah,* fine. I suppose I can do without your help for a spell. But you can only stay for the first singing. After that *Mamm* will need help gathering eggs and such."

"*Danki,* Elam." Becky flashed her dimples in her brother's general direction, then looped her arm with Emily's once more. "Let's go, Em. Maybe we can still get a *gut* seat."

Emily allowed herself to be dragged across the yard. She only looked back once to see Elam staring after them, hands on his hips and a saddened look tainting his features.

Elam was careful not to let the screen door slam behind him as he entered the house. He kept his hat on as he made his way across the living room and into the kitchen. Just a quick glass of water, then it was on to

18

milking. He stood at the sink and poured himself a drink, staring out the window at the backyard as he took a sip.

"Elam, is that you?"

"*Jah, Mamm.*"

He heard the bedroom door close behind her, then her soft footsteps as she came down the hall. He turned and waited for the woman he had called *mudder* since he was eight years old. After his own *mamm* had passed on, his father decided that two men had no business being without a nurturing hand. As far as Elam was concerned, it was the best decision James Riehl had ever made.

"Is he sleeping?" he asked as she appeared at the kitchen door. Her eyes were heavy and tired and deep lines bracketed her mouth.

"*Jah.*" She shot him an encouraging smile as if to say everything was fine, but they both knew that wasn't the truth. Things hadn't been all right in a long time.

"Where's Becky?" she asked.

"I let her stay at the wedding. They were about to have a singing."

Mamm nodded. They both wanted Becky to have as normal a *rumspringa* as possible. *Jah,* she was needed at home, but there were other things important in life as well.

Yet the attempt at normalcy was beginning to take its toll.

"Emily Ebersol offered to bring her home. Are the twins here to help?"

Mamm smiled, and this one almost reached her tired blue eyes. "They took the girls down to the pond to fish. I thought that would be *gut* for *natchess, jah*? Fresh *katzfisch*?"

"*Jah.*"

"I can call them back if 'n you need their help."

Elam shook his head. "I'll go fetch them." He needed them to sweep the floors, help with the milking machines, and tote the milk to the cooler. Even with them, there was still so much to do.

"Joy?"

At the sound of *Dat*'s call, *Mamm* turned. "I was so hoping he would sleep until supper." She sighed, the sound resigned and heavy.

Guilt stabbed at Elam. "I should hire you some help. Or at the very least make the girls help more." But neither choice sat well with him.

How much longer could they go on this way? How much longer before one of them broke?

Mamm turned back, patted him on the

cheek, and attempted her smile once again. "I am all right, Elam. If any help gets hired, it would be for you. Now go get your milking done. There is nothing to worry about here."

She made her way down the hall, but Elam knew: there was plenty to worry about. Plenty more and then some.

Emily bumped shoulders with Becky as the horse cantered along. The singing had gone almost according to plan. Billy Beiler hadn't sat with Becky, but he had talked to her a bit afterward.

Yet Emily had to cut their chat short, haunted by the somber look in Elam's eyes as he told his sister to come home right after the singing. It wasn't just his eyes though. His whole demeanor was chock-full of seriousness and woe, as if he carried a burden too big for even his broad shoulders to manage and too precious to share with others.

"Is Elam always that . . . stern?" She tried to pick a word that didn't sound so negative.

"I prefer to think of it as thoughtful," Becky chirped. It was amazing to Emily that Becky was so bubbly while Elam was not.

"Thoughtful then," Emily amended.

Becky shook her head. "Only since the accident."

How had she forgotten the terrible accident that had rendered James Riehl practically helpless? Or maybe she had thought in the year since he had been kicked in the head by a cantankerous milk cow that he had somehow become whole again.

"How is your *dat*?"

"The same." Becky shrugged, though her dancing blue eyes dimmed just a bit. Was her perpetual joy just a front to hide the stresses at home?

Regret swamped Emily. She had been so caught up in her own problems that she hadn't given the trials of others a second thought. Her father would be so disappointed if he knew. Just one more thing she needed to pray about. The Amish always cared for their neighbors, always looked after the community. That philosophy went double for a bishop's daughter. She had fallen down on both accounts.

Emily bit back a sigh as she turned the buggy into the packed dirt drive that led to the Riehls' dairy farm. She didn't know how many cows they kept, but she knew their property stretched almost into the next county. Was Elam taking care of business by himself? There were no other Riehl sons, but surely a cousin or two came around to help from time to time.

She pulled the horse to a stop. Surely . . .

"*Danki* for the ride, Emily. That was sure *gut* of you."

"*Gern gschehne,*" she replied though her attention was centered on the rambling farmhouse and its peeling paint.

She hadn't realized the Riehls had fallen on to such hard times. Did anyone in the district know? She'd have to ask her father about it the minute she got home.

"Becky," she started. "Can I stay and help you gather the eggs?" She wasn't sure where the words came from, but once they were said, she was thankful for them. She had been wallowing in her own problems for far too long.

"You'd do that?" Becky's eyes sparkled, then her smile faded. She shook her head. "*Danki,* Emily. That is a kind offer to be sure, but the chickens are my responsibility."

As if they had tarried too long, Elam emerged from the milking barn, a scowl marring his handsome features.

The thought drew Emily back. Elam was a handsome man, or at least he would be if he didn't look like he'd taken a big bite from a green persimmon.

23

"Becky, time to work."

The young girl gave a quick nod, then turned her gaze back to Emily. "Thank you again."

"Becky." Elam propped his hands onto his hips, his impatience evident. "*Mamm* needs you inside."

"*Jah, bruder.*" She turned as if to go into the house, but not before Emily saw the shine of tears in her blue eyes.

"Some potatoes for you?"

"Huh?" Emily turned as her sister Mary nudged her shoulder to get her attention. "Oh, *jah. Danki.*" She took the bowl from her sister though her thoughts were still on Elam's stern frown and the glitter of tears in Becky's eyes.

"Have you heard from Luke?" Mary leaned close as she handed off the bowl full of mashed potatoes, her voice so soft only Emily could hear. "Jonah Miller said he called his uncle yesterday."

At the mention of his name, thoughts of all others fled from her mind. "He did?" It was hard to temper her response to a whisper when she really wanted to shout with glee. Luke had called!

"*Jah.*"

Her heart thumped hard in her chest.

"Who told you that? Aaron?"

"Girls." Their father glared at them from the head of the table.

"Jah, Dat," Emily murmured, passing the potatoes on to her sister Susannah. She'd have to talk with Mary later, after supper, maybe during chore time.

As the oldest, Emily was expected to oversee her sisters, but surely she and Mary could sneak a minute or two to talk. She had three more sisters, after all.

Rose was perhaps the most demure and motherlike one of them all, even though at eighteen Mary was two years older. At twelve years old and the baby, Bea hadn't quite figured out where she fit into the family. Not as gingery as middle child Susannah nor as retiring as Rose and Mary. She was more like Emily than any of the others.

Excitement filled Emily as she thought of news from Luke. It had been months since he'd left, nearly four to be exact, but this was the first she had heard from him.

He had promised to call, but she knew how difficult that would be. It wasn't like he could call the shanty out in front of their house. Her father was as sure to get that message as any one of the Ebersol family. Nor was Luke big on writing letters. He was more into action, living, breathing, having fun.

But he had called. Emily ducked her head and smiled down at her plate lest her father see the joy she could not contain. Luke had called. He had gotten a message to Jonah Miller. He hadn't forgotten about her after all.

CHAPTER TWO

After supper, it was Mary's turn to help with the dishes and their mother's cheese making, while Emily and their other sisters headed out to the barn to help their father.

The goats they used for their mother's business had been milked at four-thirty as was their usual custom, but now the horses had to be fed, the stalls mucked out, the few cows they kept for personal use needed to be milked.

Yet all Emily could think about was Luke.

"You are very quiet tonight, *dochder.*" Her father didn't look up from his milking, but Emily was the only one around.

Susannah and Rose had gone to see to the stables, while Bea had stayed in with Mary to help their mother. *Dat* was talking to her.

"Oh, *jah?*" She tried her best to sound off-handed and casual, like she wasn't exploding inside from the *gut* news about Luke.

"Not so much at supper though." Again he didn't look at her, just kept his head down close to Sadie's belly.

His tone made Emily's heart stop in her throat. She knew she wasn't going to like what he had to say next. The fact was further confirmed as he grabbed the milk pail and stood. He handed it to Emily and slapped the cow on the rump to send her back to the pasture. Then he replaced his brimless "milking" hat with his regular one and leveled his serious blue gaze to hers. "It does not look good for the bishop's daughter to be pining after someone who has left our faith."

She opened her mouth to protest, but her *vatter* continued. "Luke Lambright has brought shame onto his family. Onto his community. It's time to move forward."

"But he'll return." Even as she said the words, she doubted them. She wanted to believe them. After all, so many who left the Amish quickly came back. It was just a matter of time, was all. Soon Luke would tire of the competition in the *Englisch* world, the strange customs, and unfamiliar faces. When that happened he would come running back, and she would be there waiting for him.

Her father's mouth twisted into a frown

above his dark beard. "You don't know that he will."

"You don't know that he won't."

At her sharp tone, *Dat* raised one brow, a sign she had gone too far.

"I'm sorry, *Dat.* I just —" She stopped as he shook his head.

"Do I have to remind you that you have already bowed your knees and joined the church?"

Emily lowered her chin to her chest. "No, *Vatter.*" Her words were apologetic and humble. But she wanted to remind her *dat* that Luke hadn't joined the church. He was not shunned in the community. He could get this out of his system and come back, kneel before everyone, and state his intentions. He could still join the church, and then they could be married, just like they'd always talked about.

"Hear me." His voice dropped and the bishop became her father once again.

Emily raised her gaze to meet his.

"You are not the only one who has been left with a broken heart. It is an uncomfortable place, but it is where you find yourself now."

She blinked back her tears. She would have been better off with his stern frown rather than his caring tone. She didn't want

29

to cry, she didn't want Luke to be gone, and she surely didn't want what she knew was coming next.

"It is time to move forward. Time to think about someone who has joined the church."

It was the very last thing she wanted to do. Yet what choice did she have?

"I will not tell you who you should consider, but only that you need to leave your heart open for the new."

She nodded and sniffed. She would not cry. She would not cry.

"I do not tell you these things to hurt you."

"I know," she whispered.

"There's always Elam Riehl," her father said. "He seems to be in your thoughts a lot lately."

True, he had been on her mind. Or at least his family had. But for no other reason than she had realized someone in her community was suffering and needed help.

Elam Riehl was about as opposite to Luke as one could imagine. Luke was just a little taller than she was, slim and trim with laughing blue eyes and a permanent smile on his lips. Elam was large, solid looking, taller than most men she knew, and as serious as a wake.

If she was remembering correctly, Elam

was three or four years older than she and Luke, which would put him close to twenty-five. If her father needed to wonder about something, it should be why Elam had never married. Thankfully she managed to keep that question to herself.

"I'll give it some thought." Emily said the words solely to appease her father. What more could she do?

He gave her a quick nod, then pointed to the milk pail at her feet. "Best get that on in to your *mudder.*"

"Jah." Emily picked up the pail and carted it to the house.

"Are you asleep?" Mary's quiet voice floated on the darkness to Emily.

"Nay." She hadn't been able to settle down enough to close her eyes, much less fall asleep. All she could think about was Luke and Elam and Elam and Luke.

Her father expected a lot to assume that Elam would even *want* to court her. Not that she would give it any more thought than she already had. But it seemed she was going to have to do something to keep her father from out and out finding her a husband.

She heard the soft patter of Mary's bare feet as she padded across the wood floor.

31

"Scoot over." Her sister lifted the covers and slid into the bed beside her.

In the darkened room, Emily could just make out Mary's sweet face so like their mother's. "You should be asleep," she said even though she was grateful to have her sister near.

Emily was the only daughter with her own room. Mary shared with Rose while Susannah and Bea occupied the bedroom right across the hall. Still she would miss nights like this when Mary married Aaron Miller, Jonah Miller's younger brother.

"So should you."

Four-thirty came early. But the goats had to be milked before the younger Ebersol girls headed to school.

"I heard about what *Dat* said to you tonight in the barn."

"Who told you?"

"Susannah."

"She is a gossip," Emily grumbled.

At fourteen, Susannah was a little more . . . spirited than the rest of them, a little more like Luke Lambright than their father would have preferred.

Mary found Emily's hand under the covers and gently squeezed her fingers. "She loves you as much as we all do."

"She is probably the one who told *Dat*

Luke called and started this whole mess."

"You don't believe that."

"*Nay.* I don't." Emily sighed into the darkness. "What am I supposed to do? Now *Dat* has this in his head about me and Elam . . . he'll never let it rest. I've already said I would go help at their house. *Dat* will probably do everything he can to make me known to Elam. How embarrassing."

"I am certain everything will work out just fine."

"I hope so."

They lay quietly in the darkness, each absorbed in her own thoughts.

"I miss him so much," Emily finally said. "I just want to talk to him, hear his voice, know that he's *allrecht* out there among the *Englisch.*"

"He will call when he can," Mary said, her tone reassuring and so very much like their mother's. She didn't even ask who Emily was talking about. She knew right away it was Luke.

"Do you really think so?" Emily hated the urgent quality in her voice. She had always been so confident when it came to Luke, never once doubting his love for her. Now everything was different, changing, and she wasn't sure what to do about it. Or if there was anything she could do.

"You know he would never call here," Mary said, her words referring to the phone shanty that sat just across the road from their farm.

"*Jah*. I know." But it didn't lessen her disappointment.

"Be strong, *shveshtah*."

She would be strong, for her, for Luke. And she would pray. Pray that soon the lure of the *Englisch* world would dull, and Luke would return to Wells Landing once again.

"Jonah." Emily raced down the sidewalk behind her friend's beau. After the conversation with her *vatter* the night before, Emily knew it was time to do something. If she sat back, her life would blow right on past her, taking Luke and all her dreams along with it. She didn't want to court anyone else; she wanted Luke, plain and simple. "Jonah Miller," she called again.

He finally heard her, stopping to allow her to catch up with him. She was breathless by the time she did.

"*Goedemiddag*," he said as she gasped for air. "Are you *allrecht*?"

Emily gulped and nodded. It had taken three blocks of running as fast as she could, but she finally managed to catch him. "I heard . . . you talked . . . to Luke."

"Oh, *jah*. He called a couple of days ago."

A couple of days? Why had no one told her? "How is he?" She was so desperate for news that she forgot herself and clutched Jonah's arm.

He looked down at her hand.

She let him go and twisted her fingers together as she waited for his answer.

"He's *gut*."

"Did he" — she paused — "did he mention me?"

Jonah rubbed the back of his neck with a grimace. "*Nay,* Emily. But I figured you had already talked to him."

She shook her head, doing her best to hide her disappointment. "My *dat* would have a fit if he called the phone shanty. You know how he can be."

Jonah nodded.

Luke Lambright had brazenly left the community. He'd walked out on the promises he'd made to Emily and the people who had known him his entire life. Cephas Ebersol did not take such abandonment lightly.

"Did he say when he was coming back?"

Jonah flashed her that pained face once again. "He's really busy right now, Emily."

"*Jah,* I know." She said the words as a pang of something she couldn't name settled in her heart. Longing? Worry? Fear?

35

Was Luke out there in the *Englisch* world having so much fun that he hadn't thought about her even once?

She shook her head. There was nothing to worry about. Luke himself had told her how special they were together. She was his girl. Whether they were miles apart or next door to each other, nothing would change that.

"I miss him," she confessed in a whisper. So much so that she had left her booth at the market unattended. That wasn't unheard of. Oftentimes, they put up a collection box and trusted the customers to pay the correct amount and take only what they bought. But she ran his best friend down on the street to find out any news. Her mother would be ashamed if she knew.

Emily smoothed her prayer *kapp* and ran her hands down the sides of her dress to gather herself back.

"I'm going down to meet Lorie. Want to walk with me?" Jonah asked with a nod toward the park.

She shook her head. So much had changed this fall. Now that Caroline and Andrew were married, Caroline only worked part-time at the bakery. Gone were the days of meeting in the park for lunch. Lorie and Jonah seemed to be getting along better. At least they had gone for a couple of months without a breakup.

With Luke away, she felt . . . lonely.

Jah, that was the word. Lonely. Alone. It was all the same.

"Have fun." She started back toward the market, but turned and caught Jonah's attention once again. "If you talk to him . . ."

His tawny eyes filled with understanding. *"Jah,"* he said. "I will."

Emily trudged back up the sidewalk. It was a beautiful October day, still early enough in the month that the Indian summer remained in control of the temperatures. But it wouldn't be long until the market closed for the season. Once the pumpkins were all harvested and the weather turned cold, her job would be over until the spring.

She sighed and collapsed onto the stool behind her booth. She missed teaching, more than she could have ever dreamed.

"Why so sad on such a beautiful day?"

Her head jerked up and her heart pounded as she shaded her eyes. *"Ach,* Elam Riehl. You scared me half to death."

"I did not mean to." He rapped his knuckles on the wooden stand. "I just wanted to say *danki* for bringing Becky home after the singing Saturday."

"It was the least I could do."

37

He seemed to mull that over. "So why are you?"

"Why am I what?"

"Sad on such a beautiful day?"

She shook her head, unable to say the words. To do so would make the reality all the more real.

"I am guessing Luke Lambright."

It was no secret that she and Luke had been intended for years. They hadn't announced anything, but everyone just assumed that one day they would marry. Then Luke learned to drive a car, and the rest was still being written. She didn't understand his need to see the world, but she tried to. She could not fathom why he wanted to drive a car in circles. She had tried. She really had. In the end, she knew she had to let him go. Yet the fact he had chosen the world over her . . . it made her feel a little like the last puppy left in the litter, the one no one wanted.

"Your *dat* sent word that he'd bring some men to come paint this weekend," Elam continued.

Emily nodded. "We thought you could use some help."

He looked away, and she couldn't read the expression in his dark green eyes.

"Danki." He turned back to her, his features blank.

Nay, that wasn't it. His expression was . . . controlled, as if he didn't want her to see what was going on behind it.

"He also said you would be coming by tomorrow to help *Mamm.* "

He did?

Emily tried not to let her surprise show. She should have expected as much. Just like she had told Mary last night, her father had set his mind to her marrying Elam Riehl. *"Jah,"* she said, hoping she didn't look too stunned. What was it the *Englisch* said? Like a deer in the headlights?

She supposed her *vatter* would get someone to take her place at the market or not open their stand at all.

"Why are you here today?" she asked Elam, then backtracked when she realized how rude she sounded. "I mean, Becky usually tends your booth."

He gave a quick nod. "Her youth group went on an overnight fishing trip."

So he had to come to the market after milking the cows and helping his *mamm* get the younger kids off to school. No wonder his eyes drooped at the corners.

"I'm sure she appreciates that," Emily finally said.

"Jah," Elam said. *"Danki* again." He rapped his knuckles against the table in front of her, then turned back toward his booth.

Elam could feel her eyes on him as he made his way back to his booth. It was strange being in town in the middle of the afternoon, and he was a little jumpy. There was just so much for him to do at the farm, but he and his *mamm* had agreed that Becky should be able to do as much as possible during her run-around time. As far as Elam was behind in the everyday chores, one more day wouldn't matter.

Oh, he kept up the milking and such. He had the girls to help him with that. But it took him nearly twice as long as it had when his father was well.

That had been just a year ago, but it seemed like much longer.

Elam was grateful that his father was still alive after the kick he'd received last September. Many a lesser man would have died. Yet as lucky as James Riehl had been, sometimes Elam could not help thinking he'd be better off if he had died.

He couldn't help those thoughts, and they stayed in his prayers each day. He didn't mind the extra work, not really, but seeing his father barely able to get around, not able to do any of the things he enjoyed made Elam grieve for his father as if he had succumbed to the crushing blow that fateful day. In a way, Elam supposed he had.

But it had not been God's will. That much Elam understood, even if he didn't understand the why.

Dan Troyer had just preached on that very subject last church Sunday.

They weren't supposed to question God. There was a wisdom in all that He did. But Elam did question, he did wonder. He prayed for forgiveness, then prayed for understanding. Then he got up at three-thirty and milked the cows.

Elam slid behind his table and checked his cooler to see how much milk he had left. Three more jugs and he would go home.

He checked the sun. With any luck he'd make it there just in time to start the milking again.

41

CHAPTER THREE

"Whoa." Emily pulled back on the reins and brought the buggy to a stop in front of the Riehl family's house. She had prayed last night that it wouldn't look as bad as she remembered, but it did. It looked . . . ragged, frayed around the edges, and in sore need of paint.

She knew her father and the other men had made plans to come tomorrow and get the house and barn spruced up. In the meantime, she and her sisters would spend the afternoon helping Joy Riehl get everything in the house spick-and-span new.

As if reading her thoughts, Joy came onto the porch drying her hands on a linen towel. She shaded her eyes against the bright noonday sun. "*Ach,* Emily Ebersol, have you come calling?"

Emily hopped down from the buggy and grabbed the basket from behind her seat. Her sisters, all save Bea, filed out of the buggy. Susannah went around to unhitch the horse.

"We came to help you today."

Joy's expression was unreadable as she looked around at all their faces.

"We brought you some bread and cookies." Mary stepped forward holding the box filled with goodies. The girls had stayed up late last night baking in order to bring the offering today.

A smile warbled on Joy's lips as if she wasn't sure whether to laugh or cry. "Come in," she said, her voice thick. "Come in."

The girls smiled and tromped to the porch, stopping to greet little Johanna Riehl as they entered the house.

"Have you come to mop?" Johanna asked them in *Deutsch*. At four, she hadn't learned English yet and wouldn't for another couple of years when she finally started to school.

"*Jah,*" Emily said, smiling down at the sweet-faced child. She was blond-haired and blue-eyed just like her mother.

Johanna popped her thumb into her mouth and solemnly surveyed the older girls.

"Are you going to help us mop?" Emily asked her.

Johanna nodded. "I'm a good helper," she said.

Emily laughed. "I'm sure you are."

She took Johanna by her free hand and led her into the house.

The girls immediately got to work. Emily and Susannah started on the downstairs while Rose and Mary made their way upstairs.

Her sisters returned a few minutes later carrying the sheets from the rooms. They laughed and joked with each other as they carted the bedclothes into the screened-in back porch where Joy Riehl kept her propane-powered washing machine.

Susannah grabbed the broom from beside the refrigerator and started to sweep.

"Where are your dusting rags?" Emily asked. She would set young Johanna to wiping down the baseboards behind Susannah.

"I — I don't know what to say." Tears filled Joy's eyes. Emily could see how tired and run-down the poor woman looked, and her heart went out to her.

"There is nothing to be said, Joy Riehl." She shot Elam's mother a quick smile.

"*Danki,*" Joy whispered.

"Why don't you go take a nap?" Emily suggested.

Joy shook her head. "*Nay.* I should help. Strip the rest of the beds . . . draw the water to mop."

44

But Emily wouldn't hear of it. "A nap," she said firmly. "You can help us most by taking a nap."

Joy grabbed her fingers and squeezed hard. "You are a blessing, Emily Ebersol. You and your sisters."

"*Danki,* Joy Riehl." Emily smiled. "Now about that nap."

Finally Joy agreed and retired to one of the downstairs bedrooms to rest.

Emily noticed there were two rooms downstairs and sadly enough Joy and her husband no longer shared a bed. She mentally chastised herself for being such a busybody. But she remembered how happy the couple had looked before the accident. Not that they showed outward affection. But a body could tell when two people were well-suited. Joy and James Riehl were one of those couples.

"Where do you suppose Elam is?" Susannah asked. She didn't bother to look up from her task of sweeping under the kitchen table, but Emily could hear the intention in her tone.

"I wouldn't know." Her voice held an edge she immediately regretted. "I suppose he is out in the pasture tending his stock."

Mary nodded, a smile twitching at the corners of her mouth.

"Why?" Emily demanded. "Are you thinking of courtin' him?"

"Emily Jane! What a thing to say. Surely you know I was asking for your sake."

"My sake?" Emily squeaked.

"*Jah.* Seems to me that with Luke gone, Elam would be the perfect choice for you."

"I don't see how," she huffed. "Besides, Luke is bound to return any day."

Susannah stopped sweeping. All the teasing had drained from her features leaving her expression serious. "You really believe he'll come back?"

Emily nodded emphatically. "*Jah.* I do. He just has to get this racing nonsense out of his system."

"And then what?" Susannah asked. "Do you really think *Dat* will let you marry him after all that?"

Technically, after a confession and shunning, the person would be welcomed back into the church. But Luke hadn't joined the church yet. He shouldn't even have to go through that when he returned.

"I don't know why not. After he joins the church."

Susannah shook her head. "That's the way it's supposed to work but . . ." She trailed off not needing to say the words for Emily to understand. Their father was honest and

46

fair to a fault, but he would not allow his daughters to consort with someone of the world. He simply would not tolerate it.

But Emily already had her argument in place for when Luke did return. What better testament to the power of God's forgiveness and supremacy than for the bishop's daughter to marry a wayward soul who had returned to grace.

"Elam's cute, though. Don't you think?" Mary asked.

Emily shrugged, unable to voice the words that ran through her mind just days ago. Elam was handsome, in a burly sort of way. Though she would never describe him as *cute.* He was steady, solid, and dependable. He sounded like one of those *Englisch* commercials for trucks she had seen on the television in the hardware store. He had nice eyes, she decided. Clear and green, though the last time she had seen him they had been clouded with pain and worry.

"All finished." Johanna smiled up at Emily, then popped her thumb into her mouth.

"Oh, no, *liebschdi.* Let's get your hands washed before we do that." Emily pulled the child's thumb from her mouth and led her over to the sink.

Johanna dutifully climbed onto the stool

47

and allowed Emily to help her wash her hands.

"You will be a *gut* mother," Susannah said quietly.

"When the time comes," Emily softly returned.

Just after three o'clock, Bea arrived. "The teacher let us out early today," she called as she marched into the house. Bea had been disappointed that their father hadn't let her skip school to help the Riehls and had vowed to join the other sisters as soon as possible.

Miriam and Ruthie Riehl followed behind her, their footsteps quiet. Were they trying to not disturb their father's rest? Emily hadn't seen him the entire time she'd been cleaning.

So far they had caught up the laundry, changed the sheets on all the beds save the ones downstairs, and swept and mopped from top to bottom.

"Emily," Norma squealed and threw herself into Emily's arms. "I have missed you."

Emily returned the young girl's hug. "I've missed you too. Have you been *gut* for Lilly Joyce?" she asked, indicating their new teacher.

Norma solemnly nodded. "She's nice,"

she said, then lowered her voice for only Emily to hear. "Just not as nice as you."

Emily chuckled and squeezed the girl a little tighter before letting her go. "Are you *hungerich?*" She took the child by the hand and led her toward the kitchen. "Come on, girls, let's get a snack before we start the rest of the chores."

"We must be quiet," Miriam said with a shake of her head. Her hair gleamed like copper in the sunshine streaming through the freshly cleaned windows.

"Elam will be angry if we wake *Vatter.*"

Elam's not here, Emily wanted to say. Yet she held her tongue. Is this how he ran his household? No wonder they all looked so . . . sad.

"Is everyone still here?" Becky burst through the front door, a pink flush topping her bright smile. "I am so glad to see you." She gave Emily a quick squeeze, then went to hug Susannah as well.

"How were things at the market today?"

Becky shrugged. "The same I suppose. I missed you being there."

"We were just about to have a snack," Susannah said.

As if on cue, Mary and Rose appeared tripping down the stairs to join the rest of the girls in the kitchen.

"It's almost like a sisters' day, *jah?*" Rose asked, smiling all around.

"Almost," Becky agreed with a grin of her own. Emily hadn't seen her smile like that in . . . *ach,* in a year for sure.

"What's going on out here?"

"*Mamm,*" Johanna squealed, jumping up and down as Joy approached.

"Have you been a *gut maedel?*"

"A very good girl." She nodded solemnly, though nothing could dim the sparkle in her clear blue eyes.

Joy swung her into her arms and sat at the table watching as the young girls bustled around preparing a snack large enough for everyone.

Emily was glad to see the purple smudges under Joy Riehl's blue eyes were not as dark as they had been before, the lines of worry bracketing her mouth not nearly as deep. The rest had done the woman some good. Emily's heart warmed at the thought.

"Joy."

A hush fell over the room as James Riehl called out to his wife. He had one hand clutching the wall and the other braced against his heart.

Uneasy glances flew around the room as all the Riehl daughters ducked their heads. Even Joy looked a little afraid that she had

50

disturbed her husband.

Afraid wasn't quite the word. More like *chagrined.* But why?

"James." Joy hastily rose to her feet, allowing Johanna to slide to the ground. "I'm sorry. Did we wake you?"

He moved his hand up to cradle his head as if the noise in the house was more than he could take. "I . . . my head hurts."

"I'll get you something." She rushed toward the back of the house. Emily could only suppose to the room where James slept. Emily had seen a variety of prescription medicine bottles on the nightstand.

She approached where James stood at the entrance of the kitchen. "Here," she said, offering him her arm. "Come sit down at the table. We were just about to have a snack."

He looked her up and down, starting with her prayer *kapp* and ending with the toes of her black walking shoes. "Who are you?" he asked.

She tried not to let her surprise at the question show itself to his watchful gaze. "Emily Ebersol."

He gave a gentle nod, but no spark of recognition showed in his eyes. He slid his arm through hers and allowed her to lead him to the table.

He wobbled on unsteady legs, or maybe it was his balance in general. He swayed as if he'd had too much dandelion wine, then collapsed into one of the kitchen chairs. The Riehl girls watched him as closely as the Ebersol girls watched the Riehls. What was wrong with everyone?

"Mary, get one more plate down, if you please."

Mary nodded, the strings of her *kapp* dancing wildly around her shoulders as she reached for another setting.

Joy returned with a bottle of pills and a glass of water, but other than her helping James take his medication, everyone else seemed frozen.

What was wrong with everybody? She looked to Becky for answers, but the young girl was too busy watching her father to pay Emily much mind.

"Would you like to go back to bed now?" Joy hovered at her husband's side. Emily could already see the grooves that bracketed her mouth etching themselves deeper.

"This girl offered me a snack," he rasped, pointing to Emily.

He was pale, wan, as if he hadn't been in the sun in months. Emily supposed he hadn't been, if he was unable to make his way from the bedroom to the kitchen without assistance.

"I'll bring you something to eat in your room. It's nice and dark in there," Joy said as if it was the best place on earth. The comment further cemented Emily's thoughts. But how could he survive in the dark? Everyone needed sunshine.

"Nay," James looked as though he tried to shake his head, but stopped the action midway. "I think I would like to eat here," he said. "With her." He raised a hand to point at Emily again.

She wasn't sure if she should be honored or frightened. One thing was certain: James Riehl didn't spend much time with his family anymore and that broke her heart. He was walking proof that God was good, life was precious, and they should all be grateful for the time they had together.

She smiled at James. "I'd be honored."

The girls relaxed a bit, though the noise level dropped. Emily was certain it was in deference to James's head injury. No one had said for certain, but she got the impression his head ached constantly and everything from light to sounds were magnified.

Yet it seemed as if the family needed something to be normal for once. Or at least for once in the last year. It was one other thing she could offer them in addition to a clean house.

Once everyone had a plate, Emily looked to Norma. "Did anything exciting happen at school today?"

The young girl glanced from Emily to her father before her gaze came to a stop on her mother. She shrugged, though Emily could tell she had something she wanted to say.

"Tell us," Emily encouraged. Something inside her said James Riehl needed this family connection more than he needed the pills his wife had brought him.

"Jacob Beiler brought a bullfrog to school today and turned it loose just before math."

"Inside the building?" Emily tried to imagine the one-room schoolhouse with a frog jumping wildly about. That shouldn't have been too much of a problem.

"Lilly Joyce is a'scared of frogs," Norma added while the twins nodded solemnly. They looked like they were about to burst with something they wanted to add, but neither one said a word.

Bea laughed. "You should have seen her face." She gave her own interpretation of the horror on the teacher's face. "She ran screaming from the building hollering, '*Mach schnell! Mach schnell!* There's a frog in the schoolhouse.' "

"She made us all leave and stand out in

the yard while she figured out what to do," Norma added.

"Then she sent Jacob back in to get the frog," Miriam finally said, unable to hold in the words any longer.

Emily was certain the Beiler family would be getting a visit from someone about the infraction, but she couldn't help the chuckle that escaped her. She was well aware of the adventures of Jacob Beiler as she taught him last year. The freckled face *bu* was a bit of a handful thanks to his playful nature.

Ruthie warmed up to the telling, adding her two cents into the mix. "But she realized he was going to take his time to collect the frog and sent Joshua in after him."

"Like his brother would be any better." Susannah laughed. This was her first year out of school. Emily couldn't tell if she missed the other kids or not. But from the look on her face right then, she did.

"So she sent me in after both of them," Bea added.

Everyone laughed.

"What happened to the frog?" James asked.

Up until that point, Emily hadn't been sure if James had even been paying attention to the story.

"I caught him," Bea said. Emily could tell

that she was suppressing her pride at accomplishing something that two boys couldn't.

"Did he pee on you?" James asked.

Bea made a face. *"Jah."*

James laughed. Not a belly-shaking laugh, but a gentle chuckle that sent a ripple of surprise through the group.

Jah, the Riehls were long overdue for some everyday joy.

"Time to finish up," Emily called. They had less than an hour before they would need to head back to their house and begin their milking. She couldn't say that she had accomplished everything she had wanted to, but she had given Joy and her daughters a jump start on getting back on track.

The girls gobbled down the last of their snacks and took their plates to the sink.

"Let's get you back to bed." Joy stood and took her husband's arm.

"I want to stay here," he said, watching as Mary started running water to clean up their mess.

Johanna climbed into her father's lap and laid her head on his chest. Her thumb went immediately into her mouth, and she closed her eyes.

"Jo." Becky reached for her sister, but James slapped her hands away.

"Leave her." His voice sounded like that of a petulant child.

"Now, James," Joy started. But whatever she was about to say was lost as a deep voice sounded from the doorway.

"What is going on in here?"

CHAPTER FOUR

Emily could feel the anger coming off Elam in waves like the ocean tide. He practically vibrated with it. But for the life of her, she couldn't figure out what he was so upset about.

"Are you going to answer me?"

She glanced around, only then noticing that Joy was gone. Where she had disappeared to was anybody's guess. Amid the earlier laughter and chattering, she might have stated her intentions, but Emily didn't hear. As the oldest, she figured it was her job to answer. Well, that and the fact that Elam's hard green eyes were pinned on her.

"We were just cleaning up from our snack." She tried to smooth the frown that puckered her brow. What was wrong with him?

He didn't say, just stood there, hands braced on his hips and nostrils flared like an angry bull. "Johanna, get down. *Mamm,* please help *Vatter* back to his bed."

Emily turned to see Joy behind her.

"Jah." The woman dipped her chin, and made her way over to her husband. She scooped Johanna from his lap and set her feet on the floor. *"Kumm,* James." She pulled the man to his feet, and the pair disappeared down the hallway.

"But . . . but . . ." James sputtered as his wife led him away.

"Miriam, Ruthie, it's time to set up the milking machines."

The red-haired twins ducked their heads and hurried out the back way.

It was as if they didn't want to pass by their *bruder* on their way out the door.

Then he turned those cold green eyes back to her.

Emily propped her hands on her hips and stared right back. Whatever was bothering Elam Riehl was not her fault. And clearly he was upset about something.

"Emily," Bea started, her voice small and hesitant. "Should I go help the twins?"

"Nay," Emily said without taking her gaze from Elam's. "It's time for us to leave."

"Jah, okay," she said.

The rest of her sisters slowly set their feet into motion, gathering their things as Elam continued to scowl at them all.

"Elam," Becky started, though her voice sounded as tiny as Bea's had earlier.

"It's time for you to sterilize the milk vats."

She looked about to protest, but obviously thought better of it. Instead she gave a quick nod to her brother and headed for the door.

"Take Johanna out with you. She can gather the eggs."

Becky backtracked to get her sister, and without a word all of the Riehl girls were gone.

"I think that's everything," Mary said. "All Joy has to do is take down the sheets from the line. Unless you want us to do it before we leave."

"You have done enough," Elam gruffed. But instead of sounding like praise, it was more of an accusation.

"Girls, go wait for me in the buggy." Emily'd had enough. They had come here to help and instead were being made to feel as if they had somehow intruded. This was definitely not the Amish way.

Her sisters didn't protest, all too ready to get away from Elam Riehl.

The door shut behind them, and Emily and Elam were left alone.

She crossed her arms and calmly met his hard gaze. "What's the matter with you, Elam Riehl?"

"What's wrong with me?" The words were barely controlled. "I came home to find my house chaotic and my father bothered with all kinds of noise and activity. What's wrong with you?"

Something in his words didn't ring true. There was more to his reaction than he was telling her. That was fine. Elam Riehl could keep his secrets. But he wasn't going to make them feel like they had been a burden instead of a help.

"Not a thing." She grabbed up the basket she'd used to bring in the baked goods. "Tell your *mamm* that we'll be by tomorrow afternoon."

Before he could say one more word, she marched out the door.

"Just who does he think he is?" she grumbled as she made her way across the yard to the buggy. One of the sisters had already hitched up their horse, and they were ready to go. Good, because she was more than ready to leave.

"What happened in there?" Mary asked as Emily swung into the driver's seat.

"*Nix,*" Emily lied.

"Well, something happened," Susannah chimed in. "Your face is all splotchy, and you're breathing like you just ran a race."

"Such a thing to say," Mary admonished.

61

Yet Emily knew Susannah was right. She *felt* all splotchy and winded.

She clicked the reins and started the horse forward. One quick turn around and they would be on their way back home.

But she had no more than gotten the horse facing the right direction when Joy Riehl hurried from the house, her prayer *kapp* strings flying out behind her.

"Emily! *Halt! Halt!*"

Emily pulled back on the reins and waited for Joy to catch up with them.

"I'm sorry about . . ." Joy waved a hand toward the house, and Emily could only assume she was talking about Elam and his surly attitude. "*Danki* for coming to help today."

Emily smiled. *"Gern gschehne."*

Her sisters echoed the sentiment.

"Will you come back tomorrow, like you said?" Joy asked.

"If that is what you want," Emily said.

Joy smiled, an honest to goodness smile that lit up her whole face. "I would like that very much."

"Then we will be here." Emily could only hope Elam would not.

He knew the minute his stepmother shut the door behind her she was angry.

Joy Riehl lived up to her name most always, but this afternoon, he could tell she would fall short on that promise.

"Elam Riehl!" she called as she stalked across the room. "What has gotten into you today?"

He didn't have an answer. He had walked into the house and chaos surrounded him.

Girls were everywhere. He'd lost count at eight, since they fluttered around, nosily chattering as they zoomed from one task to another.

There was noise, so very much noise. In the middle of it all sat his poor *dat,* Johanna cuddled in his lap even as he cradled his head in one hand. Elam had no idea the pain his father suffered. He could only guess. None of them truly knew. So they kept the house dark and quiet. When Elam had arrived home, his house had been neither.

Then his gaze fell on Emily Ebersol, and he knew who was to blame.

"*Dat* cannot take so much racket," he replied, his voice sounding rough as sandpaper.

"Your *dat* was fine. Enjoying himself even."

Elam shook his head against the truth in her words. *Jah,* his father had looked okay then, but how was he going to feel later with his head throbbing because he'd been up too much, or even nauseated from tiring himself out? "You know as well as I do it is not that simple." But he couldn't ignore the look on his father's face as he held little Johanna in his lap. She had missed her *vatter* this past year. They all had. And if the smile of contentment on *Dat*'s face was any indication, he had missed them too.

"You should apologize to Emily. And her sisters," *Mamm* continued.

He knew she was right. Just as he knew his father had seemed on top of the world. But what was right was not always the best way to do things.

"*Jah,*" he said.

"Tomorrow, when she comes back."

"She's coming back?" A muscle in his jaw started to twitch.

"I need someone to help make clothes for the girls. I have jelly that needs to be made and tomatoes that must be canned."

"I should hire you someone to help. Maybe someone from town could come in and —"

"Why are you so against Emily Ebersol coming here?"

"It's not that." He said the words even as he knew them to be a lie.

"Then what is it?"

But he had no answer. At least not one he could share with his *mamm*. "I must get to the milking," he rasped. Then he left for the barn, hoping that by the time the afternoon milking was done, *Mamm* would have forgotten all about her question and the answer he never gave.

"What is wrong with him?" Emily asked Mary as they set about their milking. Each sister had a job to do. Once the goats were in their milking stalls, Bea and Susannah cleaned their teats with the iodine solution while Mary and Rose hooked them up to the machines. It was Emily's job to clean the milk vats and pour the smaller containers of milk into the large cooler. Once she went into the milk room, she would be by herself until the milking was done.

"I do not know." Mary shrugged. "Pride maybe?"

" 'Pride goeth before destruction, and a haughty spirit before a fall,' " Emily quoted as they worked to get the goats into the milking stalls.

Normally the does were easy enough to work with. They had been through the process too many times to count, but today they seemed unusually ornery. Or maybe it was her own frustration and impatience working against her.

"Are you going to say something to *Dat*?"

"Nay." Something in the haunted look coloring Elam's green eyes had her wanting to forgive him quickly despite the anger he showed toward her. He was hurting, though Emily didn't know if it had to do with his father or something else. Though she suspected there was more to it than his *dat*'s injury.

"Well, here goes," Emily muttered to herself as she pulled to a stop in front of the Riehl house. Her sisters had been none too happy when she had left them behind, but she thought perhaps it best. They had gotten a great deal accomplished the day before. With her help today, Joy Riehl would be caught up with her housework.

Emily swung down from the buggy, her gaze drifting to the family garden. The tomatoes needed picking, as well as the squash and beans. That was just what she could see from where she stood. Those were probably the last of the vegetables for the season. With any luck she might be able to still harvest a few ears of corn.

She gathered her things out of the back of the buggy, a basket filled with bread and cookies as well as some material for dresses. Her *mamm* had sent over the latter with the intentions of Emily staying long enough to sew a dress for young Johanna.

Emily sighed. It wasn't that she minded sewing, but it was the staying. It would take a couple more trips to get the garden taken care of, and the rest of the laundry finished. Then to sew a dress on top of that . . . well, it seemed that her *eldra* expected her to come to the Riehl house every other day. Which would have been fine except for the hard stare of Elam Riehl.

She knocked on the door, and it swung open immediately.

Little Johanna stood just inside, thumb in her mouth and doll tucked into the crook of her arm. She smiled around the digit, and Emily's heart melted.

"May I come in, Johanna Riehl? I have cookies."

Johanna laughed, then ran toward the back of the house.

The high-pitched sound of her chatter floated back into the front room as Johanna spoke to someone in the back. Then Joy appeared, a sweet smile on her tired face.

"Emily, *guder mariye.* I thought you would be at the market this morning."

She shook her head. "*Mamm* sent Mary

instead." Though Emily had a feeling her father was behind the switch. First he had told her that he wanted her to not teach and to help her *mudder* with the market stand. Then he suggested she should consider Elam Riehl as a suitor. Which would happen when the goats started milking themselves. Now her father insisted she help the Riehl family and let Mary take care of the market. He wasn't fooling her. He was trying to get her to see Elam in a different light. But it wasn't Elam that spurred her father's actions, it was Luke. Her *dat* wanted her to forget Luke Lambright. As if she could ever.

"I'm glad you're here."

Emily smiled. "I'm *froh* to be here." She *was* happy she was there to help. And yet . . .

"Becky has gone to the market, but we didn't have a lot to sell. She should be home by lunch."

"Where is . . . ?"

"Elam? He's in the barn."

"Joy?" James called. From the close sound of his voice, Emily could tell he had gotten out of bed and was coming down the hallway toward them.

"James." Joy bustled over to him as he steadied himself, one hand braced against the wall.

"I thought I heard voices."

"*Jah,*" she said. "You did. Emily Ebersol has come again today to help us in the house."

"The bishop's daughter?"

"*Jah,* the one and the same."

"I like her," James said, then flashed Emily a quick smile.

"And I like you, too." She started as something touched her hand. Looking down, she found Johanna gazing up at her with those big blue eyes.

"I like you, too," she said in her high-pitched *Deutsch.* "Are you going to stay with us?"

"For the afternoon, *jah.*"

"Stay all day and all night." Johanna bounced on her toes, pulling on Emily's hand as she hopped around. "Please please please."

Emily squatted down to look into Johanna's precious face. "I will stay until it is time for the milking. Then I must go home and take care of my *mamm*'s goats. But until then, you and I are going to have a fun sisters' day, cleaning and such. Would you like that?"

Johanna's eyes lit up. "A sisters' day? You and me?"

"And your *mamm, jah.*"

"I would like that very much."

Emily smiled. "Then let's get your father settled, and we will start our day." She offered her other arm to James and supported him in his short walk to the table.

"Can we have cookies first?" Johanna asked, climbing into the chair opposite her *dat.*

"If it is *allrecht* with your *mamm.*" Emily looked to Joy who simply nodded.

"Yes, cookies, please," James said, a bright smile on his face. He looked so childlike and innocent it nearly broke Emily's heart. She remembered James Riehl as a strong man who came to help them rebuild their barn a few years back. Now he could barely walk without assistance.

"James," Joy started, her tone gentle. "Perhaps you should go back and lie down."

James gave a few shakes of his head, then stopped as if the motion was too much for him. "No," he said, sounding all the more like a petulant child. "I want to stay here with Emily and Johanna."

"But what if —"

"I want to stay here." His voice boomed, and he winced as if it hurt his head.

Johanna seemed not to notice his outburst and continued to distribute the cookies between the four places at the table. Or maybe she was accustomed to her father's mercurial moods.

"He gets dizzy spells," Joy explained, where only Emily could hear.

"Is he fine as long as he's sitting?"

Joy nodded.

"Then we will have to make certain that he continues to sit." She smiled reassuringly.

Joy's response trembled on her lips. "I'm glad to have your help, Emily Ebersol." To Emily's dismay, tears filled Joy's eyes.

"Don't cry, Joy. Perhaps you should go lie down for a bit."

"*Nay,* I cannot. James needs me."

"I will not argue with that," Emily said. "But right now, I think all James needs is someone to watch him. And I am here."

"But if he were to fall . . ."

"What do you do when he falls while you are here?"

"I go get Elam from the barn."

Emily gave a satisfied nod. "Then that is what I will do as well. Go rest, Joy, and let me take care of this for you. You look like you could fall asleep standing up."

Joy wiped the tears from her eyes. "James . . . James had a bad night."

Emily could tell that Joy didn't want to admit as much to her. "Sleep while you can.

We'll all be here when you wake up."

"*Danki,* Emily." Joy squeezed her fingers. "I wasn't sure you'd come back today."

"Why ever not?"

"Elam . . ." She shook her head. "He's a stubborn soul that one, so much like his father before . . . well, before."

"It will take more than his stubbornness to chase me off." And she meant it. Ever since Luke had left and she'd had to give up her teaching position, she had felt adrift. She'd felt like she was living in someone else's skin. But being here and helping — regardless of the scowls she'd received from Elam — she felt more like herself. As if God had been intending for her to help this family all along. "Now go rest and when you wake up I'm sure everything will be a little brighter."

Finally, Joy made her way back to her room. By then, James and Johanna had devoured almost a dozen chocolate chip cookies. She shook her head, laughing at the chocolate smears on their faces.

She could see now why James's injury had been so hard on the family. He was like a child, simple and petulant. That in itself wouldn't have been so bad. He could still do the chores of a small child, but the dizzy spells mixed with his strong will could make for some terrible accidents.

It was easy to see why Elam and Joy worried about him constantly, but some things a person had to hand to the Lord.

CHAPTER FIVE

Elam took a deep breath as he came across the hill in the pasture and saw the buggy in the side yard. A deep calming breath. What was she doing here again?

Jah, his *mamm* had told him that Emily Ebersol would be stopping by today, but somewhere in the back of his mind, he'd hoped she wouldn't show.

His heart pounded a little harder in his chest the closer he got to the house. He would have to apologize, have to come up with some reason why he had acted so surly toward her. He'd have to come up with something other than the truth.

How could he tell her that he had loved her for as long as he could remember, though he knew even longer than that she had been in love with Luke Lambright?

He couldn't remember the first time he had ever seen Emily Ebersol, but he could certainly remember the first time he'd

noticed her. She was ten and he was fourteen, in his last year of school. He'd tried so
hard that year to gain her attention, but
even then, Luke Lambright was the one she
loved.

After Elam had left school, he'd had to
settle himself with the occasional chance
meeting in town or perhaps the off-Sunday
volleyball game. Other than that, he hardly
saw her. Their four-year age difference put
them in different youth groups. Like it
would have mattered. Luke had captured
her heart long ago.

Then for Elam to come into his own
house and see the pity in her eyes . . .

It was almost more than he could bear.

He slapped his gloves against his leg and
slipped the multi-use pliers into his back
pocket. He'd been out walking the fence all
morning, after chasing down two heifers
that had somehow gotten out of the pasture.
He found the hole and patched it, but the
incident put him behind for the day. He had
two more acres of alfalfa to bale before the
cold hit. If the talk around the co-op was
right, they were in for a long winter this year.

Before he could get to the hay, he had an
apology to make.

Of course it was the hottest day on record
for early October, and he had to humble

himself before Emily Ebersol. He swiped one sleeve across his forehead.

He was grimy and dusty, his mouth full of sand and grit. It was bad enough he had to face her at all, but to face her like this . . . He sighed. It couldn't be helped.

Without another thought on the matter, he loped up the porch steps and entered the house. The sight that greeted him was yet another surprise.

His father sat at the table with Johanna. Both had a school worksheet in front of them and a crayon grasped in one hand. His father's tongue stuck out of the corner of his mouth as he concentrated on coloring.

He was coloring. Elam closed his eyes, shook his head, then looked again. *Jah,* his *vatter* was coloring a picture of harvest corn and an *Englisch* scarecrow. But whereas Johanna was working diligently with orange and brown, his father's picture was purple. Several different shades, but all purple.

Emily bustled out of the kitchen looking like a breath of spring in her violet-colored dress and crisp black apron. Her dark blue eyes settled on him and widened.

"Elam," she exclaimed. "I wasn't expecting you."

"*Bruder.*" Johanna tossed her crayon aside

76

and slid from her chair. In an instant, she had thrown herself at his legs as if he'd been gone a week instead of just the morning.

Her reaction was just another side effect of his father's injury. Anytime anyone left for too long, Johanna worried they wouldn't come back the same as when they left.

He lifted his sister into his arms.

She ran her tiny fingers down his face as if to assure herself he was the same as this morning.

"Where's *Mamm*?" he asked.

"Taking a nap," Johanna answered. "But Emily said I don't have to because I'm too big."

"Really?" He turned to Emily, who had the grace to blush.

"That's not exactly what I said."

He let Johanna slide to the floor. She raced back over to her picture and picked up the orange crayon once again. "*Dat,* you're doing it wrong," she protested. "Corn isn't purple."

Emily turned back to Elam's baby sister. "Corn can be any color your *vatter* wants it to be."

"*Jah.*" Johanna ducked her head. "Okay, then."

But Elam could feel her frustration. They all suffered from it. Frustration that a once

77

vibrant and healthy man had been reduced to coloring stalks of corn in a child's workbook.

Suddenly he wanted to march over to his father and snatch the paper away. It hurt. Plain and simple.

As much as Elam understood God's will, he didn't understand how to accept it. He couldn't see why his father with so many *gut* years left of his life needed to be reduced to a child.

He held his place and refused to allow himself the anger. "Emily." He cleared his throat. "Can I talk to you for a moment?"

She tilted her head to one side, obviously surprised by his request. *"Jah."* She straightened her shoulders as if preparing for an opposition.

"Alone," he clarified.

She raised her brows, but said nothing else on the matter. "We could step out on the porch. That way I can keep an eye on . . ." She trailed off.

"Can I have another cookie before you go?" Johanna asked.

Emily laughed. The sound refreshed the room. How long had it been since any of them had laughed? Too long, for sure. But he knew much of the beauty in it came from the woman herself.

"Nay, liebschdi," Emily said. "You will ruin your *middawk.*"

"Jah. Okay." She bent her head down over her picture, so low, even the tied strings on her *kapp* touched the table.

Elam opened the door and motioned Emily to step onto the porch.

"Jah?" she said as she steadily gazed at him. She was not going to make this easy.

"I must apologize for yesterday."

She seemed to deflate before his eyes, like one of the rafts they used to float down the river. "It is not necessary." She seemed suddenly uncomfortable and started to move past him, back into the house.

"I disagree." He caught her arm before she could leave him behind.

She looked down at his fingers against the fabric of her sleeve. He told himself to release her, but he couldn't.

He wasn't hurting her, just soaking in the warmth that was Emily.

"Please," he said. "I was just surprised, is all."

"Surprised by what?"

He shrugged his shoulders and finally convinced his fingers to turn her loose. "That there were so many people in my house."

Making noise and bustling about like . . .

like nothing in the world was wrong.

"You worry about him too much, you know?"

His gaze jerked up to meet hers. She eyed him without apology, the blue orbs steady. *"Jah,"* he finally said. But he couldn't say more through the constriction in his throat.

"Joy does, too. He needs to be up and moving."

"He falls," Elam protested.

"At least let him sit at the kitchen table."

Just like that, his charitable feelings toward Emily evaporated. "Two days of coming here to help does not make you an expert on handling my father."

She crossed her arms and raised herself up, but she still hardly reached his shoulder. "I never said it did."

"*Gut . . . jah . . .* you keep that in mind." He wanted to say more, but the words failed him.

She pushed past him and into the house.

Elam stood for the longest time staring at the door and wondering how it all went so wrong.

Milking time was both her favorite time of the day and her least favorite. Emily loved it because they all worked together in the barn, taking care of the goats that provided

80

so much for them. But she hated it because as the eldest she was assigned the sterilized milk room and didn't see much of her sisters for the two hours she was there.

But tonight wasn't so bad. She had plenty of thoughts to keep her company. Unfortunately most of them had to do with stubborn Elam Riehl. She would have much rather been thinking about Luke and his dancing blue eyes, wondering what he was doing at that very moment. His life had to be filled with excitement and fun, like only the *Englisch* could experience. Was he racing a car? Eating with friends? Maybe even playing games and watching television like the world was prone to do? One thing was for sure, he wasn't milking goats and wondering about her.

Yet as much as she wanted to think about Luke, all that came to mind was Elam. The expression on his face as she said his father needed to be up and moving around his own house told her that she had shocked him as if she had declared something utterly sinful.

Emily poured another bucket of goat's milk into the cooler.

James had been so happy to be out of his room, so tickled to color a picture with his daughter. *Jah,* it was sad for her to see him like that, but he had so much left to give his family, in smiles, if nothing else.

Little Johanna was starved for his attention. She craved his presence and spent their time before lunch instructing him on the best ways to work a puzzle.

But after Elam had come in with his weak apology, she had sent Johanna into the garden to gather the last of the food.

Tomorrow they were all headed over to paint the house and the barn. She and her *shveshtah* would work on canning the last of the garden and that would be that. Hopefully she wouldn't have to go to Elam's house anymore and be subjected to his cold heart and permanent scowl.

The look on her face was still lingering in his mind as Elam cut the bread for their supper that night. But only because she had brought over the bread. Not because her blue eyes flashed with hurt.

"Be careful *bruder,* or you will ruin the whole loaf." Becky's words brought him back to the present before he sliced into his hand instead of the bread. "What is bothering you tonight?"

"Nix." He hated how easily the lie sprang to his lips.

He carried the bread basket to the table

82

and sat down. His *mamm* had taken his *vatter*'s supper into the bedroom to feed him. His hands were not steady enough nor his balance dependable enough to allow him a place at the table. Elam could not stand the thought of the younger *kinner* seeing their father in this state, and Joy had agreed. Holding a crayon was one thing, a spoon of hot soup another.

"And then we colored pictures. Though *Dat* colored his corn purple." Johanna made a face as if she was still uncertain about the merits of purple corn.

"It's time to pray," Elam said, bowing his head only after his sisters had done so.

Here lately, the words for a prayer were harder to find. Was God even listening? Elam had asked for his father's healing, rain, and peace, but so far none of those things were his.

The last Sunday he'd gone to church, Bishop Ebersol had talked about humbling yourself before God, accepting His will. Elam had felt like the man was speaking straight to him, but he noticed that Cephas's gaze never drifted far from his own daughter.

Amish church leaders were supposed to preach off the cuff each church Sunday and talk about whatever God moved them to speak about, but Elam had a feeling there was more to the sermon than just that.

Elam pulled his thoughts back to his prayer. He thanked the Lord for the food and the health of those sitting around him. *"Aemen,"* he said, and lifted his head.

"Did you see the purple potatoes in the market?" Becky asked, passing the plain white ones to one of the twins.

"Purple potatoes?" Johanna scrunched up her nose, and Elam realized it was an expression she shared with their father. He too would wrinkle his nose when doubtful about something.

"Jah," Becky said. She scooped up a spoonful of green beans and passed the bowl to the next sister.

"But only on the outside, right?" Miriam asked.

"Nay, on the inside. They are as purple as . . . as purple as . . ."

"Emily's dress?" Johanna asked.

"Jah." Becky laughed. "I suppose so."

And as easily as that, Emily Ebersol was back in his thoughts.

Like she was ever far from them.

She was the most stubborn and infuriating woman he had ever known. Yet he found himself drawn to her, thinking about her more and more with each day.

84

Not so long ago, he had learned to curb his thoughts of her. He had come to realize the truth in her relationship with Luke. But now everything was changing, almost faster than he could keep up. All of a sudden she was underfoot, coming to his house, helping his family. *Jah,* he had managed to not think about her so much back then, but this was now, and she was becoming part of his dreams once again.

She told herself she was going to stay as far away from Elam Riehl as possible. So why did she find herself pulling into his driveway once again?

"Are you sure you want to do this?" Mary asked.

"Do I have a choice?" Emily asked.

Mary's mouth twisted into a grimace. "I suppose *Dat*'s excuse for you to drive out here is weak at best."

"I'll say." Emily pulled the horses to a stop and climbed down from the buggy. "I don't see why they can't just bring the paint over tomorrow morning when they come to do the work."

Mary nodded. "That seems more logical to me, but you know *Dat.*"

She certainly did, and her father wanted her to spend as much time as possible with

Elam Riehl. Even if it meant inventing wacky excuses for her to come to the Riehl house. Who even said he would be there for her to see? He might have a love in another district. Sure, the courting rituals weren't quite as secretive as they had been back in her father's day, but that didn't mean Elam was one to go spouting off about his intentions.

In fact, with his stern mouth and quiet nature, telling everyone about his feelings for another was the last thing she would expect from him.

"Oy!" he called from the front porch. He was wiping his hands on a towel as if he had been inside cleaning up after supper.

So much for him not even being home.

Emily had managed not to say another word to him before she left that very afternoon. She stayed out of his way and he out of hers. Becky could tell something was amiss between them. She kept looking back and forth, from one to the other whenever they found themselves in the same room together.

Thankfully, time to milk had finally come around. Emily had hugged Joy, Johanna, and Becky good-bye, even getting a quick squeeze from James before heading back home. At the time, she had wondered how she would make it through the following day when they came to paint. Now she had to figure out how to make it through this evening with Elam.

"We brought paint." Mary said the words like they were the greatest news.

"Paint?" Becky appeared on the porch behind her *bruder.*

"For tomorrow," Emily explained.

Elam nodded, then tossed the towel over his shoulder. He jogged down the steps as Emily grabbed two buckets of the paint and moved out of his way.

"Where do you want this?" she asked.

"Barn," he rumbled.

She headed off in the direction of the barn just as Mary chirped, "This paint is for the house. We'll put it on the porch."

Emily inwardly sighed as Elam followed behind her into the barn. Could her sister be any more obvious?

"Where do you want it?" she asked once they had stepped into the dim interior.

"There's *gut.*" Elam raised his chin toward the first stall. It looked like it was only used for storage.

Emily set the paint cans just inside the door, then moved back so Elam could do the same.

"If you haven't noticed, I think my sister

is trying to play matchmaker," she said in a rush. "And my *vatter,* too."

"*Jah?*" Elam set his paint cans down, then turned his attention to her.

She nodded. "I'm sorry."

"It is nothing you have done."

"*Jah,* but I thought I should warn you."

"*Danki,*" he said.

"He thinks I'm never going to get married." Why was she telling him this? She almost clamped a hand over her mouth to stem the flow of words, but she was afraid that would only draw attention to them.

"Because of Luke Lambright?"

"What about Luke?" she asked, wrapping her arms around herself. Suddenly she felt exposed. That was the second time Elam had mentioned Luke to her.

"Everyone knows that you and Luke . . ." He trailed off with a shake of his head. "Why did you stop teaching?" he asked.

"Again my father. He said it was because he needed my help with the market booth. But I think he believes that if I keep teaching, I'll never get married."

"He seems pretty determined to find you a husband."

"*Jah.*" She brushed at a strand of hay clinging to her apron.

"Is that what you want?"

88

"Does it matter?"

He was quiet for so long, Emily wasn't sure he'd even answer. She looked up and met his steady gaze. *"Jah,"* he finally said. "It does matter. Everyone should have love."

"If you're such a romantic, then why haven't you gotten married?" This time she did clamp her hand over her mouth. "I'm sorry," she mumbled through her fingers. "I didn't mean to be rude."

"I've got my hands full around here. I just never found the time to court anyone."

Surely there had been a time during his *rumspringa* when he'd had the time to court a special girl. Back then his father had been fine and whole, but Emily wasn't about to ask. Something in Elam's tone gave her pause, stilled her words on her lips. Something in his eyes made her stop, though she wasn't sure what it was. Hurt, longing, determination. She couldn't tell.

"Emily?" Mary called from the barn door. "The paint is all unloaded. Time to go."

"Be right there," she called. "I need to uh . . ." She waved a hand for him to move to the side so she could exit the stall. "Tonight Aaron is coming over to see her, and she wants to get back before he gets to the house."

"Aaron Miller?"

"Jah."

"Do you think they'll get married?"

"Of course." And that was the problem. With Mary being younger and already intended, both her sister and her father thought it was time for Emily to get married as well. What they didn't understand was how much she loved Luke Lambright. Or how long she was willing to wait for him to come to his senses and return to Wells Landing.

He would return. She knew it as surely as she knew that God was good, puppies were cute, and the sky was blue.

She just had to be patient. She needed to be understanding. And she had to avoid her father's matchmaking at all costs. It would never do for Luke to return and find Emily courting another.

CHAPTER SIX

Saturday morning turned out to be the perfect day to hold a work frolic. Between the scraping off the old paint and the application of the primer, Emily made gallons of lemonade. Beautiful day or not, lingering summer warmed the air and the men were hot and thirsty.

As she stirred yet another batch of lemonade in the big cooler, her sister Mary sidled up and slipped her arm through Emily's.

"Have you seen him?"

Emily started. "Luke's here?" Her gaze darted around the men trying to spot him in the crowd of workers.

"Nay," she said. "Aaron." She pointed to where he stood, high on a ladder as he painted the trim on the house.

Aaron Miller was as tall and lanky as his brother Jonah. Both boys had dark blond hair and tawny eyes the color of rich maple syrup. Aaron Miller was a handsome *bu* —

not as handsome as her Luke, of course. But he'd make Mary a *gut* husband.

"Mary Miller," her sister breathed, trying the name on for sound and size.

"Are you going to marry him?" Emily asked.

Mary dimpled and dropped her gaze, a sure sign she was hiding something. "That's supposed to be a secret."

"Which means he hasn't asked you," Emily said, hating the dryness of her tone.

Mary's gaze jerked back to Emily's. "You know as well as I do that he won't announce his intentions until after the wedding season."

"Which hasn't even started yet." Plus Mary still had to join the church. Baptism classes hadn't been held this year, delaying her ability to attend classes until next year. Perfect timing as far as Emily was concerned. Mary and Luke could attend classes together and maybe the following year, Emily and Luke could have a double wedding with Mary and Aaron. It would be so perfect.

"Why are you being difficult?" Mary asked, hurt flashing in her eyes.

Emily wrapped an arm around her sister. "I'm sorry. I didn't mean to be —"

"Mean?" Mary supplied.

"*Jah*. Forgive me?"

Mary returned her hug and patted her hand. "Of course."

"I just . . ." Emily trailed off, not able to adequately put into words all her worry and fears about Luke. For all her thoughts of a wedding, she worried because she hadn't heard from him. Worried that he was forgetting all about her.

She pushed the thoughts aside. *Nay,* he was the one for her, and she had to be patient and strong until God returned him to her.

"Maybe you should go talk to Aaron about it," Mary said as if she could read Emily's thoughts.

"I don't know what good it would do. I already talked to Jonah."

"You could go ask his *onkle.*"

Now *that* she could do. Maybe next week. As the plan took shape in her mind, Emily poured the cups of lemonade and took them over to the men.

"Would anyone like a drink?" she asked.

A chorus of *jah*s went up all around.

She laughed at their enthusiasm and handed out cups.

"*Danki.*"

She looked up from her task to see that Elam Riehl had taken the last drink from her tray. *"Gern gschehne."*

He swallowed deep and nodded toward the barn. "It's coming along, *jah?"*

"It looks *wunderbaar."*

"Not yet, but it will." He swept his hat from his head and ran a sleeve across his sweaty brow. "And I have you to thank."

"Me?" She shook her head. *"Nay.* I only made the lemonade."

"You told your father that we needed help."

"That is nothing."

He took a deep breath and propped his hands on his hips. "It was something to me," he said. Then he turned and went back to painting, leaving Emily to wonder where his agreeable mood had come from.

"Emily!" Becky Riehl raced across the yard, the strings on her *kapp* trailing behind her. *"Dat* wants you," she said when she got close enough that she didn't have to shout.

"My *dat?"*

"No, silly. My *dat."*

What would James Riehl want with her?

Becky slipped her arm through Emily's and led her back to the house.

They went in the front door, but James was not sitting at the kitchen table.

"Back here." Becky led the way down the

hall to James's room.

It was dark and surprisingly cool inside. James sat on the edge of his bed, his head cradled in his hands. Joy stood over him, her fists propped on her hips in a defensive pose.

"*Dat,* I brought Emily to you."

He looked up, his eyes shining with recognition. "I want to watch the men paint."

Emily glanced toward Joy who stiffened at his request. "It's too bright out there, James. It'll make your head ache."

"My head aches anyway." He pouted. "Emily, take me outside."

"Emily is not going to take you anywhere."

She couldn't tell if Joy was upset with this latest development or not. Her eyes were unreadable and her expression stoic.

"Maybe if we put him in the shade . . . ?" Emily started, quietly so that only Joy could hear.

"I do not think it is a *gut* idea." She bit her bottom lip, but otherwise her strong stance remained steady.

"Nor is allowing him to get this upset," Becky pointed out.

Joy took them by the arms and led them to a corner across the room. "I worry," she started.

Emily patted her hand. "I know. But

95

sunshine might do him some *gut.* I'll sit with him," she offered. "I'll make sure he doesn't get up or wander off."

Tears rose in Joy's eyes. "You would do that for him? For us?"

"Of course." It was all part of giving back to the community, the cornerstone of being Amish.

"Will you help me get him up and around?"

Emily wasn't sure if Joy had changed her mind about taking her husband outside or if she was tired of fighting him about staying in bed. Whatever it was, Emily was willing to help. She nodded and together the three of them prepared James for his trip outside.

Joy decided it would be easiest to take James only as far as the front porch, but Becky pointed out it might just frustrate him as he wouldn't be able to see all of the men as they worked.

"There are three of us," Emily reasoned. "We should be able to get him down the steps and to the big oak next to the shed."

James was willing enough, just unsteady on his feet as they helped him outside. Emily took one elbow and Joy the other, while Becky hurried ahead and spread a quilt underneath the tree.

In no time at all, they were settled under the big branches while the men painted and the women watched. It wasn't as bright under the tree, but Emily made a mental note to check into some of those dark glasses the *Englisch* wore when they were outside. They might hide the glare enough for James to be comfortable out in the sun.

A softball game had started among some of the children. A few were painting on the lower parts of the barn while still others ran in circles and chased the dogs. Johanna Riehl was one of these, until she saw her father had come outside. She veered off from the rest and raced to his side.

"Dat," she squealed as she hurled herself at him.

The smile on James's face was worth every bit of worry Emily had gone through to get him to the yard. Mixed with Johanna's grin, they were both brighter than the sun.

She turned and caught Elam's stare. Her own smile died on her lips at his scowl. Whatever goodwill was between them earlier vanished in that instant.

She thought for a minute that he was about to storm over to her and demand she take his father right back into the house, but someone next to him spoke and she was granted a reprieve.

But not for long. As Johanna and her *dat* played hand games and found shapes in the clouds above, Elam stalked over.

"Emily, may I have a word?"

She wanted to tell him no and remain seated under the big oak tree, but that would only fuel his anger.

"Jah." She stood and brushed her hands down the sides of her blue *frack*. Not that her clothes were wrinkled enough for much attention, but suddenly she felt a little like a child caught with her hand in the cookie jar. "I know what you are going to say," she started.

"You have no idea."

She reared back at the harshness of his tone. He spoke in low volumes so others wouldn't hear, but anger came off him like rippling waves of summer heat. "I didn't bring him out here on my own. Your mother and sister were with me. He was never in any danger of falling."

"He is always in danger of falling." His green eyes glittered accusingly.

"But he wanted to come out. How long has it been, Elam? Since he's been outside?"

"That is not what we are talking about."

His tone raised her hackles, but something deep inside her wanted to help this family that was held together by a thread and a

98

prayer. "Maybe it is what we should be talking about." She braced her hands on her hips and stiffened her spine. "I think being outside will do your father some *gut.*"

"You don't get to make the decisions for this family."

She wasn't going to get anywhere with him like this. She softened her tone, hoping to reason with him. His father needed to be outside, prone to dizzy spells or not. He needed his family and the love of those around him, not to be locked in a dark room and allowed to waste away. "I'm only trying to help."

"You are disrupting everything."

"Elam, your father wanted to come outside. He asked for us to bring him out in the sun."

"He doesn't know what he wants." Elam crossed his arms and stared down at her. His mouth was still set in a stern line, but at least he didn't vibrate with anger.

"You have to stop protecting him so much," she said, extending a hand toward him.

He jerked out of her reach. "And you have to stop . . . stop . . ." He obviously couldn't find the words. "Stay away from my family, Emily Ebersol." Then he stalked away, leaving Emily to go back to the blanket under the big oak tree on very shaky legs.

James shot her a sweet smile as she sat back down on the quilt next to him. Johanna had tired of their game and crawled into his lap. The sight of her curled up with her thumb in her mouth and her head on his shoulder was enough to warrant putting up with Elam's foul mood.

Honestly, she didn't know why he was so cranky with her. Couldn't he see that his father needed this attention? That James needed to be out among people again?

"Don't mind him," James said, rocking Johanna back and forth. His voice was so quiet she thought for a minute she might have imagined it. "He was always too serious."

Emily studied the man's face, so like his son's except for the dark beard. Their eyes were the same, though where Elam's were clouded, James's were clear with a newborn innocence.

"I know this has to be hard on him." James's words came out in short spurts, as if he had to search through files before he could find the right ones to say, even in *Deutsch.*

"Elam?"

"Jah." He leaned back against the tree to brace himself as his daughter fell asleep in

his arms. "I know I'm not the same as I was before. It must be hard for someone you depend on to get hurt."

"They love you very much."

"I know." He closed his eyes, and his hat pitched forward as he rested his head against the trunk.

Emily plucked it from its precarious position, laying it on the blanket between them. "Are you ready to go back in the house?"

"Nay." He smiled, though his eyes remained closed.

"Is your head hurting?" Emily asked. The last thing she wanted was for James to overdo it. Having Elam even madder at her resided at the bottom of her wish list.

"Not so bad right now. Joy will be by in a while to make me take pills again." He made a face as if he didn't like to take the pills.

Should she ask him why? Was it too personal? Would he even understand?

"Will you come back over next week?" he asked.

"Of course I will." The words automatically fell from her lips. So what if Elam had told her to stay away? His father wanted her close. That was all that mattered to her.

"Will you wear your purple dress?"

She smiled at his request. "It's my favorite."

"I think he likes you," Mary said as they trotted home that afternoon. They left the Riehls' house just after three, which gave them plenty of time to get home before milking began.

It had taken the better part of the morning, but the Riehl house and barn had never looked better.

"What?" Emily turned her attention from her thoughts to her sister. The horses practically knew the way home and could maneuver without much help from her, which left her wallowing in her own thoughts.

"I think Elam likes you," Mary explained.

"No more than any other *maedel.*" As she said the words, his cold stare and warning to stay away from his family flashed through her mind.

"Oh, *jah.* Lots more."

Emily shook her head. "You're wrong. He hates me."

" 'Hate is an ugly word,' " she said, quoting their mother.

"Strongly dislikes, then."

Mary shook her head, their shoulders bumping as they cantered along. "He likes you."

"He yelled at me for bringing his father outside."

"I watched the whole thing, and there was no yelling."

Emily twisted her mouth into a grimace. "He wanted to then."

Mary smiled. "You know what the *Englisch* say."

"*Nay*," Emily said, already tired of the conversation. "I don't."

"It is a short line between hate and love."

She frowned at her sister. "Are you sure that is how it goes?"

"It is something like that. It means that the person who cares about you the most can make you the angriest."

"I'm not sure I believe that," Emily said, pulling the buggy to a stop. She waited at the intersection for a beat before setting the horse in motion once again.

"Of course it is true."

Emily shook her head, her sister's intentions suddenly clear. "Oh, *nay*, you don't. Just because you are in love doesn't mean the world needs to be in love with you."

"What about Luke?" Mary asked with a self-satisfied smirk.

Her heart gave a painful thump at the mention of his name. She schooled her features to hide her inner turmoil, though if anyone knew how much she missed Luke, it was her sister. "What about Luke?"

"Does he count in your 'the world doesn't need to be in love theory?' Of course not."

Emily sniffed. "I'm just saying you shouldn't try to see feelings where there are none."

"I know what I saw," Mary insisted.

"I know he loves someone else."

Mary's eyes grew wide. "How do you know that?"

"He told me . . . sort of. I mean, he said something that, oh never mind."

"Was this before or after he 'yelled' at you?"

Emily decided it best not to answer that question. "After the milking, will you go into town with me?"

"Jah," Mary said immediately. "What do you want to do in town?"

"I want to go by the library and look up some stuff on the computer."

Mary's eyes grew impossibly wide. "On the *Englisch* computer?"

"Are there any other kind?"

"Nay . . . I mean . . . *Dat* will . . . Emily!"

"It is for a *gut* cause," she defended. "I want to check out some things." She had been hearing talk of the *Englisch* Internet where anything and everything could be

104

found. Like ways to help people who had suffered head injuries and problems with medications. She wasn't sure how she knew, but she just did: she needed to help James Riehl.

"How are you going to work an *Englisch* computer?" Mary asked.

"The librarian will help me, *jah*?"

Mary shrugged. "I suppose. But what if *Dat* finds out?"

"He's not going to," she said with confidence. "And you're not going to tell him."

CHAPTER SEVEN

Emily slid from the buggy two days later and smoothed her hands over her lilac dress. It wasn't the same purple one that James loved so much, but hopefully he would enjoy this one just as well.

She reached behind the seat and pulled out the basket of goodies she had collected. Tucked in the bottom, underneath the bag of grape jelly flavored jelly beans, the plastic school box full of markers and crayons in a variety of purple shades, and the stacks of purple construction paper was the info she had gathered at the library Saturday evening.

She had wanted to come yesterday and share what she had learned, but her family had traveled to the neighboring district to attend church. Given the length of the service and all of her regular milking duties, she hadn't had enough time to give to the visit. The delay also gave her a bit more time to gather fun things for James to do and her courage to face the wrath of Elam.

She had wanted to immediately go and put what she had learned into practice, but she didn't let herself. If Elam Riehl was upset about her taking his father outside, he would be furious at what she was about to suggest. It was best to give him a chance to completely cool off before starting up again.

She drew in a deep breath. He was not going to like what she had discovered.

"Emily?" Becky rushed out onto the front porch. "I am so glad to see you." She skipped down the stairs and looped her arm through hers. "Are you staying the entire afternoon?"

"As long as your family will have me."

Becky's smile beamed. "I'll send a messenger to your family then so they won't worry about you."

"*Jah?*"

Becky pulled her close. "Because we're keeping you forever."

We'll see, Emily silently added.

"*Mamm, Mamm,*" Becky called as she hurried up the porch steps. "Look who's here."

Emily followed Becky into the house.

Joy Riehl came out of the kitchen, wiping her hands on a dish towel. "Emily, so *gut* to see you."

Emily smiled in return and lifted her basket. "I brought some things for James."

Joy's smile was both relieved and pleased.

Emily had to admit the house had never looked better. Even as much as pride was a sin, she was proud of the job she and her sisters had done for this family. She'd just have to pray about it later.

"Where is James?" Emily set the basket on the kitchen table.

"Can I?" Becky asked, indicating she wanted to unload what Emily had brought.

Emily gave her a quick nod.

"He's napping." Joy said. She pressed the back of one hand to her forehead. As if to stay the beginning pangs of a headache.

"Are you *allrecht*?" she asked.

Joy nodded. "I'm tired is all." She slid into the closest kitchen chair. "James had a bad night. He had crazy dreams. Then he got up and rambled all over the house."

"I'm so sorry," Emily murmured. What she had printed out from the library might just be the solution this family needed, but she held back. She needed to present this gently. "What time did he finally get to sleep *gut*?"

"It was about four." Joy sighed. "Of course that was after he fell. Thankfully Elam was already awake. Together we got him back to bed."

"What's this?" Becky held up the folded papers Emily had printed at the library.

"It's just some information." She pulled the papers from Becky's grasp.

"What kind of information?" she asked.

Emily slid into the chair opposite Joy and unfolded the papers. She smoothed them flat, searching for the right words. "I went to the library the other day and printed out some information about the medications James is taking."

"Jah?"

Emily wasn't sure how to read the expression on Joy's face. Quietly open was her hope, so she pushed on. "Some of these medications have severe side effects." She pushed the papers across the table. "It's all in there. You should read it. Maybe ask his doctor. I just . . ." She took a deep breath and gathered her courage. "I think his medicine might be doing him more harm than good."

"I thought I told you to stay away from my family."

Emily whirled around as Elam stormed into the room. How long had he been standing there listening to their conversation? Long enough.

"I am only trying to help."

Joy picked up the papers and started flipping through the sheets.

"Well, you are failing." He loomed over her.

Emily stood, like that did any good against his superior height. Or his anger.

"Elam." Joy's voice was unreadable, and Emily wasn't about to look at her. She was locked in a stare-down with Elam. Why was he being so stubborn?

"Just read what's there." That was not too much to ask, to keep an open mind and seek answers.

He stalked around the table and scooped up the papers. He fisted them in his big hand, reducing them to a wad of crumpled words.

"Elam," Joy's voice admonished.

"What if it helps him?" Emily asked.

A moment hung suspended between them.

He stilled. "What if it doesn't?"

Emily kept her eyes on him, her gaze steady and reassuring. "If he were my *vatter*, it would be a chance I'd be willing to take."

He wilted a bit, his eyes filled with pain and something else. Regret? Remorse? Then he tossed the papers back onto the table and stalked out the door.

Joy and Becky watched him leave, their expressions a mirror image of confusion and apology.

"I don't know —" Joy started, but only finished with a shake of her head.

Emily pointed toward the wad of papers. "Will you read it?" she asked.

"Jah."

"That's all I can ask." She turned on her heel and followed Elam out into the bright sun.

She found him standing under the large tree to the side of the house, the very same one where she and James had watched the men paint a few days before.

"What is wrong with you?" She hadn't intended her words to come out sharp and accusing, but she'd had about all of his contention she could stand. She was only trying to help, after all.

He braced his hands on the tree and tucked his head between his arms. He said something, but she couldn't quite make out the words.

"What?" she asked, doing her best to keep her temper under control.

He raised his head. "I don't know."

She stopped. A little of the starch that had sustained her this far escaped. "I think you do." She crossed her arms and eyed him.

"Why are you so against reading that information?"

He shook his head.

"You're afraid." Big strong Elam Riehl was scared. "But of what?"

"You don't understand," he whispered.

"Then tell me."

He braced his back against the tree and slid downward until he was sitting between the roots.

Emily lowered herself to sit in front of him, so close their knees almost touched.

"He was so strong before." Elam's voice was quiet, almost hesitant.

"I remember."

He leaned his head against the tree, its trunk smashing the back of his hat. "He was my everything and to see him like that . . ."

"Now you have to be everything to everybody instead. And everything to him."

"*Jah.*" The words were spoken so quietly she almost thought she had imagined them.

"You don't have to always be strong, you know."

"I'm not." His eyes were closed, but she didn't need to see the green depths to know his pain.

"You try to be."

He didn't say anything for a long time. He just sat under the tree, his eyes closed, his breathing slow. Emily wondered if perhaps he had fallen asleep.

"*Danki,*" he finally said. His eyes flickered open. He seemed to have recovered in those few moments. His gaze was clear, his shoulders relaxed. He looked like they had just come out for a stroll.

"You're not alone in this," she told him.

He nodded. "That's what *Mamm* keeps telling me. I try to trust her. After all, she's been my *mamm* since I was eight years old."

Emily had forgotten that his mother had died when he was so young. Not that she remembered firsthand about Linda Riehl's illness and death, but she had heard the story many times in the years following. But when James married Joy Detweiller, talk of the past died down and only murmurs about the future could be heard.

"Well, she is right. You are not alone. You have her and God and —"

"You?"

Emily paused, just a half a second between when he spoke and when she answered. "*Jah,*" she said. "You have me."

Elam felt a little more in control by the time he and Emily made their way back into the house. Enough so that he managed to read the papers she'd brought concerning his father's medications. *Ach,* he tried to read them, but there were so many medical terms that he was soon way over his head.

He stroked his chin, a gesture he'd seen his father perform a hundred times. "I don't understand half of this." He turned his eyes to Emily, hoping he didn't sound half as hopeless as he felt.

"I'm no expert either, but the best I can figure, it sounds like your father's medications may be a little strong for him. He might even be allergic."

"Allergic?"

Emily nodded. "That could cause all sorts of side effects."

"Like him being dizzy?" Joy asked.

"Or falling?" Becky added.

"*Jah.* I s'pose." Though Emily sounded a little hesitant. After all her push to get them to listen, why was she pulling back now?

"That's what I've been trying to tell them."

"*Dat!*" Becky slapped a hand over her heart. "We should put a bell on you like we did the cat."

True. Without shoes on, his *dat* could make it into the room before anyone even knew he was up and about. All the more reason for them to figure out if the medication was indeed making him worse than his injury alone.

Dat shook his head, but smiled. "So you can talk about me without me hearing what you say?"

"We are checking into your medications," Becky said. "They might not be right."

"And?" James asked.

"Well." *Mamm* drew the one word out until it seemed like three.

"We're looking into it," Elam said, and the relieved expression on Emily's face made it all worth it.

This was not ridiculous, Emily told herself as she knocked on the door. It was Tuesday, three days after the work frolic at Elam's house. She'd helped out the Riehls. What difference was there in helping out the Lambrights?

She knocked again on Joseph Lambright's door, but to no answer. Her only option would be to leave the bread on the rocker out front and try another day.

Emily tucked the linen towels around the loaves. As much as she hated to leave without news from Luke, she didn't have much choice.

"*Ach,* Emily Ebersol, is that you?"

She whirled around as Joseph came out of the barn, a leather harness flung over one

115

shoulder.

Emily had never noticed how much Luke and his uncle favored one another. They were both not as tall as some men, about five foot eight inches. Which was good for her because Luke didn't tower over her like other people she knew. Both men had the same inky black hair full of waves that tended to curl under the edge of their hats. But whereas Luke's eyes were clear blue like the summertime sky, Joseph's were a stormy gray of the clouds before it rained.

"I brought you some bread, Joseph Lambright."

He smiled. "I bet you've come for news from Luke."

The heat rose into her cheeks but she kept her gaze steady. *"Jah,"* she said. "I have at that."

"Come on in the house." He climbed the porch steps and led the way inside. "You wouldn't happen to have any pie in that basket would you?"

Emily laughed. "Only bread. But there is a loaf of pumpkin spice."

Joseph grinned. "We'll have some coffee and a snack then, while I tell you what my nephew has been up to."

"Is he doing all right?" Emily asked after the coffee had been brewed, the cups poured, and the bread sliced and served.

"I s'pose so." Joseph took a bite of the pumpkin bread and smiled around the crumbs. "That's delicious," he said and bit off another large hunk. "He called last week. Said something about getting a sponsor for his car."

Emily didn't know if that was a good thing or a bad one. From the look on Joseph's face, neither did he. "Did he ask about me?"

"*Jah, jah.*" Joseph nodded. "He said to give you something." He stood and went to his desk, shuffling through papers before finding what he was looking for. He located it, then handed it to Emily.

She took the folded piece of paper, and her heart thumped in her chest. Her first news from Luke since he'd left. She opened the paper to find numbers written on the other side.

"It is his cell phone number. He said for you to call him anytime."

Joy burst inside of her. She could call Luke, hear his voice, talk to him, and find out firsthand how the *Englisch* world was treating him. "*Danki,*" she said, slipping the paper into her apron pocket. She took a sip of her coffee and tried to appear calm when she was anything but. She wanted to jump up from the table and race to the phone shanty out front. She wanted to call Luke that very second and hear his beloved voice. But she would have to wait. At least until she finished her visit with Joseph Lambright.

"Go on," he said, his eyes twinkling. "I know that is why you came all the way out here. Not that I don't appreciate the bread and such. You go on home and give him a call."

Emily smiled and pushed back from the table. "*Danki*, Joseph. I'll come back in a couple of weeks and check on you."

He smiled. "Next time, could you bring some pie? I really love pie."

Emily was so very aware of the piece of paper in her pocket as she drove the buggy back to her house. It seemed to burn straight through her clothes, which was silly, but she supposed love could do that to a person. Turn them silly.

She wished they lived closer to each other. She was so anxious to call Luke, she was bursting at the seams. As it stood now, it would be another half an hour before she could even think about calling him, and that would mean she would only get to talk to him twenty minutes or so before it was time to start the milking again. Coupled with the fact that church was at the Ebersols' house this week, it would be days and days before she could call him again.

She sighed. She would take anything she could get. She just hoped Luke answered when she called.

The phone rang three times before he answered.

"Hello?"

Emily's mouth went dry. It had been months since she had talked to him, but he sounded close, as if she could reach out a hand and touch him. "Luke?"

"Emily. It's so *gut* to hear your voice." His smile floated across the lines as clear as his words.

"You, too. How is everything for you?"

"It's amazing here." She listened while he chatted about sponsors, dirt tracks, and safety gear. She understood none of it, but listened as closely as she could. He seemed happy, so much so her heart gave a lurch. It wasn't that she wanted him to be unhappy, but how would he ever return to Wells Landing if the *Englisch* world was tempting him with fulfillment of his dreams?

"I share a place with three other guys," Luke said, finally taking a break from racing talk. "It's sort of crowded, but we all seem

119

to get along."

"When are you coming home?" Her time to talk to him was quickly evaporating, like mist in the summer sun.

Someone spoke on the other end of the line. Not Luke. "Listen, Emily, I have to go."

"Jah," she said, trying not to let her disappointment taint her voice. She really needed to get off the phone before she raised her *dat*'s suspicions as well.

"Call me tomorrow, okay?"

"I can't. We've got church here this week and —"

"Then call me when you can, okay?" His tone seemed distracted.

"Jah," she said, pushing her frustration deep inside. *"Ich liebe dich."*

"I love you, too," he said, and then he was gone.

CHAPTER EIGHT

The next two days were filled with cleaning and cooking and otherwise getting ready for the church service to be held at their house.

As was their usual custom, they had started cleaning weeks ago, washing down the walls, cleaning the baseboards, and polishing the windows.

Emily told herself that she had been too busy to tell Mary about her conversation with Luke, but the truth was she wanted to keep it all to herself. She only wished he had answered her last question, and she knew when she could expect him home.

"Mamm?" Emily started just after breakfast Friday morning. "I know there is still a lot left for us to do, but I was hoping to ride out to the Riehl farm today and visit with James."

Helen turned from drying the dishes. "I think that's a fine idea."

"I promised him I would be by this week,

but the time seems to have gotten away from me."

Mamm nodded. "That is the way of church week, *jah*? So much to do."

"So much that you wouldn't be able to ride out there with me?"

"Me?" *Mamm* stacked the dry plates, one on top of the other, and lifted them into the cupboard above her head. "Why, I don't know."

"Please, *Mamm*. It's just . . ."

Her mother dried her hands on a dishcloth and studied her with those pale blue eyes. "What is on your mind, Emily Jane?"

She never could get one over on her *mudder*. Too many years as the bishop's wife had honed her skills to a fine point. "I want James to come to the church service this week, and I don't think Joy or Elam will let him attend if I ask. But if you were to invite him . . ."

"You think I would be more successful?"

"Jah." In fact, she was sure of it.

"Come to think of it, I haven't seen James around much at all since his accident. He was outside a few minutes at the work frolic last week."

"He has headaches," Emily explained. "Joy and Elam are afraid he's going to fall."

"Now, Emily, I know you are trying to be

helpful, but it seems to me they know his limitations better than you or I."

Then she definitely wasn't telling her mother about the information she'd given them earlier in the week. "But it would be *gut* for him to come to church, *jah*?"

Her *mamm* nodded.

"And since we are hosting this week we could make sure he is comfortable."

"Jah."

"And safe."

Mamm nodded again.

"I think it would be *gut* for everyone. Joy and Elam could both attend the services, and James could be here, too."

Her *mamm* smiled. "Tie your *kapp* strings and get in the buggy. We've got some convincing to do."

Elam looked less than convinced two hours later as Emily and her *mamm* sat at the Riehls' table sharing a pot of coffee with him and Joy.

"I don't know," Elam said, but his tone was anything but happy. It perfectly matched his stern frown.

Emily had thought she'd made such progress on Monday. What a difference a few days could make.

Joy, on the other hand, seemed intrigued

123

by the idea. Intrigued and perhaps a little frightened.

"I am ashamed I did not think of this earlier," *Mamm* said. "I s'pose I just got used to seeing only one of you at the service and didn't think twice about it."

"It's *allrecht,*" Joy said, stirring a teaspoon of sugar into her second cup. "It's a big district, and you have a lot to accomplish of your own."

"That is no excuse. Thankfully, Emily here pointed out my shortcoming."

Elam scowled at Emily. She shifted in her chair and glanced out the window to keep from having to meet his hard stare.

"*Danki,* Emily," Joy said, but she shook her head. "I don't know how we would manage though."

"Like we always do," *Mamm* insisted. "Together. I will send Mary over that morning, and she can help you get the girls ready. All you have to do is get James into the buggy and over to our house."

"I don't know," Joy said again, though Emily could feel her weakening.

"I want to go."

They all turned as James's voice sounded from the hallway. He stood, arms braced on either side of him as he balanced himself between the rooms.

"James." Joy was on her feet in an instant, Elam right at her side. "You should be in bed," she admonished. She tried to get him to let go of the walls and follow her back down the hallway, but James was too busy looking past her to their guests.

"You said you would come."

Emily smiled. "A promise is a promise."

"And you wore your purple dress."

"I said I would."

James smiled. "Will you wear it to church on Sunday?"

"If that is what you want."

"*Jah,*" he said. "I'm going to church on Sunday." He sounded like a child about to throw a fit.

"Right now you need to go back and lay down." Joy's voice was unwavering.

"But I want to see Emily and her purple dress."

"Does your head hurt? I'll get you some pills," Joy continued as if he hadn't spoken.

"I do not want pills. They make me dizzy and go to sleep."

"We will talk to the doctor about that next week. For now, you need to sleep," she soothed.

"But I want to see Emily's dress."

Emily shifted uncomfortably in her seat as both her mother and Elam stared at her.

Almost like she had done something wrong. Well, at least that was the way Elam was staring at her.

"You can see it Sunday," Joy promised. "But only if you go back to bed."

James hesitated. "*Jah,* okay then." He smiled at Emily. "*Danki* for coming to see me again."

"You are welcome," she said, returning his smile.

Joy led him down the hallway, their voices drifting away as she managed to get him back to his room.

"It seems my *dat* has fallen a bit in love with you." Elam's words held an accusing edge, but he didn't look as angry as he had before. That had to be *gut, jah*?

"We only want to help him," her *mamm* said, saving her the trouble of coming up with a suitable response.

His green eyes softened until they were the color of a spring meadow after the rain. When he looked like that, not so mad, his face filled with love, and not worry, he seemed like a different person.

Emily wanted to reach across the table and smooth the last of the wrinkles from his brow. Once they were gone, the transformation would be complete. Elam Riehl would be changed from a worried soul into a handsome man.

"*Danki,* Emily . . . Helen. Your care and concern have been most welcome."

She wasn't so sure about that, but Emily was certainly glad she brought her mother along for the trip. There was something about the bishop's wife that made everyone sit up a little straighter and see things a bit clearer.

Her *mamm* stood and smoothed non-existent creases out of her *frack* and flawless black apron. "So we'll see you Sunday morning, *jah*? All of you." It wasn't really a question, more of a confirmation of an order.

"*Jah.*" Elam nodded. "We will be there."

"That Emily Ebersol seems like a *gut maedel.*" Elam's *mamm* took a sip of *kaffi* and eyed him over the rim of her cup. The look on her face was far too innocent to be anything but a ruse.

"*Jah?*" Elam leaned one hip against the sink and feigned his own guileless expression.

"So considerate and kind."

He allowed his gaze to drift out the window over the sink. Johanna, Norma, and the twins were playing their own version of Corner Ball. Becky served as the referee while the last litter of pups danced in and out between their legs and nipped at the hems on their skirts.

Emily was considerate and kind, but it wasn't something he wanted to think about. He had mulled it over too many years to count. That time was over now. If it had ever begun.

"She'll make some man a *gut fraa.*"

Elam poured the rest of his coffee down the drain and rinsed his cup. "*Jah* . . . Luke Lambright."

Mamm's forehead puckered into a frown. "I thought Luke had run off to join the *Englisch.*"

"He'll be back." With a girl like Emily Ebersol waiting for him, Luke would be a fool not to return to Wells Landing.

"It seems to me that he's not here. And you are."

Elam sighed. Time to meet this head-on. "What are you suggesting, *Mamm*?"

She delicately shrugged and took another sip, that too-innocent expression settling back over her face. "Nothing."

He waited, sure there was more to come.

"You have dedicated so much of your life to this farm. Maybe it's time you started thinking about marriage."

And there it was. "I hardly have time to

do my work and sleep. How am I supposed to go courtin'?"

He was twenty-five years old. Most of his friends were long-ago married. Some even had two or three *kinner.* He was the male equivalent of an old maid. A sworn bachelor. Wasn't that what the *Englisch* called it?

A lot like Abe Fitch.

But Abe just got married, the voice inside him whispered. Old Abe had waited years and years for the one woman he wanted and now that their lives were half over, they would get to spend the rest together.

Is that what Elam wanted? To wait until it was almost too late and then try to find someone to spend his days with?

"A man can find the time if he so chooses." *Mamm* stood and brought her cup to the sink, rinsing it out and setting it next to Elam's. "We'll find someone to help us," *Mamm* started. "We've put it off too long. Emily said she would come help with your *vatter.* Her sister Mary promised to ask Aaron Miller if he'd be interested in coming to help with the milking and other chores. Once those things are in place, you will have plenty of time to court and such."

"What brought all this on?" He asked the question, but he was almost afraid of what her answer might be.

129

She shrugged again. "I have just been thinking about it." She didn't look him in the eye, giving him the suspicion she was not being entirely truthful. "It is time you had some happiness. Perhaps even your own family."

He couldn't find the words to answer.

"Once we get help, you'll have more time for the sweeter things in life."

That was exactly what he needed: Time to pursue the one girl in the county he couldn't have.

CHAPTER NINE

Sunday dawned with blue skies and a thin layer of frost twinkling in the sunlight. So very soon temperatures would drop even lower and winter would officially come to Wells Landing.

Emily couldn't say she liked winter, but she enjoyed the change from one season to the next. Oklahoma winters were unpredictable at best. The morning could be sixty-five and breezy, with snow falling the same day at sunset. Such changes were hard, but expected. Though she hoped tonight would be a little more even. Especially since the youth singing would be held at their house.

But first . . .

She turned the buggy into the Riehls' driveway. So much for her mother sending Mary over to help. As the oldest, Emily felt she should be at home helping to get ready for the church service, taking care of the final details before everyone started arriving.

She parked her buggy and set the brake. For this trip she wouldn't unhitch the horses. Soon enough they would be back on the road headed toward home.

Becky opened the door, a bright smile spreading across her face. "*Guder mariye,* Emily. Come in, come in."

Emily stepped into the house and hugged her young friend.

"I was expecting Mary."

"*Mamm* sent me instead." She shrugged.

Becky smiled. "*Dat* will be pleased."

The Riehl house on a church Sunday morning was a lot like the Ebersols'. The milking had been done long ago, but five girls were trying to get ready to go. Add in James who was so excited about attending church for the first time in a year, and the atmosphere was more than chaotic.

Emily brushed out Johanna's hair and twisted it into a tidy knot at the back of her head. Then she pinned on her prayer *kapp.* She sent Johanna on her way, then did the same for Norma. In no time at all, the girls were dressed and ready to go.

"I want to ride with Emily." James rubbed his hands together and grinned. Couldn't they see how good this was for him? A high flush rode his cheeks, making him look like a kid at Christmas. His eyes twinkled, and his lips had curved into a permanent smile.

"The sun is awfully bright today." Joy shaded her eyes and cast a concerned glance toward James.

"I almost forgot." Emily pulled out the dark sunglasses she had bought for just this occasion and handed them to James.

He slid them on his face. If anything, his grin grew even wider as he swung his gaze from one side of the yard to the other.

"It'll help with the glare and your headaches," Emily explained.

The family seemed to hold its collective breath.

"That is against the *Ordnung*," Joy whispered.

Elam frowned.

"I have it on good authority that the bishop does not object."

Everyone relaxed. Except for Elam. What was his problem today? Was it outside help that he objected to or her in general?

"*Danki*, Emily." James grabbed her hand much like Johanna would have and squeezed her fingers.

"You're welcome."

Then he turned his head, this way and that, as if posing for invisible cameras. "Do

I look like a movie star?"

Everyone laughed. Except for Elam, of course.

"An Amish movie star." Ruthie chuckled.

"Maybe you could be on one of those television shows," Becky said.

"What do you know of those shows?" Elam scowled at his sister.

Becky mumbled something and looked off over the pasture.

"We'd better go if we want to get there in time." Emily had to say something to break the tension. Hadn't Elam said he wanted Becky to enjoy her *rumspringa*? What harm was there in a little bit of television? Emily had certainly never been afforded such freedoms during her own run-around time. Sometimes being the bishop's daughter was harder than anyone knew.

"I want to ride with *Dat,* too." Norma took his hand into hers and bounced on the balls of her feet.

The twins joined in, chanting that they wanted to ride to church with their *vatter* as well.

Elam let out a shrill whistle that Emily was certain he used to summon his live-stock. "Of course everyone is going to ride with Dat. Now get in the buggy. *Dummle.* Hurry, before we are late."

James crossed his arms and frowned, looking all the more like a spoiled *Englisch* movie star in Plain clothes. "I am riding with Emily."

All at once the chatter began again as the girls argued as to who would ride with Emily and their father.

Elam whistled again. It was a handy trick for sure.

The girls immediately fell silent.

"Not everyone can ride in Emily's buggy," Elam said.

Immediate protests sprang up.

Elam frowned.

As if sensing they had pushed their *bruder* beyond the limits of his good nature, the sisters fell silent once again.

Obviously he didn't like the disobedience he received from his siblings. He had been head of the household for a year and evidently had grown accustomed to everyone following his orders.

"I could drive your buggy," Emily said. "And you can drive mine."

The buggy she'd brought could only comfortably seat four, but the Riehls' buggy could hold the entire family.

"That's a perfect idea." Joy nodded.

Elam looked like he wanted to protest, but the words didn't come.

The girls cheered, and they scrambled into the large buggy without another word.

Elam helped his father climb inside. He was still frowning, his scowl the direct opposite of his father's soppy grin.

"He'll be fine," Emily said quietly. She didn't receive so much as a grunt in response. Had Elam even heard her?

He slid the door closed. "Hang on here, if you feel dizzy."

James patted his son's hand where it rested in the open widow of the buggy. "I am fine. Emily will take *gut* care of me."

Elam gave a stern nod, then disappeared from view.

Emily set the horses in motion.

James laughed and grabbed his hat as they started down the road. Everyone seemed happy, content, even excited to be on their way to church.

Couldn't Elam see that? His family needed normalcy, something to let them know that despite their hardships, God was good and watching over them all.

"Why such a look, Elam?" *Mamm* asked him as they drove Emily's small buggy back to her house.

He relaxed his features into what he hoped was an impassive expression. It seemed the more time he spent around the bishop's oldest daughter, the more he scowled.

"No look," he said.

But from the frown on *Mamm*'s face she wasn't convinced. "I think perhaps this has something to do with our new helper."

"I don't want to talk about Emily Ebersol." His voice came out sterner than he intended.

"Why not?"

Elam shook his head. The woman had upset everything about his way of living. She had come in unwanted and started rearranging what Elam had spent the last year carefully stacking into place.

How could he explain that to *Mamm*?

"She would make a good *fraa*."

Elam grunted. "So you've said." She would make a *gut* wife for someone. Nor would he admit that out loud. She was kind and caring, beautiful even with her chocolate brown hair and eyes the color of twilight. She was smart and brave, but her heart belonged to Luke Lambright.

"Do you really think I don't know?"

He turned his attention from the road to stare at her. His heart gave a hard pound of apprehension. "Know what?"

"That you are in love with Emily."

An immediate protest sprang to his lips.

"She is in love with someone else."

Mamm shook her head. "Luke Lambright is not coming back here, and Emily's not leaving her family. Seems to me you have a *gut* opportunity to show her you care."

He pulled his gaze from *Mamm*'s to stare over the swaying rears of the horses. "I don't know."

"I do." He saw her nod out of the corner of his eye. "It would help if you would stop glowering at her whenever she gets near."

"I don't glower," he lied.

"You do." A small laugh escaped her. "How is she supposed to know you care if you keep trying to scare her away?" She stopped. "That is it, *jah*? You don't want her to know that you care."

"I don't know what you are talking about," he said, feeling very much like a bug trapped in a jar. "She is a menace." A beautiful menace, for sure.

"Mm-hmm," *Mamm* murmured. "Be sure to add these lies to your prayer list today."

Back before Elam could even remember, Bishop Riehl had built on a special room to his house for when church services were held there. The room was open and airy with large unadorned windows that let nature be a part of the service. Elam wasn't sure which he liked best: the dark cool services held in the barns or the bright service held in what the Ebersols referred to as the "bonus room."

He supposed it served two purposes. It gave them extra room for when they hosted church. But it also gave the family a place to gather to play games and enjoy each other's company.

Today it was filled with rows of benches from the bench wagon. As usual, there was a walkway through the middle. The women gathered on one side and the men on the other. Special cushioned seats had been set up across the back for the elderly and infirm.

"James, you sit here." Emily guided him to one of those chairs and held his arm to steady him while he lowered himself into the seat. He was still wearing those dark glasses. If anyone thought it strange, they hadn't said. More than anything, the district seemed happy to see James up and about.

"And you sit here." He patted the seat next to him.

"I'll sit with you," Elam said.

"But I want Emily to sit here."

"I don't mind," she said.

But Elam did.

He bit back his protests. Everything that

sprang to mind seemed petty and unwarranted. Emily was only trying to help, but his pride had reared its ugly head. She wanted to help now. But where had she been the past year?

He tamped down the memories of her bringing by casseroles and pies those first couple of months.

If he could admit the truth to himself, then he needed to stay a little angry at her. Otherwise he might find himself head over heels for her once again.

The three-hour service seemed to fly by for Emily. Maybe it was because James found such joy in the Word. He kept his glasses on during the service to help with the glare streaming in from the large windows, but she could tell. He only took his gaze from the speaker when the congregation was asked to kneel and pray.

His happiness was nearly tangible like the heat rising off the pavement in August. She could feel the elation he had for being out, being in church, and just being.

At the end of the service, the benches were flipped over and pushed together to make tables for the food service. Both Joy and Elam tried to take over the care of James, but he wouldn't hear of it. He looped his arm through Emily's for balance and did his best to talk to everyone he saw.

Emily could tell it was both fun and hard for him. Some people he remembered right off, while others had names that eluded him. In the end, she would allow him a chance to remember, then she'd whisper the name as to not allow him to get frustrated.

"Will you eat with me?" James asked as the women began serving the meal.

Emily hesitated. The men were served first, then the women and children. As in church, the males and females separated from each other, sometimes even sitting across the yard from one another.

"I know that it's not . . . not . . ."

"Customary?" she supplied.

James smiled. "*Jah,* but I want to talk with you more."

"Okay," she said, unable to refuse him. He was such a kind soul. His family had been through so much. If he wanted to talk while they ate, then that was what they would do. If the church elders had a problem with it, then she would deal with it later. "I will find us some place shady to eat."

James gave a small nod. He looked tired,

as if the morning had been too much for him.

"Are you sure you don't want to go home and rest?"

"Nay," he said. "I can rest next Sunday."

She made them both a plate and together they walked to the shade of the large maple tree. Already the leaves had begun to change, turning a brilliant orange against the clear blue sky.

They garnered a few looks as they settled down together under the branches, but no one said a word. Among those looks was the hard stare of Elam Riehl. She couldn't tell if he was angry or thoughtful.

"My son is jealous," James said as if he could read her thoughts.

"W-what?" she stammered.

James took a bite of the cheese and cracker stacks she had made for him. She had purposefully chosen food he could eat with his fingers, things he wouldn't spill with his unsteady hands. "I think he would rather be over here eating with a pretty *maedel* instead of with the men."

Emily laughed. "Did you do this on purpose?"

James dropped his chin to his chest, but not before she caught the quick flash of his grin. "*Jah.* A man must seize his opportunities."

"Is that what you call it?"

"For sure and for certain."

They ate in a comfortable silence while everyone around them chatted amongst themselves. James seemed to be content to just be outside, be among the others, even if he couldn't participate as he had before the accident.

"I am different now than I was before," he said, startling her out of her own thoughts. Could he read her mind? "I know this."

"It does not mean the change is bad."

"I know I'm not as quick-minded as I used to be."

She didn't know how to respond, so she kept quiet and let him continue.

"*Danki,* Emily Ebersol, for treating me like I am."

Emily swallowed hard, unable to get the last bite of her biscuit past the lump of emotion in her throat. "I only treat you like a person."

He shook his head. "Joy and Elam," he slowly started. "They coddle me. They won't let me do for myself."

"They love you very much."

"I know."

"They are only trying to protect you."

"I don't want to be protected. I want to live."

Emily fell silent. She supposed a nearly fatal accident would do that to a person. It would definitely make her want to make the most of the life she had left.

"James." Joy approached, her expression unreadable. "You have kept Emily to yourself for too long now. Are you ready to go home?"

"Can we stay just a little longer please? I haven't had dessert yet."

Joy's brow puckered into a frown, but otherwise her expression remained unreadable. "It's time for your pain medication."

"I would rather have a piece of Esther Lapp's banana cream pie."

"Esther Fitch," Emily corrected. "She got married, you know."

James tilted his head at a thoughtful angle, like a pup deciphering a sound. "She got married?"

"To Abe Fitch."

He turned his eyes to his wife. "Why didn't you tell me?"

Joy shrugged. "It didn't seem important."

"It is very important," he insisted.

If the pitch of his tone was any indication, he was about to have a meltdown. As a former schoolteacher, she had seen it too many times to count.

Emily laid a comforting hand on James's sleeve. "What Joy means to say is, in light of your injury and healing, the news about the wedding had to be prioritized."

A frown wrinkled his strong brow, almost hiding the scar that ran from one temple and disappeared under the brim of his hat. "I don't know what that word means now."

"It means things are placed in order of importance," Emily explained. "The wedding wasn't as important as allowing you time to heal."

"Bet it was to Esther and Abe."

She couldn't stop the bark of laughter from escaping. "I'm sure you are right about that, James Riehl."

"Emily, will you help me get him up?"

She stood, even though she knew James did not want to go just yet. She had pushed the boundaries with his family enough for one day.

"I want dessert." James stuck out his bottom lip, but allowed them to hoist him to his feet.

"How about I get you a piece of pie to take home with you?"

James smiled, the look full of sheer ecstasy. "That would be *gut, jah.*"

■ ■ ■ ■

Emily was getting her own slice of pie when Becky hustled over. "You're going to be here tonight for the singing, *jah*?"

She hadn't really thought much about it. She had long since passed her days of youth groups and singings after church. "If you want me to be."

Becky nodded. "*Jah*. Of course."

She ran her arm through Emily's and pulled her along toward the barn.

Everyone had eaten, and the cleanup was nearly complete. Some families with smaller children had already begun to pack up for home.

"There is one other thing," Becky said.

"*Jah?*"

"You need to talk Elam into staying."

Emily's feet stuck to the ground as if they had been nailed there. "Why do I need to do that?"

"So he can get to know Billy Beiler a bit more."

"Are you sure that is all?"

Becky sighed. "All he does is work and take care of the farm. He is doing the job of two men. I'm afraid he's going to be old before his time."

146

"And attending the singing will help?"

"Jah." Becky nodded so vigorously her prayer *kapp* nearly flew off her head.

Yet Emily knew there was more to it than Becky was letting on.

"If you ask him, I am sure he will stay."

"I would not count on that." All he had for her these days was a scowl, a frown, or a moody look. Sometimes all three.

"It's because he likes you, you know?"

"What?" Emily must have heard her wrong.

"Isn't it obvious?" Becky said. "My *bruder* is smitten."

CHAPTER TEN

Becky's words echoed through her head as Emily went in search of her friends Caroline and Lorie. She wanted to see them before everyone left for the afternoon. Since Caroline had gotten married, it seemed she didn't see them as much anymore. Well, that and the fact that she wasn't in town as much these days.

"Emily." Caroline pulled her in for a quick squeeze. "I'm so glad to see you. It has been ages."

"It's been two weeks," Emily protested.

"That's ages to me." Lorie pulled Emily close as soon as Caroline released her.

How she missed her friends.

"I saw you eating with James Riehl," Caroline said. "I wanted to come sit with you, but Emma started fussing."

"Where is Emma?" Emily glanced around to find Caroline's dark-haired toddler.

"Andrew has her. No doubt she's asleep

on his shoulder while he's talking manure and growing seasons." Her eyes sparkled as she spoke of her husband. Her cheeks held a pink flush, and her lips seemed unable to do anything save smile. "I'm glad I found you two," she continued. "I wanted to tell you something."

"You're having a baby?" Lorie guessed.

Caroline nodded. "But you can't tell anyone."

"Caroline, I'm so *froh* for you." And she was, she thought. Even as she pushed aside the small twinge of jealousy. She could only hope that Luke would give up this crazy notion of driving a race car and come back to Wells Landing.

As it stood now, it would be Lorie's turn before Emily's, even with the on-again, off-again relationship she shared with Jonah Miller.

"I wanted you to be the first to know," Caroline said. "Aside from Andrew."

"And your *mamm* and *dat* . . . and Emma," Lorie said dryly.

"Hush." Emily swatted their friend on the arm. "Be happy for Caroline."

Lorie smiled, the motion lighting up her pretty face. "I am. So happy."

They each gave Caroline another hug and promised not to say a word about it. Pregnancies weren't talked about much in the Amish districts. Talking too much about the baby before it was born was considered a bit on the prideful side.

"Caroline, are you ready?" Andrew Fitch called from near their buggy. As expected, Emma was cradled high in his arms.

"Andrew has a horse about to foal."

"Already?" Emily asked.

Andrew had given up working in his *on-kle*'s furniture store in order to move to the country and raise horses. The move hadn't been that long ago, much too soon for one of the new horses to be giving birth.

Caroline shook her head. "Not one of his. The mare belongs to one of the stables that leases his land. But still he has to be there when the time comes."

She gave them each a quick hug. "I better get over there and take Emma. He's *gut, jah,* but not *gut* enough to harness the horses with one hand."

"I have to be going, too," Lorie said. "Jonah said he wanted to do something special this afternoon, but it's a secret."

Emily hugged her friends and watched them both walk away toward the men they loved. Jealousy was a sin, for sure, but it had certainly raised its head with her today. Maybe instead of trying to convince Elam to stay and help chaperone the singing, she should spend a little more time in prayer.

With a sigh at her own foolishness, she went in search of the frowning Elam Riehl.

"Nay." Elam shook his head with such conviction, Emily wasn't sure if she would ever change his mind. But she had promised Becky, and she would try.

"Why not?"

"I have too much to do." He continued to harness his horses and get the buggy ready for the trip home. It was three o'clock, and soon it would be time to milk again. On both farms.

"Jah, I understand, but Becky wants you to get to know Billy Beiler a little better."

"She is too young to start courtin'." His words brooked no argument.

"She's sixteen. Plenty old enough to start to know her mind. Wouldn't you rather be around for it than not? Your father won't be able to make these decisions about her future. That will be up to you."

His hands stilled. "I have too much to do," he repeated. "And Becky does, too."

Emily propped her hands on her hips and glared at him. Well, at the back of his head. "Stop talking out of both sides of your mouth, Elam Riehl. First you say you want her to have a normal *rumspringa,* then you won't let her attend any singings. It can't be both ways."

She would have thought his frown couldn't get any worse, but somehow it turned into an out-and-out scowl.

"You have interfered with my family enough for one day, Emily Ebersol. I'll thank you to leave us alone for a while."

"What if I come help you?"

He stopped, turned back to her as if contemplating the idea. Then he shook his head. "You have your own milking to do."

"My *shveshtah* can take care of that."

"Milking cows is different than milking goats," he protested.

"Not so very." She propped her hands on her hips. "With all of us working, we can be done in no time."

"Why would you do that for us?"

"I like Becky. I want her to have a *gut* time, too. I would do it for any of my sisters." Why was he being so stubborn?

He seemed to mull over her answer.

She could almost feel his resolve slipping. She pushed a little harder. "Is it help in general that you object to? Or is it help from a bunch of girls?"

"*Jah,* fine. Okay then."

■ ■ ■ ■

He wasn't sure how he got talked into this. He looked around his barn. Once again his world was filled with more girls than he could count.

True to her word, Emily had come for the milking, bringing all her sisters with her. He had to admit that more hands made the job go by a lot faster.

In no time at all, the cows were milked, released back into the pasture, and all the milk had been stored.

They even fed the chickens, mucked out the stalls, and gathered the eggs.

"Are you ready to go back?" Emily asked as she smoothed her hair down on each side.

His fingers itched to do the same. Instead, he shoved his hands into his pockets. "I'm not going to the singing."

"Why not?" Her eyes twinkled, and he had the feeling he was being set up for something he wasn't going to like.

"Please, *bruder.*" Becky was immediately at his side, pulling on his arm as if somehow that would change his mind.

"I am too old for such . . ." He stopped himself before saying nonsense. "Activities," he finished.

"You could chaperone," Becky said.

"That is what the Ebersols are there for."

"Come on," Emily cajoled. "It might be fun."

"Are you serving as chaperone?" he asked her.

"*Jah.* Of course. I gotta keep an eye on Mary and Aaron."

Her sister turned as red as a *riewe.* How could two *maedel* be so different even though they were kin? "Okay."

Wait . . . who said that? The word sprang to his lips without any direction from his brain. He didn't want to sit around while the young people sang and courted.

But you do want to sit around and visit with Emily. Anything to be close to Emily.

"Yay!" Becky did a little dance, then seemed to remember herself. She stilled her feet and smoothed her hands down her apron. "You'll be able to meet Billy Beiler." She grinned as she said his name.

What had he gotten himself into? "I've met Billy before."

"Well, you can get to know him better."

"You're not courtin', and that's final. You can't even join the church until next year when classes start again."

"*Jah,* but . . ." She stopped. "Okay. But you are coming."

Ach, him and his big mouth. "I s'pose."

Instead of having the singing in the house, the youth decided to gather in the barn. Emily secretly thought they believed they would get more privacy in the barn; after all, mules tell no tales. But her father sent her and Elam out as soon as the decision was made.

That was how she found herself sitting on a hay bale next to Becky's brother while the boys sang their songs for the girls.

In a little while, they would serve lemonade and cookies, but for now she was content to sit next to Elam and soak in the sweet voices.

"Look at them," he groused. "They can't keep their eyes off each other."

"Mary and Aaron?" she asked. "*Jah,* I expect he'll ask for her hand after the next wedding season." After all, Mary had to go through her baptism classes as well.

"*Nay.* Becky and Billy Beiler."

"They have liked each other for a long time."

"Why am I just now finding out about this?"

Emily shrugged. "I saw them together at school. They always ate lunch together and wanted to sit together at special events.

Does it bother you?"

"Becky's too young for such matters." He picked at the hay beneath them, tossing the straws aside one by one.

"Not so very. If she joins the church next year and is spoken for the year after, she'll be almost nineteen when she gets married. That's about normal."

The light in his eyes said he knew she was right, but he didn't say the words.

"She seems so young because she is your *shveshtah.*"

"I guess you are right," he finally grumped.

"I know I am."

The singing stopped, and kids started milling around, each getting a glass of lemonade and a stack of cookies.

"Come on." Emily tugged on Elam's sleeve. "Let's go before they notice we're gone."

"Go where?" he asked, but he stood none-theless.

"To get some stuff to decorate one of the buggies."

"Whose buggy?"

Emily scanned the sea of youthful faces. "John Bontrager's buggy. He'll be taking Leah Yoder home tonight. Let's leave them a surprise."

156

She would have decorated Aaron Miller's buggy, but he wasn't taking Mary home since she was already there.

"Decorate how?"

"Crepe paper, flowers, whatever we can find. Didn't you ever do this when you were in a group?"

He shook his head, but allowed her to quietly tug him from the barn.

She had thought that his father's illness had spawned his somber attitude, but it seemed that Elam's serious nature was a gift from God. She chuckled at the thought.

"What's so funny?" he asked as they walked toward the house.

"You."

"Me?"

She shook her head. "I take that back. You are not funny. But you are way too serious. You should lighten up a bit."

"I don't know what you are talking about." He stopped in the middle of the yard and crossed his arms. Between the twilight sky and the dark brim of his hat she couldn't see his eyes. She didn't need to. She knew they were hard green with anger.

"*Jah,* you do."

"There is a lot about my life that is serious."

"And there's a lot that needs to be

changed as well." She skipped up the porch steps. "Are you coming in or not?"

He climbed the steps, then collapsed into the wooden rocker next to the front door. "You go on ahead. I'll wait here."

"Suit yourself," she said, then made her way inside.

Too serious? She honestly thought he was too serious? He was only as serious as his life warranted. He had responsibilities, an injured father, a family to care for, a farm to run.

He didn't have time to be carefree and frivolous. He had responsibilities.

"You already said that."

He jerked around as Emily appeared on the porch once again. He hadn't realized that he had been talking out loud. She would think he was *ab im kopp.* Off in the head.

"Don't worry. Your secret is safe with me."

As she tripped down the steps, he noticed that she held a bulging sack in one hand. "What secret?"

"That you mumble to yourself when you think you are alone. Which one of the buggies is John's? Do you know? Did you see him drive up?"

He followed her down the stairs, his

concentration on the line of buggies parked to one side of the barn. It sure beat staring at her pretty form washed in moonlight.

What did Luke Lambright have that he didn't?

Everything.

Luke was fun-loving, adventuresome. All the things it seemed Emily Ebersol wanted. Why else would she be waiting for him to return?

"I think that's it." Elam pointed to the third buggy in the row.

"Gut, gut." She set the bag down near one of the wheels and started pulling out decorations. "Here." She handed him a roll of blue crepe paper. "Run that through the spokes."

He did as she asked, working the paper ribbon though the wheel.

"You're sure this is John's buggy?" she asked after a bit. "I mean, if it's not . . . how funny would that be?"

Elam laughed, the sound rusty to his own ears. How long had it been since he'd laughed at something . . . anything? Maybe a year. Since his father's accident for sure, but long before that too.

Emily stopped, her gaze seeking him out in the dark night. "You should laugh more often," she said. Her head was tilted at a thoughtful angle. Then she started back again, throwing flower petals onto the floor of the buggy.

"That's it." She stepped back to survey her work. She was so close. He could have reached out and touched her, but he managed to keep his hands at his sides. "Do you think they will like it?"

"*Jah,*" he said, his voice nearly unrecognizable.

She turned to look at him, and the moment froze in time. Had it not been for the sounds of the crickets chirping and the young people singing, he would have thought they were alone in the world.

How easy it would be to reach out, touch her face, pull her close. Kiss her lips.

Her eyes grew wide and darkened to the color of the nighttime sky.

Did she feel it too?

Her lips parted, and a small sigh escaped them.

His hand went up, the backs of his fingers brushing against the smooth curve of her cheek.

"What are you two doing out here?" Becky's voice cut through the night.

He took a hasty step back.

Emily did the same, running her hands down the skirt of her dress. "We . . . uh . . ."

"We were decorating one of the buggies."

His *shveshtah* looked from one of them to the other. Her eyes sparkled. "Well, *kumm* on back inside. We have something to talk about."

Elam gave a quick nod and motioned for them to precede him into the barn.

It appeared the singing was over. The young people milled around talking and pairing up.

Becky led them over to a group of about eight young people, one of which was Billy Beiler.

"We want to go on the haunted hayride," Becky started.

The others nodded while Emily shook her head. "We do not celebrate Halloween."

"Not for Halloween," Becky backpedaled. "Just because."

"Just because." Emily crossed her arms, and Elam got a glimpse of what it must have been like to have her as a teacher.

"*Jah*. It's fun to be scared."

"Fun?" Emily repeated.

"There's nothing in the *Ordnung* against being scared," Billy Beiler said.

"True. But what is the difference in celebrating a holiday and participating in *Englisch* customs?"

"It's not like we want to hang up black

161

and orange decorations or go door to door asking for candy." This was from another *bu.* Elam did not know his name.

"How do we fit into all of this?" Elam asked.

"We want you two to go with us."

"Go with you?" Emily raised her eyebrows so high, Elam couldn't tell where they ended and her hair began.

"*Jah,* please." Becky bounced on the balls of her feet, shaking Emily's hand as if that would clench the deal. "If you go, then the bishop is less likely to protest."

"And you want Elam to go, too." It wasn't quite a question.

"We need at least three chaperones," another girl explained. Melanie, he thought her name was, Lorie Kauffman's sister. "My *shveshtah* has already promised to go. We just need a couple more."

"Please." Becky did her begging dance again.

"I'll do it." Had he just agreed to chaperone his sister's buddy bunch on a hayride? His own words surprised him.

Evidently, they surprised Emily, too. She turned to stare at him, her mouth open. "*Jah?*"

"*Jah.*" She didn't think he was fun or that he knew how to have a *gut* time. Well, he would show her. He could be just as fun-loving and carefree as Luke Lambright. Just wait and see.

CHAPTER ELEVEN

"Hello?"

At the sound of his voice coming through the phone line, Emily collapsed on the corner bench in the phone shanty. "Luke?"

"Emily? Gosh, it's *gut* to hear your voice."

She smiled, a warmth spreading through her from her heart to her fingertips. "Yours, too."

"I was beginning to think you weren't going to call again."

"It's hard to get away, you know?"

"*Jah,*" he said. "I understand. Here, too."

"So everything is *gut*?"

She braced her feet on the opposite wall as she listened to Luke. Just as their last conversation, he talked about racing, racing, and more racing. The excitement in his voice was near tangible, like she could touch it had she been sitting next to him instead of miles away.

"I finished first. It was incredible, Em."

"That sounds great." She tried her best to inject some excitement for him into her voice. She must have succeeded or perhaps he didn't notice that she was a bit distracted.

"That'll bring me a sponsor for sure. And once I sign with someone, the sky's the limit. New car, my own crew, everything." She could hear the smile in his voice. "Are you proud of me?"

"*Hochmut* is a sin."

"Spoken like a true bishop's daughter." He laughed. "Well, hang on to your prayer *kapp,* because I'm about to make the big time. You'll be proud of me whether you want to be or not."

Emily's heart fell. "It's not that I don't want to be proud of you."

"I know." He fell silent on the other end of the phone line as if his excitement could only carry him so far.

"When are you coming home, Luke?"

"Coming home?" His voice sounded suddenly distant. "Em, I don't think you understand. I'm not coming home. I'm about to break into the circuit. I can't leave it now."

"But —" she sputtered, her words getting trapped somewhere below the lump in her throat. "I thought you'd be back by now," she finally managed to choke out.

"I can't leave yet. Not when I'm this close.

Oh, Emily, it's right there . . . I can almost touch it. You'll see," he said. "Someday soon I'm going to be a champion race car driver."

Suddenly, she felt sick to her stomach. Luke wasn't coming home. She had lost the battle between her and race car driving. He loved the *Englisch* world more than her. She jumped to her feet. "I've got to go, Luke. I —" Unable to take it any longer, she hung up the receiver and slammed out of the shanty.

Luke stared at the phone in his hand. "Bye," he whispered.

He turned off the phone and sat down on the edge of the bed. It wasn't much. Really just a single mattress on the floor. He had the attic room in the old house. The last one to arrive always got the attic room, they said. He didn't mind. He was free. Free from the confines of his conservative Amish life.

With a sigh, he leaned back against the angled wall and stared at the picture across the room. His hero, Dale Earnhardt Jr. One day . . . one day he'd drive for a big sponsor like Dale Jr. did. Luke would have all the accolades, all the glory. And Emily would have no choice but to come with him. She'd be overcome with pride for him. And all would be right with the world.

"Luke, are you up here?" Tony Stoltzfus popped his head into Luke's room. Tony was another ex-Amish kid trying to make it in the *Englisch* world. But unlike Luke, Tony only had dreams of working construction, moving out of the transition house, and buying some land of his own. "We're about to order pizza. You want in?"

Luke shook his head. Pizza sounded wonderful, but he only had ten dollars to last him until payday. No one told him living in the *Englisch* world was so expensive. Without an education, he had to work at a fast-food restaurant while he studied for his GED and tried to get time in on the track. At least he ate for free at work. It had only taken a month, and he was already tired of hamburgers.

"Suit yourself." Tony disappeared, and Luke reached into the plastic basket by his bed. He had a bag of chips and a can of peanuts. Not that either one would be able to compete with the enticing aroma of pepperoni pizza. But for now they would have to do.

"Emily?"

At the sound of Mary's voice, she wiped the tears from her face. After hanging up on

Luke, Emily had climbed into the barn loft and succumbed to the tears that threatened.

She thought she had cried them all out, but with one word her sister brought them back again.

"Are you *allrecht?*" Mary knelt down into the hay next to her and wrapped her in a sweet embrace.

"He's not coming back," she sobbed. "He loves the *Englisch* world, and he said he's not coming back here. Mary, what am I supposed to do?"

"Shhh," her sister soothed, rubbing a hand down the side of her face and rocking her back and forth. The action was so much like their mother's, Emily's tears came faster. She needed her mother right now more than ever, but *Mamm* wouldn't understand. She had heard her *eldra* talking about her and Luke and Elam Riehl. They thought Elam was good for her, steady and strong, and he would take her mind off Luke.

Instead, she was heartbroken. Shattered. Luke was never coming back to Wells Landing. How was she supposed to go on?

"You just do," Mary said, her wisdom far beyond her age and experience. Mary had been born old, understanding more than most people three times her age. "If Luke means to stay in the *Englisch* world, that proves it is God's will."

"I don't want it to be God's will."

Her sister smiled against her hair. "That's one of the hardest things about it, *jah?*"

Emily pulled away so she could stare into her sister's sky blue eyes. "I've never loved anyone else. Ever." Not since the third grade when Luke Lambright had shared his lunch with her and pushed her in the big tire swing all recess long. They had been inseparable since then.

Until *rumspringa* and race car driving had reared their ugly heads and turned Luke's attention away from her.

"Did he say it out right? Did he use those words? 'I'm never coming back'?"

"He didn't have to." Emily sniffed one last time and pushed herself up straight.

Her sister let her go and settled down in the hay beside her.

This had always been their safe place, the place to go when things turned bad, when trouble started. Not that they had many trying times in their lives. But this was the worst.

"If he didn't tell you he wasn't coming back, there's always a chance he will."

Emily shook her head. Talking about it helped. "You didn't hear his voice." She took a shuddering breath, her sobs finally subsiding. "He was so excited."

"As hard as this is, you know what this means." Mary gently took Emily's hand into her own.

Emily squeezed her sister's fingers in understanding. "That it wasn't meant to be."

"*Jah.*"

"I just . . . I mean, I always . . ."

"Of course you did."

"I've never even looked at another boy." As the words fell from her lips, Sunday night with Elam drifted into her thoughts. He had almost kissed her. She knew enough to know that he had wanted to. Had his sister not interrupted them, he might have done just that.

And a part of her — a small part — had wanted him to.

She shook the thought away. She had never wanted to kiss anyone but Luke. Had never kissed anyone but him.

With all the talk of weddings and engagements, she must be getting sentimental. *Jah,* that was all there was to it. She was falling prey to the romance of romance and not the crisp fall night and a pair of meadow green eyes.

"This is going to be so much fun." Becky

linked arms with Emily and smiled. Emily couldn't help but return the gesture. She wasn't sure *fun* was the right word for it. How had she allowed herself to be talked into a haunted hayride? She hated being scared. She hated even thinking about it. Yet here she was about to be terrified witless on an *Englisch* adventure. All in the name of chaperoning a friend.

"Are you ready?" The driver tipped his cap back, revealing weird yellow eyes with pupils like a cat.

Emily gasped.

Becky laughed. "They are contacts, silly."

The driver smiled. She supposed he was trying to take the edge off her terror, but she wasn't sure that was possible.

"Let's get this over with," she muttered.

"Eight to a wagon," the driver said. He pushed his cap back down and slapped his gloves against one thigh before heading toward the lead wagon.

Emily shivered. It was a chilly night. Or was it the anticipation sending goose bumps skittering across her skin? She pulled her wool coat a little tighter around her.

"We're riding in the second wagon," Lorie said, pulling Jonah Miller along behind her.

There were three wagons in all. Emily did a quick count and figured out that four couples could ride in a wagon, but not if she and Elam each rode in the other two. She started for the front wagon to find it full with four smiling couples. One of which was Becky and Billy Beiler.

Please, her eyes begged, and Emily immediately understood. Becky wanted a little time alone with her boyfriend.

"I've got one more spot in the back," the driver of the third wagon called.

That meant she'd be riding with Elam. How foolish would she look if she protested?

Resigned, she made her way to the last wagon. A plastic milk crate had been placed bottom-up to provide a makeshift step stool.

She stepped up, and then Elam was there. He was already in the back of the hay-filled wagon, extending a hand.

She allowed him to pull her up beside him. His grasp was warm and solid, a lot like the man himself.

"I saved you a spot." He gestured toward the far end of the wagon closestto the driver. "I thought you might be more comfortable with your back protected."

Was her fear that obvious?

"Danki." Her hand still enclosed in his, they picked their way between the feet and legs of the other riders.

Elam let go of her hand to settle himself

on the hay. The only spot left was the one right next to him.

She held herself in check as the driver clicked the horses into motion. They set off down a dirt road with trees lining both sides. Only the moon and a battery-operated lantern provided any light at all.

The driver wasn't kidding about there being no more room than eight to a wagon. As it was, she bumped shoulders with Elam with each step the horses took.

"Relax," Elam whispered next to her. "You're scaring the kids."

She hadn't realized she was clenching her teeth until he said something. At the rate she was going, she would grind her molars to dust before they finished the ride. "Is it that obvious?" she whispered in return.

"That you are terrified? *Jah.* That Norma would be a better chaperone for a haunted hayride? *Jah.* That my sister is falling over herself to get us together? Double *jah.*"

She chuckled in spite of her fear. "You think Becky is trying to get us together?"

He shook his head. "I don't think. I know she is."

"But you volunteered to come along tonight."

"*Jah.* I did."

"Why?"

He took her hand into his own. At first Emily had been chastising herself for not wearing thick gloves; now she was glad she hadn't. His hands were warm and strong, callous and tough. The kind of hands that took care of things. "I didn't want you to think I don't know how to have fun."

"Why would I think that?" she asked, when she should have really inquired as to why it mattered to him. Somehow she knew.

He turned her fingers over and studied her palm in the dim lantern glow. "I've always thought you were special. But you only seemed to have eyes for Luke Lambright." His sweet words washed over her. It wasn't the response she had expected, but it answered so much more.

Had Elam had a crush on her all these years? Was she the reason he never married?

She shook the thought away. Ridiculous. She couldn't have been the reason. He'd dated girls . . . hadn't he?

Her eyes met his, and she couldn't look away. She needed to say something . . . anything to break the spell she was under.

She opened her mouth, then screamed as a mummy jumped out from behind the trees at the edge of the forest.

Echoes of screams and laughter sounded all around them as the "haunted" part of the hayride began.

Terrified, she drew up her knees and buried her face in her skirt. Not the most dignified position, but it was better than risking an accidental glance at the monsters she could hear stirring in the surrounding woods.

Beside her Elam chuckled. Then she felt his arm around her as he pulled her close and tucked her chin into the shelter of his shoulder.

Warm and safe. Those words perfectly described how she felt next to him. She was still scared out of her mind, but at least she knew he would be there to help her.

"Why did you agree to come on this trip?" His voice sounded just above her ear. She felt it before she heard it, as the question rumbled up from his chest before crossing his lips.

"Because I like your sister."

He chuckled again. "Tell me how much you like her after this ride is over."

Emily shook her head and buried her nose a little deeper into the edge of Elam's coat.

Some chaperone she was turning out to be.

Elam smiled to himself as Emily snuggled a little closer to him. Having her this close was sweet torture. He wanted so badly to tell her how long he had waited for this moment, but would it really change anything?

That it might, the logical side of him countered. He would never know unless he told her how he felt.

His heart thumped in his chest at the mere thought of confessing his love for her. He was twenty-five years old, and he had never once talked about his feelings with another. Especially not the girl he loved more than life itself.

The past couple of weeks had been even harder for him. To see her at his house, surrounded by his family . . . She had helped his *dat* come out of his shell, she had helped his *mamm* and his sisters with their work. And even helped him so they could chaperone the youth singing. Her constant presence only reinforced the fact that he wanted her with them, as part of his family for always and forever.

And how had he responded? With disdain and anger. He hadn't meant to treat her poorly, but he had to protect his heart and his family. Yet here he was with her wrapped in his embrace like she never wanted to let him go.

Dare he hope?

There was only one way to find out.

Chapter Twelve

"Emily," he whispered into her hair.

"Hmmm?" She didn't lift her head, which was okay with him. He might have more courage to say what needed to be said if he didn't have to stare into those midnight eyes. Plus, he loved the warmth of her soft breath on his neck.

"I'm sorry about the way I've acted toward you. I know you were only trying to help."

"It's *allrecht.*" She snuggled down a little closer; he was sure to block out all the noise going on around them. Monsters he couldn't identify jumped out from behind trees and haystacks. The youth group delighted in being scared. The girls screamed while the boys laughed and pretended to protect them.

"Can I . . . uhum . . . can I tell you something?" His voice cracked like a young teen's, and he was glad for the cover of the darkness. It hid the hot flush creeping up his neck.

"Jah."

"It's just that I —" Before he could finish the sentence the driver hollered, "Whoa," and the wagon slowed to a stop.

"Is it over?" Emily lifted her head, her gaze hesitantly bouncing around. She still had her hands fisted in the lapels of his coat

"I don't know," he said, looking around. "Maybe."

But if he were going to end a hayride, it certainly wouldn't be in the middle of the woods. Yet the teens stood up and climbed from the back of the wagon. Stretching and . . . waiting? Perhaps they would serve refreshments.

Elam pushed up from the wagon and reached out a hand to help Emily to her feet. He loved the feel of her fingers entwined with his and was loath to let her go. What would she do if he didn't? What would she do if he just kept holding her hand all night long?

The question wouldn't be answered as he hopped down from the back of the wagon. He couldn't very well stay glued to her side as he jumped to the ground. Even better, he got to place his hands on her waist and hoist her down beside him. His fingers longed to stay on her waist, just linger there, absorbing her warmth and the essence that was Emily. He knew he couldn't stay that way for long. After a while, someone was bound to notice and say —

"Zombies!"

Emily's eyes widened in fear. Elam glanced around and sure enough, zombies lurched from the woods. They walked slowly toward the groups of youngsters who squealed and laughed and scrambled back into the wagons. Elam lifted Emily into the buckboard once again, following behind her with a laugh.

"I don't see what is so funny, Elam Riehl."

"Not a thing." He did his best to squelch his chuckles, then executed a quick head count and whistled for the driver to set the wagon in motion once again.

He smiled to himself as Emily tucked her head into his shoulder once more. If he'd known this was what it would take to get close to Emily Ebersol, he'd have scheduled a haunted hayride years ago.

Emily pressed her face into Elam's coat and tried her best not to breathe too deeply. Every breath she took pulled in more and more of his scent. It was an odd combination of outdoors, laundry detergent, and shave cream. Somehow, on him, it was irresistible.

His chest rumbled beneath her fingertips.

"It's not funny, Elam Riehl."

Suppressed laughter gained a voice, and his chuckles filled the air around them. "I have it on good faith that it is."

"To you maybe."

If she hadn't had her face pressed against him, she wouldn't have felt the small hitch in his breath. It was tiny, just a little catch that would have otherwise gone unnoticed.

Her own breath lodged in her throat. This was too intimate by far. She was cuddled up to Elam, more than likely giving him the wrong idea about her . . . about them.

She pushed herself away from the protective warmth of his embrace. "I'm sorry," she whispered into the night. She didn't want any of the youths to hear. After all, she had come along as an escort. Instead, what kind of example had she been setting for the group?

"You don't have to apologize," he said, but he let her go.

Had she imagined the intimacy of his tone or the implications that he wanted to say more to her?

She must have.

"I shouldn't have come," she said. "I should have known better."

He shook his head. "You were trying to do something nice for someone else. That is not without its own rewards."

Confusion swamped her. She had started this as a favor to Becky, but now it seemed like so much more was happening. Or had she just imagined it? Had Elam held her with more tenderness than he would have anyone else?

She chanced a quick look in his direction. Whether it was the cover of the night or something else, she couldn't tell. His expression was unreadable.

Maybe she had imagined the whole thing.

As October faded into November, the market closed, and the wedding season geared up.

"Are you ready to go?" Emily tied her black travel bonnet under her chin and waited as Mary came hurrying out of the kitchen.

"I'm coming. I'm coming."

"Do you need an extra blanket?" *Mamm* called as they grabbed their wool coats and plain black scarves. It was cold for early November, but the sun shone brightly in the sky, promising warm temperatures as the day wore on.

"I think we'll be *allrecht.*" Mary tied her

bonnet, and Emily shifted from foot to foot.

She had been more than a little impatient these days. Her normally even disposition seemed to be a bit on edge, like she was waiting for something to happen. She felt like she had when the monsters jumped out at their wagon during the haunted hayride. Whatever was about to happen could occur at any minute, and she wasn't quite ready for it.

"Tell Jonah's *mudder* I'm sorry I have to miss it," *Mamm* said, pressing the wrinkles out of Bea's *fur gut* apron.

"She understands, *Mamm.*" Emily tried her best to take the edge out of her voice, but a tad of it crept in anyway. There were three weddings today. And that was in their district alone. Her *mamm* and other sisters were heading to one wedding while she and Mary were heading off to another.

"Be safe, girls," *Mamm* called as they headed out the door.

"*Was iss letz,* Emily? You've been acting strange all day," Mary said as they hurried along toward their buggy.

"I have not."

"You're right," Mary said with a quick nod. "It's been longer than that. You've been acting strange since you chaperoned the hayride for Becky Riehl. . . ." Mary's words

182

trailed off and a grin took their place on her lips. "Did something happen between you and Elam?"

The heat started somewhere under the collar of her dress and worked its way clear up to her hairline. The flush was so great, the cold November air seemed like an Arctic blast against her skin. "I do not know what you are talking about."

Mary's smile widened, and Emily did her best to ignore it, to act natural. Yet her every step seemed forced and jerky. "It is a sin to lie, Emily Jane."

She sighed. She never could keep anything from her sister. "Nothing happened," she said. "Not really. But something . . ." She climbed into the buggy, and Mary followed suit. Her sister pulled the thick wool blanket from the back and set it between them, ready in case they needed the extra warmth.

"He likes you, you know," Mary said once they were both seated.

Emily pretended to be wholly concentrating on turning the buggy around and heading the horses down the driveway, but in truth she didn't know how to respond to such a claim. "He does not," she finally sputtered.

Mary nodded. "Oh *jah,* he does. I've seen how he looks at you when he thinks you won't see."

"That is ridiculous."

"During church, after church, at the market that day." Mary ticked off the places on her gloved fingers.

Emily harrumphed. Not exactly the most convincing argument, but the best she could do considering. She had been wondering the same thing. Wondering if Elam was somehow holding back from expressing himself to her. Or if she had imagined the whole thing. It was so confusing. To make matters worse, she couldn't erase the memory of his scent as she buried her face in his strong form. Looking back, she found her behavior childish, but at the time she had been scared. Oh, what he must think of her now. If he cared about her before, he must surely think she was a ninny now.

"You know I love Luke." The words almost stuck in her throat, but she managed to get them out into the chilly afternoon air. "He's going to come back soon, and then none of this will matter."

Mary stared at her. Emily could feel the sting of her crystal blue eyes. "Are you trying to convince me or you?"

As much as she hated to admit it, she was trying to get herself to believe the words to be true. Her last conversation with Luke haunted her. "I'm not coming home" echoed inside her head over and over like the music they played in the bank. There was no escaping it.

Luke said he wasn't coming back. And if he didn't . . .

"Maybe Luke is the reason Elam has never confessed his feelings for you."

The words were like an iceberg, so much hiding below the surface.

Emily shook her head. There was more to it than that. Or nothing at all. "Elam doesn't like me."

"And there, my dear sister, is where you are wrong."

In keeping with tradition, the wedding was a huge celebration. The bride's family had spent weeks getting ready, making food and desserts, cleaning the house, and otherwise sprucing up everything. Four hundred people or more were in attendance. The wedding was a bit loud, a little chaotic, and filled with food, fun, and fellowship.

After the sermon and the exchanging of vows, everyone settled down to eat while the attendants fluttered about making sure the guests had everything they needed.

Emily's gaze drifted toward the newlywed couple. They sat in the *eck,* the special

185

corner of the table reserved just for them. They looked so happy, a bit bashful, and genuinely enjoying themselves as they were surrounded by friends and family.

Suddenly she wanted that more than anything.

"You're not eating very much."

Emily whirled around, pressing her free hand to her chest. In the other, she held the plate of food in question. "Elam, *gut himmel,* you scared me." A small laugh escaped her as she sucked in a gulp of air to bring her heart rate under control.

He smiled, revealing his even white teeth. Now why hadn't she ever noticed that before? Because he never smiled? Or because of her sister's crazy words about him liking her? "Maybe you are a bit jumpy still from the other night."

"Of course not." She laughed again, suddenly feeling like everyone in the room was staring at her . . . and Elam . . . and talking about them. Which was ridiculous.

"I've missed seeing you at the house this week." His words were so quietly spoken, she almost didn't hear them at all.

She swung her gaze to his, meeting his unreadable green eyes. "I've been busy."

"*Jah.* Getting the market shut down and such."

She nodded. It had been almost three weeks since she had been to the Riehls' farm. "Mary's been by, *jah?*"

"For sure. But *Dat* has missed seeing you."

Truth was she had missed him too, but she hadn't wanted to risk running into Elam. She hadn't wanted him to get the wrong impression about her. Or an even worse one than he already had.

"Maybe you could drop by this afternoon and say hi."

Emily looked down at her deep purple dress. "I am dressed for it, for sure."

Elam smiled. "It would mean a lot to me . . . I mean, to him." A red flush started at his neck and worked its way up. Mary's earlier words tossed around inside her head. *He likes you, you know.*

"*Jah,* Elam Riehl, I will come by this afternoon."

After the second cake was served, the young people started gathering in the barn for an evening of singing.

Emily was lingering, talking with Caroline and Lorie and otherwise enjoying this afternoon off. Her sisters had promised to take care of all the milking for her and Mary today as long as the two of them took care of everything tomorrow. And of course the

187

promise of a piece of wedding cake brought home to them only sweetened the deal.

"Aaron is staying." Mary sidled up behind Emily and whispered in her ear. "Can we stay, please?"

"I promised Elam Riehl I would come by this afternoon and visit with his *vatter*," Emily said.

Lorie nudged Caroline in the ribs. "I told you."

"You told her what?" Emily looked from one of them to the other, but their faces were pulled into innocent expressions. She looked to Mary, who quickly glanced away. "Told her what?" she asked again.

"That there is something going on between you and Elam Riehl," Caroline answered.

"There is nothing going on." She looked to Mary who shrugged.

"That's not how Johnathan Miller tells it." Lorie's smile was cheesy and full of sass.

"Aaron and Jonah's *bruder*?" Emily swung her gaze from one *maedel* to the other.

"Johnathan was in the wagon with you and Elam during the hayride," Lorie added. "He said the two of you were all cuddled up together as if you were the only ones there."

"We . . . I . . . uh . . ." She couldn't manage to form one sentence in her defense. She had been cuddled up to Elam, but that didn't mean anything. And how could she have not noticed Johnathan Miller in that wagon? "Mary, why didn't you say something?" She turned her accusing eyes to her sister. After all, she dated Johnathan's older brother.

"I tried to."

Emily crossed her arms. "You most certainly did not."

"Earlier today, in the buggy."

Emily shook her head.

"So what about it?" Lorie asked.

"What about what?" Emily asked.

"You and Elam," Caroline said. "I mean, you just said you were going over to his house this afternoon."

"To see his father," Emily argued. Why was everyone trying to see romance where there was none? Had wedding fever taken ahold of everybody's good sense?

"You know he will be there," Lorie pointed out.

"If I go at milking time," Emily said, "he'll be in the barn." And that was exactly her plan. She could get in, visit, and get back out before he even realized she was there.

"I want to stay for the singing," Mary said, bringing the conversation full circle.

"I —"

Mary grabbed Emily's hand and bounced up and down in apparent excitement. "I know. Why don't you ride with Elam to the house, and then I can come by and get you later?"

"Or better yet, Elam can take you home." Caroline nudged Lorie, and they both smiled like crazy.

"I'll go ask Elam." Mary released her hand and raced away.

"Why do I feel like I've been majorly set up?" Emily asked no one in particular.

Her *freinden* smiled in return. "Because you have."

That was how Emily found herself swaying beside Elam Riehl as his buggy rocked along the road.

"You don't seem very happy today, Emily Ebersol."

She shrugged, unable to line up all her emotions and get a handle on them.

"You did not have to come," he continued.

"It's not that." She picked at an invisible spot on her apron and tried to put to a voice what was swirling around in her thoughts. "Did you know everyone is talking about us?" She cast a glance at him from the corner of her eye, but he kept his attention straight ahead.

"I don't think it's everyone."

"Close enough!" Emily threw her arms up, then let them slap back to her sides. "They are saying that we're not doing a very good job at hiding our courtin'."

"I guess that much is true. We aren't hiding it very well."

"We're not courtin'." She did her best to keep her tone even, but despite her efforts, the last word was close to a shout.

He cleared his throat. "We could be."

Emily stopped, the bluster seeping out of her. "What?"

"I said we could be." His words were quiet and steady, almost as if he had been practicing them, but hadn't meant to say them just yet.

She mulled over what he'd said. Did he really mean what it sounded like he was saying?

"Would courtin' me be such a bad thing?" he asked. This time there was no mistaking his intent.

He pulled the buggy to the side of the road. The horse shook his head at the interruption to the trip. He stamped his feet, but otherwise held steady as Elam turned in his seat to look at her.

"I hadn't planned to do this . . . yet." His

voice washed over her, warm and true, and sent shivers down her spine. She pulled her coat a little tighter around herself. "I think you are a fine woman, Emily Ebersol, and I know you have set yourself by Luke Lambright all these years. Well, Luke's gone, and I'm still here. And if you've so a mind, I'd be happy to court you."

Emily blinked, unsure of how to respond. She had expected Elam to get upset, maybe even rage a bit concerning those who were gossiping about the two of them. The last thing — the very last thing — she expected was for him to ask to court her.

He cleared his throat, then gave a terse nod. "I see that I have misunderstood." He checked the traffic, then turned his gaze back to the road. With a slap of the reins, he clicked his tongue and set the beast into motion once again. "Giddyup."

Emily laid a hand on his arm.

He pulled the horse to a stop. The beast snorted and shook his head again, eager to be on his way back to the warm barn.

"*Nay.* I'm sorry. I'm just surprised is all."

He turned to study her face. His eyes searched, for what she did not know. "*Gut* surprised or bad surprised?"

She really hadn't given it a lot of thought. She had been so caught up in Luke and when he was coming home and how soon before they could start their life together that she hadn't given much attention to anything else. Elam was steady and true. He was loyal to his family and to his church. And she had to admit when he stopped frowning long enough to smile, he was as handsome as they came.

"*Gut* surprised," she heard herself say. Her ears hummed with excitement and something more. A new beginning, perhaps?

His green, green eyes studied her. Were they looking for signs of deceit or regret? Then they softened to that dew in spring color she loved so much. "*Jah?*" His smile flickered, then stretched its way across his face.

"*Jah.*" This time she said it with more conviction. With more certainty. She hadn't thought about it before, or maybe she hadn't let herself think about it. But there was something special about Elam Riehl. Something that drew her in, pulled to her, called her, and captured her all at the same time.

He raised a hand to touch her cheek, the backs of his fingers covered by warm leather gloves. "I'm so very glad, Emily Ebersol."

Elam clicked his horse back into motion

and willed his heart to quit beating so fast. If he wasn't careful he would end up in the emergency room before the night was over. But never in his wildest dreams had he imagined that Emily Ebersol would agree to date him.

Slow down. She didn't agree to marry you, he told himself, but he couldn't stop the stupid grin from spreading across his face.

"Next week, Caroline and Andrew are having a Thanksgiving party. Perhaps you would go with me?" she asked.

Elam checked his smile once more. "I'd like nothing better."

The wind didn't seem quite so cold or the sky as dreary. The morning had started off sunny, but as the afternoon wore on, the clouds had begun to gather.

"I appreciate you coming to visit with *Dat,*" he said, feeling a bit awkward.

"You're welcome." She folded her hands in her lap.

She seemed uncomfortable and stiff. Maybe he should have kissed her. Yet he hadn't wanted to overstep his bounds with her. What was he thinking? They had agreed to date. Surely she would expect him to kiss her eventually.

But he didn't want their first kiss to be on the side of the road in plain view of anyone who happened by. They had already started too many tongues to waggin' and nothing had even happened between them yet.

"Your *dat*," he started, not knowing exactly how to proceed. "I suppose I should come and talk to him about . . . everything . . . you know, since there are rumors and such."

Emily nodded. "That might be a *gut* idea."

"After church then?"

Emily nodded. "*Jah.* Okay. I'll tell him to expect you."

Then the doubts started to creep in. "Emily," he said as they rocked along. They were almost to his house now. He'd have to get this settled before he got home. Before his *mamm* and *dat* saw them together and drew the same conclusions everyone else in the district apparently had. "Are you sure about this? I mean about courtin'?"

"Why would I not be?"

He shrugged. "Luke." The name was bitter on his lips, and he vowed to pray about it that night. It wasn't Luke's fault that he had so readily captured Emily's heart. But he had left her for the pleasures of the world. Couldn't Emily see that?

"It's time I faced a few facts where Luke is concerned," Emily said. "He's not coming back, and I can't go. That leaves me and you."

Emily might be in love with Luke Lambright now, but Elam promised them both, before the next wedding season was over he would make Emily Ebersol love him instead.

CHAPTER THIRTEEN

Danny Fitch and Julie King got married. Since Danny only had two brothers of his own, his cousin, Andrew, served as an attendant as well. Caroline was left to attend on her own, and Emily was more than happy to accompany her. Lorie readily joined them. How long had it been since the three of them had done something together?

"Too long," Lorie said, clearly enjoying their girl time. "Now that you are married, Caroline, it seems like we never see you."

Caroline nodded. "It's true, *jah.*" She glanced over to where a group of children played with a variety of push toys, both plastic and wooden. Her daughter Emma was among those happy toddlers.

The wedding had gone off without a hitch, and Mr. and Mrs. Fitch were happily entertaining their guests. Most had a plate of cake and a glass of punch as they celebrated the union.

"What about you?" Caroline asked Emily. "It seems you are never in town since you stopped teaching."

"That's because she's courtin' Elam Riehl."

"What?" Thankfully the room was loud enough that no one around them paid any attention to Caroline's outburst. "I mean, what?" she said, softer this time. "You and Elam?"

"It's nothing serious. We're just taking things as they come."

"So did me and Andrew, and you know how that turned out."

Emily shook her head. "This is different."

"Because of Luke?" Caroline asked.

Strangely enough, Luke wasn't the barrier between her and Elam. "He's so busy trying to take care of his family. He's brother and provider." She shrugged. "That doesn't leave a lot of time for much else."

"But he did say he wanted to date," Caroline pushed.

"Jah."

"It's exciting." Lorie grinned from ear to ear as if she was somehow responsible for the match.

Caroline shot a pointed look at Emily. "She doesn't look excited."

Emily squirmed as Lorie turned her inquisitive brown eyes to her. "Are you not happy?" Lorie finally asked.

"It's not that." Emily shifted from one foot to the other. She had been wanting to talk to someone about this, but hadn't found the courage. Confiding in her mother or her sisters was next to impossible, but her friends . . . "He has not kissed me." There, she said it.

"What?" Lorie's eyes grew wide.

"Esther," Caroline called. "Keep an eye on Emma for me."

Esther Lapp nodded her head, and Emily found herself being hustled out of the house. Before she realized what had happened, she was standing in the yard, her friends staring at her with mouths agape.

"Not even once?" Caroline asked.

"Not even during the hayride?" Lorie added.

Caroline shook her head. "It's strange. I mean . . . I'm all for taking this slow, but . . ." She trailed off, unable to get any more out.

If the heat radiating from Emily was any indication, she had to be bright red. They just didn't talk about stuff like this.

Lorie straightened her back and crossed her arms. "If the way he was looking at you the other day was any indication, it won't be long."

"You think?" Emily hated the gush of relief coloring her voice. She didn't want to sound desperate, but she was new at this dating business. She had no idea how it went. "I've never dated anyone but Luke."

Caroline gave her a knowing smile. "I think you might find kissing Elam a bit different than kissing Luke."

Emily covered her mouth with one hand, her squeal trapped somewhere in between.

Lorie swatted Caroline on the arm, but her smile conveyed it was all in good fun. "Such talk. Married women should not go around corrupting the minds of the maidens."

Caroline rolled her eyes. "You know what I mean."

Strangely enough, Emily did know. Luke was the same age as her, actually a couple of months younger, and Elam . . . well, Elam was four years older. He had been through more. Seen more in his life. When she looked into his eyes, she felt as if she was looking into another world she had never known about. Of course his kiss would be different. But would it be as thrilling as when she kissed Luke? She could hardly wait until she discovered it for herself.

■ ■ ■ ■

"I'm looking forward to tonight," Elam said as they bounced along the road. They were on their way to Abe Fitch's old farmhouse to the Thanksgiving party being held by Caroline and Andrew Fitch.

Elam would be glad when they finally got there. It wasn't that the night was too cold or the wind too strong. No, sitting by Emily, alone and not being able to touch her, was slowly driving him out of his mind. He wanted so badly to reach across and brush her prayer *kapp* strings behind her shoulders, run his fingers down the sheer pink the cold had stained on her cheeks. Or even just hold her hand in his own. Yet he had told himself he should take this slow. And he would. Even if it drove him mad in the process.

He was under no illusions that Emily loved him. He knew she still harbored feelings for Luke Lambright. But Luke was no longer a part of their community. The younger man had his chance with Emily and walked away from it. Elam wasn't about to make that mistake. Nor was he going to press his hand. He might not have to compete with Luke the man, but he would still have to triumph over his memory.

Elam would show Emily how it felt to be cherished and loved. How it felt to be wooed and cared for, appreciated and valued.

Thankfully the driveway to the Fitch place came into sight before Elam lost all control over his promises to himself.

He pulled into the yard, parking his buggy next to those belonging to the other guests. He had no idea who all might be here. He hadn't given it much thought other than he and Emily would be together. Now he wondered if he would be accepted into this grown-up youth group.

He was doing this all backward. He was well past the time for acceptance and "buddy bunches." He was almost too old to consider courtin'. And the good Lord knew he was too old to be worried about what people thought of him now. But he was as *naerfich* as a mouse in a barnyard full of cats as he swung down from the buggy.

"Are you *allrecht*?" Emily asked as he came around and helped her to the ground.

"*Jah*. Of course." But it was a lie. This was his first public outing with Emily Ebersol, and he wanted everything to be perfect. Sure she had agreed to court him and see if they could come out on the other side more than friends, but that didn't mean she couldn't change her mind along the way.

Being alone with her was one thing, but being out, at a party with the eyes of the community on them . . . that was another altogether.

He took her arm and steered her toward the house. His legs were stiff, his footsteps weighted down by trepidation.

A bark of laughter escaped Emily. She stopped as she continued to laugh, nearly doubling over with her mystery mirth.

"What is so funny?" He planted his hands on his hips and patiently waited for her to get herself back in control. Yet in truth he was even more anxious now to get this night over with. What was wrong with her?

"*Nix.* Nothing." She gulped in air and pressed the back of her hand to her mouth as if to stop more laughter from bubbling out.

"That didn't seem like nothing." He waved a hand in front of him for emphasis.

"It's us." She sucked in a shuddering breath as she wiped happy tears from her eyes. At least, he hoped they were happy tears. "You're all like . . ." She walked with stiff legs, her arms out in front of her much like the Frankenstein monster at the hayride. "And I'm all like . . ." She cupped her

203

hand over the side of her face and played a quick game of peek-a-boo with him. "Trying to see if you're looking at me or not looking at me and . . ."

"I don't understand how this is funny." He frowned.

"It's not. It's just all very . . . confusing," she finished on a rush. She sucked in another breath, then stopped as if she had only then realized they were standing alone in the middle of Andrew Fitch's front yard.

"Why?" he asked, hoping her answer was just as simple as his question.

She shook her head. "I feel too old for this."

How amazing that he was just thinking the same thing. "What do you mean?"

She folded her arms across her middle, but the action somehow seemed protective instead of defensive. "I'm too old to be sitting in a buggy wondering if and when a *bu* is going to kiss me." Her words trailed off until the last two were barely audible on the chilly night breeze.

He cleared his suddenly dry throat. "Perhaps the *bu* is thinking the same thing."

Her gaze jerked to his and all at once they seemed connected. Connected in a way like never before. What was it about Emily Ebersol that had him tied in knots? Whatever it was, it had been there the first time he saw her, and it was still there today. "What do we do about it?" she asked.

Even in the pale light from the harvest moon, he saw her eyes darken. Such beautiful eyes. "I can think of only one thing." He took a step closer to her.

"Jah?"

Another step and he could reach out and pull her close. "This is not what I had planned for us," he said quietly.

"You had plans?" she whispered in return.

He nodded. "I was going to take you home tonight. Maybe sit on your front porch and watch the stars. I wanted you to have time to get used to the idea of . . ."

"Of what?"

Did he imagine it or had she stepped a little closer to him? "Of me and you. Of us. Together."

"You think I need time for that? Any other man would have stolen a kiss long ago."

Oh, he had thought about it. "I don't want to be like anyone else to you."

She smiled. "Trust me," she said, taking one more baby step in his direction. "You're not."

Emily was certain no man had ever spoken sweeter words to her than those that had just tumbled from Elam Riehl's lips. He wanted to be different from any other man. He was different. Couldn't he see that?

Maybe not.

"I didn't want to steal a kiss. I wanted to share a kiss with you."

She was wrong. *Those* were the sweetest words she had ever heard. "Okay," she heard herself saying.

"Okay?" His voice sounded a little like he'd stepped on a frog.

"*Jah,*" she said. "That is what I want, too."

"Tonight," he croaked. "When I take you home?"

She shook her head. "What's wrong with now?"

In an instant he closed the small gap between them. Perhaps he too had been nearly tortured by the wait, the anticipation of wondering if the actual kiss would live up to the expectations building in their minds.

His arms wrapped around her as he lowered his head. His hat bumped her ear and fell to the ground at their feet, but she hardly noticed. She was too focused on him.

His lips were cool on hers, his kiss warm in the fall night. It was gentle and strong, soft and firm, and everything she could have asked for. And it was more.

She melted right there in the November

night air. But it was okay, because he was there to hold her up. He was there to catch her sigh as he continued to kiss her like he couldn't get enough.

Never before had she been kissed with such tenderness and passion all wrapped up in one restrained package. She never wanted it to end.

"Elam, is that you?"

Emily stepped back as Elam lifted his head. His eyes were dark and unreadable, but something in the light sparkling there told her they were lucky they had been interrupted. How long they would have stood there, locked in each other's warm embrace was anyone's guess.

"Jah." His voice sounded rusty as he bent down to retrieve his hat.

How had they not heard the door to the house open? Or Andrew Fitch, Caroline's husband, step out onto the porch? Even worse, how long had he stood there watching before he called out to them?

Shame stained her cheeks with a heat that could only be as red as Andrew's horse barn. Shame and something else.

"Are you coming in?" Laughter colored Andrew's tone.

"Jah." Elam slapped his hat against his thigh, but never took his gaze from her. He

placed the hat back on his head and offered her his arm. "We'll be right there."

Unfortunately Andrew waited for them to come into the house, leaving them no time to talk. Not that Emily could have put words to it. She wasn't sure what had happened between them. She knew it was special and unexpected, but other than that, she was lost.

"Are you *allrecht*?" Lorie grabbed her elbow and steered her away from the milling party guests.

Caroline had set up a table across the back of their living room. She had piled it high with bread, turkey, all sorts of finger foods, some kind of meatballs, and a variety of chips. Emily couldn't eat a thing.

"*Jah*," she lied. She wanted to tell Lorie the truth, but she couldn't find the words. Didn't even know how to explain what happened to herself.

Lorie crossed her arms and eyed Emily with that pinning stare. "Tell me another lie, and I'll report you to the deacon."

Emily didn't answer. Instead she glanced to the other side of the room where Elam stood. Andrew Fitch appeared to be giving him as much trouble as Lorie was giving her.

It didn't take long for her friend to figure out what had happened.

"Oh, *gut himmel.*" Lorie grabbed her by the arm and dragged her into the kitchen.

Caroline stood at the stove stirring a large pot of something that smelled pretty *gut,* but Emily had no wits about her to tell what it was from its aroma alone. Joanie Yoder stood next to her.

"Joanie, Samuel King was looking for you."

The girl dropped the stack of paper plates on the counter and hurried from the kitchen.

"Lorie," Caroline admonished. "That wasn't very nice. She's had a crush on him forever." She replaced the lid back on the pot and wiped her hands on a dish towel. "My word," she exclaimed. "What happened to you?"

"Nothing," Emily said, then shook her head. These were her friends, her best *freinden.* She could tell them anything. "Elam kissed me."

"It must have been some kiss for you to be this dreamy-eyed," Caroline said.

Emily shrugged. "It just surprised me is all." That was what it was. Surprise. She had never kissed anyone but Luke. Elam's kiss took her by surprise. *Jah.* That made perfect sense.

Surprise and nothing more. The next time wouldn't be like that at all.

Elam waited until they were almost to Emily's *haus* before he spoke. They had spent the entire evening avoiding each other. Not very mature of either of them, but he didn't trust himself not to kiss her once more just to see if it would be that fantastic again.

Or maybe he was the only one who felt sparks fly.

It was a cold night. Instead of scooting closer like couples do to share their warmth, Emily held herself stiffly away from him.

Maybe courting was a bad idea. Maybe she wasn't ready to move on from Luke.

He cleared his throat. "I won't bite, you know." He did his best to make his voice light and teasing, but somehow it sounded as rough as a cob. "I mean, it's cold, and if 'n you want to scoot closer . . ." That didn't sound any better.

"I'm fine." Evidently Emily thought the same thing.

He shouldn't have waited so long to talk to her about what happened at the party. But he hadn't known how to handle it. He'd been a little too stunned to think clearly, then Andrew on the porch. Elam hadn't been left alone with his thoughts for more than three minutes all night long. How was he supposed to sort through this myriad of emotions while a party carried on around him?

If he had been smart, he could have pulled her aside at the house, in the warmth, and talked to her there. As it was, he wanted to pull to the side of the road and clear the air between them before they went one foot farther, but it was too cold to sit in a buggy and hash through feelings he couldn't decipher on his own.

He pulled the buggy into the drive at the Ebersols'. First off, he noticed the lights shining in every window. It looked as if no one was asleep.

"So much for coming in and being alone," he muttered.

"What?" Emily finally turned toward him. If he wasn't mistaken, it was the first time she had looked at him since their kiss.

"We should talk about this." He pulled the horses to a stop. "But it's a little too cold out here."

She bit her lip as she glanced at the house, no doubt coming to the same conclusion he had. There would be no privacy for them there. "The barn," she said.

"What?"

She slid from the buggy without waiting for his help and raced toward the big double doors. He had no choice but to follow.

The inside of the barn was dark and quiet, the night interrupted only by the soft breathing of the stabled animals.

Emily lit a lantern and turned to face him. "Talk."

"I shouldn't have kissed you tonight. At least not in the middle of Andrew's yard."

She nodded. "I shouldn't have asked you to."

Not exactly the productive talk he had imagined. "Well, that clears things up." He shoved his hands into his pockets, pretending like he needed the warmth when in truth he didn't know what to do with them. They wanted to reach out and brush the wisps of escaped hair back from her face, show her that he could be kind and loving, everything she could want from a boyfriend and suitor.

"This is awkward." She sighed. "But I feel I need to be honest with you."

"You haven't been?"

"Not totally," she whispered. She took a deep breath, then let it out slowly. "I have loved Luke Lambright for as long as I can remember."

He tried to hide the frustration her words

caused. Luke had left her behind for the pleasures of the world.

"When he left, I held the hope that he would forget about race car driving and come back to Wells Landing." She stopped, as if gathering her thoughts. "I talked to him the other day. He's not coming back. Not ever."

Elam wanted to call him a fool, but he was sure it wouldn't change Emily's feelings on the situation.

She raised her shoulders and let them fall, the gesture more defeated than he would have imagined. "I just need some time is all."

He nodded. There was only one thing worse than her being in love with someone else, and that was her *thinking* she was in love with someone else.

But it was *allrecht*. He was a patient man.

Chapter Fourteen

"Are you awake?" Emily crept into Mary's room. She needed to talk to her sister in the worst way. But she didn't want to disturb Rose.

"Jah," Mary whispered in return.

Emily heard the sound of the covers shifting as Mary scooted over to make room for her in the bed.

As quietly as possible she climbed into the bed next to her sister.

"Was iss letz?" Mary asked. "What is wrong?"

Emily sighed. She had seen the look of concern on her sister's face when she'd entered the house that evening. Her talk with Elam hadn't gone exactly as planned. But neither had the kiss. What had she been thinking, asking him to kiss her and get it over with?

And then the kiss itself.

"Elam kissed me tonight."

"What?" Mary's voice rose, and Emily shushed her. Across the room Rose turned over in her bed mumbling something before her breathing evened out once again. "What?" Mary repeated in a whisper this time.

"Elam kissed me."

"What did you do?"

"I kissed him back."

"Emily Jane, that is not what I meant, and you know it."

"I told him that I'm still in love with Luke."

Mary studied her in the darkness. Her sister had their mother's eyes, the kind that could see through to the bones of the matter. Wise eyes that missed nothing. "Are you?"

"Still in love with him? Of course." But as she said the words doubts crowded in. How could she love someone who'd left her for the outside world? Someone who would rather drive a car in a circle than bend his knee and follow God's instruction. What made her hold on to the hope that he would change his mind and come back to her?

"It won't be the same you know." Mary's words hung in the darkness between them.

"What do you mean?"

Mary shifted in the bed and took Emily's

215

hand into her own. "When Luke returns . . . *if* Luke returns. He won't be the same. Things between the two of you won't be the same. No matter how badly you wish for it to be different, this separation will change you both."

As much as Emily wanted to tell her sister she was wrong, she had a feeling Mary was right. But change didn't always mean for the bad.

"He says he's not coming back," Emily whispered. "But I can't believe that he won't. I can't imagine Wells Landing without Luke."

"You've been living in Wells Landing without Luke," Mary pointed out.

"You're right." How come she had never seen it before? She had been living without Luke and he without her. He seemed so happy to be living out this crazy dream of his. She might not understand it, but that didn't make it any less important to him.

"Just take things slow with Elam," Mary advised. "Who knows where that might lead?"

It could be nothing or everything. Only time would tell.

"Luke? Your phone's ringing."

Luke dropped the air hose and made his

way over to the toolbox where he'd left his phone. He'd heard the melodic sound, but wasn't yet accustomed to it being associated with someone wanting to talk to him. Most probably because no one ever called him.

He knew Emily was busy and had a hard time getting away from her father long enough to call and chat. Her mother kept her busy with the goats and her sisters were always underfoot. She was as busy as he was these days. And it wasn't like they had a great deal to talk about. He wanted to be able to call and tell her that he'd made it to the circuit, that he would move up from the amateurs to the dirt tracks. From there it was just a hop and skip to the big time. He had to be patient, pay his dues, and not give up. No matter how homesick he had become lately.

"*Jah?*"

"Luke?" The voice on the other side of the line was as familiar to him as his own.

"Jonah. Good to hear from you." A wave of nostalgia and longing washed over Luke. He loved being a part of the *Englisch* world. He loved the excitement of race car driving and the freedom to wear blue jeans and soft cotton T-shirts, but there were a lot of things he missed about Wells Landing. A lot of

217

people.

Luke tucked the phone between his shoulder and his ear and wiped his hands on an oil-stained rag. He smiled as Jonah told him about the buggy race that happened between two of their friends, young men who hadn't yet joined the church. Even still, they needed to pray the bishop never found out about their shenanigans. Luke listened and laughed and tried not to let the loneliness creep into his voice.

"Speaking of the bishop," Jonah said in a not so smooth attempt to change the subject. "I saw Emily the other night."

"Oh, *jah?*" His heart gave a hard thump at the sound of her name. He had been so eager to come to the *Englisch* world that he had given up the best girl ever. Some days he thought he deserved a kick in the pants for leaving her behind. But once he made it . . .

"She came to Andrew Fitch's Thanksgiving party."

Thanksgiving. He had almost forgotten. It was the day after tomorrow. It wasn't like it was a big holiday for the Amish. More often than not they had a wedding to attend instead of the big family dinner like the *Englisch* preferred.

"With Elam Riehl."

His heart skipped a beat. Just because she went to the party with another guy didn't mean a thing. Maybe they had become friends since Luke had been gone. Emily was a sweet and caring girl. That was what it had to be.

"I don't really know if I should tell you this." Jonah let out a reluctant bark of laughter. "Of course I have to tell you. I'm just not sure how to."

Luke's mouth tasted like ash. "Will you just tell me already?"

"Okay, now I didn't see this with my own eyes, but Andrew swears he saw them kissing in the front yard before they came into the party."

His heart fell to his feet. Emily. His Emily. Kissing another. And not just anybody, but Elam Riehl. He was so . . . *old.*

"Andrew said it looked pretty intense, but I don't know. I thought you should hear it from me instead of someone else."

"Do you . . ." He cleared his throat. Suddenly it was clogged with more emotions than he could name. "Do you think it was serious?"

He could almost hear his friend shrug. "I don't know about that. But neither one of them would look at the other the entire time they were at the house. It was sort of weird."

Good weird or bad weird? Luke wanted to ask. But he knew the answer. He was losing his girl.

He thanked Jonah for calling and hung up the phone.

"Bad news?" the garage owner asked.

"Something like that," Luke mumbled. He sat down on a stained plastic chair and watched the others around him. They worked on their cars, changed the oil, filled up the tires, and topped off the fluids as if nothing earth-shattering had just happened. He supposed for them, nothing had happened. But for Luke . . .

He needed to get back to Wells Landing as quickly as possible. He didn't have the money to travel back, but he had to. The season was over. He wouldn't miss a race if he snuck away for the weekend, dropped in to see Emily. Let her know that he loved her and he would be coming back for her.

In all honesty, he hadn't expected her to hang on this long. He'd hoped by the end of October she would give up her stubborn decision to stay with the Amish and would join him on the circuit. But she hadn't.

Now he would have to do everything in his power to let her know that he cared about her. He wanted her, and she would always be his girl.

Emily had just laid her head on the pillow when a *plink* sounded at the window. She rolled over, convinced she had imagined it.

Plink.

She glanced toward the door to her room, thinking for a minute that her ears were playing tricks on her. But her door was firmly closed. Not a sister in sight.

Plink.

She flung back the covers and made her way to the window. The glass chilled her fingers as she pushed the sash up and looked down into the yard.

A young man stood below the window. He was wearing jeans and sneakers, a thick woolen coat of the Amish, and a baseball hat like the *Englisch buwe* preferred.

Despite his eclectic manner of dress, she would have known him anywhere. "Luke?" she whispered.

He waved at her, his smile lighting up the night.

Luke had come back for her!

"I'll be right there," she whispered, hoping he would hear her quiet words, praying he would still be there when she got outside.

As quietly as she could, she raced down

221

the stairs, stopping only long enough to snatch her heavy coat off the peg by the back door. She slipped it on and hurried into the yard, straight into Luke Lambright's arms.

"I can't believe you came back." She touched his cheek to prove to herself he was really there. "You came back."

"It's so good to see your face."

"Kumm," she said tugging him toward the barn. "It's too cold out here."

And it would be no *gut* a'tall if her father caught them together in the middle of the night.

The barn wasn't much warmer, but at least they were out of the wind.

Emily turned on one of the battery-operated lanterns and settled herself down on a hay bale next to Luke. Her talk in the barn with Elam was brought to mind, but she pushed the memory away. Luke was back, and for now that was all she wanted to think about.

"I can hardly believe you are actually here." Emily folded her hands in her lap, suddenly uncomfortable. It had been so long since she had seen him, that was all. But Luke was different. He had changed, was changing still. It wasn't just the clothes and hat. The light in his eyes shone with a determined intensity. She was confused about how to handle it.

He took her hand into his and squeezed her fingers. "I had to come back. I heard that my girl has been going around with someone else."

Her gaze jerked from their entwined hands to his pale blue eyes. "What was I supposed to do? You told me you weren't coming back," she whispered. "I was just trying to move forward."

"I didn't think you'd start going with another."

"It's not like that," she whispered, though she felt a pang of guilt at her words. What was she saying?

Luke lifted her fingers to his lips and pressed a sweet kiss to each one. They tingled where his lips met her skin. How she had missed him.

And yet she wanted to pull her hand from his grasp. She was just so confused.

"There will be a time when we can move forward together," he promised. "You just have to be patient."

She nodded, unable to get a response past the lump in her throat. That was what she wanted, wasn't it? To move forward with Luke?

What about Elam?

She had been in love with Luke longer than she could remember, yet the thrill of Elam's kiss still colored her dreams.

How was a girl supposed to keep her head straight in times like these? Luke was all she had ever wanted, and yet he was just out of reach. Elam was becoming very important to her as well. He was there, strong, steady, and true. Was it possible to love two men? Did she love Luke still? Or had Elam captured her heart?

"You're not staying." Emily searched his face for something, anything, a promise that it would really be okay. She found nothing but a tinge of sadness and that ever-present spirit of adventure.

"I have a job and meetings with sponsors. It's not going to be long before the season starts again. I'm not sure my car can handle many more races."

"I have to go," she whispered. She turned her eyes away and pulled her hand from his grasp. She couldn't think as long as he was touching her.

"Emily?" Luke whispered.

But she shook her head and stumbled from the barn without looking back.

She thought she heard him whisper her name to call her back, but she couldn't be sure. He wouldn't get loud and risk waking the entire family. A fact Emily used to her advantage. As much as she wanted to wrap herself in Luke's arms and forget about everything else, she couldn't. Oh, how she wished she could.

She stifled back a sob — or was it a laugh? — as she let herself into the house. Quietly she shut the door behind her and hung her coat back on its hook. She was aware of every creak of the floorboards as she made her way across the room and back up the stairs. Almost there.

"Where have you been?" Mary hissed in the darkness, scaring Emily nearly half to death.

She clamped a hand over her mouth to stifle her scream. Sucking in a deep breath, she pressed a hand to her pounding heart. "Mary, you frightened me."

Her sister propped her hands on her hips, not one to be put off the subject easily. "Well?"

Still so confused about what had just happened, Emily shrugged. "Luke was here."

Mary's eyes grew wide. She grasped Emily's hand into her own and tugged her toward Emily's bedroom.

Emily allowed her sister to pull her along. She supposed such a declaration warranted an explanation.

Mary pushed her down onto the bed and waited impatiently for her to begin.

Emily quickly recounted Luke's visit.

"What are you going to do?" Mary sank down next to her.

"I don't know," Emily whispered. "I just don't know."

CHAPTER FIFTEEN

December came and brought with it an early snow. With over six inches covering everything from the streets to the barns, the *Englisch* kids rejoiced in their "snow day" while the Amish kids went on to school.

It had been nearly a week since Luke had snuck into her barn, a week since he had confused her to the point of not knowing her name. How was a girl supposed to go on if the past kept coming back? If the past kept making her want things that were never going to be?

She pulled the buggy to a stop in front of Elam's house. Someone, most probably him, had cleared a spot for others to pull in without having to park on top of the snow.

"Em, are you okay?" Mary asked from beside her.

"*Jah,* why?"

"Because you're sitting there, staring off into space."

Emily shook her head. "Just thinking."

Mary frowned. "You've been doing a lot of that since Luke's visit."

She whipped around to face her sister. "You haven't told anyone, have you?"

"*Nay.* I promised I wouldn't." Her tone clearly conveyed her hurt. She had made a promise, and she would keep it.

"I'm sorry," Emily said. "It's just that —"

"The deceit is making you *naerfich.*"

Crazy. It was as good a description as any.

" 'A good name is to be chosen rather than great riches, loving favor rather than silver and gold.' " Mary quoted, her hands folded primly in her lap.

" 'The heart is deceitful above all things, and desperately wicked: who can know it?' " Emily shot back, then she pushed the buggy door open and retrieved the basket from behind the seat.

The last thing she wanted to do was deceive Elam, but how could she explain something she didn't quite understand herself? It wasn't like she and Elam had pledged their love and devotion. They weren't in line to get married. They were just . . . dating, seeing where things might go from there.

Emily trained her gaze to the ground beneath her feet, carefully stepping in the pressed-down snow. The path was comprised mostly of tire tracks and made Emily remember that James had gone to the doctor the day before.

She hoped they'd received good news. "Come on," she urged Mary. "Let's see how James made out yesterday."

Their previous disagreement forgotten, Mary linked arms with Emily and together they picked their way toward the house.

Mary knocked on the door. It was promptly answered by a smiling James.

"Emily! *Mamm,* come look. Emily and Mary are here."

Emily blinked and resisted the urge to check the numbers on the mailbox. They were at the right *haus.* But things inside seemed so much different than before.

James wore a dark purple shirt almost the same color as Emily's dress that he favored so much. A big pot of something bubbled on the stove. Emily wasn't sure, but it smelled a lot like chicken pot pie.

Johanna skipped around, her lilac dress twirling around her ankles. It was a completely different household than when she and Mary had first visited.

Something must have happened at the doctor's appointment, and it was *gut* if the atmosphere in the Riehl house was any indication.

"Emily Emily Emily!" Johanna grabbed her hand and pulled her all the way inside. "Did you see the snow? Did you?"

Emily laughed. "Of course I did, *liebschdi.* I drove all the way here in it."

Johanna's face fell. Then quick as a wink, she bounced back. "Can we go play in it? Please, please, please!"

"That is something you will have to discuss with your mother."

"Mamm, Mamm, Mamm." In a flash, Johanna was gone, racing into the kitchen to ask her mother about playing outside.

Emily handed her basket to James. "Will you take this for me? I need to go see to the horses."

He accepted it with a quick smile. "Are there any more of those grape jelly jelly beans in here?"

"Maybe, but you wait until I get back before you open it, you hear?"

James feigned a pout, his sparkling eyes giving away his true emotion. "I guess, but hurry, *jah*?"

"I will."

She pulled her coat a little tighter around herself and started outside. But her horse was no longer hitched to the buggy. She changed her course and headed for the barn.

"Elam?" she called as she slid the door open.

"Back here."

She followed the sound of his voice and the soothing scrape of the brush against horsehide.

He was in the third stall down, brushing Clover, the gentle mare that Emily preferred.

"I didn't want her to get too cold," he explained.

"I was coming back out for her."

He stopped and smiled, one of the first genuine smiles she had ever received from him. That was when she noticed he seemed different somehow. Like the scene in the house, he was more relaxed. His shoulders weren't quite as stiff, his jaw not quite so rigid. When he looked like that, so at ease and happy, he was as handsome a man as she had ever seen. "I know."

"Your father," she started.

"It's a miracle, *jah*?" Elam gave Clover one last pat on the rump and left her alone with her oats. "And we have you to thank."

Emily shook her head. "*Nay,* not me. I didn't do anything but run the printer at the library. And even that was the librarian's doing."

"But you thought about it. You brought it to our attention. It was you who pointed out that the medications might be having a negative effect on *Dat*."

"And were they?"

"*Jah.* You saw him. He's like a whole new person."

"God is *gut*," Emily whispered, so thankful that she had played even a small part in James's healing.

"*Jah.*" Elam reached for his coat, then slipped his arms into the sleeves. "Let's go see if *Mamm* has any *kaffi* made."

Emily smiled and allowed him to follow her outside.

The sun sparkled in blue lights over the snow-covered ground. The temperature dipped down to below freezing, but if Oklahoma's previous snows held any indication, the ground would be nearly cleared by tomorrow afternoon.

As beautiful as the snow could be, Emily was glad. It was so hard to get around in. Her rubber boots were cumbersome at best, stiff from the cold and a little too big. They slowed her down, but at least her feet were dry.

As if he sensed her struggle, Elam took

her hand and pulled her along behind him. "It might be easier if you step where I step," he said over one shoulder.

"*Jah,* it might if your legs were half their size."

He stopped and looked back at their deep footprints in the snow. Her steps were two to his one. His grin flashed, almost as dazzling as the sunlight on the snow. "Sorry."

Funny, but he didn't seem sorry as he took another giant step forward. The snow was deeper here, having been blown toward the carriage house in the night. The small building sat between the house and the barn and served as the only break between the road and the pasture.

"Elam Riehl, you are doing this on purpose."

He shot her an innocent look. "Can you not make it?"

There had to be four feet between his steps. Maybe five. *"Nay,"* she said. Was he being playful or deliberately thick-headed?

"Well, then. I guess I should carry you."

She barely had time to register his words before she found herself scooped into his arms. "What are you doing?" Instinctively she kicked her feet against the air, her arms flailing in surprise.

Elam grunted as one hand connected to

his throat.

She felt as if she was falling. She *was* falling! She threw her arms around his neck in desperation, but the motion was a bit too much. Together they both toppled into the snow.

Emily landed with a soft thud as Elam managed to catch himself before tumbling headlong on top of her. He rolled to the side and ended up on his back right next to her.

She sucked in a breath, the air knocked from her lungs as she hit the ground.

"Are you *allrecht*?" Elam raised up on one elbow to look at her. His hat had been lost in the fall and snow dusted his dark hair. In the bright light, hints of red shone in the strands like the roan horse her *dat* kept for the *kinner* to ride.

"*Jah,*" she said, turning her thoughts away from his hair and onto the fact that the snow was trickling down into the collar of her coat. She shivered and shifted, hoping to avoid any more unwanted cold running down her back while she tried to catch her breath. "Why couldn't we have walked down the regular path?"

Elam's expression turned suddenly serious, though the playful light in his eyes took all the starch from his words. "You were the one who started walking over here. I was following you."

"You were leading."

"Okay, I was."

The air seemed suddenly warm between them, or was it thick? Something hitched, and Emily realized it was her breath in her throat.

One small move and she could press her lips to his. She could see if the attraction between them at Caroline's party was real or a trick of the night.

He seemed to sense it, too, this intimate position they had landed in. His eyes darkened from bottle green to the color of the fields in late June, rich, fertile green filled with promise and hope and so much more.

Was she imagining things or was he closer? So very close . . .

He seemed to find himself. "I guess I'm not much good at this courtin' thing."

Or maybe she had imagined it all. "I think you're doing just fine."

"We want to play." Johanna slammed out of the house, bundled from head to toe. James stood next to her, his eyes twinkling with excitement.

Elam pushed himself to his feet, then reached out a hand to help her up. "Where's *Mamm* and Mary?"

"Inside by the fire." James made a face as if to ask why anyone would want to be inside and warm when there was snow on the ground.

Emily chuckled at his expression.

"Go get them, Jo. Tell them I said they must come play, too."

With a quick nod of her head, she disappeared back into the house, returning in a flash. "They rolled their eyes at me. Like this," she said, demonstrating the action.

"Then what happened?" Elam asked.

Johanna smiled. "I called them chickens, and they went to fetch their coats."

All six of them were still out in the snow when the schoolkids came home a couple of hours later.

The teacher had let them out early, knowing their concentration wouldn't be on learning with so much snow covering the ground. Oklahoma weather was unpredictable at best. It could snow next week or not again until next December. Emily considered it a smart move on the teacher's part to release the kids for some extra playtime.

But after sloughing to school and back in the stuff, Miriam, Ruthie, and Norma were more than happy to huddle around the fire inside and drink hot cocoa.

After building two forts, a snowman, a snow pig, and creating countless snow angels all over the yard, Emily was more than ready to go inside as well.

"Awh . . ." Johanna's lips protruded in a sweet pout.

James scooped her into his arms and rubbed his nose into the crook of her neck.

She squealed.

"We have to go in and warm up, *liebschdi,*" he said. "We don't want to get sick."

Johanna nodded. *"Jah, Dat."*

"Besides," James continued, "I sneaked a peek into the basket Emily brought. There are pictures in there for us to color."

"Can we color them purple?" Johanna asked.

"You can color them any color you want," he answered.

"I want to color them purple, the same as you like to do."

James nodded. "Purple, it is."

Emily smiled to herself. Not one of the coloring pages were pictures of things that were traditionally purple. And that was just fine with all of them.

The snow melted away by the weekend, leaving muddy fields and wet streets on the afternoon of the school Christmas pageant.

Nothing gave Emily a sweeter thrill than seeing James at the pageant. He was sitting in the back in the chairs reserved for the infirm. Johanna was perched on his lap. They were both wearing purple.

She smiled at the pair, then went in search of Joy and Elam.

His eyes lit up when he saw her, and she couldn't help but compare the Elam of a couple of months ago to the man who stood before her today. To an outsider, he might not even look like the same man. He had changed that much.

"Hi." He bent close and said the one word for only her ears.

Joy smiled her greeting, then discreetly turned her attention to the front of the schoolroom. In the crush of milling parents and older siblings, his hand found hers and squeezed.

"I brought my buggy," he said. His gentle breath stirred the strands of hair tucked so neatly under her prayer *kapp.*

"Jah?"

"I thought I might drive you home. We never seem to have any time together anymore."

Her heart jumped at the thought. They had been chaperoning Becky's youth group and watching them during the singings, but keeping an eye on fifty teenagers was not an intimate way to spend an evening.

"Jah?" She tried to make her voice sound normal. Not as excited as a schoolgirl with her first crush on a *bu.*

She was excited. She enjoyed being with Elam. He was steady and strong. He loved his family and would do anything for them. He loved God and their church, his community, and the work he did at the dairy farm.

But he's not Luke.

Nor did she want him to be. She hadn't spoken to Luke since the night he'd come into the barn and asked her to wait on him. Was she really supposed to wait? For how long?

She had looked up race car driving on the Internet in the library, and it was not easy to make it "big," as Luke called it.

Did he want her to wait for years while he chased his dream in the *Englisch* world?

One thing she knew for certain: the longer he stayed gone, the harder it would be for him to return.

Luke Lambright wasn't the only one with dreams. Emily had a few of her own. Like most Amish girls, she wanted to get married, start a family, set up house somewhere, and watch her children grow. In the great spectrum of dreams, she supposed they were modest. But they were hers, and she would see them through.

She bit back a sigh as the teacher welcomed everyone to the pageant. She told a little about the school and the scholars who would be performing. Then she announced that she was certain some of those there tonight had been hearing rumors and yes, they were true. Even though the wedding season wasn't quite over yet, her intended had proposed, and she would not be returning as the teacher the following fall.

She was three years younger than Emily.

How long was she supposed to wait?

She squeezed Elam's fingers, unintentionally tightening her hand around his.

"Are you *allrecht*?" Elam asked.

She nodded, then smoothed the frown from her brow. No sense in giving herself wrinkles. She smiled strictly for his benefit and loosened her grip.

Elam seemed about to say something, then the first performer stepped forward and a hush fell over the entire crowd. Whatever he'd wanted to say would have to wait until later.

Punch and cookies were served after the

pageant. Parents strolled through the small one-room schoolhouse while others immediately headed home.

Elam too was ready to get in his buggy. He had been thinking about this evening for a couple of weeks. Was it wrong to want to spend some time alone with Emily?

He loved the time she spent with his family. And he loved everything she had done for his father. She had given them all a new lease on life. But no matter where they seemed to be, with nine sisters between them, someone was always around.

"Are you ready now?" he asked, trying his best to hide his impatience. A body would think he had never been alone with a *maedel* the way he was carrying on, but Emily was different. So very different.

"Jah." She seemed to be enjoying herself, not stalling, and Elam immediately felt ashamed of his hurry-up attitude.

Emily had worked here as a teacher up until last year. Aside from her sisters, the other scholars had been in her charge. As caring as she was, he knew she enjoyed talking and visiting with the families just as much as she had the pageant.

"It's okay," he backpedaled. "We can stay for a bit longer."

She smiled at him. "I'm sorry. I didn't realize it was getting so late." She tossed her plastic cup still half filled with punch into the trash can and prepared to leave.

"Are you sure?" All of a sudden he felt like a bully just for wanting to be alone with her.

"Jah, jah." She held out her coat for him to help her with it.

She had no more slipped her arms into the sleeves than Becky sidled up. If the mischievous look in her eyes was any indication, this was no chance encounter.

"You're not leaving now, are you?"

"Yes," Elam said with as much conviction as he dared. "We are."

"But you can't leave. You . . . haven't tried a piece of Abner Chupp's peanut butter fudge." She looped her arm through Emily's and led her away. Elam had no choice but to follow.

Fifteen minutes later, after sampling Abner's peanut butter fudge and his cookies and his cream bars, Elam finally set his foot down.

"Go find *Mamm* and *Dat,"* he told Becky with a nudge. "It's time for me to take Emily home." He couldn't stop the thrill his words created. He was taking Emily Ebersol home. And if everything went as planned . . .

242

"*Jah,* okay," Becky said. "You're welcome." Then she smiled and sashayed away.

"What was that all about?" Emily asked.

Elam shrugged, hoping his expression
didn't give away anything. He'd hate to
spoil the surprise now.

Emily nodded. "It was like she was trying
to keep us in here for some reason."

"Hmmm." He took Emily's elbow and
steered her toward the door.

"This way," he said, helping her down the
schoolhouse steps. "I parked over here —"

He wasn't able to finish the sentence as
he caught sight of his buggy.

Just as he and Emily had decorated a
buggy for one of the courting couples in
Becky's group, the teens had in turn decorated for them.

He had asked them to do this something
special for Emily, but he hadn't expected it
to come out so utterly perfect.

Red ribbon had been wound around the
horse's tack and all around the reins. Pine
boughs shaped into wreaths were tied to the
door and the entire thing was covered with
a pristine white sheet. The horse tossed his
mane as if anxious to be on his way and the
sound of jungle bells filled the night.

"Oh, Elam." Emily sounded close to tears.
"It's beautiful."

And it was. "Come," he said, his voice sounding like a bucket full of rusty nails.

He was overly aware that everyone around was watching them closely as they made their way to the buggy. He helped Emily inside and slid in next to her, doing his best to pretend this was another ordinary evening.

But it wasn't.

The inside of the buggy smelled like apples and spice. Mixed with the scent wafting in from the pine wreaths, he felt cocooned in Christmas.

"This is really nice," Emily said.

"*Jah.*" He handed her a thick plaid blanket, aware that the entire scene looked like an old-timey *Englisch* Christmas card. That was fine with him. He needed tonight to be special, extra special.

"*Danki.*" She spread the blanket across both their laps.

His hands shook as he took up the reins and set the horse into motion.

She half turned in her seat to stare at him. "You set all this up, didn't you?"

He shrugged. "Maybe."

"Maybe, my foot." But she smiled when she said the words. "What's this?" She pulled a basket from behind his seat. It contained a thermos and a container filled with cookies.

"Apple cider and buttermilk cookies."

She placed the basket behind his seat once again, that smile still lighting up her face. "You thought of everything."

This time he couldn't help but return her smile. "I wanted tonight to be special for you."

"It is." He could hear the sincerity in her tone.

"Extra special."

"Why is that?"

His heart gave a nervous thump. "You'll just have to wait and see."

Riding along next to Elam was magical. It was the only word she could find to describe it. She felt as if she was living a dream, or maybe playing a part in one of those *Englisch* movies. The night seemed perfect, just enough lingering chill to say Christmas was coming. The stars twinkled, the wind was still, and the sound of jungle bells filled the air.

"Where are we going?" It had only taken a few moments before she realized they weren't headed toward either of their houses.

Elam shot her a smile over his right shoulder. "You'll see."

Emily snuggled a little deeper into her coat. Not because she was cold, but for the cozy feeling she got from sitting next to Elam.

Then to her surprise he began to sing. His voice was rich and deep as he sang "Love Is Patient and Kind." She had heard the song many times before, but never had anyone sang it to her.

Emily leaned back and found herself nestled against him as the buggy swayed with each step. Magical, *jah.* The night was perfect.

"We're here."

Emily opened her eyes hardly aware she had closed them until he spoke. She blinked and leaned forward, staring out at the town of Wells Landing below them. Main Street was lit with the old-fashioned street lamps that lined both sides, but it was the multicolored twinkling Christmas lights that took her breath away.

"It's beautiful," she whispered, her voice hesitant, as if mere words could shatter the night.

"*Jah.*" He shifted uncomfortably in his seat.

"Is something wrong?"

"*Nay,* no, just uh . . . would you like some cider?"

Emily smiled. "Very much so."

He retrieved the thermos and filled the attached cup with the warm brew. "There are no other cups." He handed the lid to her.

"We can share." She took a sip and passed it back, wholly aware of the intimacy of the action. Yet somehow it felt . . . right. Her and Elam, the magical night, and a cup of toasty apple cider.

"Emily." Elam cleared his throat, then started again. "Emily, you have come to mean so much to me and my family over these past few weeks."

"I feel the same," she said, unable to stop her frown. "Is everything okay?"

Elam swallowed hard, then took one of her hands into his. "I have something I need to tell you."

"Okay." She resisted the urge to jerk away from him. Maybe if he wasn't touching her, he wouldn't seem so stern or serious. But she loved the way his callous palm seemed to envelop her entire hand, warming her fingers halfway up her arm.

"I have loved you my entire life."

"What?" she breathed.

He shook his head. "Let me finish. Please." He took a deep breath as if gathering courage. "I have loved you my entire life, but I know that you and Luke Lambright . . ." He stopped. "I'm making a mess of this." Elam sighed and looked to the sky as if asking for help. "Emily, will you marry me?"

CHAPTER SIXTEEN

Emily started to tremble. She opened her mouth, but nothing came out. She was speechless in the face of his proposal.

She closed her mouth, then opened it to try a second time. Not that she knew what her answer would be.

Elam laid one gloved finger over her lips. "You don't have to answer now. I know you don't love me. But I'm willing to take a chance that one day soon you will . . . that you might come to care for me."

"I . . . I don't know what to say."

"Say you'll think about it."

"*Jah.* Of course."

"I think my feelings for you are clear." His voice sounded unpracticed in the cool night air. "I would do anything to make you happy. You have come to mean so much to my family, to me."

She swallowed hard. "I care about you all." It was the truth.

"That's all I can ask for." He gave a satisfied nod and set the horse into motion once again.

Emily bumped shoulders with Elam as the horse pulled them back down the small incline. It was a nice feeling, sitting beside him, brushing against him with the sway of the buggy. Elam was a *gut* man, steady and true, but the idea of loving anyone other than Luke was as foreign to her as Spanish.

She chanced a peek at his handsome profile as he steered them toward her house. Her father was right: Elam would make a fine husband, a *gut* father. But she wasn't ready to make that commitment yet. She needed a little more time to get used to the idea that Luke was gone. He wasn't coming back and life in Wells Landing had to go on.

If nothing else, Elam deserved that much. He deserved to know that she was over Luke, and no matter what, his memory wouldn't come between them. She would wait until then before she gave him her answer.

Luke stared at the pathetic Christmas tree. Someone had placed the drooping two-foot pine on the chipped dining room table.

Of all the things he wanted to experience

in the outside world, an *Englisch* Christmas topped the list. Maybe not with Santa and reindeer, but a beautiful tree like the one they put up in the hardware store in Wells Landing. There was something special about that tree. Luke wasn't sure if it was the twinkling red and white lights or the glitter-covered ornaments, but just looking at that symbol in the frosty window of the store made Luke feel like God was behind it.

He knew how ridiculous that sounded and how the bishop would feel about such a statement. But Luke didn't care. That tree stood for everything good about the *Englisch* world, and how they felt about God.

Looking at the scraggly thing on the table just made him sad. It made him want to go back to Wells Landing, even only for a night or two, and look in the hardware store window.

He had fifty dollars to his name. His car wouldn't take him from Van Buren, Arkansas, to Oklahoma without an oil change, a new set of spark plugs, and a tank of gas. But right then, he would have given anything to be back on Main Street.

Chris Troyer slapped him on the shoulder, startling him out of his melancholy thoughts. "Why so glum, chum?" Chris laughed, the permanent smile on his face not one bit dimmer by the thought of spending Christmas away from his family.

He never said as much, but Luke had the feeling that Chris's home life wasn't happy. All Luke knew about him was he had eleven brothers and sisters and he never quit smiling. But his grin stopped long before reaching his eyes.

So Chris'd had a hard life. He'd left the Amish to start again. And he wasn't looking back. But Luke had left more behind than Chris.

Emily's sweet face materialized in his mind.

"Girl troubles?" Chris asked.

"Something like that," Luke muttered. But it was more than just Emily. He missed . . . everything. He missed his uncle, his friends, the Christmas tree in the window at the hardware store.

"Come on in here," Chris said, waving him toward the living room. "We are going to watch a Christmas movie."

Luke shook his head. He didn't want to watch a movie about Christmas. He wanted to live it. He wanted . . . "I think I'll go lay down."

Chris shrugged in his whatever-you-want sort of way and plopped down on the worn couch. The other two ex-Amish who lived in the house were already gathered around the television waiting on whatever it was to start.

Luke hovered in the space between the dining room and the living room. He couldn't even talk his feet into moving toward the attic stairs. The Christmas tree before him stood as a mockery to everything he had dreamed. It wasn't like he thought it would be. Nothing had been like he thought it would be. Not . . . one . . . thing . . .

"You okay, man?" Tony Stoltzfus asked.

Luke could barely nod. "I think I'm going out for a while."

"I thought you were going to lay down."

Luke frowned. "I'm going to go home for Christmas."

"I've never been picked up for a date on a tractor before." Emily eyed the big green machine with mistrust.

"Then it's time you got out a little more." Elam smiled at her, and Emily's doubts melted away. Well, most of them. "When did you learn to drive one of these?"

"During my *rumspringa*. Now are you going with me or not?"

"Where are we going again?" She was being difficult, but she couldn't help herself.

"It's a surprise."

Emily crossed her arms. "I don't like surprises."

Elam cocked his head to one side. In the golden light of the setting sun, she couldn't read his expression, but she had a strong feeling it fell somewhere between laughing and exasperated. "Everyone likes surprises."

"Everyone likes *gut* surprises."

He herded her toward the tractor. "Are you implying that my surprise might not be *gut*?"

"Are you feeling guilty about your surprise?" She stopped when her knees bumped against the green painted metal. "Whose tractor is this anyway?"

Before he answered, he wrapped his hands around her waist and hoisted her into the cab. "It's Andrew Fitch's tractor."

"And he just let you have it?"

"For the night, *jah*. Are you going to complain about it all evening or have you decided to try and enjoy yourself?"

"I think . . ." She tapped one finger against her chin, trying to appear as if she had a big decision to make. "I'll enjoy myself."

"Gut," he said. "Hang on to your *kapp*. You are in for a ride."

Emily couldn't remember the last time she had been on a tractor. Even though the night air held the chill of winter, she enjoyed the fresh air and being so close to Elam.

And okay, so maybe she did like some surprises. But she wasn't prepared when he pulled the tractor across the highway and down the road that ran between the Millers' cornfields.

"Are we going to the pond?"

The weather wasn't cold enough for them to even think about skating on the water.

Elam shook his head. "You'll see."

They drove past the Millers' and continued on. Emily began to notice the power lines on the sides of the road. Street lamps and security lights began to show the way.

"Almost there," Elam said, turning down the lane with dormant fields on either side.

Several buggies, a few tractors, and many, many cars were parked to the side. Elam pulled Andrew's tractor alongside the other vehicles and turned off the engine.

"I still don't know where we are," she said as she hopped down.

"We're in Bethlehem."

She tilted her head, studying his expression from one way and then the other. Was he serious? He looked serious enough. Then he smiled as he handed the man at the front gate two tickets and led her into a field.

"This *Englisch* farmer sets this up each year. He uses the kids from the local high

255

schools to act out the Christmas story." As he finished, they came upon the first part of the journey.

A young man stepped forward and recited these words: " 'And it came to pass in those days, that there went out a decree from Caesar Augustus, that all the world should be taxed.' "

Behind him a light turned on, shining on a man dressed in full Roman armor. Emily guessed he was supposed to be Caesar Augustus as he signed a paper with flourish. The light went out, and the narrator continued, this time walking forward down a path. The spectators followed.

" 'And all went to be taxed,' " the narrator continued, " 'every one into his own city. And Joseph also went up from Galilee, out of the city of Nazareth, into Judaea, unto the city of David, which is called Bethlehem; To be taxed with Mary his espoused wife, being great with child.' "

Behind him another light shone down this time onto a weary man who led a donkey. On the back of the beast sat a tired, pregnant woman. Man, woman, and beast appeared as if they were ready to collapse any minute.

For the first time in her life, Emily thought about what it meant for them to walk from

Galilee to Bethlehem. She had no idea how far it was. But the journey couldn't have been easy. Especially not when pregnant and close to delivery.

She and Elam walked along with the crowd, following Mary and Joseph. They ambled along, Mary perched on the back of the donkey, Joseph's heavy footsteps leading the way.

Once they reached the destination, the lights went out and a single spotlight focused on a new narrator. " 'And so it was, that, while they were there, the days were accomplished that she should be delivered.' "

The lights came back on, and there sat Mary with the baby Jesus.

Tears sprang into Emily's eyes at the beautiful depiction. She moved a little closer to Elam, sharing his heat and the sight with him.

"It's beautiful, *jah*?" he whispered.

Emily nodded, unable to force words past the lump in her throat.

" 'And she brought forth her firstborn son, and wrapped him in swaddling clothes, and laid him in a manger; because there was no room for them in the inn.' "

As the fictional Mary laid the baby in a wooden trough, Emily wiped away her tears with the back of one hand. The baby stretched and fussed a little about being put down. Emily was both shocked and overjoyed that the presenters used a real baby for the exhibit.

The light remained on Mary, Joseph, and the baby Jesus, but another light snapped on to their left. As Emily turned, the narrator spoke.

" 'And there were in the same country shepherds abiding in the field, keeping watch over their flock by night.' "

The shepherds milled around, herding their lambs and sheep who bleated in response. Everyone laughed at one little lamb who wanted to play rather than be herded.

" 'And, lo, the angel of the Lord came upon them, and the glory of the Lord shone round about them: and they were sore afraid.' "

The shepherds fell to their knees and bowed their heads as an angel appeared.

Emily wasn't sure how they accomplished such a feat. The angel fairly glowed, suspended above the shepherd and the flocks of milling sheep.

" 'Fear not,' " the angel said. " 'For, behold, I bring you good tidings of great joy, which shall be to all people. For unto you is born this day in the city of David a Savior, which is Christ the Lord. And this shall be a sign unto you; Ye shall find the babe wrapped in swaddling clothes, lying in a manger.' "

The narrator spoke again, " 'And suddenly there was with the angel a multitude of the heavenly host praising God, and saying, Glory to God in the highest, and on earth peace, good will toward men.' "

They continued to watch as the shepherds made their way to Bethlehem to see the new baby. The wise men came from the faraway lands, bringing the new babe precious gifts. The kings wore long, jewel-colored robes and gold crowns on their heads. Above the manger, a bright star shone, brighter than any Emily had ever seen.

Elam clasped her hand into his own, and Emily smiled at him. What a wonderful gift to see such a production. He returned her smile, squeezed her fingers, but kept her hand in his.

Hand in hand they walked through the field, enjoying the remarkable story with the others who had come. There were Amish and *Englisch* alike, all celebrating the special birth.

At the end of the trail to Bethlehem, vendors were stationed. There were places selling food, hand warmers, Christmas ornaments, and various other holiday goods.

Elam led her to a stand selling hot drinks. A couple was ahead of them in line, each trying to decide what to get.

Emily scanned the menu. "What's a hot vanilla?"

"I s'pose it's like a hot chocolate, but vanilla instead," Elam replied.

Emily made a face.

"You don't like that idea?"

"Why would I drink vanilla when I can have chocolate?" she asked in return.

"I think it sounds good." He took a step toward the counter as the other couple took their drinks and left. "I'll have one of those."

The man behind the counter poured the drink.

"*Jah?*" Emily asked.

Elam shrugged. "It's *gut* to try something different for a change."

For some reason his words rang like a challenge. Was he talking about hot vanilla drinks or the two of them? "Okay then, I'll take one, too."

They took their drinks, wandering around looking at the wares for sale.

Emily sipped her hot vanilla.

"Do you like it?" he asked.

"It's delicious." Better than delicious. So

much better than she thought it would be. Rich, creamy, and surprising, the hint of cinnamon deliciously unexpected.

He shot her a knowing look, but refrained from actually saying, *I told you so.*

A large Christmas tree loomed over the booths, shedding fractured sparkles of light as the decorations turned in the wind.

"It's like magic," she whispered, watching the lights dance along the ground.

"This from the bishop's daughter." Elam laughed.

"So because the bishop's my father, I can't believe something is wondrous?"

"You didn't say wondrous. You said magical."

"Are you going to tell on me?"

"Not a chance."

He took up her hand and led her past the giant tree to where another manger had been set up. This one didn't have a real baby inside, but the man in the Santa Claus suit was. He knelt by the baby, his hat in his hand and his head bowed.

The sight brought tears to Emily's eyes. "It's so *schee,*" she said.

The entire evening had been picture-perfect, but this one demonstration embodied Wells Landing at its finest. The town was a seamless mix of *Englisch* and Amish, of Christianity and the world. She was so blessed to be a part of it all.

Elam pulled the tractor to a stop in the side yard and switched off the engine. All in all, he considered tonight a success. His goal was to take Emily out, show her a good time. He thought he'd succeeded on all accounts.

"Danki." Emily swung down from the tractor like she had been doing it her entire life.

Jah, he admitted that the tractor hadn't been entirely necessary, but he wanted a little edge. He might be Amish and planning to stay right where he was, but he was modern, progressive even.

"I had a *gut* time," he said, climbing down next to her.

Not once had the proposal come up, and that was just the way he planned it. No pressure. A fun evening with just the two of them. And fifty other people who happened to be milling around at the same time.

"Would you like to come inside and warm up before you go home? I'm sure *Mamm* has some pie left from *nachtess.*"

He would like nothing more than to stay with Emily for as long as possible, but tonight was about courting, and he was determined to keep it that way. He patted his stomach. "I think I had enough at the Christmas show. *Danki*, anyway."

Together they walked up the porch steps.

"Would you just like to come in?"

He shook his head. After their scorching Thanksgiving kiss, it'd be better if he got back on the tractor and hightailed it home. "Four-thirty comes mighty early."

Her brow puckered into a frown. Had she expected him to jump at the chance to be with her? His goal was to change her expectations, show her a different way. Surprise her.

"It's better like this," he said.

"How so?" she asked. Her voice dropped to a low whisper that Elam found hard to resist.

"It gives you more to think about." He took a step closer to her, loving the way she smelled like outdoors and cinnamon.

"*Jah?*"

"*Gut nacht,* Emily." He pressed a kiss to her forehead, then loped off the porch without a backward glance.

Christmas Eve held an expectant air. There was just something about the celebration of Christ's birth that made the day seem heavier. More important, different somehow.

263

Emily said her prayers and crawled into her bed. Tomorrow morning she would spend the day with her family, then in the afternoon she was going over to Elam's with the gifts she had made for Elam, James, and the rest of the Riehls.

Their date had been one of the most spectacular evenings of her life. Though being left at the door with only a chaste kiss to the forehead left her anxious to spend more time with him.

He had kissed her at the Thanksgiving party, so why didn't he kiss her after their date? Did he want to kiss her?

She rolled onto her side and punched her pillow to smooth out the lumps. All she did was make it worse. She sat up, fluffed the pillow again, and lay back down with a frustrated sigh.

She shouldn't be thinking about such matters. She was supposed to be concentrating on the holiday and all it meant to her and her family. Yet after their date, Elam would be forever intertwined in her best memories of Christmas.

Plink.

Just like before, she rolled to the side, listening to the soft sounds of the night.

Plink.

Only one person threw stones at her window.

She pushed out of the bed and rushed to the window. Up went the sash and she gazed out into the yard. "Luke?" she whispered into the starry night.

"Emily." He looked much the same as he had the last time she had seen him. Plain coat, blue jeans, baseball hat. He had his hands shoved into his pockets as he stared up at her. "Meet me in the barn?" His voice barely carried up to her window, but he pointed as he spoke.

She hesitated, then nodded.

Part of her wanted to tell him no, crawl back in bed, and pretend she had never seen him. But then this other part . . . that was the part that raced down the stairs, grabbed her coat off the hook, and hurried out the door while still trying to put it on.

The barn door slid open with minimal effort and there he was. "Luke." Emily fought against the confusion raging inside her. She was so happy to see him, but her feelings were tangled as well. She wrapped her arms around herself and held on. "What are you doing here?"

He tilted his head to one side. "You aren't happy to see me?"

"I did not say that."

"You didn't have to." A frown puckered his brow, and his demeanor turned from open to surly. "I hitchhiked all the way here to be with you on Christmas, and this is the reception I get?" He pulled a piece of hay from the bale he leaned against and tossed it away.

"You hitchhiked? That's dangerous."

He shoved his hands into his pockets and shrugged. "I didn't have any other way to get here."

"What about your car?"

He shrugged again. "It's not always that easy, Em."

"I don't understand."

He shook his head. "I don't expect you to."

She stood, silently watching him stare at the ground. So many changes.

He wasn't the same *bu* he had been when he'd left. He had been carefree and adventurous. Now he seemed tired . . . defeated.

"Luke," she started, her voice low in the night. "If you are unhappy, why don't you come back here? To stay, I mean."

He stared off at nothing.

Her heart hurt for him as she watched him. She wanted to put that sweet smile back on his face, but was it her responsibility to make sure he was happy? He had to

266

want it as well, and as he stood there she knew the *Englisch* world still had ahold of his heart.

"I'm looking toward the future, Em. Surely you can understand that."

"A future with me or a future driving a race car?" She wasn't sure she wanted the answer to that.

"Why can't I have both?" His words were quiet, heartfelt, and so much like Luke. In his mind, he had the world by the tail, and he didn't understand when things didn't go his way.

"Do you think we can have a future if you can't even knock on the front door? You sneak in to see me, slink out the way you came." She shook her head as if that could help her work the kinks out of her thoughts.

And then there was Elam. Sweet, loving Elam who only wanted her to be happy. Who only wanted her.

"Emily, you just have to be patient. All I need is a little time and —"

"Elam Riehl proposed to me."

He stopped, the expression on his face unreadable. "You told him no, *jah*?"

"I haven't told him anything."

"But you are going to tell him no."

There was a part of her that wanted to say of course, why would she marry Elam if she was in love with Luke, but she wasn't so sure anymore. Not just about her feelings, but Luke's as well. Elam? She knew how he felt. He had been forthcoming from the start. It was refreshing and real to know that he loved her. It was special and made her feel warm inside. Almost as if he was there holding her. "I don't know what I'm going to do," she whispered. Yet deep down, the choice was obvious.

"You have to give me some more time, Em."

"For what?" She wanted promises. Was that too much to ask?

"Just hang in there with me," he begged. "Please."

She shook her head. "I . . . I'm just so confused."

"You don't have to make up your mind right now." His voice held an urgent edge. "Just don't tell Elam yes."

CHAPTER SEVENTEEN

"What's wrong, *liebschdi?*" *Mamm* asked the following afternoon.

Emily had been unusually quiet even for a reverent Christmas Day, but she couldn't tell her *mudder* why. She needed to talk about it, get it out in the open, and examine all the pieces that made up this puzzle of her life, but she couldn't talk to *Mamm.* She just couldn't.

"Do we have any ginger cookies left?" she asked.

Mamm nodded. "*Jah,* a dozen or so. Why?"

"I thought I might go out to see Caroline and Andrew today."

Her mother smiled. "I think that sounds like a perfect idea. It's a beautiful day for visiting."

And that was how Emily found herself swaying along under the blue sky. The air still held the chill of winter, but it was a *wunderbaar-gut* day to get out and visit with friends. Course'n it didn't hurt that she needed to talk to her friend in the worst way.

Caroline herself had recently had to choose between the two loves of her life: Trey Rycroft, her baby's *Englisch vatter,* and the handsome Andrew Fitch. Thankfully Trey had stepped aside, allowing Caroline and Andrew to get married and raise sweet little Emma on their own. Emily wasn't sure what it cost Trey emotionally, but she could imagine the pain he felt at walking away and leaving his child with another. Yet he had done it for the good of everyone involved. Everyone but him.

Emily had almost lost her friend to the *Englisch* world and now was about to lose Luke to the same.

Is Luke really mine to lose?

She didn't know.

She pulled into the drive at the horse farm and guided her mare up the lane.

Caroline was on the porch before she was even parked. "Merry Christmas," she called.

"Merry Christmas," Emily returned, looping her arm through the basket handle and hopping down from the carriage.

"Come in, come in. I'll have Andrew see to your horse, *jah?*"

270

Emily smiled in gratitude and made her way up the porch steps. Caroline enveloped her in a quick hug and steered her into the house.

"Where's Emma?" Emily asked after she'd taken off her coat, and Caroline had sent her husband out to see to Emily's horse.

"She's down for a nap."

Emily nodded and picked at an invisible spot on her apron.

"Come, sit." Caroline waved her into a chair. "You unpack whatever is in that basket, and I'll get the coffee."

Emily nodded. Somehow Caroline knew she needed to talk and for that she was grateful. "I thought Esther and Abe would be here," she said as she took the lid off the container holding the cookies.

"They will be by later. For now they wanted to give us some private time on our first Christmas together."

"Oh." Emily started to put the cookies back into the basket. "I've intruded. I didn't think . . . I —"

Caroline carried the coffee to the table and laid a gentle hand on Emily's to stay her action. "You have not intruded."

"It's just that I —" She bit her lip.

"Have something big on your mind." Caroline nodded.

"Jah." She was grateful her friend understood. What would she have done if Caroline had gone back to Tennessee and lived
with Trey Rycroft? She definitely needed to
thank the Lord for that small miracle.

"Sit," Caroline instructed. "And tell me
what is bothering you. You look like you are
about to explode."

Emily slid into the chair and glanced
toward the door. "Andrew?"

"Is a smart man," Caroline finished. "He
won't be back from the barn for a bit."

The air left Emily in a rush. She felt
herself almost wilting under the strain.
"Luke Lambright came to see me last
night."

Caroline's eyes grew wide. *"Nay."*

Emily nodded. "That's not all. Elam Riehl
asked me to marry him."

Caroline collapsed in her seat, snatching a
cookie on her way down. "Are you joking?"

"I wish I was."

Her friend took a quick bite and studied
her as she nibbled on the treat. "What are
you going to do?"

"I wish I knew."

Emily was still wondering as she pulled into
the driveway at the Riehl house later that
afternoon. Though she hadn't gotten any

firm answers during her talk with Caroline, she felt better having confessed all that had been going on.

Caroline hadn't said as much, but Emily knew her friend thought Elam's proposal to be worth consideration.

And it was.

But Emily had been pining after Luke for so long, she wasn't able to let it go just yet. Maybe with a few more days of prayer . . .

"Emily's here! Emily's here!"

She smiled and swung down from the buggy as Johanna did a little dance on the front porch.

"*Dat, Dat!* Emily's here."

But it wasn't James's smiling face that came to the door, but Elam's.

"Merry Christmas," she called.

"Merry Christmas." She loved when he smiled. It was as if the simple gesture turned his face back ten years. Suddenly he looked young and carefree. What she wouldn't give to see that look on his face for always.

"I'll get the horse." Becky pushed past them and hustled over to Emily's rig, then she turned back toward them with a stern frown. "But no opening presents until I get back, *jah*?"

Emily laughed. "I promise."

Elam let her in the house and once again

273

Emily marveled at how different it was now compared to the first time she had come to visit.

Pine boughs decorated the mantel over the fireplace where a fire cheerfully crackled and burned. Cream-colored streamers of ribbons and purple snowflakes hung from the ceiling on strings. A wooden nativity scene sat on the table, little bits of hay scattered around it. But it wasn't only the decorations that brought in the differences, the entire atmosphere of the house was more cheerful . . . hopeful. *Jah,* that was the word. The Riehls had hope now and she was pleased that she had played even a tiny part in the transformation.

Joy stood at the kitchen door, wiping her hands on a dish towel. Johanna had gone back to putting a puzzle together with Norma while James sat at the table.

"Emily. I was hoping you would come by today. It's Christmas, you know." James stood from cutting snowflakes from the construction paper she'd brought him. Little pieces of purple paper littered the wooden floor like forgotten confetti.

"I do know. Merry Christmas," she said. Elam was behind her. Steady and true. He didn't have to touch her for her to know he was there. His presence was comforting and joyful, and she was so glad to have it.

"Merry Christmas." James grinned. "*Guck*. None of them are the same." He unfolded the paper to reveal the cuts he'd made.

"That's beautiful, James." She blinked back sudden tears. What was wrong with her? But she knew. She was overcome with happiness and indecision. Anyone else would feel the same if they stood in her shoes.

"Miriam and Ruthie showed me how to cut them."

The twins flashed her grins of their own.

"And you taught us," Ruthie said as Miriam nodded.

She had made a difference. The thought was humbling.

"You'll stay for *nachtess*?"

"*Jah,*" Emily replied. "Mary said she might stop by later. She was going over to see Aaron when I left."

"That would be *gut,*" Becky said as she came back into the house. "Your horse is all taken care of. Did I miss anything?"

Emily laughed. "Not a thing. But . . ." She held up the basket of treats and presents she still carried. "I have a few things for you."

"For me?" James and Johanna said at the

same time.

She couldn't stop her smile at their eager expressions. "For all of you."

Elam had wanted to sit beside Emily as they exchanged gifts, but James had quickly claimed one spot and Johanna the other. Elam was forced to take up a place across from her. It wasn't his first choice, but the view was right nice.

"Me first, me first." Johanna bounced on her toes as she chanted the words. Elam was about to counsel her in the virtue of patience and waiting her turn when he realized that she didn't want to open her present first, but wanted to give Emily the present from her before anyone else gave her theirs.

He nodded his consent. She went to the table where the presents were laid out and brought her gift back to Emily.

"Danki." Emily took the sack from his youngest sibling. He loved the look on her face as she peeked inside. "Oh, my," she said, pulling out a pair of purple mittens. "Did you make these yourself?"

Johanna smiled. *"Nay,* but I picked them out in town."

"I love them," Emily said, giving Jo a quick hug.

And so started the exchange of all things purple.

New purple markers, more purple paper, lavender soap, lavender seeds, purple ribbon, even purple glitter and glue.

Somehow during all the excitement, Johanna had abandoned her place and Elam had quickly claimed it as his own.

"Now this is for everyone." Emily popped open a tub of folded-up cookies. He had seen them once before at the Chinese restaurant in town, but these were purple, of course.

He leaned in close to her. "Does the bishop know that you are passing out fortunes?"

She had the good graces to blush. "I'll have you know that I made these myself, and they are not fortunes."

"Oh, *jah*?" He snagged one of the cookies from the tub and broke it in two before pulling out the tiny strip of paper inside.

Cast your burden on the LORD, and he will sustain you; he will never permit the righteous to be moved.

Psalms 55:22

He stared at the paper as everyone grabbed a purple fortune cookie and read what Emily had tucked inside. All encouraging Bible verses. It was as if she had known all along what he needed to hear. What they all needed to hear.

Quite simply, she was amazing.

He had tried to be patient about his proposal, hoping that giving her time would allow her to make the best choice: the choice to marry him. But his impatience was starting to get the better of him. He wanted to do anything and everything he could think of to get her to say yes.

But for now he would bide his time and pray.

Dat rose to his feet and gathered the last gift bag from the present stash and handed it to Emily. "These are for you," he said, grinning at her with such pride, Elam figured he'd have to pray about it later.

Emily took the bag, a bit of surprise in her eyes. "For me?"

His *vatter* nodded. "*Jah,* from all of us."

"That's right," Norma chimed in as the others nodded.

Emily smiled and pulled out the first wad of tissue paper. She reached into the bag again and retrieved a clothespin . . . a purple one.

Elam chuckled.

"Read it," *Dat* said.

Emily turned it over until she found the words. " 'A purple a day keeps the doctor away.' "

Everyone laughed as she dropped that pin back into the sack and pulled out another one. " 'All's fair in love and purple.' "

More laughter. She grabbed another one. " 'Purple is as purple does.' "

"They're all *Englisch* sayings," Becky explained.

"But we added the purple part." James nodded.

"And painted them," Johanna added.

Emily looked up from the sack, her gaze flitting to each one of them in turn. "I love them. *Danki.*"

"You're welcome," *Mamm* said. "Anyone *hungerich*?"

"Come, come." Miriam and Ruthie clapped their hands together. "It's time to eat, *jah*?"

Everyone stood to gather around the table when a knock sounded on the door. Norma went to open it, and Mary stepped into the house.

"Merry Christmas, Mary Ebersol," the Riehls called to her.

Norma barely gave her time to unbutton her coat and take off her bonnet before grabbing her by the hand and dragging her toward the kitchen table. "It's time to eat."

This time Elam purposefully sat across from Emily. He wanted to be able to see her face as they ate. It was sappy, he knew, but that was how he felt all the same.

They sat down, bowed their heads, and prayed over their food. Elam also prayed for a bit more patience where Emily and his marriage proposal were concerned and that God would guide her heart in the right direction. Couldn't she see how much she had come to mean to him? To his family?

Dat lifted his head to signify the end of the prayer and everyone followed suit.

Becky lifted her brows in *Mamm*'s direction. *Mamm* nodded in response, and Becky rose from the table. What were they planning?

A few seconds later, Becky returned to the table carrying a covered dish. "Ahem." She cleared her throat, gaining everyone's attention. "In light of this being such a special day, *Mamm* and I came up with a special dish."

A series of *yum*s went up around the table.

Becky paused, allowing the drama to build. "Mashed potatoes," she announced.

Norma and Johanna's mouths fell to frowns, while the twins tried to put on uninterested faces.

Becky pulled the lid from the pot to reveal mounds of violet. "Purple mashed potatoes."

Elam couldn't stop the chuckle that escaped him.

"Did you do that with food coloring?" Emily asked.

"Nay." Becky smiled and handed the pot to Mary. "I found purple potatoes in the market. Awesome, *jah?"*

A chorus of *jah*s went up all around the table as everyone took their turn trying the purple treat.

He looked around at his family, so different today than it had been a couple of months ago, and all thanks to one person. He caught Emily's gaze in his own. She smiled in that sweet way she had, and he was overcome with his love for her. She was so beautiful inside and out, so caring and lovely. He wanted nothing more than to marry her and make all of her days as happy as she made him and his family.

"What?" she asked, dropping her gaze to her plate then raising it back to his.

"Nix," he replied. But it was more than nothing. So much more.

After supper, Emily and Mary helped the girls clean the kitchen while Joy and James went to the living room to play with the new presents. Emily couldn't have been happier with the joy she had seen on James's face at the purple gifts that had been exchanged. But there was one more gift still left to give. Her heart pounded in her chest at the mere thought of handing Elam the present she had brought for him. What if he hated it?

She dried her hands on the dish towel as the rest of the girls finished putting the dishes away.

Only one way to know how he would feel about it and that was to give it to him.

Mary caught her eye with a knowing smile.

"I need to, uh, find Elam."

The girls all turned to her, all except Johanna who seemed oblivious to the relationship between Emily and her big brother. They smiled and nodded, their eyes twinkling with more than Christmas cheer.

"I think he's in the barn," Becky helpfully supplied.

And that was exactly where Emily found him. He had his back to her, as he tended one of the mules. He was bent low over the task, the beast's right front hoof braced on Elam's thigh as he worked.

"Hi," she said, cautiously approaching.

Elam released the mule and turned to face her. "Hi." He adjusted his hat where he had tipped it back to better see as he worked. Emily hated the gesture because she couldn't see his eyes as well shaded by the brim as they were then.

She pulled the gift bag from behind her back and held it out to him. "I have something for you."

He looked at it, then at her as if unable to say anything at the sight of the gift. Then he took the rag that had been tucked into the waistband of his pants and wiped the dirt from his fingers. "For me?"

Emily smiled at his childlike expression. "*Jah.* It's not much, but . . ." She shrugged.

"I'm sure it is perfect."

She hated the way her hand trembled as she held the sack toward him.

He tucked the rag away. His expression turned solemn — or was it thoughtful? — as he pulled the tissue-paper-wrapped present out.

"It's the song," she said while he studied the framed picture she had given him. "The one you sang to me after the school Christmas program." The librarian had helped her type all the words to "Love Is Patient and Kind" into the computer, then Emily printed it on some pretty paper and framed it in a hand-painted frame. It had taken a lot of time, effort, and patience and now she wanted to jerk it away from him before he started laughing at her for being so silly. Her heart couldn't take that.

"It's *wunderbaar,*" he said, his voice thickened with something she couldn't name. Was he happy? Laughing? Trying not to choke at her childishness?

If they had been eighteen and just starting to court, it might not have seemed so silly. But they weren't eighteen. They were well past that.

"I —" she started, not really sure how she was going to complete the sentence. Thankfully she didn't have to as Elam pulled her close and pressed a kiss to the top of her head.

"It's beautiful," he said as he released her from his embrace. "So thoughtful."

She flushed with pride and maybe a little bit of something else. Love perhaps? But she pushed the thought away. Loving Elam made things even more muddled than they already were, and she had enough confusion on her plate to last all the way through to next year.

"Come on back to the *haus.* I may have something for you." He looped his arm through hers and steered her back toward the porch.

"You might?" She smiled up at him, loving the warmth of him beside her. Again she nudged the thought aside. Way too confusing, way too much to sort through on the Lord's birthday.

"*Jah.* I might."

He smiled all the way to the house. Emily knew this because she kept casting glances his way. He looked younger when he smiled, more than just happy. He looked content, as if God had somehow set his feet on a well-lit path.

He opened the door, and she stepped inside. Strangely enough, no one was in the living room when they came in. Emily was certain she had seen the shades on the front windows stir as they had walked up the porch steps, but there was not a soul around. Must have been a trick of her eyes.

She took off her coat and hung it by the door while Elam did the same.

"Wait right here," he said, then he took the steps two at a time.

Suddenly uncomfortable, Emily smoothed her hands down the front of her dress. Where was her sister?

The only sounds that could be heard were the tick of the clock over the mantel and the fire still burning in the grate.

That in itself was strange. There were eight people in the house not counting her and Elam, and no one was making a noise?

Once again his footsteps echoed on the stairs.

"It's not a lot," he started.

Emily loved the flush of red that had crept into his cheeks. She was certain he would blame it on the cold, but she had a feeling it had more to do with the large box he held in his hands.

"Elam, I —"

"Just open it," he said.

Emily took the package from him and perched on the edge of the sofa. There was no wrapping paper, but someone had placed a large purple bow on top. It was a bit lopsided, and Emily was certain James and Johanna were responsible for the decoration.

The box was heavy, and she took her time opening it. Somehow she knew the contents were fragile. But in no time at all she had the present out of the box.

"Oh, Elam."

She wasn't sure what to say. Delicate white glass decorated with hand-painted purple violets, it was without a doubt the most beautiful lamp she had ever seen.

"It was my *grossmammi*'s," he explained as he turned it over in her hands. "The batteries go in here —"

Emily shook her head. "I can't accept this." She started to put it back into the wrapping, back into the box, but Elam laid a hand on hers, stilling her motions.

"She would love knowing you have it."

"But this is so valuable. It should stay in your family."

He shrugged and gave her a small smile. "Once you accept my proposal, then it'll be back in the family."

Emily swallowed hard. Part of her wanted the beautiful gift. It was lovely, exquisite even. She would place it in her room and every time she saw it, she would think of Elam and James, Joy and the rest of the Riehl girls.

But to accept the gift, after he made such a statement . . . she was just so confused.

"Forgive me," he murmured. "I promised not to put any pressure on you for an answer. Whatever you decide, the lamp is yours. It's the least we can offer you after everything you have given us."

"Nay." She shook her head. "I didn't give you anything."

"You gave us hope." He reached up and brushed the backs of his fingers against her cheek. It was a motion she had become familiar with. It was comforting, sweet, and exciting all at the same time.

Then the confusion was back.

"*Danki,*" she whispered.

"*Gern gschehne,*" he said in return.

The moment hung between them. For a minute, she thought he might kiss her.

Then Johanna bounded into the room.

"Emily, Emily, Emily! *Mamm* said we could have another piece of pie. Will you cut it? Please, please, please?"

Elam shot her an apologetic half smile as she allowed herself to be dragged into the kitchen.

CHAPTER EIGHTEEN

An hour later Elam stood on his front porch and waved as Emily and Mary drove away.

It had been such an enjoyable day. He'd felt . . . blessed as he spent the day with his family and Emily. It made him wonder if today was how the rest of the holiday celebrations would be, once they got married.

He tried to keep his thoughts about Emily's answer to his proposal on the positive side. He needed to believe that finally, *finally* she would be his.

The screen door slammed, and he turned to find Becky stepping out onto the porch.

He looked back to the street as Mary and Emily disappeared from view.

"Are you going to stand out here all night?" Becky asked. "*Mamm* was wondering if you wanted something else to eat."

He shook his head. He'd eaten more today than he had all week.

He'd be lucky if his pants would fasten shut tomorrow.

Becky crossed her arms, bit her lower lip, and tilted her head to one side as if mulling over something of great importance. Then again, with Becky a body never knew if it was a grave matter or simply which color dress she should wear to the youth meeting.

When she didn't speak right away, he turned back to face her. "Something on your mind, Becky?"

She shook her head, then seemed to change her mind. *"Jah,"* she said.

Elam propped one hip on the porch railing and eyed his *shveshtah.* "And?"

She hesitated for a moment longer then the words burst from her like water from a garden hose. "Jonah Miller told his brother Aaron who told Mary who told me that Luke Lambright is back." She sucked in a big gulp of air.

"It is a sin to gossip," Elam said, though the news stabbed his heart. He just needed a little more time to make Emily fall in love with him. Was that too much to ask?

"Mary said she even thinks Emily is sneaking out to see him."

He wouldn't allow himself to believe the words. He couldn't. To believe that would mean to give up hope, all the hope he had built for himself over the last few weeks.

Emily and Luke had been a couple for a long time, and they had known each other even longer. There was no way her father — the bishop — would let a wayward soul like Luke swoop in and take her away from Elam.

Well, her father wouldn't want Luke to hang around and show the youth of Wells Landing how to live a double life.

That was the thing about a *rumspringa*. It had to end. And when it didn't, the person in question had to move on. It was too much of a distraction to let those wayward souls stay around and suggest to the youth that they could have all they wanted: the thrill of the outside world and the comfort of their Amish home.

"Elam?" Becky's words brought him 'round to the here and now.

"*Jah?*"

"I think she loves you."

His heart jumped at the thought. More than anything in the world he wanted Emily's love in return. But love was a fragile thing, so easily damaged, so hard to grow.

And then there was Luke Lambright standing between them. How was Elam supposed to win her heart if Luke was there to constantly distract her?

"I hope so," he replied. "I surely do."

Luke stirred the noodles on his plate and wondered where things had gone so wrong. All he had ever done in his life was exactly what he was supposed to. He'd plowed fields and gone to church. He prayed when he was told to, sang when it was expected of him, everything. He had done everything in line with the Amish way.

Then he turned sixteen and learned to drive a car.

The thrill of his fingers curled around the steering wheel, the rumble of the engine vibrating throughout his body. It was like no other feeling on earth. He'd been hooked since the first time he ever sat in a driver's seat.

Now he had a chance to drive for a living, feel that buzz every day, get paid for it even. How could he let that go?

He stirred the chicken casserole around on his plate a bit more. He tried to pretend he was eating, when too many thoughts occupied his mind.

"Something wrong?" his *onkle* asked.

Something . . . everything . . . *"Nay,"* he lied.

It was so far from the truth, *Onkle* Joseph

frowned at him. "You want to try that again?"

"Emily." Her name brought a faster beat to his heart, a warmth to his blood, and a comfort to him like none other. He had loved her as long as he could remember.

His uncle nodded, understanding everything from the one word. "It is hard to balance two loves," he said.

That was exactly what Luke had to do: balance the things he loved most in the world.

"Elam Riehl asked her to marry him." Once he said the words out loud, they were even scarier than they had been inside his mind. If anyone outside the two of them knew how much he loved Emily, it was *Onkle* Joseph.

His *onkle* leaned back in his seat and narrowed his eyes. It was his thoughtful expression, though to an outsider it might have looked more like anger. "Did she tell him yes?"

"I asked her not to."

Onkle nodded. "Then there is still time."

"Time?"

"To prove your love to her, to show her a life that Elam cannot give her."

Luke nodded slowly. His life among the *Englisch* had been sparse at best. His living conditions other than electricity had been worse than they had when he lived with his uncle. But he had seen the magazines; the *Englisch* world was a beautiful place. One day it would all be his: fortune, fame, a big house, nice cars, and a big diamond ring for his Emily like the one the sponsor's wife wore.

They just had to be patient.

He would do just as his uncle said and show Emily the life that would soon be hers. The freedoms she could have outside of Wells Landing, the fun and excitement. And he knew just how to do it.

Plink.

The sound had become familiar to Emily. She threw back the covers and tiptoed over to the window. Tonight she didn't raise the sash. She just nodded at Luke and crept down the stairs.

She wasn't sure why, but going to him like this, in the middle of the night when everyone else was asleep, seemed wrong somehow. Very wrong. Yet she hadn't done anything sinful. She had no plans to.

But with the confusion that raged in her heart, she had to know. Did she still love Luke? Or had he become like an old familiar blanket, warm and comfortable, easy? Was she willing to wait on him to return to the Amish life where they had grown up? Oh, she knew he said he wasn't, but how long could he survive in the *Englisch* world driving cars in a circle?

She grabbed her coat and slipped it on, careful not to let the screen door slam behind her as she made her way outside.

Luke was nowhere to be seen, so she headed for the barn, sure he had gone in there for shelter from the cold.

"Luke?" She poked her head in first, then stepped inside as he turned on one of the battery-operated lights her father kept close to the door.

"Emily." The light cast shadows onto his tired features. "I've missed you so much." He set the lamp on a hay bale and pulled her close for a quick hug.

The thrill of being held in his arms didn't zing through her like it used to. But maybe that was because the cold night air had frozen her legs to icicles. She should have pulled on some stockings before coming down to meet him. As it was, her flannel nightgown offered little warmth below the line where her coat ended.

Being held by Luke was much like hugging her sister Mary.

He released her and stepped back. If he

noticed anything different about the embrace he didn't say anything. Instead he fished into his jeans pocket and brought out a small box. "I have something for you."

"For me?"

"It's not much."

She looked at the box and back to his face. She had been so busy getting everything ready for her sisters and the Riehls for Christmas, she had forgotten to get anything for Luke. "I don't have anything for you," she whispered, unable to take the box from him.

He held it closer to her. "That's all right."

She took the box and untied the red ribbon, careful not to let it fall to the barn floor. Inside was a piece of slick paper, the kind like she had seen in an *Englisch* magazine. This page had been folded up so it fit into the tiny box.

"Here." Luke took the paper and unfolded it, smoothing it against his thigh before handing it back. "That's what I'm going to get you someday. Soon," he added.

Emily stared at the picture. An *Englisch* ring lay on top of a bed of ivory rose petals. She knew enough to know the square stone set in the middle of a band of smaller stones was a diamond and considered very valuable. But the Amish didn't wear jewelry.

She frowned. "I don't understand."

"I . . ." Luke faltered. "I don't have the money to get you that now, but one day . . . one day I will. You'll see."

"But —" It was her turn to stutter. "When you come back, I . . ."

"I've almost got a sponsor, Em. I got this guy, Gus Hardin's his name. He wants to sign me."

"But you haven't signed?"

"Not yet, though it's just a matter of time before everything goes through. He likes my story — Amish kid learns to drive, makes good on the dirt tracks. That sort of thing."

"What does this mean exactly?" she asked.

"That I'll have money for a car, for races, for things like this." He tapped the paper she held in her hands. The picture of the expensive *Englisch* ring.

"I don't want a diamond."

"You may not now, but trust me, one day you will."

"Luke," she started, but wasn't able to finish as he clasped her hands in his own, crumpling the paper a bit as he squeezed her fingers. "Come with me tomorrow night. There's a party at a friend of mine's house."

"Who?"

Luke shrugged. "You don't know him."

"Luke, I —"

"Just promise you'll come with me."

"I don't know." Emily bit her lip. "I'll have to sneak out." Her father would not let her go anywhere with Luke Lambright, that much was certain. But since everyone in her family went to bed early, leaving the house after everyone was asleep would still leave them plenty of time to be together.

"So?" He shrugged again. "You're twenty-one years old, Emily. The *Englisch* believe that's old enough to make up your own mind about things."

I'm not Englisch popped to the tip of her tongue, but she bit back the words.

"I'll be by at ten to get you."

"You'll come here?"

"Only to the stop sign at the end of the lane. Can you walk down there and meet me?"

It was a quarter of a mile to the stop sign, but Emily nodded. "I'll be there."

She felt like she was in her *rumspringa* again, though never had she done anything like sneak out in the middle of the night. The worst she had done was listen to pop music on a friend's music player.

But Luke was right. She was twenty-one years old. Most Amish women her age were married and having babies. If a person her age could be trusted with an infant, surely she could be trusted to spend the evening with a friend.

"Hang on to that picture," Luke said, releasing her hands so he could refold it. "That's going to be yours someday." He pressed the small square of paper into her palm as he landed a chaste kiss to her cheek. "See you tomorrow."

And then he was gone.

"What are you doing?"

At the urgent whisper, Emily stopped midmotion, one arm up in the air as she pulled on her heavy black coat. She turned, then wilted with relief at the sight of her sister. "Mary," she whispered in return. "You scared me half to death."

Mary braced her hands on her hips and pursed her lips. The action was so like their mother, Emily had to stifle a giggle. "That did not answer my question."

"I'm going out." Emily finished putting on her coat and reached for her black bonnet.

"That's obvious. It's the where to that I'm worried about."

"Quit frowning like that. You'll be more wrinkled than Maddie Kauffman if you keep that up."

Mary shook her head, but smoothed her forehead all the same. "I'm worried about you, *shveshtah.*"

"Why ever for?" Emily tied the bonnet strings under her chin and reached for her scarf. The minute her fingers touched the soft yarn, memories of Elam surfaced. Becky had crocheted the scarf for her. The purple hue was the deep dark shade of an eggplant, nearly black. Perhaps that was the only reason why her father let her wear it, but having it in her hands . . .

She pushed the thoughts away. She would never be able to figure out her mind if she kept avoiding the issue. She had to go tonight with Luke, work through whatever feelings she had left for him. Elam was waiting for an answer from her. He was a *gut* man, but he wouldn't wait forever, just as it was unfair to ask him to do so.

Still Luke's gift from the night before confused her. She didn't want a ring. She didn't want to leave the Amish. And if she was truly being honest with herself, she didn't want to go to this party. She felt adrift, jumbled, and confused.

"You're going to meet Luke, aren't you?"

"Mary . . ." She wasn't sure what to say to her sister. "Surely you understand. You've been in love with Aaron all these years."

"Jah," Mary said, frowning again.

"And I have loved Luke."

"But he's gone, and Elam . . ."

"I know." Emily closed her eyes, doing her best to form the words she needed to make her sister understand. Yet how was she supposed to explain it to Mary when she didn't understand it herself? "My mind is befuddled," she finally whispered. "I don't know what to do, except I promised Luke I would meet him tonight."

"Oh, Emily, that's a terrible idea."

"How else am I supposed to know what I should do if I don't spend time with them both?"

"You could pray about it."

"You think I haven't done that?" She shook her head at it all. "I've prayed and prayed, but it's as if God is telling me that I have to figure this one out for myself."

"Oh, Em." Mary pulled her close for a hug. Then she pulled back, her hands still braced on Emily's shoulders as she looked her square in the eye. "Just promise me you'll be careful. I don't trust Luke. After what I've been hearing about him . . . promise, *jah?*"

Emily nodded. "I promise." But this was Luke they were talking about. Her Luke.

"And wake me up when you get home."

"Okay." She let out a small laugh. "You'll make a *gut mudder,* Mary Ebersol."

Mary frowned and released her.

Emily grabbed a flashlight and slipped out the door and into the dark cold night.

No moon graced the sky, and the night seemed so very dark. Emily pulled her coat around her, fighting off the Oklahoma wind as she hurried to the spot where she was supposed to meet Luke.

The lights of the car glowed up ahead, and her steps grew faster. Whatever Mary said, this was the only way to know what to do. Emily was just so confused. How was she supposed to make up her mind? Spending time with Luke and spending time with Elam was the only way. And if spending time with Luke meant slipping out without her *eldra* knowing, then so be it. What other choice did she have?

She was practically running by the time she reached the door of the car. She wrenched it open and slipped inside, the warm leather seat enveloping her as she slid into its comfort.

Luke smiled, his face lighting up like a child at Christmas. "I was beginning to think you weren't coming."

"Sorry."

He took her cold hands into his, warming

them with his touch. She hadn't been able to don the purple mittens that Johanna had given her for Christmas. The scarf brought back too many memories as it was.

"Are you ready?" Luke smiled, releasing her hands to put the car into gear.

"Jah." She swallowed hard as she said the word. Was she ready? She didn't even know where they were going, only that a friend of his was having some sort of party. "I thought you left your car in Arkansas." She gazed around at the lights on the dashboard and the multitude of knobs and levers that made up the vehicle.

"This belongs to a friend of mine."

"It looks expensive."

"His *dat* has a lot of money." Luke shrugged. "But just wait, one day I'll have one even better."

One day . . .

She was about to ask him when that day would be and what would happen then, but he reached out and turned on the radio. Loud rock music filled the car and cut off any chance for conversation between them.

It seemed like they were going way too fast, but she wasn't sure if she felt that way because he was speeding or if she was just so accustomed to moving at a horse's pace. She decided to try to relax, to sit back and watch Luke as he drove. He seemed at ease. His hands were loose on the wheel, his thumbs beating out a tempo to match the music blaring through the car.

This was not exactly how she thought tonight would go. *Jah,* he said they were going to a party. She knew she wouldn't have him all to herself to talk about the future and what it would mean to the both of them, but she had imagined they would at least have a bit of time to talk about things.

"Luke." She raised her voice to be heard over the music. Evidently not loud enough, because he kept his eyes forward, his thumbs still tapping on the steering wheel. "Luke!" This time louder.

"Huh?" He glanced toward her.

"I want to talk to you."

"About what?"

"Can you turn down the music?"

He did as she asked, though she thought he might argue about it.

"Can you just turn it off?"

He frowned and switched it off, blessed silence filling the car.

"Danki." She smoothed her hands down her dress.

"Are you going to be this uptight at the party?" he asked, his gaze centered back onto the road ahead of them.

"What's that supposed to mean?"

"It's just that . . ." He trailed off with a shake of his head. "You need to loosen up. This is a party we're going to."

She frowned. "I need to be loose to attend a party?"

"You need to be . . . well, not so uptight. Take off your prayer *kapp* and your apron. Maybe take down your hair."

Her hands automatically flew to her head. "Are you serious?" He *looked* serious.

"Yeah . . . how can you have a good time, with all this hanging around you?" He waved a hand in her general direction.

"I need to defy the *Ordnung* in order to have a good time?"

"My point exactly." Luke pulled into the driveway of an older house. The white painted brick could have used another coat, and even in the dark of the night she could tell the yard was covered in dead weeds and leaves. The glowing porch lights testified that it was *Englisch*-owned and the music booming from inside told her she was as close as she wanted to be.

"I'm just saying that you might have a better time if you could blend in a bit more, that's all."

"Blend in," she repeated, watching as the

door of the house swung open and a young girl stepped onto the porch. She was about Emily's age, scantily dressed and holding a cigarette in one hand and a drink in the other. Somehow Emily knew it wasn't lemonade in the plastic cup. "Like her?" she asked.

Luke looked at the girl, then back to Emily. "Sort of. I mean, the *Englisch* world is different, Em. You can be who you want to be here. You don't have to worry about the bishop or the *Ordnung.*"

"The bishop is my *vatter.*" She pulled her arms around her, hugging herself as a young man joined the girl on the porch. He hooked one arm around her waist and hauled her to him, kissing her with such intimacy that Emily blushed. "I think you should take me home, Luke."

He turned to face her in the dark interior of the car. "What if I don't want to take you home?"

On the porch the young man continued to maul the girl, groping at her with drunken hands. She didn't seem to mind, pawing at him in much the same way. Emily was embarrassed for the two of them.

"You care so little about me that you would make me stay someplace that is uncomfortable for me?" She dropped her gaze to her lap, unable to look at him or the sloppy couple on the porch.

"Em, I love you, you know that." He cupped one hand on her chin and tilted her eyes up to meet his once more.

"Do you?"

"Jah." It was the first time he had said anything in *Deutsch* since he had picked her up. The one word was comforting, a soothing balm against her raging turmoil.

He lowered his head, his intentions clear. Yet if she had thought his kiss would clarify anything, she was wrong. It only made matters worse. Where was the drop in her stomach, the excitement, the breathless anticipation?

"Are you ready to go in?" Luke asked.

"I . . . I want to go home," Emily replied.

Even with only the streetlights illuminating the interior of the car, Emily saw his eyes darken from the color of the sea to a turbulent blue of stormy skies. "Why?"

"I don't belong here with those people." She nodded her head toward the porch, but the kissing couple had disappeared. It didn't matter; her meaning was clear.

"You belong with me." His words rang with an emphatic note, a certainty she no longer felt. The change made her itchy, uncomfortable in her own skin.

"Do I?"

"What are you saying, Em?"

Emily shook her head. "I don't know," she whispered.

Luke's expression turned as unsettled as his eyes. His back stiffened. "Is this about Elam?"

She shook her head and, surprisingly enough, it was true. This wasn't about Elam. This was about her and Luke and feelings that had been in place so long they had become stagnant and not grown as the two of them had. Elam was another matter entirely. He was the future — of that she was certain — and Luke . . . Luke was the past.

Tears filled her eyes. "Please take me home."

"I don't understand. I came back here for you."

"I know."

"I quit my job and —"

"You quit your job?"

He shrugged. "It was a dumb job. But I wanted to be here with you. And now you're telling me that we're through."

"I never said that."

"You might as well have," he huffed.

Emily laid her head back against the car seat and closed her eyes. "I never wanted any of this to turn out this way."

"Yet you still went out with Elam Riehl."

"That's not fair." She swung her gaze to him. A muscle in his jaw bunched and jerked as he ground his teeth together.

"Are you denying that you went out with him?"

"You left!"

"To make a better life for us."

"What's wrong with the life we had here?"

"Everything!"

Emily sucked in a deep breath. "Why are we yelling at each other?"

Luke leaned forward and propped his head on the steering wheel. "I don't know."

"What are we going to do about it?"

"I don't know that either."

"Do you think maybe we've been in love so long that we just don't love each other anymore?" The quiet question hung in the air.

He looked up, meeting her gaze in the dim interior of the car. "That's dumb."

She sighed. "Love is dumb."

"Do you love him?"

"Elam?"

"Yeah."

"I don't know."

"I meant what I said, Emily. You are mine, and I don't want to lose you. I'll do anything to keep you."

"Does that include leaving racing behind and joining the church?"

Dead air filled the space between them. Outside the music blared, traffic raced by, and people shouted to one another. Yet there, in that expensive car, only silence could be heard.

"I love racing," he finally said.

"More than me?"

"That's not fair," Luke said, repeating her earlier sentiment.

Emily nodded, pleating a crease in her apron. "None of this is."

A heartbeat pounded between them, then another.

Luke reached for the keys and started the engine. "I'll take you home."

Emily sat back and pulled her seat belt across her lap once more.

She tried to relax, but her thoughts were all a jumble. When had life taken such a complicated turn? Or maybe the question was why?

All she had ever wanted was to marry Luke, have babies, and live her life out as one of the Amish in Wells Landing.

Then Luke went to the *Englisch* world, and Elam professed his love. Now everything was so confused, she didn't know whether she was coming or going. One thing was certain . . . Luke Lambright was not part of her future.

She looked over at him, his eyes straight ahead as he studied the road.

His fingers tightened on the wheel, and his lips pressed together. If she didn't know better, she thought the car went a little bit faster.

But she didn't know, and she couldn't gauge such fast speeds.

The tires squealed as they rounded a turn.

"Luke?" Emily braced her arms at her sides, one on the center console and the other on the car door. "You're driving too fast."

He scoffed. "Don't be such a wuss, Em. I'm a race car driver, remember? We're supposed to drive fast."

"This isn't a racetrack." Her voice trembled, and she cleared her throat to bring the warble back under control.

"Do you think I don't know how to drive?"

"Luke," she begged. "You're scaring me."

Once again he made a derisive noise. "I got this, Em."

But she was certain he slowed just a bit. Or maybe it was the curve warning up ahead.

"Holy crap." Luke braked hard.

Emily braced herself and looked through the windshield just in time to see a stalled truck in the middle of their lane. Red lights flashed, and the tires squealed as Luke worked to get the car under control and avoid the truck.

"Hold on," he told her, turning the wheel this way and that. The smell of burning rubber filled the night air, mingling with the words of Emily's silent prayer.

Then as if everything sped up and slowed down at the same time, Luke gritted his teeth, turned the wheel as far as he could, and pushed the brake pedal down as far as it would go. His struggle to control the car was the last thing she saw before she heard the sickening thud of the crash and the clatter of breaking glass.

CHAPTER NINETEEN

Emily blinked. Her head hurt. Her lip hurt. Her arm hurt. She blinked again. Everything was blurry, out of focus, and a bit too bright so she closed her eyes again.

"Em?" Was that Luke?

"Is she coming around?" This from a voice she didn't recognize.

"Luke?" she whispered. "What happened?"

A warm palm touched her cheek. "You're going to be okay, Em. You hit your head."

"My head?" She raised a hand to the throb pounding just above her eye. Wet sticky warmth met her fingers.

"Don't do that," Luke gently admonished. "You're bleeding."

Emily held her fingers out in front of her, staring at the red stain with fascination. "What happened?" she asked again.

"We had a wreck."

A wreck? "The horses?"

"We were in a car, Em."

"Should I call an ambulance?" the unfamiliar voice asked.

An ambulance? Weren't those expensive? *"Nay."* She wanted to shake her head, but it hurt too badly. She struggled to sit up, then realized she was trembling with the effort. She closed her eyes against the wave of dizziness.

"Just lay back, Emily."

"Luke?"

"I'm here." His voice washed over her and made her feel safe once more. "The ambulance is on its way."

Three hours later, Emily sat up in the emergency room hospital bed. A bandage covered the six stitches above her eye. Her right arm had been wrapped in an elastic bandage and placed in a sling. The nurse told her that once the swelling went down, tomorrow or the next day, the doctors would bind it in a cast to allow the break to heal.

Someone had brought her a cup full of pain pills, gave her a shot of antibiotics and something else. Now she waited.

They had told her that her parents had been notified. That she was in the medical clinic in Pryor, a neighboring town to Wells

Landing. She hadn't paid much attention to where they were headed as Luke had been driving, only that she was with him. Now she was far from home, injured, and waiting for the worst that was sure to come.

"Emily Jane?" Her mother rushed into the small room, tears shining in her pale blue eyes. "Oh, Emily." *Mamm* wrapped her arms around her and gently pulled her close.

Tears stung her own eyes at the fear and concern she saw in her *mudder*. She hadn't meant to worry anyone. Had never before done anything like this.

"I'm so sorry, *Mamm,*" she cried into her mother's shoulder. The familiar scents of soap and lavender filled her senses as she held her mother close.

Mamm pulled away, but remained near. "It was a miracle for sure that you weren't hurt any worse. Your father is getting your things so you can go."

"And Luke?"

Mamm's lips pressed together. "We can talk about Luke Lambright tomorrow."

"But he's *allrecht*?" Emily asked. No one would tell her how he was, or where he was, or even if he was hurt. Since he was not her family, they wouldn't let him in to see her.

Her mother's sharp gaze ran over her face and settled on her wrapped arm. "I'll say he

315

fared better than you."

Emily sighed. She and Luke might've had their differences, they might even be growing in completely different directions, but she couldn't bear the thought of him being hurt.

There was a quick knock on the door, and her father was there with a plastic bag containing what remained of her things: her coat, her bloody prayer *kapp,* and her ruined apron. "*Ach,* we're leaving now."

He barely cast a glance her way, a sure sign that his patience was thin enough to read through.

"*Kumm.*" *Mamm* held out a steadying arm and helped Emily to her feet. She swayed slightly, the mild concussion mixed with medications to make her woozier than she'd been before.

On her *mamm*'s arm, she made her way out of the hospital and into the cool winter night. Her father stopped long enough to dig her coat from the plastic sack and hand it to her.

"*Danki,*" she murmured as *Mamm* slung it over her shoulders and steered her toward the waiting car.

Jay Tyler, their *Englisch* neighbor, sat behind the wheel, attesting that her parents had been distraught when they got the news. They hadn't even called their regular Mennonite driver.

"I'm so glad you're okay, Emily," Jay said as her father climbed into the front seat and her *mamm* helped her settle into the back.

"Danki," Emily said. "Me too."

Then without another word, Jay Tyler drove them back to the farm.

It looked like every lamp in the house was on when Jay turned into their drive forty-five minutes later. Forty-five completely silent, incredibly tense minutes later.

Her mother was typically silent. Helen Ebersol was more apt to observe than speak, a trait that made her words all the more powerful when she finally did utter them.

Her *vatter* was another matter entirely. Emily could almost feel the angry vibrations rolling off his skin. Or maybe that was a side effect of the pain medication.

No matter. As soon as she got home, all she wanted to do was crawl beneath the covers and sleep and sleep. Tomorrow or the next day she'd deal with her father, the broken arm, and all the disappointments she had suffered this evening.

Jay pulled his modest sedan to a stop and unlocked the doors. He left the car running as he went around and opened the door for her mother. Emily fumbled with the handle, but her father was there, opening it for her.

He reached out a steadying hand to help her from the car.

She wanted to say something to him, apologize for the trouble and worry she had caused, but her mouth felt like it had been stuffed with cotton. Before she could form the words, her mother was there taking her away as her father turned to pay Jay for his time.

"Emily!" Mary jumped up from her seat in the living room. The quilt wrapped around her shoulders flew out behind her as she rushed to Emily's side. "It's all my fault," she moaned.

"Mary, I'm okay." Emily tried to smooth back her sister's hair but missed. "Oops." She giggled, then burst into tears as the medication, the night, and everything else proved too much for her.

"Up to bed you go, Emily Jane." Her mother steered her toward the stairs, but not before she saw those pale blue eyes pin Mary to the spot. "We'll discuss this in the morning."

Emily allowed her mother to escort her up the stairs and get her into bed. Her head had started to hurt again and her arm was beginning to ache. *Mamm* managed to get her into a nightgown, get her into bed and settled in, with her arm propped onto a pillow for support.

Emily couldn't say it was easy. In fact, she had never hurt so bad as she did in that moment. The pain in her arm brought tears to her eyes, and her head throbbed with each beat of her heart.

Once she was back in the bed, *Mamm* disappeared with the assurance to return with more of the medication to help her sleep.

As promised, she returned moments later with a glass of water and a couple of pills for Emily to swallow.

Her eyes were already closed when her mother pressed a cool hand to her brow. *"Ich liebe dich,"* she murmured, then quietly moved away.

"I love you, too," Emily whispered in return as her mother closed her bedroom door.

"Emily?"

How long had it been since she had gone to bed? The shadows in the room looked the same. Outside her window, the sky was still dark. Could have been a few minutes, or it could have been hours.

"Mary?"

Her sister was at her side in a moment, falling to her knees and burying her face in her shoulder. "I was so afraid when Jay came to the door."

"Jay?" Emily murmured, wishing she could reach her sister, smooth back her hair, and assure her that everything was going to be all right.

"After the crash, Luke called his *onkle.* Joseph called Jay to come tell *Vatter* what had happened."

"Don't cry, Mary. I'm fine."

"I'm so *froh,*" Mary sobbed. "So very glad."

"Will you stay with me?"

"*Jah,*" she said.

Emily opened her eyes enough to see her sister drag the rocking chair over to the side of the bed. Mary sat down and grabbed Emily's uninjured hand into her own and squeezed.

"I'll be right here, the minute you wake up."

Emily smiled and drifted off into a drug-enhanced sleep.

Luke stared at the ceiling and tried to get the images out of his mind. But no matter how hard he tried, all he could see when he closed his eyes was Emily's face covered in blood, her arm sitting at a strange angle, and the fear in her eyes when they took her into the ambulance.

All he had wanted was a chance to show her how things could be between them when she finally realized there was a place for both of them in the *Englisch* world. Yet all he had succeeded in doing was hurting her more. He wouldn't blame her if she never wanted to see him again. He was quite certain her father would be just fine with that.

There had never been a great admiration between him and Bishop Ebersol, but whatever there had been certainly hadn't survived the night.

Luke rolled to his side and pounded out his frustrations onto his pillow. He might have been raised conservative, noncombative Amish, but right now he just wanted to hit something. Like it would do any good. The damage was done.

Thankfully he had only clipped the bumper of the truck. The large vehicle had sustained minimal damage. Even his friend's car wasn't completely totaled. But he had hit on Emily's side of the car, resulting in a direct impact for her.

He flopped over once again, wishing he had a way to ease his spinning thoughts.

You have a way.

The words were spoken in his mind, clear as day.

You have a way.

Luke rolled out of bed and knelt at its side, propping his hands on the mattress as he prayed.

How long had it been since he had taken his concerns to the Lord?

Way too long, if the time it took to form his thoughts into prayers was any indication. He had so much to pray about. Emily, the wreck, his career, his job. So much had gone wrong lately. He so desperately needed for this to turn out right. He needed Emily like he needed air. He had messed up where she was concerned. And he was afraid that it would take more than prayer to get her back. It was going to take a miracle.

Two days later, Ben Smith, their regular Mennonite driver, drove Emily and *Mamm* to the clinic in Pryor. Thankfully the X-rays showed a clean fracture that wouldn't require surgery. The swelling had gone down enough for them to place it in a cast and the pair plus Ben headed back to Wells Landing.

"*Dat* is still angry," Emily said as they drove home. Dormant fields of winter wheat lined the highway between the two cities.

The sky sparkled blue in the winter sun, but Emily's heart weighed in her chest like a stone.

Mamm sighed. "Your *vatter* and I are having trouble understanding what happened."

"We had an accident."

She closed her eyes and for a moment Emily wondered if she was praying. "You know that is not what I mean."

"I know." She stared at her hands in her lap, one fine and whole, the other covered in a purple cast. They had asked her to pick a color and at the time she'd said she had no preference. Imagine her surprise when the purple came out.

It was like some sort of omen, a sign that she needed to get her priorities straight and fast.

"Is he ever going to talk to me again?"

"Emily." *Mamm* shot her a look. "Your father is a hard man, but he is fair."

And he was. Emily recalled earlier in the year when Caroline had confessed the truth about Emma's father to the bishop. He had decided that a shunning would do more harm than good and had agreed to keep Caroline's secret. But it seemed he had a different set of rules when it came to Emily.

Her *mamm* frowned when she said as much. "That's not it a'tall. He was so upset

when we got the news. You have to understand. We thought you were safe in bed. And
to find out that you were not . . . Give him
some time, Emily Jane."

But Emily was afraid it would take a lot
more than time to heal what was broken.

"Can I go with you?"

Elam turned as Becky skipped down the
porch steps and raced over to his buggy. He
had been trying to leave without drawing so
much attention to the fact. He had only told
Mamm that he was going to visit Emily.

It had been three days since the accident.
Three days of prayers and thanks. Three
days of wondering what truth could be
found in the gossip flying around the district. Had Emily really been with Luke
Lambright? Had they really been to a wild
Englisch party?

He had even heard that she hadn't been
wearing Amish clothes, but instead something the *Englisch* would wear. That didn't
sound like Emily, and he had trouble believing such tales.

He had gone over to see her the day after
the accident, but her mother wouldn't let
anyone in. Helen Ebersol's tired eyes were
apologetic, but her tone was firm. He would
have to wait.

"Becky, I . . ." Elam didn't know what to say. His sister loved Emily like her own sister, but there was more at stake here than care and concern.

His sister's eyes widened as the truth hit home. "You're going to break up with her." She backed away from him as if horrified at the thought.

Elam sighed. He'd be lying to say the thought hadn't crossed his mind. If half of what the wagging tongues of the district alleged was true, he was in for certain heartache. "I don't know."

"Please don't." Becky's voice trembled as she begged. "Give her a chance to explain."

"Jah," he said. "You know I will." But the truth of the matter was he wanted this more than Emily. She had her heart pinned to Luke for so long, she couldn't see the harm the relationship could cause her. Just because that danger had been realized didn't mean she would be any less blind to the perils. And just because he treasured Emily with a love beyond the stars . . . well, no amount of prayers and hopes could make her care for him in return. Not when her sights were set on another.

"I'm going to see about her," he said, but even as the words left his mouth, his heart broke a little more. "We need to talk about what happened. It might be today, or next week, but we will have to discuss this."

Becky nodded. "*Jah,* okay. Tell her we are all thinking about her and praying for her."

"*Jah.*" Elam swung himself into the buggy. "Tell *Mamm* I'll be home after 'while."

The ride to the Ebersols' was slow and torturous. Part of Elam wanted to spur the horse to trot a bit faster while another part wanted to pull on the reins and slow her to a snail's pace.

He dreaded talking to Emily as much as he knew it had to be done. If only he could put it off a bit longer, maybe he would have to adjust to the inevitable.

All too soon he pulled into the driveway at Emily's *haus.*

Mary came out onto the porch and watched him as he swung down from the buggy.

"*Guder mariye,*" she called as he walked on stiff legs toward the house.

"*Guder mariye,*" he said in return. He held up a paper sack filled with goodies his family had gathered for Emily and the rest of the Ebersols. "*Mamm* sent over some bread and the twins made cookies for everyone."

"*Danki,*" Mary said. "That is most appreciated."

Elam felt like he was in a school program,

stiff and controlled, not part of what was really happening, but involved all the same.

"Come in," Mary continued, taking the sack from him. "I'll give this to *Mamm* and get Emily for you."

Emily was already waiting for him in the living room, or maybe that was where she had been all along. She waited like a lamb for the slaughter as she fidgeted with the pleats in her apron.

His eyes drank her in, her dark hair covered with her prayer *kapp,* her blue eyes appeared even bluer as they reflected the indigo dress she wore. Tiny black stitches bisected a large bruise above her right eye and a clunky purple cast encased her right arm. But she was whole and alive.

Seeing her brought forth all the "what ifs" and all that could have happened. She could have been hurt worse, even killed in such a crash. Elam thanked God that she wasn't. She might not love him, but he couldn't bear the thought of her simply not being any longer.

"Emily." He couldn't stop his feet as they carried him to her. He dropped to his knees in front of her, clasping her good hand into his own. "I thank God you are *allrecht.*"

Tears rose into her eyes. She blinked them back and swallowed hard.

"Will you take a ride with me?" he asked. It was Saturday and with four girls under-foot and the watchful eyes of her *mamm* and the bishop trained on them, a buggy ride was the perfect opportunity to get away, be alone, and talk about all the things settling between them. "There are things we need to talk about, *jah?*"

She nodded, her eyes sad.

Elam stood and pulled her to her feet.

"Mary, tell *Mamm* where I've gone please. I'll be back shortly."

Mary nodded as Emily made her way to the door. She grabbed her coat from its peg and started for the waiting buggy, Elam right behind her.

CHAPTER TWENTY

"Are you warm enough?"

Emily nodded, though she tucked the woolen blanket a little closer around her legs.

"Do you feel like driving out to Millers' Pond?"

"If that is what you want." Even as she said the words, she felt like she was being difficult.

"Only if you feel like walking down there from the road."

Ach, this is hard. Why did everything have to be so complicated? "Whatever you want is fine with me."

She felt him frown more than saw it, sensed the look of consternation and something else she couldn't name. Why were they making a play at this? Why was he dragging this out? He was angry, she knew. And he had reason to be. She wished he would say what he came to say and get it over with.

The suspense was driving her batty.

"It's a pretty enough day to walk down there. It should give us some time alone to . . . talk."

Emily didn't miss his slight pause before "talk." If that was all they were going to do, why did it sound so ominous? It was a nice day, but dark clouds hung over the two of them, like sad souls in *Englisch* cartoons.

Elam turned the buggy down Millers' Road and in no time at all, they were parked at the edge of the field.

The rows of burned corn stubbles still stained the ground despite their early snow. In the spring, Eli Miller would plant more corn and the youth of Wells Landing would wade through the fresh green stalks to get to the popular swimming hole.

Elam was as sweet as he ever was, helping her down from the buggy and making sure she got through the fence gate without snagging her dress or her coat.

They walked the few yards in silence and entered the copse of trees that surrounded the small pond.

Though their leaves had long since turned brown, the trees still provided shade and coverage from the sun. Emily wrapped her coat a little tighter around her and wished she had grabbed her bonnet on the way out the door.

The pond was murky and looked cold, so different than it did in the summer with stray rays of sunshine making their way through the trees to sparkle against the water.

Emily perched on a stump near the water's edge and waited for Elam to get comfortable. At least she waited for him to settle himself on a fallen log.

"I'm sorry," she said.

"I know." His voice was quiet and sad.

She wanted to say more, that it wasn't what it looked like. That she had made a terrible mistake. That she realized now more than before whatever had been between her and Luke was part of the past. Elam . . . he was her future. Or at least he might have been.

"I . . ." he started, his voice breaking on the one word. He cleared his throat and started again. "I was so scared when they told me you were hurt."

"I didn't mean to worry anyone." She stared at her hands as they rested in her lap.

"Then when I realized where you had gone and with who . . . I knew I had pushed too hard."

She raised her gaze to look at him, but he was staring out over the rippling pond.

"What do you mean?"

"I thought I could make you care about me the same as I care about you."

She started to respond, to tell him that she did. Somewhere along the way she had started to care about him in a manner so different than her feelings for Luke.

But he held up his hands and stopped her words. "Please," he begged. "Let me finish."

She nodded, her throat clogged with worry, regrets, and unspoken emotion.

"I was wrong to pressure you. Wrong to push you."

"You didn't push me," Emily managed to squeeze out.

"*Jah,* but I did."

There was no merit in arguing with him, so she let him continue.

"I've not hidden the fact that I have loved you for longer than I can remember. But I've learned something these past couple of months. Loving someone who doesn't love you in return is tragic. But loving someone who loves another is hell."

"Elam, I —"

"I release you, Emily."

"W-what?" Her heart stilled in her chest.

"I release you. You won't have to worry about me any longer. I won't pressure you. I take back my proposal. I should have never offered it in the first place. I knew you loved Luke, and I foolishly thought I could switch your affections."

Tears fell from her eyes and streaked down her cheeks. She wanted to jump to her feet and shout her love for him to the treetops. But what good would it do? It would only serve to make her look like the biggest fool.

Jah, she had loved Luke once upon a time with a girl's heart, but Elam . . . she loved him as a woman. He was strong and secure, loving, responsible, God-fearing, steady, and true.

She could've had everything, and she messed it up. Now she had nothing.

Nothing but the shredded pieces of her pride. Mentally she pulled them around her while pushing away the Bible verse she had quoted about Elam so long ago.

Pride goeth before destruction.

But her destruction had already come to pass. And her pride, what remained of it, was all she had left.

She wiped her tears away with the back of her left hand and vowed to cry no more. She had made this bed she found herself in, and she would lie in it as the saying went.

"I'm tired," she said, and it was the truth. "Can you take me home?"

■ ■ ■ ■

Emily managed to hold in her tears until Elam pulled into the driveway at her house. All the way home she kept her thoughts from centering on the conversation they'd just had.

Instead she thought about the goats, making cheese, sewing a new prayer *kapp* to replace the one she had ruined. Anything except the heartbreak that was sure to come.

Elam pulled the horses to a stop and set the brake, then came around to her side of the buggy to help her to the ground.

She would have liked to have rebuffed his efforts, but with her arm in a cast and still quite painful, she needed the extra help.

Once her feet were on the ground, he let her go. "I guess I'll be seeing you." His voice was thick, rusty sounding, and a bit choked.

"*Jah,*" she whispered in return, her eyes on the scuffed toes of her shoes.

Then he moved away. Back to the other side of the buggy. She started toward the house as he set his horse into motion. And as she promised herself, she did not look back.

"Emily." Mary knocked on the door frame

to her room even though it was open.

"*Jah?*" She looked up from her Bible. Like she could concentrate on anything lately. It had been two days since Elam had dropped her off. Two days of fighting back tears, reliving mistakes, and trying to put her feet back on the right path.

Thankfully it was a non-church week, and she wouldn't have to worry about seeing Elam until next Sunday. She dreaded the thought of attending church with him, even if there would be another two hundred souls milling around them. It would leave him and her alone with all the mistakes she had made.

"Aaron is here."

Aaron Miller, Mary's longtime beau had come calling. Mary had mentioned that the two of them were heading to another's house to play board games. "Have fun."

Mary shook her head. "He has something for you."

"For me?" She set her Bible aside and rose from the wooden rocker. She had spent so much time in her room the last few days, she almost dreaded leaving it. She would have to eventually. Now was as good a time as any.

Her father was nowhere around when Emily made her way downstairs. *Mamm* and

Aaron stood in the living room waiting for her. Aaron shifted from one foot to the other, looking almost as uncomfortable as she felt.

"Hi, Emily." He nodded his blond head toward her. "I'm glad you are *allrecht.*"

She wouldn't go that far. She may have survived the car crash, but it had left lasting marks.

"Jonah asked me to bring this over to you." He held an envelope toward her. The handwriting on the outside was as familiar to her as her own. Luke.

"Danki." She accepted the letter, tucking it into her apron pocket.

Aaron glanced toward *Mamm,* then back to Mary. "Are you ready to leave?"

"Jah." She grabbed her coat and bonnet.

"You'll need to be back before milking time," *Mamm* reminded her.

"Jah," Mary said, then squeezed Emily's hand before hurrying out the door, Aaron fast on her heels.

"Is that from Luke?" *Mamm* asked.

"Jah." The letter burned white hot in her pocket, but she wouldn't take it out. Not yet. She wasn't ready to read the words Luke had taken the time to write to her.

Like most Amish men, Luke hated to write, hated everything about it. For him to put pen to paper and compose a letter to her . . . well, whatever he wrote had to be of great importance. Could be *gut,* could be bad. She'd only know when she read it, but now was not the time.

"He tried to come by and see you," her mother softly admitted.

Emily swung her gaze to *Mamm*'s face. "Luke?"

"At the hospital and again once we got you home."

"But *Dat* wouldn't let him in," Emily finished.

"Your father tries to be fair, but you know he is very protective when it comes to his *dochdern.*"

Her father was protective of his daughters; that much Emily could not deny. "I've known Luke my entire life and so has he. Why would *Dat* not let me see him?" She had been doubly heartbroken thinking Luke hadn't come by. That their argument had somehow torn a rift between them.

She knew their relationship might not ever be the same, but he would forever and always be her friend.

"Oftentimes it's not so simple," *Mamm* softly replied.

Emily couldn't dispute that. Her life had always been under more scrutiny than others in their district. Watchful eyes were trained on them, the entire family. It came with the responsibility of having a bishop for a *dat.*

"Are you going to read that?" *Mamm* asked.

"Later," Emily said.

"You never did tell me how your buggy ride with Elam went."

Emily collapsed into the kitchen chair, unable to stand under the weight of her mistakes. "Oh, *Mamm.* I really messed this one up." She propped her elbow on the table and rested her forehead in her good hand.

Her mother slid into the seat next to her and ran a soothing hand down the side of her face. "Do you want to talk about it?"

"Nay." Emily sniffed and straightened herself. Nothing good would come from breaking down now. She wiped her tears away and tried to smile.

"Elam is a *wunderbaar-gut* man," *Mamm* said.

Emily nodded. "But I realized it way too late."

Luke opened the letter from the lawyers' office, wondering why someone sent him the official-looking post.

He pulled it out and scanned it, the legal jargon like trying to read Greek. But he didn't need more than an eighth grade education to determine that the father of the friend whose car he'd wrecked wanted repayment for the insurance deductible.

He understood. It was only fair that he pay the money, but where was he going to get five hundred dollars?

He shook his head at his own stupidity. He had quit his job at the burger joint so he could go and see Emily. A lot of good that did him. He had already lost her to Elam Riehl. He hadn't been able to find another job in the week since he'd been back. The small stash he had in his pocket was quickly dwindling away. As it was now, he was living off tap water and ramen noodles with no end in sight.

He hadn't heard from Emily, not that he really expected to. But he had given the letter to Jonah and asked that Aaron give it to Mary to give to Emily. It was the only way he knew to get a message to her. He was so very sorry. He needed to tell her that. And how much he loved her. But he couldn't say those words if her father wouldn't let him in the same room with her.

He took out his cell phone and stared at the home screen. No new messages. What did he expect? For her to run out to the phone shanty and call him right away? Knowing her father, he hadn't let her out of his sight since they got her back home.

He really couldn't blame the man. But Luke had never intended to hurt Emily, not emotionally, not physically. And yet he had.

He had ten dollars left in his pocket. He could put a couple in his gas tank and head over to the track. Maybe the boss-man might have something for him to do. Or maybe he should ask his potential sponsor for an advance. He hated to, but what choice did he have?

He refolded the letter from the attorney and put it back into its envelope before shoving it into the back pocket of his jeans.

He'd go over to the track first and see what was going on. With any luck and God on his side, he would have the money by the end of the week.

It was late afternoon before Emily found time alone to read Luke's letter. She tied her bonnet over her prayer *kapp* and pulled her wool coat around her as best she could.

Normally she would have crawled into the hayloft to assure her privacy, but her right hand was practically useless. She couldn't risk climbing when her cast had barely set.

Instead she found a clean, empty barn stall and shut herself inside. She just needed a little time to absorb Luke's words.

She didn't need to be a genius to figure out that his words were an apology and most likely his good-bye to her. She had made her feelings pretty clear. She was not willing to leave Wells Landing, and Luke had his own dreams to follow. Yet as much as her heart pounded in anticipation, she dreaded breaking the seal and actually reading what he'd written.

She hunkered down into the corner of the stall and slid open the envelope.

Her fingers shook slightly as she pulled the lined paper from inside and unfolded it. Luke's childish scrawl ran across the page, its simplicity and familiarity bringing tears to her eyes.

Dear Emily,

There are no words to tell you how scared I was the other night. I held you close while we waited for the ambulance and prayed for God to let you live. In those long minutes I realized how selfish I've been. I've only been thinking of my own hopes and dreams for the future. As I held you, I came to realize that you have hopes and dreams as well. The only problem is your dreams center around Wells Landing and mine do not.

There was a time when our dreams were the same, back before I fell in love with cars. I wish I could tell you they don't mean anything to me now, but even as I write this, I long to get back to the racing world and make my mark.

Your mark is different. You want a husband, a family, a house. One day I would love to give you all of those things, but it wouldn't be in Wells Landing. I can never return. Never be satisfied with planting corn and milking cows for the rest of my days.

I know farming is a noble profession, but it's not for me. I need excitement. I need the crowd, the fame, and the thrills that I can only find in the *Englisch* world.

After today, I'm sure your father will never let me see you again. Not that I blame him. I'd probably do just the same if you were my daughter. But I still wanted you to know that despite the differences that now separate us, I still love you. I always have, and I always will. It's this love which makes me understand it's time to let you go.

This is not an easy decision for me to

make, but it must be done. So go, Emily, love. Go to Elam and get married. Accept his proposal and live happily ever after as the *Englisch* fairy tales say. If there is one person in this world who deserves to be that happy, it is you, my dear Em.

Wherever you go and whatever you do, know this one thing above all else. I will always love you.

Luke

Two cars sat in the parking lot when he pulled in twenty minutes later. One belonged to the boss-man, as they called the track manager, and the other was an old-fashioned Cadillac with a longhorn rack attached to the hood.

The car could only belong to one person. Perhaps luck was on his side. Or maybe it was God answering his prayers.

Luke smiled and pocketed his keys. For the first time in a long time, he felt everything was going to be okay.

He whistled under his breath as he let himself into the office, but he stopped short when he saw a girl sitting at the boss-man's desk.

"Hi."

She stood, watching him with dark brown

eyes, as she ran her hands down her sides. "Hi, yourself." She stretched, her gaze never leaving his. "You're Luke, right? Luke Lambree?"

"Lambright," he gently corrected. "Have we met before?"

She shook her head, her blond curls brushing the tops of her shoulders. "I've seen you around. And Daddy talks about you."

"I'm sorry?" Then her words struck home, and he realized who stood before him. "You're Sissy Hardin."

"Nice to meet you." She leaned one hip against the cluttered desk. If Luke had to guess, she was close to his age, but he'd heard the other guys talking. Sissy Hardin had one more year before she graduated from her *Englisch* high school.

It was hard for him to tell though. The *Englisch* were so different. She looked so much older, so *knowing.*

"Where's Johnny?" he asked, referring to the boss-man by his given name.

She nodded her head toward the upstairs office. "He's talking to Daddy."

Luke nodded. "So he's in?" he asked, his heart thumping. "Gus is going to grant my sponsorship?"

Her eyes sparkled. "From what I heard,

344

yes. Does that make you happy?"

The air left him in a rush of relief. "Oh, *jah*. I mean yes. I've got bills stacking up and . . ." He shook his head. "I don't mean to bore you with talk of money."

She pushed herself off the desk and came around it to stand close to him. Really, really close to him. He wanted to move away from her but his feet seemed stuck to the floor. She smelled good, like clean clothes and honeysuckle.

"I find money very, very interesting," she said, moving even closer.

Luke tried to move away, but Sissy grabbed one of his hands and placed it on her hip.

"Where are you going?" she whispered. Her tone was filled with sultry promise. "Stay here and let's get to know each other better."

"I, uh . . ." Was she coming on to him?

"Did you say you needed some money?" She grabbed his other hand and directed his arm around her.

"I don't think this is right." His protest was weak at best. He had never found himself in a situation like this. What was he supposed to do? Step away? Pretend like it never happened? Play along until he got what he needed? Nothing in his Amish upbringing had prepared him for this.

She laughed a throaty sophisticated sound. "You Amish boys are so funny. So sweet and innocent. Did you know you are all pink with embarrassment?"

He swallowed hard and shook his head.

"You know the only way to get what you want is to ask." She ran a thumb over his lower lip. "What is it that you need, Luke?"

He shivered. "I need five hundred dollars." Was he the only one dealing with her advances? Did Gus know? Did Gus care? How was Luke supposed to find out either way?

Her thumbnail scraped against his chin. "Not exactly what I mean, but I'm sure we can work out something."

He wasn't sure what *that* meant and was about to ask when a booming voice cut through the room.

"What in the sam hill is going on here?" Gus Hardin stormed down the stairs, looking from Luke to his daughter and back again.

Sissy's hands were suddenly in the middle of Luke's chest. She pushed him away yelling, "Get your hands off me" as if she hadn't initiated the touch in the first place.

He stumbled backward, catching himself before he tripped over the chair Sissy had been sitting in when he came in.

"Luke?"

He turned to face Johnny Johnson, otherwise known as the boss-man to all the drivers.

"I —" He didn't know how to explain. He hadn't done anything. Yet it looked like he had.

Sissy ran her hands down herself as if putting her clothes to rights.

But nothing happened!

"I think it's time for you to leave, son." Gus's booming voice lowered to a deadly level.

"What about my car?" He looked from Johnny to Gus. What about his dreams? Driving a race car? Making the big time?

The big man shook his head. "That's not going to happen. Not if I have anything to say about it."

Luke pulled his coat a little tighter around himself and ducked his head against the wind. Aside from when it had snowed, this was the coldest day of the year so far. And he was walking.

He'd left his car with his friend, a big FOR SALE sign in the front window. Anything they could get for it over the five hundred dollars Luke still owed him, his friend promised to send to his uncle's house.

And that was where Luke was heading, back to his uncle's, back to Wells Landing, his dreams in shreds.

CHAPTER TWENTY-ONE

The first church Sunday after Elam and Emily's breakup was held at Caroline and Andrew's house. It had never been taken out of rotation when Abe married Esther and placed back in under the newlyweds' names, but Caroline assured the church elders she could handle the load. Emily thought she was putting on too brave a face, but agreed to help out that week in getting the house ready.

Not that she was much help at all. Her heart was bruised and sore, her pride had taken a beating, and her spirit seemed to need constant rest. And that didn't even account for her physical injuries. Her arm still ached, and whenever she was up for too long a time, her head began to throb.

"Here," Lorie said, taking the dust rag from Emily who had been polishing the baseboards. "You look dead on your feet."

Emily sat back on her heels and rubbed

her eyes. Dead on her feet — that was a perfect way to describe how she felt.

She felt dead. Walking around, dead like one of those zombies in the haunted hay-ride, but still having to move among the living.

She had lost Luke to race car driving, and she had lost Elam to her own stupidity.

Now she was fairly certain neither one of them would talk to her. Oh, Luke would always be her friend, but he was off in the *Englisch* world. Despite what Elam had said, she knew he would avoid her like the plague. Why would he want to be friends with her when she had rebuffed every attempt he had made at a relationship with her?

But at night, when she was alone in her room, she thought of the kiss they had shared. It seemed like so much more than a simple kiss, or had time and longing turned it into so much more than it truly was?

She'd never know.

"Emily? *Emily.*" Lorie brought her back to the present.

"*Jah?*"

"You've not heard a word we've said."

"Of course I have."

Caroline gave a sage nod. "Of course.

Then I'm sure you heard Lorie say Luke is back."

"What?" Emily shook her head. "You're just saying that because I wasn't paying attention."

Lorie rolled her eyes. "Now she admits it."

Caroline shrugged and dropped down into the nearest chair.

"Are you feeling all right?" Lorie asked.

She nodded. "Just tired."

"And the baby?"

Caroline beamed as she placed a protective hand over her still-slim midriff. "Right as rain, as my *dat* would say."

Emily returned her friend's smile, happy, so very delighted for Caroline and Andrew. She couldn't imagine two people who deserved a more perfect union than the two of them. "Is Luke really back?" She hadn't meant to ask the question. The words just slipped out all on their own.

Lorie nodded and braced her rear against the sideboard. "Jonah said he got back late Thursday night."

"You haven't seen him?" Emily shifted to sit cross-legged on the floor.

"*Nay.* Jonah acted like something was wrong, but he wouldn't tell me what."

After reading the letter Luke had left for

her, something would have to be wrong for him to return. He had big plans and dreams in the *Englisch* world.

"Is Joseph okay?" she asked.

"His uncle? I s'ppose." Lorie shrugged. "I'm surprised you didn't know."

Emily shook her head. "Things aren't the same between us anymore."

Her friends nodded sympathetically. But how could they understand something she didn't even herself?

"And what about Elam?" Caroline asked.

Emily tried to smile, but tears rose in her eyes instead. "Elam broke up with me."

"Oh, Em." Caroline moved to her side and, in an instant, she was wrapped in a warm hug.

"I'm so sorry." Lorie's arms were there as well, sweet and comforting.

Emily swiped at the tears with the back of her hand and took a deep breath. "I can't blame anyone but myself. He was patient and understanding, but that can only take a man so far."

And she had been a fool. She missed Elam terribly, but she also missed James, Johanna, and the rest of the Riehls. She had started out helping them as an act of good will, but they had done so much more for her. They had given her back her joy when Luke left and her purpose after teaching.

Elam had said that he wanted to remain friends, but how could she go to his house and spend time with his family knowing she had failed him and embarrassed him in front of the community? She'd had everything she could have ever asked for in Elam, and she had foolishly thrown it all away in the name of girlish dreams.

She sucked in another shuddering breath. "Well, this is not getting the house clean for sure and for certain." She rose to her feet and looked at each one of her friends in turn. Compassion and worry showed on their faces, but Emily smiled bravely. "Come on now. We have lots of work to do."

Elam did his best to keep his mind on the sermon that Sunday. Not that he succeeded. His father sat to his right, hands clasped between his knees, eager gaze straight ahead. And all Elam could think about was that none of it would have been possible if not for Emily Ebersol.

His heart broke all over again at the mere thought of her.

Breaking up with her had been the hardest thing he had ever done, but he knew. He had been a fool from the start thinking he could compete with the likes of Luke Lambright. Elam would never be able to be so carefree and fun-loving. He wasn't as handsome as Luke, by far. To most Amish girls, Elam knew he was *gut* husband material, but not for the bishop's daughter. Luke had captured her heart long ago and locked it away so no one else could touch it.

And now he was back.

Three rows up and two seats over, Luke Lambright sat next to Jonah Miller, each one of them looking like they wished they were someplace else. Perhaps off with Lorie and Emily. How soon before they announced their intentions? Luke hadn't joined the church so it would be another year before he and Emily could marry, but the lapse in time wouldn't do anything for Elam. She would wait for Luke, he knew.

"There's Emily." His father leaned close and pointed one finger toward the women's side of the congregation. Like Elam needed a reminder as to where Emily was. "She's wearing green today." *Dat* frowned.

Just another proof that she was over them all. Elam squeezed his father's hand reassuringly. "She can't wear purple all the time."

Once the service was over, the benches were flipped into tables, and the food was served. Prayers were said, and the eating began.

"I want to take my plate and eat with Emily," *Dat* said. His chin had taken on that stubborn slant Elam knew all too well.

"You know that is not allowed."

"I have eaten with her before."

Elam shook his head. "We've talked about this. You know the men are supposed to eat together and the women eat together."

"That is dumb." His father pouted.

"It may seem that way, *jah,* but that is how we do it."

His father's mouth twisted into a frown. "If we can't eat with Emily, let's find the bishop and eat with him."

Dat turned on his heel and started through the milling church members.

Elam had no choice but to follow behind him. Eating with the bishop was the last thing he wanted to do, the very last thing. And not because Elam was so intimidated by the bishop, but because he was Emily's father.

Elam wondered how much Emily had said to her family about their breakup. He didn't even know how her father felt about her accident and her being out with Luke Lambright. The bishop might hold hope for Luke yet.

But regardless of Elam's feelings, he couldn't leave his *vatter* alone. With his childlike mind had come an impulsiveness that had to be monitored. Secretly Elam believed his *dat* could control it more than he let on, but he supposed it was a small compensation for all that James had suffered. He had lost so much in one afternoon, that Elam couldn't find fault. Still there were times when he wished his father would try a bit harder to behave. Like now.

He found the men in the barn. They held their plates in their hands and ate while looking at one of the beautiful horses Andrew Fitch boarded for breeders.

Elam had heard Andrew was about to embark in horse breeding himself and he was interested in knowing more, but not at the price of eating with the bishop.

"There he is." His father's words insinuated that he had been talking about him before he came up.

Elam winced. He could only imagine what *Dat* had been saying.

"Bishop." Elam nodded to Emily's father, then turned to the man he was talking to, Dan Troyer, the minister.

"I was just telling the bishop here about you and Emily."

Elam cleared his throat. "I'm sure Cephas

knows all there is to know."

"Nay." His father shook his head. "We both agree that we don't know why the two of you broke up. And he says Emily has been beside herself ever since."

How long *had* his father been talking to the bishop?

Elam shifted from one foot to the other. "This is not something I'm comfortable talking about."

The bishop pinned him with those blue eyes so like his daughter's. "But you do care for Emily?"

He couldn't lie. Not to the bishop. "Very much so."

Cephas nodded. "Maybe you should come by the house and talk to her. Perhaps the two of you can clear up these matters."

He wished it was that simple.

But before he could respond, his father did. "Elam thinks now that Luke is back, Emily will want to marry him instead."

"Dat!" Short of grabbing his *vatter* by the arm and hustling him out of the barn, all Elam could do was shoot him a warning look.

Dat simply smiled in return.

The bishop frowned and cast his own look at Luke as he stood at the end of the stalls with Andrew Fitch and Jonah Miller. *"Ach,"* he said with a shake of his head. But Elam had the feeling he wanted to say more.

He couldn't imagine the bishop would approve of his daughter running around with a wayward soul like Luke. As much as Elam wished otherwise, Luke had done nothing wrong. He had not joined the church. He was free to come and go as he pleased, though his run-around time was quickly drawing to a close.

Cephas Ebersol loved his daughters and would want to see them all well married and happy. Happiness for Emily would mean Luke. It was a fact that Elam was still coming to terms with.

He wrapped his free hand around his *dat*'s arm. "Come on, *Dat*. I think *Mamm* is looking for you."

Elam nodded to the bishop and the minister, then quickly led his father away.

"But I thought the men and the women weren't supposed to eat together."

"You're not eating," Elam said, tossing his own plate into the trash barrel just outside the barn doors. "You're walking 'round with a plate and causing trouble."

His father grinned and pulled away from Elam's grasp.

Thankfully he made no move to go back and harass the bishop, and instead grabbed a cheese-covered cracker off his plate. "Uhmm, this is *gut*. Is this the goat cheese that Emily's family makes?"

"Stop." Elam raised his hands in surrender. "Just stop, please."

"You'll never win her over with that attitude."

"I tried to win her over, and I failed. Luke won."

Dat shook his head. "Not according to the bishop."

Elam sighed. It was times like these when his father's injury became even more apparent. How could Elam explain? It wasn't as simple as his *dat* wished it to be, and that was that. "One day soon, she'll marry Luke Lambright," Elam said. His heart gave a painful lurch as he said the words out loud. "I've accepted that," he lied. "And you should, too."

Emily took a big gulp of her lemonade and wiped a quick hand across her forehead. The congregation had been served food and drink and now everyone was milling around, finishing their sweets and visiting with one another.

Thankfully the day had turned out sunny and cool, but not as cold as January could typically be.

Several of the older church members had asked about her cast, but all in all, the news of her accident with Luke had spread through the community like a wildfire through dry grass.

She absently scratched at the top of the purple cast as if somehow that would ease the itch inside. She hated the cast, hated everything it stood for and all that it reminded her of. All that she had lost.

She had seen Elam earlier, following his *dat* into the barn, but she hadn't said a word to him. She had used the fact that she was still helping everyone get served as an excuse, but in truth she wasn't ready to face him.

"Hey, Emily."

She turned as Luke came up, his bright smile a bit dimmer these days. "Luke." She hadn't talked to him since he had come back. "It's *gut* to see you at church today."

He shoved his hands into his pockets and shrugged. "It seemed like the thing to do."

But it was one step closer to where he needed to be.

"And dressed as an Amish man again."

"*Onkle* thought it best." He shrugged as if it was no big deal, but it was. It was huge. So many nights since he had been gone she had prayed for his return. At first so they could be married, but as things changed and her feelings for Elam grew, she prayed for Luke's soul. How was he supposed to fight the temptations of the world?

"Joseph Lambright always was a smart man."

"It feels weird, you know?" He rolled his shoulders as if he was still trying to adjust to the fit and feel.

"You've come back, and it's God's will, Luke. You know that."

"Jah." But he glanced off into the distance, as if he wasn't sure he believed it himself.

Emily was confident. Luke had been led back to Wells Landing. She didn't know why or how, but he was there once again. God's touch was all over it. "It's a *gut* place to be." She swept a hand around, gesturing to all the people milling in the Fitches' yard. "You have support here. You'll see."

He shrugged again. "I s'pose."

"Luke." She quietly said his name.

He swung his gaze back to her.

"You're Amish," she said. "Born and raised. Everyone here understands you and loves you. They're — *I'm* here for you."

"I appreciate that so much, Emily, especially after —" He broke off as his gaze flickered to her cast.

"Everyone makes mistakes. And God forgives."

He nodded and swallowed hard as if unable to speak.

"You're not the only one who's left and come back," she continued. "Just give it a chance."

Elam tried not to stare when he saw Emily talking to Luke. He had seen it too many times to count in situations just like this. After church as the congregation milled around, talked about the weather, the sermon, and all the what-nots of the community. But that was before . . . everything.

"Why don't you go talk to her?"

He spun around as his *mamm* strode over from where she had been watching him. "Where's *Dat*?"

"He talked Becky into taking him and Johanna over to see Andrew's puppies."

Elam had heard talk of a new litter of border collies born a couple of weeks ago. "I s'pose they want one."

Mamm smiled and nodded.

"And I s'pose you'll let them."

"Elam, he's doing so much better now that we've got him off medications."

And they had Emily to thank.

"*Jah?*" Elam asked. He never asked about

362

their relationship, deeming it none of his business, but he'd noticed that Joy had moved her things out of the spare room downstairs and back in with her husband.

"He's not the same, and I know that he never will be. But I love him. He's a *gut* husband. He's a *gut* father."

"I know."

"He only wants what's best for you."

So they were back to that. "I can't go talk to her." He sighed. "Luke is back and —"

"Elam Riehl, I never suspected you for a quitter."

"I'm not a quitter." But he knew when a battle was lost.

He glanced back over to where Emily and Luke still talked. She laughed at something he said, looking happy and content and all the other things Elam had wanted to make her but hadn't.

She was beautiful when she smiled, and when she laughed, she took his breath away. She deserved someone who could make her laugh and smile and give her the world. As much as Elam hated it, that person was Luke Lambright.

Emily stared at the ceiling and watched as the shadows moved across the room. She had made it through the church service without completely breaking down. She didn't fall to the ground at Elam's feet or beg him to reconsider.

Nor did she get to talk to James. She missed her time spent with Elam's father, with all the family. But she couldn't go visit them and run the risk of running into Elam. That would be too heartbreaking to bear.

But she had talked to Luke about church, and that was the shining moment of her day. Luke had experienced his time in the *Englisch* world. But now he was back. She could see it in his eyes, the wonder and searching. He needed the church like he needed air to breathe. He just didn't know it.

That was up to her. She might have lost him and Elam, but she could show Luke that Wells Landing was where he needed to be. The temptations of the *Englisch* world were too great. If nothing else, she would help him save his soul.

The thought brought a smile to her lips.

"Emily?" Mary's voice floated to her from the doorway of her room.

"Come in, *shveshtah.*" Emily scooted toward the far side of the bed so Mary could slide under the covers next to her. They hadn't had a chance to talk all day. Mary had spent the afternoon with Aaron, then

364

there had been milking and supper.

"Did you talk to Elam today?" Mary asked once she was settled in the bed next to her.

Emily shook her head. "I wanted to, but then I didn't, you know?"

"*Jah.*"

"I mean, what *gut* would it do?"

"It might do a lot if 'n you give it a chance."

Emily shook her head. "I talked to Luke though."

"Oh, Emily." Mary's tone was sad and chastising.

"What?"

"Don't you think you should stay away from him?"

"We've known each other our whole lives."

"He's trouble, Emily. He's been out in the *Englisch* world." She said it as if he was somehow diseased from exposure.

"You're overreacting. He's home now."

The covers rustled as Mary shook her head. "You don't really think he'll stay."

"*Jah,* I do. In fact, I hope he does. He's unprotected out there with the *Englisch,* and his soul is in danger. If he's here . . ." She shrugged.

Plink.

"What was that?" Mary's eyes widened.

"Luke." Emily threw back the covers and

slipped from the other side of the bed.

"What's he doing here?" Mary asked.

"I guess he wants to talk. That's why he usually comes."

"He's done this before?" Mary pushed herself into a sitting position.

Emily went to the window. As expected, Luke was waiting down below, but unlike the last time he had been there, he was dressed in Plain clothing.

He pointed to her and then to the barn. Emily nodded.

She reached for her stockings, perching on the edge of the rocker while she pulled on the leg coverings.

"You're not going down there," Mary protested.

"I am." Emily tugged her stockings into place and reached for her shoes.

"But you can't."

"Why not?" Emily tied her shoes and stood.

"*Dat* will have a fit."

"*Dat* will be happy when I bring Luke back into the church fold."

Mary shook her head. "Last time you snuck out with him . . ." She looked pointedly at Emily's casted arm.

"Nothing is going to happen in the barn, Mary."

"If you're not back in thirty minutes I'm coming after you." Mary crossed her arms as if that somehow weighted her words with importance.

Emily smiled at her sister. "Deal."

She crept down the stairs, lest she disturb anyone else in the house, and pulled her coat over her shoulders. Actually putting her casted arm through the sleeve was impossible. She did the best she could and hustled out into the winter night.

Luke waited in the barn, his feet propped on a hay bale as if he hadn't a care in the world. "I didn't figure your *dat* would let me visit any other way."

"You're probably right about that."

Luke smiled, but the action didn't reach past the corners of his lips. Normally sparkling and bright, his eyes shone dull in the lamplight.

"What's wrong, Luke?" She moved to sit closer to him. She might not be in love with him anymore, but he had been her friend for so long. She hated to see him in pain.

He sighed, as if mulling over words too hard to speak. "Did you ever want something so badly, but then realize it's not going to happen?"

Elam's face swam before her eyes. *"Jah,"* she whispered.

"I lost my sponsor." He smiled again. Typical Luke, making light of every situation.

"I'm sorry." She said the words, but she didn't really mean them. Not like he thought. She was so very sorry that he was disappointed, but she was extremely grateful that her prayers had been answered. Luke was back in Wells Landing. This time to stay.

"Without him I don't have enough money to stay in the *Englisch* world." He pushed himself up and started to pace. "Everything is so expensive. I couldn't get a decent job without my high school diploma, and the classes were so hard. Not at all like here." He stopped and whirled around to face her. "Why do dreams have to hurt so bad when they fail?"

Tears stung at the back of her eyes. "I don't know. God's will?"

Luke snorted. "Why does God care about my petty little issues? There are so many more big problems out in the world."

Emily had never wondered about that. All her life she had been told that everything happened for a reason, and that reason was because God had deemed it so. "I don't know," she whispered.

Luke ran his fingers through his hair,

pushing his hat off in the process. "I lost everything: racing, my car, you."

"You haven't lost me."

He picked up his hat, slapping it against his thigh to knock the hay off before settling it back on his head. "I have, and we both know it."

She shot him a sad smile. "I will always love you, but —"

"Just as a *freind.*"

"*Jah.*"

He took one step closer and then two, until he was standing within touching distance. "If you ever . . . change your mind, you know. I'm here for you." He ran his fingertips down the side of her face.

She captured his hand in hers. "I know." She squeezed his fingers for a quick moment, then released them. "I have to get back in before Mary comes looking for me."

"Mary knows I'm here?"

Emily nodded. "Don't worry. She won't tell *Dat.*"

"She and Aaron looked pretty serious today."

"*Jah,* I think they'll get married in the fall. I know it'll be sort of rushed because they'll just be finishing up their baptism classes." She shrugged. So badly she wanted to ask Luke if he had plans to join the church in the upcoming year, but she didn't want to pressure him.

"A brand-new year," he mused.

"Jah." Two more days until the New Year began. It wasn't a big celebration for the Amish like it was for the *Englisch,* but Emily could see that it held some significance for Luke. Perhaps a new year obeying God and adjusting back to life in Wells Landing. She could only hope.

CHAPTER TWENTY-TWO

"I miss Emily."

Elam didn't need to look up to know that his *vatter* was frowning.

"Me, too," Johanna said as the other girls chimed in.

But none of them missed her as much as Elam. And a lot of good it did them. Now that Luke Lambright was back, Emily was lost, if she had ever been his at all.

He stirred his food around on his plate as if searching for the perfect bite when all he wanted to do was push back from the table and pretend there was some emergency in the barn. Anything rather than sit there and see his family heartbroken over the loss.

"You don't really think she'll marry Luke after . . . well, after everything, do you?" Becky's question was quietly spoken, so low that Elam wondered if anyone else at the table heard it.

He shrugged. "I knew she loved him from

the very beginning."

"But that's ridiculous," Becky hissed.

That Emily could still love Luke after all he'd put her through, *jah.* That she couldn't see the love Elam had to offer, double *jah.* But it seemed as if God's will was not on his side. It was a fact he was learning to live with daily.

"She made her choice, Becky. It wasn't me."

"But she cares about you. I saw it in her eyes," *Mamm* said.

Elam tossed down his fork, unable to eat another bite.

Thankfully, at the other end of the table, the conversation about the best purple item they had given Emily for Christmas drowned out the solemn words from his end.

"I do not want to talk about it." He said the words without lifting his gaze to meet those of *Mamm* and Becky. He could not bear to see their eyes filled with pity. He had made the best play for Emily that he could. And he had lost. It was simple as that. The sooner his family realized it, the better off they would all be.

"You look tired, *shveshtah.*"

"*Nay,* I'm fine," Emily said.

The sun had set long ago, the milking completed, and the Ebersol household wound down as everyone prepared for bed.

Emily flashed Mary her best smile and continued to brush her hair. It was not easy, brushing left-handed, but she was getting the hang of it. By the time she had mastered the action, it would be time to remove the awful cast. And not a day too soon. She had come to hate the constant reminder of her shortcomings.

Mary took the brush from her and continued the task.

"Danki," Emily murmured.

"Your hair is so *schpass.*"

"Pretty? My hair?" Emily scoffed. "It's the color of mud."

"It's the color of chocolate."

If her sister hadn't been in the middle of a long stroke, Emily would have shaken her head. She didn't have the honey blond hair that Mary had gotten from their mother. Or the pale blue eyes. She favored their *vatter* in both looks and temperament, which was a blessing as well as a curse.

"Are you going out to meet him again tonight?" Mary asked.

Emily shrugged. She didn't need to ask who Mary was talking about. "If he comes, I guess."

"He's been here every day this week. You know he'll come tonight."

"Perhaps," she said, though Mary was right.

"Don't go meet him." Mary's words were heartfelt and softly spoken, a plea between sisters.

"Why not?" Emily turned and Mary was forced to stop brushing her hair and step back.

"It'll be *baremlich* when *Dat* finds out. Worse than terrible. And you know he will find out."

Emily took the brush from her sister and gave her hair one last hard yank before pulling it back for bed. "It's not like that."

She and Luke had come to an understanding of sorts. They didn't talk about the future, and they didn't talk about the past. Dreams were also off the list of acceptable subjects. They simply . . . talked. She brought up church and God every chance she found, and she knew Luke was listening. It was only a matter of time before he saw the truth in her testaments. Only a matter of time before he realized God's plan and consented to join the church.

"*Dat* will think the worst."

She shook her head. She had no intentions of starting her relationship back up with Luke. They were simply friends. Funny how her dreams of marrying Luke and having a family had turned into marrying Elam and starting a family with him. That was truly what she wanted, and since she couldn't have it, she wasn't sure she wanted to settle for less.

"*Dat* is not going to know." She smoothed a hand over her sister's forehead. "Now quit frowning before you're as wrinkled as Maddie Kauffman."

Mary managed only a smile at her joke. "Think about what I said, okay?"

Emily smiled. "It's all going to be okay, Mary. Stop your worrying."

Luke came as expected. Emily met him in the barn, and they talked for a couple of hours. Was it too much to ask to enjoy this new friendship that the two of them had forged?

Mary was right: If her father were to find out about her meetings with Luke, *Dat* would be furious. But only if he were to find out before Emily had a chance to change Luke's mind about staying in Wells Landing and joining the church. Once that happened, her *vatter* would be so happy to welcome Luke back into the fold. And Emily was about to make that happen.

Luke had been such an important part of her life for so long, she was unwilling to give him up entirely. They may not love each other in a romantic sense, but he was quickly becoming her best friend again. She cherished all the time she could spend with him, even if it meant hiding out in the barn in the middle of the night.

"I can hardly believe it's New Year's Eve," Luke said.

"Soon it will be Three Kings Day," Emily added since it was a much bigger holiday for the Amish.

Luke plucked a straw of hay from the bale where he sat and pitched it at her.

She dodged it with a laugh, and it fell harmlessly to the side.

"All my friends are out at parties," he said with a wry shake of his head.

"Is that where you want to be?" It was the first time she had asked him how he felt about leaving his new life behind. She hadn't wanted to pressure him, but support him in his decision to leave the *Englisch* world.

"I don't know anymore." His eyes grew dim with confusion. "All I ever wanted was to be with you, and then I discovered racing."

Strange, but losing Luke to racing didn't

hurt as much as it used to.

"Then all I wanted to do was drive a car. Now . . . I don't know what I want anymore."

She pushed herself off the hay bale and made her way across to where he sat. "You don't have to decide right now." Baptism classes wouldn't start until next spring. He had plenty of time to get used to being back among the Plain people.

She knelt down in front of him and took his hands into her own. "Give yourself some time. Who knows what you might decide?"

He worked one of his hands free to trace the healing scar over her right eye. "I'm so sorry I hurt you, Em."

"I know."

"What is going on in here?" At the sound of her father's voice, Emily pushed to her feet. She whirled around to face the bishop's angry, accusing glare. She only had a split second to register his fierce expression before she was blinded by the glare of his flashlight.

"Nix." She raised one hand against the harsh light.

Then he moved the beam to pin it on Luke.

He pushed to his feet and squinted into the glare. "Nothing," he repeated.

Emily hastily smoothed her hands down the front of her coat. Even though it was buttoned up against the cold, the fact that she wore only her nightgown underneath was evident.

"This does not look like 'nothing' to me."

"*Dat*, I —"

"Go to the house, Emily Jane."

"*Dat.*" She moved to stand in front of Luke as if the action alone could protect him. She had come so far in helping him, she didn't want to give up on him now.

Her father stopped, and for a moment, the night stilled as she defied him.

"Now, Emily."

"We've done nothing wrong," she said, silently urging Luke to say something — *anything* — in their defense.

What had happened to her fair and objective father?

"I'm going to pretend you didn't say that to me. Now get back in the house."

"*Dat* —"

"Now!"

"Emily, go."

Had it not been for Luke's words she might not have obeyed her *vatter*. It was hard to say. But until Luke spoke, she had no intentions of leaving. Yet staying and making her father angrier would not help either of them.

She glanced back at him one last time. Luke nodded, and she stiffly left the barn.

She could hear her father's voice as she hurried toward the house, but she couldn't make out any of the words he said. His tone was enough to let her know he was upset. Cephas Ebersol didn't yell or raise his voice when he was really angry. He became quiet. Almost too quiet. And it was enough to scare even the worst sinners in their district.

Emily didn't catch the screen door as she entered the house. It snapped behind her like the pop of a child's balloon. She anticipated the sound, but still she jumped from nerves.

"Oh, my, Emily, you scared me." Mary hopped to her feet, one hand pressed over her heart.

"Did you tell him I was out there?" She didn't mean for her words to sound so harsh. She shook her head and rubbed her eyes with her good hand.

"I didn't mean to." A sob hitched in Mary's throat. "He came in and asked me where you were. I think he already knew."

Emily immediately regretted her tone. "Shhh . . ." she hushed, pulling Mary close as she wrapped comforting arms around her. "It's *allrecht.*"

"I was so afraid you would be angry with me." She hiccupped into Emily's shoulder.

"You're my *shveshtah.* I could never stay upset with you."

"What about Luke?" Mary asked. She cast a quick look at the door as if that could tell her what was going on outside in their barn.

Emily pressed her lips together. "*Dat* is overreacting." But tomorrow, after he calmed down a bit, she would talk to him, explain what she had been doing in the barn with Luke. How she wanted to give Luke a new view of the Amish church and all the reasons why he should attend the baptism classes in the spring. Not because she wanted to marry him, but because it was the right thing for him to do.

Her father was in a foul mood when he came back into the house twenty minutes later. He simply brushed past them, telling them to go to bed as he went by.

Nor had his demeanor changed after milking the next morning. Emily tried to talk to him, but he wouldn't discuss the matter at all. Instead he hitched up his buggy and headed out.

"Where do you think he's going?" Mary asked.

Emily shrugged. "He could be going

anywhere." But she had a feeling he was on his way to Joseph Lambright's to talk to Luke. Maybe in the light of day Luke would have more to say about what had happened in the barn. Or rather what had *not* happened.

Perhaps her father would listen to him. For sure and for certain, he was not willing to hear Emily out.

Emily sighed.

"What's wrong, *shveshtah*?"

"At the beginning of the summer I was worried that my life would be boring."

Mary chuckled.

"I had to quit teaching and work in the market. Luke left, Caroline got married."

"Since then your life has been anything but dull."

"*Jah.*" What she wouldn't give for a little bit of that boring back.

Luke heard the rattle of the horse and buggy and went to the window. He was not surprised to see the bishop's rig pull to a stop.

Cephas Ebersol hopped down from the carriage and made his way to the house. His steps were sure and true, each one with a deeper purpose. The fact that he hadn't unhitched his rig told its own tale. The bishop had a plan, and he wasn't staying long.

Luke walked out onto the porch to face the talk head-on. As he stepped out of the house, his uncle ambled around the corner from the backyard to see who had come calling. Despite the crisp temperatures, Luke didn't grab his coat, and he wasn't about to invite the bishop in.

"I thought we cleared the air last night," Luke said instead of a greeting.

His uncle's eyes widened at his gruff words, but he didn't say anything to correct Luke.

The bishop stopped before reaching the porch steps. He stroked his beard and squinted as he faced the midmorning sun. "I prayed all night for God to give me answers."

"Did you get them?" He knew he was being insolent, rude even, but he had taken a tongue lashing the night before, and he wasn't willing to do so again. He and Emily had done nothing wrong. He had apologized for the wreck and all the trouble he'd caused. Couldn't her father see past it all to the fact that he loved Emily more than anything in the world?

More than racing?

He pushed the thought aside and concen-

382

trated on the man before him.

"Luke Lambright, you have reached the age of baptism."

He couldn't argue with that. Instead he nodded and crossed his arms, waiting for the bishop to continue.

"You've left our community for the pleasures of the *Englisch* world, and now you've come back. As the bishop here, I must say it's time for you to bend your knee and join the church."

"And if I say no?"

"Then I'll ask you to go back to the *Englisch* or into another district. The teens entering *rumspringa* have enough temptations. You are not setting a *gut* example."

Luke stiffened. He had been afraid it would come to this. What was he going to do? "I'll be gone by the end of the week."

"Luke —" *Onkle* started, but Luke shook his head to stop his words. He had made his decision long ago. Regardless of everything that had gone wrong for him in the *Englisch* world, he could not remain with the Amish.

The bishop issued a curt nod. He turned on his heel to leave, then stopped. Facing Luke once again he said, "And I'll thank you to steer clear of my *dochder.*"

As he watched, the bishop swung himself

back into his buggy and set his horse into motion. Luke remained on the porch, not moving until the bishop's buggy disappeared down the road. Then he collapsed into the old lawn chair his *onkle* kept on the porch.

"Are you really leaving again?"

He had almost forgotten his uncle was there.

"Jah," Luke said as *Onkle* made his way around the house and eased down onto the middle step.

Joseph Lambright stared out at the pasture as if it held the answers to all life's problems. "I tried my best all these years to do right by your parents —"

"That has nothing to do with it."

He waved a hand as if to brush away Luke's protests. "I could have done a better job. Looking back I see that. What can a bachelor offer his brother's child?" He shook his head.

"This is not your fault."

"It is," Joseph said. "If I had only done more for you."

"You took care of me after my *eldra* died," Luke said, his voice suddenly thick with tears. "A *bu* can't ask for more than that."

"If I had done more," Joseph continued as if Luke hadn't spoken, "then maybe you wouldn't be leaving."

"Nay." But the truth was, they would never know. Joseph had been ill-prepared to care for the young son of his recently deceased *bruder.* But as the next of kin, the burden had fallen to him.

Luke couldn't complain. He had been grateful not to have to leave Wells Landing. His uncle had done the very best for him that he knew how. Perhaps there were times when he wasn't strict enough or stern enough, but Joseph was too easygoing to hold Luke accountable. Still, Luke had been loved, and that was enough.

Joseph stood, his knees popping with the motion. He turned back to Luke, his eyes full of hope and sadness. "You be careful out there among the *Englisch.*"

CHAPTER TWENTY-THREE

Supper time and Emily's *vatter* still hadn't said more than two sentences to her. They had worked in the milking room side by side in complete silence, then trudged into the house to eat. The atmosphere around the table was strained at best. Everyone looked to the others to see who was going to cave first. Who was going to initiate the conversation from which there was no return?

After they ate and prayed again, Emily helped her sisters clean the kitchen, then went to find her father. Enough was enough. Time to get it out into the open. The thought of confronting her father made her a little sick to her stomach, but she couldn't let him go around believing the worst in her, believing the worst in Luke.

She pulled on her coat and went in search of her *dat*. She found him on the porch smoking his pipe. The habit was sporadic at best since her mother frowned upon it. That he was smoking now was a testament that he was just as upset as she was.

"*Dat?*"

"*Jah?*"

She could barely make out his face in the dim porch light. He had lit a lantern on the table behind him, but his expression was hidden. Only when he took a draw on his pipe did the shadows disappear enough for her to see his eyes.

"About last night . . ." She drew her coat a little tighter around her.

"It is done, Emily Jane."

"What do you mean?"

"Luke is leaving Wells Landing." His tone was unreadable, flat and matter-of-fact.

Her heart gave a painful lurch as her stomach tightened. "Why?" she whispered.

"Because I asked him to."

Her knees trembled even as her teeth wanted to chatter in the cold. But it wasn't that chilly. "Why would you do something like that?"

"It's not your place to question my judgment. I did so as the bishop of this district."

"You did it out of spite." The words flew from her mouth unheeded.

He stood and in an instant loomed over her. "I'll not have my authority questioned, Emily Jane. I did what was best for the community."

Hot tears stung her eyes. "You never liked Luke."

"I do not like what he has done."

"We weren't doing anything wrong. I've been trying to get him to stay and join the church." The tears she had been fighting spilled down her cheeks. She dashed them away with the back of her uncasted hand and continued. "And you ruined it."

Her father took a step closer, his eyes steely. "What's done is done. We will not speak of it again." He pushed the words through gritted teeth, the closest she had ever seen him to yelling.

But she wanted to yell, to scream and stomp around. Luke was one of the best friends she had ever had and her father had sent him away. Just like that. He hadn't given him a chance to join the church or even think about it.

She opened her mouth to say more, but no words would come. Not even a squeak. She pivoted on one heel and stormed back into the house.

"Emily?" Mary sat on the sofa working on some sewing, but Emily didn't acknowledge her sister's concern.

Instead she stormed up the stairs and slammed her door shut. With a decisive click, she locked the door and threw herself on her bed. Then and only then, with her face pressed into the pillow, did she let go of her sobs, her screams, and her overwhelming frustration with it all.

Elam, her father, Luke, everyone thought they knew what was best for her, yet no one knew what she was going through, nobody bothered to ask how she felt about it.

A soft knock sounded on her door followed by "Emily?"

Mary.

"Go away," she said, knowing the words would hurt her sister but unable to face her care and concern.

"Will you not open the door for me?"

"*Nay.* I — I need some time alone."

"I understand," Mary said. "But I don't think you should be by yourself at a time like this."

Emily rolled over and stared at the plain white ceiling above her bed. That was her life: plain, white. All her life had been plain and white. The entire Amish existence: plain and white.

"I don't want to talk about it right now, Mary. Maybe later."

A small thump sounded, and Emily imagined her sister resting her head against the plain varnished wood of the door. "I will leave you only if you promise to come to me when you are ready to talk."

"I promise." Fresh tears welled in her eyes at her sister's concern. But these were silent.

"Ich liebe dich," Mary said.

Emily let the tears fall from the corners of her eyes. "I love you, too."

For once Emily was grateful that she had a room to herself.

She could hear her sisters moving around their rooms, getting ready for bed and such. They were talking in hushed tones she couldn't understand. Mary must've told them about her request to be left alone. No one laughed out loud, no one knocked on the door to talk to her.

Then it was time for bed, and the house grew quiet.

Emily flopped over once again, unable to bring herself to get up and actually ready herself for bed.

Why had her father done that? Why had he asked Luke to leave without even talking to her once about it?

He hadn't asked. He hadn't taken the time to find out the truth.

She had worked so hard to get Luke to open up to her. He was so close to giving up his crazy dream of driving a car and instead joining the church where he belonged.

She needed to talk to him. Now. Right now.

She sat bolt upright on her bed. She would go to him. *Jah.* She would go over to Luke's house, convince him to stay for a while longer, give his Amish upbringing another chance.

She jumped to her feet, straightening her clothes as her mind whirled in a dozen different directions.

A soft knock sounded on her door. She stopped, sure she had imagined the sound. But there it was again.

"Emily." *Mary.*

She crossed to the door and cautiously opened it.

"I heard you moving around," Mary said.

Emily pulled her into the room and quietly shut the door behind them.

"You're not ready for bed."

"I'm going to talk to Luke."

"You think that's a *gut* idea? I mean *Dat* will be upset."

"Mary, really. He'll be furious. But he's already mad, so what do I have to lose?"

"Don't go," Mary pleaded. "Wait until tomorrow."

Emily moved toward her sister, giving her

a quick squeeze. "It's not like I'm cutting my prayer *kapp* strings or anything."

Mary was reluctant to let her go. "Please, Emily."

Emily stopped, her sister's tone cutting her straight through.

"It's dark outside. If you wait till tomorrow you can take a buggy. You'll be so much safer. I could go with you."

Her urgency deflated in the face of her sister's arguments. She sank to the edge of the bed beside Mary. "What if he's already gone?"

"He won't leave that quickly."

"You're probably right. Okay," she agreed. "I'll wait until tomorrow."

Mary smiled through her tears. "*Danki,* sister. It'll all work out. You'll see."

Emily felt stiff and conspicuous as she went through her morning chores. As much as she wanted to speed through them and hustle out the door, she had to bide her time.

The skies were gray and dull, promising rain and reflecting her mood. Maybe she should have gone last night. But Mary was right. She would be much safer in the light of day.

She felt terrible about deceiving her *mamm*

and *dat* once again, but she had to take one last chance to save Luke from the perils of the *Englisch* world. She should have done more to make him stay the first time. She would have, had she known it would come to this.

Once the milking was complete, chores done, and the family fed, Emily hitched up the smaller buggy under the guise of visiting with Caroline. She gathered a basket of goodies and prayed that no one asked her friend how she liked the cheese bread.

"I'm leaving now," Emily called as she headed for the door.

"Okay," *Mamm* called back. "Give Caroline my best."

Guilt panged inside her.

"Are you sure you don't want me to come along?" Mary asked as the sisters made their way to the front yard where the horse and buggy waited.

"I'm sure. This is something I need to do by myself." She didn't add that it was best Mary not involve herself in case their *dat* found out.

"*Geb acht,*" Mary said. Be careful.

"I will." Emily smiled at her sister and set the horse into motion.

"I've got a little money put away." *Onkle*

Joseph wrapped his hands around the coffee mug and lifted it to his lips.

"I don't want to take your money." Luke took a sip of his own *kaffi,* using its warmth as a balm to his spirit. He never thought he'd find himself where he was now, caught between two worlds. "I'll figure something out." He didn't know what, but he'd think of something. Eventually.

He had spent a long sleepless night trying to figure out what. He had no money, no sponsor, no job. His future seemed so bleak, he actually considered staying in Wells Landing and joining the church. How crazy was that?

His *onkle* stood and retrieved a coffee can from the top of the refrigerator. He popped off the top, then pulled a wad of bills from inside. "It's the least I can do." He placed the money on the table and nudged it toward Luke.

"Danki," Luke managed to squeeze past the lump in his throat. He wanted to push the money back, tell his uncle that he'd be fine. But he was only kidding himself. He wasn't able to say more as a knock sounded.

"Who could that be this time a'morning?" His uncle set the coffee can on the table and made his way to the door.

But Luke wasn't prepared for who stood

on their porch. "Emily?"

His uncle stepped to the side as Emily made her way into the house. "I'm so sorry about my *vatter.*"

He stood as Emily rushed to his side. "It's all right, Em."

His *onkle* looked from one of them to the other. He took a step back, then started out the door. "I'll just go see to your horses."

"Danki, Onkle."

Emily murmured her thanks, and the two of them were alone.

"I was afraid you would leave without coming by," she said.

Hope rose in his chest. Maybe all of his nights going to Emily's house, wooing her while everyone was asleep were about to pay off. *"Jah?"*

"My *vatter* should have never come to you."

Luke shrugged. "I'm not going to worry about it."

"But . . ."

"Listen." He took her hands into his own. "I love you, Emily. But I have to leave. And this time, I want you to come with me."

Her eyes widened, her lips parted, and she shook her head. "I don't understand."

"I want you to come with me," he repeated. It was simple enough. "We can get married like the *Englisch* and live out our days together."

"But . . . but I don't want you to go."

She had such a big heart, just another of the reasons he loved her so. "I wish it was that simple," he said. He wanted to reach out and touch her face, show her how much she meant to him, but he held back. Something in her eyes kept his touch at bay.

"It is. Just be patient. I know you can convince *Dat* that you have sincere intentions."

Sincere intentions? "What are you talking about?"

"I'm talking about you, joining the church."

He scrubbed his hands down his face. "Why would I do that when you're coming with me?"

"To the *Englisch. Nay.* And neither are you. You need to stay here, *jah?*"

They were going in circles. "Is that what all of this has been about? Getting me to stay?"

"And join the church, *jah.*" A frown puckered her forehead. "What did you think it was about?"

"Me and you." He reached out then, gently fingered the side of her prayer *kapp,* a constant reminder of all that separated them. "Just think about it." He lowered his tone and reached for the pins that held her *kapp* in place. "We can be together, like we always talked about. Just the two of us. Without the church or your *dat* there to stand between us."

She pulled away from him, gasping as her *kapp* remained in his hands. Her own flew to her head as if to protect it. "That's not why I'm here." She snatched the white linen out of his hands, crumpling it between her own trembling fingers. Her ill treatment of the near-sacred item was proof of her distress. "You are supposed to stay here."

"And get married under the watchful eyes of the church?" he scoffed. "I want more for us than that."

Emily shook her head, backing away from him as she spoke. The look on her face was a cross between shaken and disturbed. "There is no us."

"So you've been leading me on?" He rubbed his eyes.

"You came to my house."

"You let me in," he countered.

To his dismay, tears rose in her eyes. "This was a mistake. I was wrong to come here." She stumbled toward the door.

"Emily," he called after her, but she waved away his plea.

"I'll pray for you, Luke Lambright."

Before he could say another word, she slammed out the door, out of his house, and out of his life once again.

Emily ignored the tears that streamed down her face as she swung herself up into her buggy. She had been such a fool. A stupid, stupid fool!

She wrapped her casted arm around her a little tighter as the winter wind blew. The sharp breeze cut right through her woolen coat. The smell of rain hung in the air.

She had thought Luke had changed, unwisely believing he was finally growing up and ready to live the life expected of him. How wrong could one person be?

She had jeopardized everything she held dear for him. Her relationship with her father would never be the same. And Elam . . . he would never trust her again. Stupid, stupid puppy love. If only she had listened with a woman's heart. Then she might have seen that Elam's feelings for her were real, and Luke's were superficial.

Or maybe Luke really did love her in his own way. The thought made her feel only a little better. At least it stopped her tears.

She pulled the buggy onto the road heading the opposite way. She couldn't go home.

Not yet. She had too many thoughts to work out. Maybe she should head over to Caroline's. At least then all of her words wouldn't be a lie.

As the horse clopped along, the rain started to fall. Its patter on the roof steadied her nerves and joined the rhythm of the buggy.

Jah, she would go to see Caroline. Her *freind* would know what to do.

A thump jarred her from her thoughts. The carriage lurched sideways. Emily pulled back on the reins, slowing the horse to a stop at the side of the road. Just in time, too. A loud pop sounded, followed by a crack. The front right side collapsed.

Emily's head bumped the side of the buggy. Tears stung her eyes. What now?

She slid open the door and stepped into the cold January rain. Her teeth began to chatter almost immediately.

Her horse, Clover, tossed her mane and snorted as Emily walked around in front of her to check for damage.

The wooden wheel had broken in two, split by wear and tear. Or maybe God was trying to tell her something. She shouldn't be out on a day like this. She shouldn't have lied to her *mamm* and *dat.* She shouldn't have asked her sister to lie for her, and she shouldn't be pinning her hopes on a way-ward soul like Luke Lambright. Regardless that her intentions had started off for the good.

She bit her lip to hold fresh tears at bay. Crying would do no good now. Still she wanted to. She wanted to sit on the side of the road with the rain pounding down and bawl like a baby.

Instead she unhitched Clover and led her down the road. Her teeth chattered, her heart ached.

The sound of a car engine could be heard over the rain. She moved farther onto the side of the road. A car whizzed past, the blare of the horn scaring her nearly out of her frozen skin.

She had to find shelter soon or she might freeze to death. A small building loomed in the distance, a phone shanty. Perhaps she could call someone, but she didn't know any phone numbers by memory. But a phone shanty meant a house was close. There was a driveway up ahead, maybe fifty or more feet in front of her. Once she got there, she would stop and ask for help, whether they were *Englisch* or Amish.

She shivered as she walked, keeping her head down and hurrying her footsteps for both warmth and speed. She needed to get out of the cold damp before she caught pneumonia. She needed to get Clover to shelter, too. It was no fit day for girl or beast.

Emily turned down the drive. She was halfway to the house before she faltered.

Elam's.

Of all the farms in all of Wells Landing she had to be at the Riehls'.

She squinted and stared up at the sky as the rain continued to fall. "I don't know if this is Your will or some kind of joke." But she got no answer.

Her father would tell her that God didn't joke about things, but coming to Elam's house as a matter of God's will was more than she could fathom at the moment. She ducked her head and continued on.

She led Clover into the barn, shutting her in a stall with the promise to return with a blanket and a brush. Clover snorted her consent, happy to be out of the freezing rain.

Emily was soaked to the bone by the time she made her way up the familiar porch steps. Wet, shivering, and beyond cold, she raised her hand and knocked on the door.

Noises sounded from the other side of the door. Feet shuffled, voices murmured, then the door opened and there he stood.

"Elam." Tears rose in her eyes, grateful and sad tears. Then she threw her arms

around him as if she never wanted to let
him go.

CHAPTER TWENTY-FOUR

She smelled warm and sweet and even better than he remembered.

Elam inhaled the scent of Emily plus rain and wrapped his arms around her.

"What are you doing out on a day like this?"

She pulled away from him, and it took all that he had not to pull her back. Too much had happened, too much stood between them. It would never be the same again.

Tears mixed with rain streamed down her cheeks.

"*Gut himmel,* Elam. Let her get dried off, then ask your questions." *Mamm* came downstairs, a stack of towels in her arms.

"I'm c-c-cold," Emily chattered.

What was wrong with him? He led her to the fire, stoking it until it roared with warmth.

"Get out of that wet coat, Emily," *Mamm* said. "It's just holding in the chill."

She rolled her shoulders, alerting Elam to the fact that he still had one arm around her. He cleared his throat and stepped back, dropping his hold as modestly as possible.

"My horse is in the barn." Her teeth chattered as she spoke.

"You rode your horse here in the rain?" What was the matter with her?

"Of course she didn't." *Mamm* stepped in, helping Emily shrug out of the sodden wool. "You are soaked to the bone." She turned back to him. "Elam, go up to Becky's room and find a dress for Emily to wear."

He stared at her.

"Go on," she urged. "Then you can check on her horse."

His father bounded into the room before Elam could take the first step to completing the chore.

"Emily." *Dat* smiled his toothy grin. But his expression fell as his gaze took in all of her. "What happened? Why are you all wet?"

"The wheel on my buggy broke a ways down the road." At least her teeth weren't chattering quite as violently now.

Dat turned to Elam. "Go get her something dry to put on before she catches pneumonia."

Elam's feet weighed heavy as he headed up to his sister's room.

"Something purple," his *dat* called behind him.

Elam shook his head at the wonder of it all. He could hear their voices as they floated up from the living room. He couldn't make out exactly what they were saying, but he was certain Emily was telling his *mamm* and *dat* how she came to be there.

He wanted to believe it was God. That the good Lord had a hand in putting her on their road today, but he couldn't get his hopes up. His house was between the bishop's *haus* and Caroline and Andrew's place. Emily hadn't started out to come see him. Or had she?

He grabbed the first dress hanging on the pegs inside Becky's room and headed back downstairs.

But only Emily remained. She was bundled up in a quilt, huddled close to the fire. Her hair had been wrapped in a towel and for the time being her teeth had stopped chattering.

"Where's *Mamm*?" he asked.

"Making coffee."

"Dat?"

"Taking care of Clover."

"Are you warm enough?"

She nodded and pulled the quilt a little tighter around herself.

He wanted to ask the dozen or so questions spinning around inside his head. Instead, he held the dress toward her hooked on the end of one finger. "Here's a *frack.*"

She took it, and he nodded toward the back hallway. "There's a bathroom down the hall."

"I know." She moved past him, the quilt wrapped around her like an overlarge cape.

She returned a few minutes later wearing Becky's dress with the quilt still pulled across her shoulders.

Until that moment he hadn't realized she'd not been wearing any clothes under the quilt when he came back downstairs.

The heat started at his collar and worked its way up until his entire face felt hotter than the top of his buggy in late August.

"Here we go."

He whirled around as his *mamm* came into the room.

She placed the tray on the table and handed one of the steaming mugs to Emily. *Mamm* took one for herself and passed the other to Elam.

"You're a very lucky *maedel,*" *Mamm* said. "Buggy accidents can be very serious."

"I know." Emily ducked her head over her cup.

Her lips trembled and her chin shook.

Mamm came closer, smoothing a hand over the side of Emily's face. "Whatever it is," she said, "God has a plan."

Emily nodded, and to his dismay two tears streaked down her cheeks.

"I think I'll go see about *middawk.*" *Mamm* started for the kitchen. "Or bake a pie. Or something."

Elam waited until she disappeared before joining Emily on the couch. "Do you want to talk about it?"

"There's nothing to talk about."

He let out a quick chuckle. "You arrive at my house soaking wet and crying, and there's not a story behind it?"

"Talking about it won't change a thing," she mumbled, then took a big gulp of coffee.

"You're all right, though . . . right?" He dropped his voice so low it was barely louder than the crackle of the fire. Until that moment it hadn't occurred to him that someone might have hurt her intentionally, physically. "No one . . . ?"

"Oh, *nay.*" She raised those midnight eyes to meet his, then quickly looked away. "It's . . . complicated."

Why had he expected her to say *heartbreaking* instead?

He took one of her hands into his own, loving the slim curve of her fingers. Such pretty hands.

She had given them so much. And yet she had taken from them, too. She definitely had stolen Elam's heart before she'd broken it in two. That was what he needed to remember in times like these when she looked so irresistible in the firelight. When it would be so easy to lean in and steal a kiss or two. Or five.

His *mamm* had said it all.

God had a plan for them. But one thing was certain: His plan for Elam and His plan for Emily were two entirely different things.

He dropped her hand and stood, needing as much distance between them as possible.

"No one cries like this just because their buggy broke down." He was pressuring her, *jah,* but something in him wouldn't let it go.

She swiped at her tears. "Where is everyone?"

"Becky took Johanna to town to look for material for a new dress. The twins and Norma are at school."

"I went to see Luke today."

His heart dropped at the sound of the other man's name.

"My *vatter* asked him to leave Wells Landing yesterday."

"Why?" Elam asked, though he had a pretty good idea as to why the bishop wanted Luke Lambright out of the picture.

"*Dat* doesn't feel he's setting a *gut* enough example for the youth of the district."

Elam couldn't argue with that. "You asked him to stay."

"And join the church, *jah.*"

So they could get married.

He released his pent-up breath not realizing until that moment he had been holding it. If Emily was crying, then . . .

"What did Luke say?"

She sniffed. "He doesn't want to stay here. He doesn't want to join the church."

"He's leaving again?" His words were thick, as his own emotions clogged his throat. He turned to the window, looking out at the falling rain.

How he wished they could go back in time. Maybe he could do things differently to get Emily to change her mind about him. See him in a new light and forget all about Luke Lambright. But it was too late for that.

"I've just made so many mistakes. I thought it would all work out. But it didn't. It just didn't."

Elam nodded. He understood perfectly.

Outside his father closed the barn door

and dashed back to the house, jumping over mud puddles much in the same way Johanna and Norma did.

Dat opened the front door, shaking off the rain and hanging his hat on the peg just inside. "Clover's all taken care of."

"Danki," Emily said.

"You want some more coffee?" Elam asked.

"That would be *gut.*"

"Can I have a cup, too?" James asked. He crossed the room to the rolltop desk, opening it and pulling out a deck of cards. "Will you play with me?" he asked Emily. "I've missed playing with you." He made a face at Elam. "Nobody here likes to play as much as I do."

"I'd like that." Emily's smile trembled on her lips, though she managed to keep any new tears at bay.

Elam was grateful for that. He didn't think he could take many more of those before he pulled her into his arms and never let her go.

His *dat* plopped down into the chair opposite Emily and started shuffling the cards. "Will you teach me how to play poker?" His eyes twinkled.

Emily had the presence to look shocked. "I'm sure I don't know how to play such a wicked game as that."

Dat smiled, as Elam turned to fetch their coffee. "Rummy, it is."

James barely waited until his son was out of the room before he spoke. "He's not been the same since you two broke up."

Emily tried to smile. Neither of them had been.

"He's been cranky and moping around the house. You have to do something, Emily." He started to deal the cards for their game.

"There's nothing I can do, James. He broke up with me."

He shook his head and set up the "draw" and "discard" piles on the coffee table. "Why would he do something so stupid?"

"I guess you could say I started it."

"I don't understand." He frowned and picked up his cards.

"I did something pretty stupid first."

"Everybody does stupid stuff from time to time. That's no reason to break up."

"I guess he feels differently." She swallowed back her tears. So many mistakes. So many stupid mistakes on top of bad choices. "It's not always that easy, James."

James pouted. "It should be." He stopped when Elam came back into the room carrying their coffees.

"I'm going to the barn to check on Sally Ann," he said. "I'll take you home when the rain stops."

"Okay." She watched as he made his way to the front door and prepared to go outside.

"Sally Ann is our mule," James explained. "Something got a'hold of her leg the other day. Elam's been doctoring it."

"Huh?" Emily said.

James shot her a knowing look. Despite the innocence in his expression, Emily could see the intelligence underlying lighting his eyes. "You miss him as much as he misses you."

"It's not that simple, James," she said again. "I wish it was. I hurt him."

"You both are making it way too complicated." James shook his head. "He loves you, you know."

"Love isn't always enough," Emily replied, ignoring the quick beat of her heart at the thought of Elam loving her. He had said he did, but she had stomped on his feelings too many times to gain back his love now.

"What if it is?" James asked. "What if all you need to do is talk to him? Hmm? What then? How will you know until you ask?" He spread his cards on the board.

"Rummy," he called.

One thing was certain, whether Elam loved her or not. If she was going to have a prayer of winning even one game against his *dat,* she was going to have to pay better attention.

But how could she when thoughts of a second chance with Elam swam around inside her mind? Was love enough? Could their feelings for each other bridge the chasm that had yawned between them? Or was it simply too late?

By midafternoon the rain had stopped. The girls weren't home yet. After countless games of Rummy, Go Fish, and War, Emily had decided that James might just have a point. How could she not give them both a chance? She had tried to tell Elam that she loved him the night he broke up with her, but the words got lost somewhere between her conservative upbringing and her pride.

But she would forever be kicking herself if she didn't put her heart out there and tell Elam how she felt.

He was silent as he drove down the lane from his house. Clover followed behind the buggy and slowed their journey. Emily would have plenty of time to talk to him, if only she could find her courage.

Sucking in a deep breath, she laid her hand on his arm.

He flinched as if she burned him.

"Elam?" she asked.

"Hmmm?" He didn't take his eyes from the road, as if leading the horse required all of his attention.

"Can I talk to you for a minute?"

"Sure, *jah.*" But once again he refused to look at her.

"*Nay,* I mean talk. Really talk."

He tensed, then rolled his big shoulders, bumping against her as they ambled along. "Do I need to pull over for this?"

She shook her head. "When we get to the house we could maybe sit in the barn for a while." The ground was too wet and the air too damp and cold to stay out in it longer than absolutely necessary.

"The barn," he repeated. "*Jah,* okay."

Emily sighed and tried to smile, but she was more nervous now than she'd ever been. It was nerve-racking enough to sit beside him and think about talking with him later and another matter altogether to sit next to him *knowing* they would be talking in the very near future.

Thankfully she had stressed over the asking long enough that they were almost at her house when he agreed. She only had fifteen or so minutes to sit next to him and twist her hands together before they pulled into the driveway.

Elam had no sooner set the brake than *Mamm* flew out of the house. She had a dish towel thrown over one shoulder and a concerned light shining in her eyes.

"Emily, praise be, you're *allrecht.* Dan Troyer called to say he saw your buggy on the side of the road with no horse or driver. I couldn't imagine what had happened to you." She wrapped Emily into a quick hug. "I've been worried sick and praying non-stop."

"I didn't mean to worry you." She returned her mother's embrace. "I guess Dan Troyer told you about the wheel?"

"*Jah,* your father took Mary and Susannah to go look at it, and I promised to stay here until you got home." She turned to Elam. "Thank you, Elam Riehl, for bringing my Emily back home."

He gave her a quick nod. "I'll take Clover into the barn and get her settled." He unhitched the horse and led her away.

Emily disentangled herself from her mother's clingy arms. Normally *Mamm* was as calm and cool as they come, but with all the recent accidents and upheavals, her nerves seemed a bit rattled. "It's okay,

Mamm. I'm fine. Truly."

Mamm gave her one last squeeze and let her go. "Come on in the house. I'll make some *kaffi.*"

But Emily shook her head. "I need to go talk to Elam."

"Oh. *Oh.*" *Mamm* gave a sage nod. "Okay then." She started back toward the house and out of the cold. "Just don't take too long, okay?"

Emily smiled. "I won't."

Elam was sitting on a bale of hay just inside the door when she walked into the barn. It was almost the exact spot where Luke had been sitting just two short nights ago. Had it not even been forty-eight hours since her *vatter* had told Luke to leave? It seemed as if a lifetime had passed since then.

Ever the gentleman, Elam stood when he saw her, tossing away the random pieces of hay he held and dusting off his pants. "Emily."

Her name sounded like a prayer on his lips and gave her hope. More than anything she wanted to save whatever she could between them.

"I wanted to talk to you," she stuttered. Where were all the words she needed to tell him that she loved him?

416

"*Jah,* you said that much already." He settled himself back down, crossed his arms over his chest, and eyed her suspiciously. Guarded. That was the best way to describe his demeanor. Not that she could blame him. They had been through too much. Yet she longed to wipe away the look of distrust and replace it with one of love and joy.

"I love you."

He blinked those green eyes. "What?"

Gut himmel! Could she find the courage to say it again? "I love you."

He rose from his seat on the hay bale and started for the door. "Good-bye, Emily."

She rushed after him, stopping him with a hand on his back before he could set one foot out into the new rain.

The muscles under her fingers bunched and jerked.

He shrugged her hand away and turned around to face her. "You don't love me."

His words cut her to the bone. "But I do," she protested.

"Nay." He sighed and propped his hands onto his hips. "You have always loved Luke Lambright. Now he's gone for good, and I'm all that's left." He shook his head. "I thought I could compete with him. I had big hopes that one day you would come to care for me the way you do for him. I

417

thought that was God's will for us."

Tears slid down her cheeks and dropped off the edge of her jaw.

"But I can't be second. I love you too much for that."

"You're not second." Her voice hitched on a sob. She wanted to reach out to him, show him that she loved him. He said he loved her. Surely there was still a chance for them. "I've made so many mistakes," she said. "But this isn't one of them."

"It's over, Emily. Luke's gone, and I'm here, but I won't be a poor substitute for what you really want."

"You're what I want," she cried. "I love you."

"You'll never know how much I wish I could believe that."

And then he was gone.

CHAPTER TWENTY-FIVE

Sissy Hardin pressed her foot to the brake as she came around the tight corner. She was a city girl, born and raised, and these winding roads in the backwoods of Amish country were more than she had planned for. No wonder country folks took so long to get anywhere. They drove miles out of the way just in curves.

Beside her in the passenger seat her cell phone chirped, alerting her to a new message, but she ignored it. She had made the pledge to not text and drive, and there was no way she was chancing it on these unfamiliar roads. It was one of her friends, anyway, and that could definitely wait. It couldn't be her father. He always picked up the phone and called.

She slowed even more as she neared the intersection. Before her was a stop sign that said WHOA and a telephone pole with a hand-painted sign announcing local honey and brown eggs. That was her turn.

She steered her car down the tiny dirt lane and flipped the heater up a little higher. She'd heard that it was colder in the country than in the city, and this trip just proved it.

If the directions the woman at the bakery had given her were correct, the third house on the left belonged to Luke Lambright. Or rather, it belonged to Joseph Lambright, Luke's uncle.

She passed the first drive and realized the houses were farther back from the road than she'd expected and nearly miles apart. But she was diligent. She had to find Luke and set things right.

Her phone chimed again, and she resisted the urge to pick it up. No distractions or she'd miss the house altogether.

She passed the second drive and down this one she could see the white paint of the house through the trees in the yard. Off to one side was a field of bright green. Who knew things grew in the wintertime?

Drive number three was so narrow she almost missed it entirely. As it was, she jerked her car into the dirt lane and winced as the bottom of her car scraped the frozen ground. She pressed her foot back on the brake and held it there as she eased along the hard-packed lane.

She didn't have far to drive before she saw the house. It seemed typical of the farmhouses in the area. The two-story structure was painted white and rambled in all different directions. The porch stretching across the front was dotted with a mix of lawn chairs and wooden rockers. A man sat in one of the chairs as if waiting for her to arrive.

He was Amish. Or at least she thought he was. He wore a plain black coat, over a blue shirt and black pants. His black hat had a wide brim and hid most of his face from her view. The bottom half was shaved smooth. Which seemed weird. Didn't Amish men have beards?

She sure hoped she was in the right place. And if luck was on her side, he was Joseph Lambright, Luke's uncle.

She pulled her car to a stop and got out. As she tugged on the tail of her shirt and the arms of her winter coat, the man stood.

"Hi," she called. She waved to the man as she picked her way across the yard. She hadn't exactly worn the right shoes for walking across a country lawn.

"Goedemiddag," he said in return. She had no idea what that meant, but he seemed harmless enough as he shuffled down the steps. "Can I help you?"

"I'm looking for Luke Lambright."

"*Jah?*" He tipped his hat back a bit and Sissy could finally see his eyes. They were stormy gray, but somehow they brought to mind Luke and gave her hope she was at the right house.

"My name is Sissy Hardin. My daddy owns a bunch of fried chicken restaurants."

He studied her as she spoke, but didn't interrupt. She took that as a sign to continue.

"Luke came to Daddy wanting him as a sponsor for a race car. But things sort of fell through." Okay, so that wasn't *exactly* what happened, but she was here to make things right and that was the most important thing, wasn't it?

She shifted from one foot to the other, wondering for a second how much this man knew.

"Luke is not here."

She didn't try to hide her disappointment. She had driven a long way to find him. "Will he be home soon?"

The man shook his head. "*Nay.* He's gone for good this time, I s'pose."

"For good? But where did he go?"

"Back to the *Englisch.*"

Her eyes widened. "He went to England?"

The man laughed. "That's what you are.

Englisch. "

O-kay. "So he's here?" She didn't mean to play dumb, but she was seriously having trouble understanding him. And she so needed to make up for the mistakes she had made concerning Luke.

"He went to catch the bus back to Arkansas."

She was too late.

The man looked to the sky and back to her. "If you hurry you just might catch him."

She didn't know what he saw in the sky, but she was hopeful.

"He's in town then?"

"Jah."

"Thank you," she said, mincing back across the sparsely covered ground.

"Anytime," the man said. "Anytime."

Luke stretched his legs out in front of him and tried to look bored. He didn't want anyone to think that he was excited or hurt or any of the number of emotions racing through him. He hadn't wanted to leave Wells Landing. And he sure hadn't wanted things to end between him and Emily like they had.

But it was too late for apologies. Too late to go back. Too late to wish for things to be different.

He stood and walked to the large plate glass window that looked out over the road. His ruse was not fooling anyone, not even him.

A big part of him, the part that was a born dreamer, was glad to be going back to Arkansas. But a huge chunk of his heart would always be in Wells Landing with Emily. He had loved her too long to stop now. Maybe one day . . .

A shiny red car eased down the road as if the driver wasn't sure where they were going. As Luke watched, the car stopped, hung a quick turn, and disappeared into the side parking lot.

There was something vaguely familiar about the car, but he wasn't sure why. He had been obsessed with cars for years now. Most probably the sleek lines and shimmering paint were what drew him in like a fly to honey.

"Luke?"

He turned to find Sissy Hardin standing near the door that led outside. Her blond hair billowed around her shoulders like a cloud of spun gold, her cheeks pink from the cold.

"What are you doing here?" He turned away from her. As nice as she was to look at, she had ruined everything for him. A fact he wasn't forgetting anytime soon.

"Your uncle told me you were here."

"In Oklahoma," he clarified.

She started toward him, the keys in her hand clinking together as she came nearer. "Listen. I know you're mad at me, and you have every right to be. But I came to make amends."

"Amends?"

She reached into her purse and pulled out an envelope. "Here." She thrust it toward him.

He took it, staring at her and the thick white envelope in turn. "What is it?"

"Five hundred dollars."

"Five hundred —" He thumbed open the envelope to stare at the bills inside. "Why are you giving me this?"

She shoved her hands into her coat pockets and shrugged. "Because my father would have given you that and more if I hadn't of —" She stopped and he didn't miss the fact that she couldn't meet his gaze. "I'm sorry. I shouldn't have — well, the truth is I like you. A lot. I had seen you around the track, I just wanted to get to know you better. And then . . ." She shook her head. "I felt just awful."

"*Jah?*"

"I know you needed that money. The

425

other guys told me what happened with the wreck and . . . so I wanted you to have it."

"Thank you." He was humbled. What else was he supposed to say? In light of her apology, what else could he do but forgive her? The ability to forgive was one part of his Amish upbringing he hoped he never lost.

"I talked to my daddy and explained what happened." She shrugged again. "I would have been here sooner, but he grounded me." She made a face. "Anyway, he's agreed to talk to you some more about a sponsorship. If you're still interested."

"Are you serious?" Hope surged inside him — hope for the dreamer, hope for the future.

"Yeah. He likes the way you drive."

"Yeah?" He tried to play it cool, but he couldn't stop the grin spreading across his face. Gus Hardin liked the way he drove.

"Me, too," she added.

"That's awesome." He slapped the envelope containing the money against his leg, loving the *whack* it made.

"There's just one more thing," Sissy said. "Can you forgive me for what I did? I am terribly sorry."

Luke smiled. She was just so pretty, how could a guy not forgive her? Still, he couldn't make it *too* easy for her. "On one

426

condition."

"What's that?"

"Give me a ride back to Van Buren?"

She smiled, and the world seemed a bit brighter. "You got it."

Elam pulled his buggy back into the driveway at his house and just sat there for a moment. He'd turned the battery-operated heater off long ago, its hum nearly driving him to distraction.

Walking away from Emily a second time was the hardest thing he had ever done. Even harder than the first time.

He rubbed his eyes with one hand. If only he could believe her when she said she loved him. That was all he ever wanted. But he wasn't willing to settle. He knew plenty of men who would, even more who *had.* But he couldn't do it. He was an "all or nothing" sort of man.

With a sigh, he got out of the buggy and unhitched the horse. With heavy footsteps and an even heavier heart, he made his way to the barn.

He led the horse to his stall and grabbed the brush for a quick rubdown, his thoughts still whirling around inside his head like a swarm of angry hornets. He couldn't catch any one, so he let them be, preferring instead to ignore them as he completed his task. Mindless. That was the best way to go. At least until he was ready to look at the situation with clear eyes. At the rate he was going, that would be never.

"Elam?"

His father's voice pulled him out of his own misery. "Back here," he called.

Footsteps shuffled in the hay, and then his father was there, a frown on his brow. "I didn't expect you back so soon," *Dat* said.

"Why not?" Elam finished the brushing and filled the horse's oat trough.

"Thought you might stay and spend a little time with Emily."

He knew his father well enough to know when the man was digging. "What are you talking about?"

"I'm talking about you and Emily and love," his *dat* said.

Elam sighed when he wanted to howl in frustration. "Emily and I broke up," he said as gently as he could manage. Still his voice was rough and rusty.

"But you are going to get back together again, *jah*?"

"*Nay.*"

"But she told me she loved you." His *vatter*'s frown deepened until his entire face was involved.

428

"That seems to be the rumor."

"And you love her," *Dat* prodded.

"Is this conversation going somewhere?" This whole love thing was making him snippy.

"Did she or did she not tell you that she loves you?"

Elam really didn't want to talk about it, but since his head injury his father seemed more determined than ever. He was like a bulldog who latched on to something and wouldn't let go. *Dat* wouldn't let this subject drop until he had all his questions answered.

"She told me she loved me." A fist squeezed his heart as he spoke. How long had he wanted to hear those very words from her? How long had he waited for her to realize that he would do anything and everything he could to make her happy?

The Amish believed that everything that happened was a part of God's will. Elam just didn't understand why God thought he needed a broken heart.

"Then what's the problem?" his *dat* asked.

"She loves Luke more."

His father propped his hands on his hips. "What gave you that fool idea?"

"She's always loved Luke."

Dat shook his head. "That doesn't mean she loves him more."

But it did.

Didn't it?

"That *maedel* loves you," his *vatter* continued. "Now what are you going to do about it?"

"There's nothing to do."

Dat shook his head. "You mean you are just going to let her go?"

Elam shrugged, tired of the conversation. He didn't want to forget about Emily nor could he accept her and what little she had to offer him. "*Dat,* you don't understand."

Dat took a step closer, hands on his hips as his amiable demeanor vanished. "Now, son, I know I'm not as smart as I used to be. But I'm sharp enough to know when a *gut* thing is in front of my face. And Emily Ebersol is a *gut* thing."

Elam took a step back, thoroughly chastised. "I —"

" 'Purple is as purple does,' " *Dat* quoted.

Elam sighed. "I don't even know what that means." More now than ever, he wanted to escape to the house and forget today ever happened.

His *dat* grinned. "I don't either. But I think it means that you should be true to yourself. Be the person you are and the one that you want to be. Once you do that, it'll come to you."

"What will come?"

Dat held his hands out, palms up. "Whatever it is that you want."

Could it be that simple?

His *dat* watched him closely, then shook his head and started back to the house. "Let me know when you come to your senses."

"Pass the potatoes," Miriam requested.

The evening milking had been completed, and the product stored. Still Elam was no closer to an answer than he had been earlier.

"Elam. *Elam.*"

"Jah?" He shook himself around. "Did you say something?" He looked to each of his sisters.

"I asked for the potatoes." Miriam nodded toward the bowl that sat in front of him.

He passed it to her as *Mamm* spoke. "You're not eating much tonight."

"Elam's in love." His *dat* turned twinkling eyes on him. *"Jah,* Elam?"

"We all know that," Johanna said. She was wise beyond her years. Or were his feelings that transparent?

"Did you know that Emily loves him, too?" *Dat* asked.

"Dat," Elam dropped his voice, hoping it would serve as a warning. He wasn't accustomed to chastising his *vatter,* but he

would if given no other choice.

Ruthie made a face. "Of course."

"What about what she told him today, and he said . . . what is it the *Englisch* say? 'Too bad so sad'?"

A chorus of "whats?" flew around the table.

"Why would you do that?"

"I hope she stomped on your foot."

"That's terrible."

Along with a few other phrases he couldn't make out.

"Elam," *Mamm* said. "Why would you do something like that?"

"Danki, Dat," Elam said, shooting his father a wilting look.

His *vatter* sat back, seemingly satisfied with the trouble he had caused.

"She loves Luke Lambright," Elam explained. "You all know that as well as I do."

"But Luke is gone," Becky said. "Jonah told Aaron and he told Billy and —"

"It is a sin to gossip, Becky Ann," *Mamm* said with a stern look.

Becky wilted.

"Just because he's left Wells Landing doesn't mean she doesn't love him any longer," Elam said. He had to put a stop to this and quickly.

"I think you should go after her." Norma

licked the applesauce off her spoon. Then pointed it at him. "She's *gut* for you."

Elam tried not to laugh. The situation was far from humorous, but tiny Norma's serious expression was his undoing.

"What's so funny?" Johanna took another bite of her applesauce and stared at him as if he'd taken leave of his senses.

Elam cleared his throat. "I think this conversation has gone on long enough."

"My thoughts exactly." Ruthie jumped up from the table and raced to the door to get his hat and coat. "You should get over there immediately and get this straightened out." She thrust the items toward him. "Now would be *gut, jah*?"

He closed his eyes and said a quick prayer for patience. Had his entire family lost their minds? "I am not going over there this time a'night."

"Why not?" *Dat* asked.

Another chorus of similar sentiments went up around the table, but Elam had had enough. "I'll be in the barn if anyone needs me." He stood and started for the door. But he stopped before he got there, turning around and pinning each of his family members with a stern stare. "For something important."

■ ■ ■ ■

But no one in the household was willing to let things go.

Couldn't they see it was hard enough for him to put one foot in front of the other each day without their silly notions that he and Emily belonged together?

Yet they were relentless, taking every opportunity to slip Emily's name into the conversation. Or mention the color purple. Or any number of references to make him recall the sweet time when he thought things might be different for him and Emily.

Thankfully the church-going Sunday brought some relief. At least no one talked to him about Emily during the three-hour service. Even better, she sat behind him so he didn't have to keep his gaze off the back of her head.

Pathetic. He was simply pathetic where she was concerned. But time was a healer. Maybe in a year or two he would be able to hear her name and not want to fall at her feet and beg for crumbs.

After the final prayer, the women prepared the tables and got the food ready to serve. Outside the barn, it began to snow. The sky had been threatening all morning, and the temperature dropped until the white flakes started falling. The children oohed and aahed and begged their parents to let them go outside and play. Yet all Elam could think about was the day in the snow with Emily. Maybe after five years everything, including the weather, wouldn't bring her to mind.

His father grabbed his plate and shot Elam a pointed look. "I'm going to find Emily."

Elam sighed. "*Dat,* I thought we had already covered this. The men and the women do not eat together. You can talk to her after the meal."

His *vatter* raised his chin to that defiant angle Elam was coming to know all too well. "I want to eat with Emily." He turned on his heel and disappeared into the milling church members before Elam could stop him.

As he saw it, he had two choices. He could follow after his *dat* and risk running into Emily — which was probably *Dat*'s plan from the beginning. Or he could let his father alone to do as he pleased. It wasn't like Elam could make his father behave.

That was the hardest part of his father's injury. A two-hundred-pound man-child was hard to control. With another sigh, he filled his own plate and found a quiet corner to eat his *middawk* alone.

"I want to eat with you today."

Emily whirled around to find James standing directly behind her. She pressed one hand to her beating heart. She had been on edge all day just waiting for the inevitable confrontation with Elam.

She had prayed to avoid it, but she had to prepare for it all the same.

All during the service, she had stared at the back of his head, nearly willing him to turn around and acknowledge she was there. She knew he wouldn't, but this dancing around each other was about to drive her batty. If she kept this up she'd have to move to a different church district to keep from having to see Elam every other week. And to keep her sanity.

"James, we talked about this. Men and women are supposed to eat separately."

"You sound like Elam." He made a face. "I see no reason why we shouldn't be allowed to eat together. You ate with me once before. Besides" — he lowered his voice for only her to hear — "I want to talk to you about something." He graced her with one of his innocent smiles. How could she say no?

She had missed him almost as much as she missed Elam. Almost. James and the rest of the Riehls had become so very important to her. It was a shame that she couldn't stand to go over to help them now that she and Elam were no longer courting. But she couldn't risk running in to him. It would be easier if he worked in a factory or even at a restaurant or furniture store. But dairy farmers were home all day long.

"Please?" James turned his green eyes to hers, the mischievous light almost drowned out by the sincerity she saw there.

"*Jah,* fine," she said with a sigh.

"Goodie."

She and James found a place out of the way and not as visible to most of the district. She settled down on a milking stool while James sat cross-legged in the hay.

"I've missed you coming by the house." James took too large a bite of his peanut butter sandwich.

Emily suppressed a laugh at the face he made.

"Yuck," he said, swallowing the bite nearly whole. "It's the creamy kind."

"What's wrong with creamy peanut butter?"

"It's not crunchy." James wiped off his tongue with his napkin, bringing laughter to

Emily's lips once more. She had been with him less than fifteen minutes and already she had laughed more than she had all week.

"So will you come by again?" His question was so innocent, it somehow seemed anything but.

Emily put the cracker she had been eating back on her plate. "Oh, James. I don't know if that's such a *gut* idea."

"It was a *gut* idea before."

"*Jah,* well, that was . . . before."

They sat in silence for a moment. He ate around his sandwich while she pushed the food on her plate in circles.

"He still loves you, you know."

Emily shook her head. "I hurt him."

"If he didn't love you, you wouldn't have the power to cause him pain."

Emily dropped her hand into her lap and stared at James. What happened to the childlike man who wanted everything purple? She could still see him lurking in those green eyes of his, but somehow they had taken on an edge of wisdom. Now James was a dangerous combination of a child who wasn't afraid to speak and a man who knew too much. "You know what I think? I think you use your injury to your favor. That way you always get what you want."

"Does that mean you'll come by the house for a visit?" He shot her a sly grin.

"James."

"What if I promise he won't be there?"

"How can you promise that?"

He shrugged. "You leave that up to me."

"I don't know."

"Please," he said. "We all miss you so much."

Emily's resolve started to crumble. "Why don't you come to my house?"

James shook his head as his lower lip protruded into an all-out pout. "That won't be the same."

"*Jah,* fine, okay." She hardly believed she had agreed to that.

"That's *brechdich.*" He grinned.

She wasn't sure exactly what was so magnificent about it, but his smile was worth it all.

CHAPTER TWENTY-SIX

"I still think this is a bad idea." Emily hopped down from the buggy and stared at Elam's house. Why had she agreed to this?

James. Plain and simple. She could deny the man almost nothing. In the short time that she had been coming to his house and helping him, she had fallen in love with him. Almost as deeply as she had his *sohn.* The courage in his eyes, his renewed joy for life, and his love for his family. And the color purple. All that endeared him to her more and more. She'd be lying to say that she wasn't grateful to be visiting with the Riehls once again. Yet it would be another lie to say she was calm and collected.

"Because you know it's the right thing to do." Mary slid out of the opposite side of the buggy and reached for the box of supplies behind the seat. "Even so, you made me come along."

"I told you why I need you here." The

snow from the day before had barely made it to the ground before melting back away. Emily couldn't even use the weather as an excuse.

Mary shot her a look. "You told me that you wanted my help. I know that I'm here as an extra buffer in case Elam comes in."

"James promised he wouldn't be here," Emily muttered.

"And you think he's not telling you the truth?"

Emily recalled the spirited light in the man's eyes. "I wouldn't put it past him, no."

As she spoke, Becky came out onto the porch, a scarf wrapped around her head and ears. "I'll take your horse, *jah?*" She skipped over to where Emily stood torn between the warmth of the house and the inevitable run-in with Elam. "Unless you want to take her. Elam's in the barn."

Mary laughed as Emily handed the reins to Becky and together the sisters made their way to the house.

They knocked once, and a muffled voice instructed them to come inside.

Emily looked to Mary who shrugged. Then she opened the door to the largest amount of purple things she had ever seen.

"Surprise!" James, Johanna, and Joy all stood behind the couch. Smiles stretched across their faces at their own handiwork.

Purple helium balloons hung from the ceiling, their purple ribbons trailing in the air. Purple hearts cut from construction paper decorated each one. There were purple streamers, a purple tablecloth on the table, and purple place mats and plates. Even the plastic cutlery was lavender.

"What is this?" It wasn't her birthday, or any one of theirs that she knew of. She turned to her sister. Mary shrugged, but her eyes sparkled with delight.

"It's for you and —"

"Would someone like to tell me what's going on here?"

Emily whirled about at the sound of Elam's voice.

His cheeks were pink from the cold, and he was breathing heavily as if he had sprinted into the house all the way from the barn. "Becky told me you slipped and . . ." His gaze fell on each of them in turn.

"That was my idea, *sohn,*" James said. "Forgive me, but I didn't know any other way to get you inside."

"Coming and asking me might have worked." Elam's mouth twisted into something akin to a frown.

"I had nothing to do with this." Emily threw her hands into the air in surrender and turned to make her way back outside. She hated harnessing Clover so soon after sending her to the barn, but she couldn't stay here.

"Now just hold on." James stepped forward. "We went to a lot of trouble to get this ready for the two of you, and you are both going to stay, have some cake, and talk this out."

"Talk what out?" Emily and Elam said at the same time. She turned to glare at him to find him already glaring back.

"This." Joy waved a hand between the two of them.

"It's gone on long enough," Johanna said.

She was so much like her *bruder,* Emily couldn't stifle her laugh.

"Take off your coat, and *kumm* over here." James waved her toward the table, pulling out a chair for her to sit in. She did as he asked, shedding her coat, her black travel bonnet, and the purple scarf she had been given by this caring, wonderful family.

As she walked across the wooden floor, she noticed it was covered with silk hydrangea petals and what could only be homemade purple confetti.

"Now you." James motioned for Elam to join her.

She closed her eyes for the merest of moments, praying that he would do as his father asked. Nothing might ever come of this afternoon, but his family had gone to a lot of work to make this possible. The least they could do would be pretend to enjoy it before going their separate ways.

She opened her eyes at the sound of Elam's steady footsteps drawing closer.

His chair scraped against the floor, and then he was seated across from her.

"On today's menu," James started, sounding for all it was worth like a proper *Englisch* waiter, "we have lilac cake." He took the lid off the domed cake stand to reveal a shockingly purple cake with creamy white frosting.

"It's okay," Johanna whispered. "It doesn't taste like lilacs." She pulled a face and made even her brother chuckle.

"We are also offering purple hearts and flowers." Joy opened the container of gelatin painstakingly cut into bite-sized shapes.

"And purple grape juice." Johanna swung her arm toward the pitcher, missing it by mere inches. "It's really red grape juice, but it looks purple to me."

Joy laughed and scooped her out of the chair and placed her feet safely on the floor. "We wanted you to have some time alone to . . . talk about . . . whatever. Perhaps you two will be able to work through this."

"And when you do, I want a new purple dress for the wedding." Johanna pointed her finger at each one of them.

"Now, if you'll excuse us . . ." The three of them put on their coats, and together with Mary and Becky, they tromped outside.

Emily had no idea when Elam's sister had come back into the house, but she was there all the same.

Once the door closed behind his family, Elam turned to her. "I'm sorry," he said.

"It's *allrecht*. I'll give them time to get down the road, and then I'll go." Her voice cracked on the final word. The last time she had talked to him, she humiliated herself, laying her feelings at his feet only to have him reject her.

"You don't have to do that." He laid his hand on top of hers where it rested on the table. His touch warmed her straight through. "I mean, they obviously went to a lot of trouble."

As much as she wanted to soak in his warmth and presence, she slid her hand from under his and stood to serve them cake.

Elam looked at the combination of purples before him. "This has my *dat* written all over it."

Emily couldn't stop her smile. "*Jah,* it does for sure." She poured them both some grape juice and sat back across from him.

She bowed her head to say a prayer before eating, but only words of hope and new chances came to mind. *Lord, if it be Your will . . . please let it be Your will . . .*

Emily lifted her head and picked up her fork. She set it down again. "I'm sorry." She tossed her napkin onto the table and stood. "I cannot do this."

In an instant, she was on her feet and heading for the door.

"Don't."

His one, quietly spoken word stopped her in her tracks.

"Don't what?" She said the words toward the door, unable to turn and face him. If she did, she would be more apt to break down than hold herself steady. She couldn't embarrass herself like that again. Pride might be a sin, but she had to hold on to what was left of hers.

"Don't leave."

She heard the scrape of his chair and closed her eyes against all the emotions raging inside her. Love, hope, faith.

"Have you ever made a mistake?" he asked, his voice drawing nearer with each step.

"Jah," she whispered, still unable to find the courage to face him. What if he didn't mean what she thought? She couldn't take any more heartbreak. She just couldn't.

"I made one of those."

"When?" she asked.

"Many times," he whispered in return.

She turned, her eyes flying open. He was close, so very close she could reach out and lay a hand on his chest over the spot where his heart beat. Did it beat for her? Dare she hope?

"As did I." She licked her suddenly dry lips. "I thought I was in love with someone, but it turns out I was wrong."

"Jah?" he returned.

"That's not even the worst part. See, I let the man I truly love walk away."

"I'm here now." His words were barely above a whisper.

Oh, how she wanted him to take her into his arms and kiss her. Instead he took a step back and another. His hands shook as he pushed his hair off his forehead.

Had she misunderstood? "I love you." She sighed the words, unable to say them louder than the sound of butterfly wings.

"I love you, too."

It was more than she could have hoped for. "You do?"

"Did you think I stopped?"

She shook her head. "But I wasn't sure if you could ever forgive me for all the foolishness I put you through."

"Can you forgive me for not being patient?"

"Of course."

"Does that mean we can have a second chance?"

Emily smiled. "I would like that very much."

Elam's eyes drifted closed for a second, as if he was saying a small prayer of thanks. Then he opened them again and smiled. "*Gut,* then. Let's have some purple cake to celebrate."

They ate the cake, laughed, and talked, but as much as they had promised second chances, something was amiss.

Emily tried not to show her disappointment. She so badly wanted Elam to take her into his arms and seal their new promises with a kiss. But he remained distant, jovial, and caring, but apart from her just the same.

And she couldn't help but wonder where it would really go from there.

"I don't know, Mary," Emily said that night

as she lay beside her sister. "Something is wrong."

"How so?"

"I thought he would have kissed me, you know. I wanted him to."

"And he didn't?" Mary turned on her side. "Not even once?"

"Nay." Emily hated admitting that. It just brought home all the mistakes she had made and all the times she had hurt Elam, not even realizing she held that power.

"Has he kissed you before?" Mary asked.

Emily's cheeks flushed with heat at the memory of the kiss she and Elam had shared in the front yard at Caroline Fitch's house. "Oh, *jah.*"

"Then perhaps you should ask him."

Emily sucked in a sharp breath. "I could never do that."

In the darkness, Mary smiled. "You will if you want that kiss."

Mary's words stayed with her all during the night and into the next morning. For once Emily was glad that her job at milking time forced her to be alone. She needed time to think things through. Maybe she was being fearful for nothing. After all, Elam had said he loved her.

She recalled the look on his face as he said

the words. She was certain he meant them. Yet maybe he needed a bit more time before he could fully get over the trials of their relationship.

She looked down at the purple cast. The doctor said her arm was healing nicely. A couple more weeks and she could have the cumbersome thing removed. It was a constant reminder of the foolish mistakes she had made.

Mary poked her head into the milking room. "We are done, *jah?*"

She gave the aluminum vat one last swipe. *"Jah."*

"Gut. Come on," Mary challenged. "I'll race you to the house."

How many times had her sister called those words to her over the years? More than she could count.

"You're on," she said and sprinted for the door.

Mary was on her heels as she rounded the barn and passed their other sisters. Susannah took off after them, while Rose and Bea shook their heads and continued to walk.

Her sisters' footsteps pounded the hard ground behind her. Emily turned up the speed. She ducked her head as she ran, then looked toward the porch. Elam sat in the rocker as if waiting. Her footsteps faltered, and she stumbled to a halt. Mary and Susannah laughed and continued toward the porch.

Elam stood as Mary and Susannah raced up the steps. Mary saw him first, grinding to a surprised halt. Susannah laughed as she rang the bell, the clear winner of the race. Then she saw Elam and stopped.

What was he doing here?

Emily couldn't read his face. Somehow she made her feet move toward the porch. Despite her sprint, the brisk January wind cut right through.

"Let's go into the house." Mary cast a pointed glance toward Susannah.

"But this looks interesting," Susannah protested.

Mary grabbed her by the arm and tugged her inside.

Rose and Bea finally caught up. *"Guder mariye,"* they called as they bounded up the steps.

"Guder mariye," he repeated, though his gaze never left Emily.

Her sisters giggled, then slammed into the house.

Emily was left alone with Elam.

His expression was unreadable. "I don't think we've ever met," he started. "My name is Elam Riehl. I've seen you at church and in town." He cleared his throat.

Hope rose inside Emily. Hope for the future and the promise of second chances. "My name is Emily," she returned. "Emily Ebersol. I'm the bishop's daughter."

He smiled. "I know. I asked around about you."

"You did?"

"*Jah.* See, I think you're real pretty and word is you are sweet and funny. Caring, I believe came up several times."

Is that how he saw her? She didn't need to go inside against the cold. His compliment warmed her straight through. "I'm the bishop's daughter. I'm supposed to set a *gut* example for others."

"*Ach,* it is more than that. I heard of this family whose *vatter* was injured. Folks say you helped him regain a lot of his life back. He was unable to feed himself at times and now he's back to being a husband and father. He's even working on his dairy farm again."

Tears welled in her eyes and blurred her vision as he spoke. "I only did what needed to be done."

"That may be," he continued. "But that family is mighty grateful. So grateful that they told their son to come over here and ask to marry you."

"Is that so?" Happiness burst inside her. How could she have ever thought she loved Luke? Not when what she really wanted — what she really *needed* — was standing in front of her now.

"He told them he needed some time first."

"Oh?" Her heart stopped.

"*Jah,* he wants a little time to court you. Get to know you. See, he missed out on a lot, and he wants to share that with you. Are you willing to court him for a while and perhaps marry him next November?"

"*Jah,*" she said, somehow managing not to throw herself at him in joy. "But only if he's you."

Saturday night racing was always a good time. Luke was happy for the first time in a while. He loved the mixed smells of the track: burnt rubber, burnt popcorn, and oil. The hum of the engines was like a mother's lullaby. He had gotten the sponsorship, paid his friend for the damage to his car, and gone to work in one of Gus Hardin's fried chicken restaurants. Life was good.

Sissy sashayed up next to him. She stood close enough that he could breathe in the sweet scent of her hair and the honeysuckle body lotion she preferred. But she did not touch him. He found it refreshing, this do-over they now shared.

He knew she was used to *Englisch* boys and their dating habits, but he was bound and determined to court her the same as he would if she were Amish. They were taking things slow, but he enjoyed taking the time to get to know her.

She leaned in a bit closer to be heard over the roar of the engines. "Let's get something to eat."

The track wouldn't officially be open for a couple more months, but Johnny was good to let them practice whenever they wanted.

"Okay." He wasn't scheduled on the track for another hour. Plenty of time to get a bite to eat and get ready to race.

He turned, placing his hand at the small of Sissy's back to escort her to the break room.

Behind them, tires screeched. He turned as metal crunched, scraped the side wall of the track, and then there was fire.

Luke didn't think twice. He let go of Sissy and raced down the stairs and into the arena.

Car number thirty-two. His friend Justin's car.

He wasn't the first one on the scene. The guys who worked the pits were there, each one holding a spewing fire extinguisher.

Why wasn't Justin out of the car?

Luke ripped off his jacket and raced toward the burning vehicle. He could hear the shouts around him, but he couldn't tell if they were yelling for him to stop or to keep going. But he knew what he had to do.

He stuck his head into the car's window hole. Justin was slumped over the steering wheel unconscious. Luke wrapped his coat around Justin's body and used it to drag his friend from the car.

The fire roared in his ears, the heat burned his face. The smell of burnt hair and fabric permeated his senses. But he had to get Justin to safety.

Protect him, whispered through him as he dragged Justin away from the wreckage. A sixth sense kicked in. Luke doubled his efforts to get Justin to safety. Then he shielded his friend, throwing his body over Justin's just in time. All the air was sucked from the arena. A whoosh followed. Then the world slowed down. The explosion rocked the ground beneath him and everything went black.

CHAPTER TWENTY-SEVEN

"I like this new heater," Emily said. The battery-powered warmth heated the air around their feet and legs and made today's buggy ride possible.

"Now I know why we court in the spring and summer and marry when it gets cold," Elam groused.

She laughed. "Having second thoughts?"

"About you? Never. About the weather? Definitely."

"How about this?" She scooted a little closer to him.

"Better."

It had been just over a week since she and Elam had decided to start over. He had yet to kiss her, instead taking things slow as they learned to trust each other again. Luke's name had not been brought up once.

Emily had gone over to Elam's house every day of the week. She played cards, dice, and board games with James and Johanna, loving the time she spent with this *wunderbaar* family. She could hardly believe James was the same man she had seen just a few months before. She could hardly believe that in another few months, she and Elam would be married.

Her father had already granted them the *zeugnis,* the contract they needed to get married. A small part of Emily wished Elam would break tradition as her friend Caroline had, to get married out of season, but the two of them didn't have the same excuse to go against the way things were done. Caroline's family had to travel all the way from Tennessee to attend the wedding. Andrew had been worried about his future in-laws running into bad weather to prevent their travel to and from Wells Landing. Who could have known that Caroline's *dat* would announce that his family was moving out to be closer to their *dochder* and *grosskind*?

"Where are we going again?" she asked.

"I told you, it's a surprise."

"And I told you I don't like surprises."

"You're going to like this one." Elam smiled. "Well, the truth is, it's more of a surprise for *Dat* than you. But I still wanted you to come along."

"Now I'm really intrigued."

Elam pulled on the reins, and the horses

made the turn down a familiar driveway.

"Why are we going to Caroline and Andrew's?" she asked.

Elam braked the buggy and switched off the heater. "I'm going to get *Dat* a dog."

Emily smiled and slid from the buggy. "Did you bring me along to help you pick one out or so I could hold him on the way home?"

He returned her grin. "Both."

"*Goedemiddag,*" Andrew called from the front porch. He wrapped his scarf around his face and ducked his head against the wind.

"Perhaps I should have picked a warmer day to choose a pup," Elam said.

Emily pulled her coat a little tighter around her. "*Jah,* maybe."

They followed Andrew into the barn where the puppies scampered in the hay.

"They're all good dogs," Andrew said. "Esther and my *onkle* Abe got one from the first litter."

Emily was well acquainted with Moxie. He had been intended for Caroline and Emma and somehow wound up staying in town with Abe and Esther. They now lived behind the bakery Esther owned with Moxie serving as guard dog and companion. Abe Fitch still ran his furniture store and produced some of the finest handcrafted pieces around. Though these days he was more apt to be snacking with Esther while his other nephew, Danny, worked the cash register.

"Are you keeping one?" Elam asked.

Andrew pointed to the smallest one in the litter. A tiny female dog that seemed a little more timid than the rest. "Caroline wants that one." He shook his head. "She is always for the underdog."

Considering what all Caroline had been through, moving to Wells Landing alone and pregnant with an *Englischer*'s child, it was no wonder she rooted for those who fell behind.

The puppies rolled and tumbled, playing in the hay without a care in the world. One in particular caught Emily's attention. She had one black ear and one white one as if God had drawn a line down her face and only painted one half. She was a bit smaller than the others, though not as small as Caroline's choice, and she gave as good as she got.

Emily laughed as the puppy crouched down on her front paws, her rear sticking up in the air as she barked at her litter mates.

"She's the one," Elam said, pointing to her as he chuckled.

"I think so, too."

"Then she's yours." Andrew scooped up the puppy, depositing her into Emily's arms.

The pup immediately starting licking her face and neck above the scarf she wore to ward off the chill.

"She's perfect." Emily cradled the dog in her arms as the three of them made their way out of the barn.

The rattle of a buggy rig met her ears.

"That's Jonah Miller," Andrew said.

"He's driving real fast," Elam added.

Jonah was going a bit faster than necessary, but not enough to be dangerous. He pulled over when he saw the three of them and jumped out. He ran to them, breathless with the effort.

"It's Luke," he wheezed. "He's hurt."

Fear squeezed her heart. "What?"

"Someone from the racetrack called Joseph. Luke's in the hospital. In Intensive Care."

Dear Lord, please don't let this be happening.

"Where is he?" Andrew asked.

Jonah sucked in another gulp of air. "He's in Tulsa. Joseph is already on his way there."

Emily turned to Elam. "I have to go to him."

All she could think about was Luke alone

with the *Englisch,* lying injured in a hospital bed with no one to care for him.

If only he had stayed . . .

Elam's mouth pressed into a hard thin line. *"Jah,"* was all he said.

She thrust the squirming puppy into Andrew's arms. She couldn't handle all that unbridled joy when she felt as if she was coming undone.

This was all her fault. If somehow she could have talked him into staying. She should have tried harder. And now he could die.

Dear Lord, please help him.

She turned her eyes to Elam, silently begging him to understand. She and Jonah were among Luke's best *freinden.* She couldn't abandon him in his time of need.

"I'll go call Ben Smith."

They rode in silence all the way to Tulsa. The drive wasn't extremely long, but with each pounding of her heart she feared for Luke. *What if . . . what if . . . what if . . .* kept hammering through her brain.

She glanced over to Elam who sat next to her in the backseat of Ben Smith's car. The Mennonite driver knew Luke as well and didn't charge them anything for the trip. Emily decided to bake him some cookies or

461

a cake in appreciation for his generosity.

Elam faced the front, his eyes on the road ahead. His hands rested in his lap, but there was a tension about him that fairly hummed.

She was afraid she had hurt him once again. And she was afraid this time the gap between them could not be bridged.

"I'm not sure if they'll let us all in to see him," Ben said, glancing in the rearview mirror at them. "But we can try."

They didn't even know how badly he'd been hurt. Only that there had been a wreck and an explosion and now Luke was in the hospital.

"Jah." It was the first word Elam had uttered since they'd gotten into the car.

"I'll drop you two off at the door and find a parking space."

Emily nodded gratefully. The last thing she wanted to do was trudge through a sea of cars to get to the hospital doors. She just had to see Luke and know that her lifelong friend was going to be okay.

Emily did her best not to race into the automatic doors of the hospital and over to the elevators. She took a deep breath to calm herself. They were there. And about to see Luke. There was no sense losing her head at this point.

She and Elam garnered several curious stares as they made their way across the lobby. Emily hated the squeak of her rubber-soled walking shoes against the overwaxed tiles. The sound was obnoxious in the hushed solitude of the hospital lobby.

Elam walked directly to the elevators.

"Shouldn't we check the map to know what floor?"

"I know what floor." His words were somber and heavy.

Emily bit her lip. She stepped into the elevator cautiously. It seemed to shift under her feet. She reached out for Elam to steady herself, but given the dark look clouding his expression she grabbed the handrail instead. "Is this where they brought your *dat*?"

He gave one small nod and pushed the button to take them to the sixth floor.

The elevator ride seemed to take the longest time. Her own nervousness mixed with Elam's withdrawn behavior and the blatant stare from their riding companions set Emily's teeth on edge. Finally they reached their floor, and she raced to the waiting room.

Joseph sat slumped in a chair, his head at an odd angle, a cup of coffee on the table next to him. Others waited for their loved ones, but he was the only person there for Luke.

Her decision to come solidified in her mind as she knelt before Luke's uncle.

"Joseph." She touched his shoulder, and he jerked awake. Blinking several times, he rubbed his eyes and yawned. "Emily."

"We came as soon as we heard. What happened?"

Joseph pushed himself up in his seat. "I'm not going to lie. It's bad. We almost lost him a couple of times in the night. But he's stable now."

Emily blinked back her tears. She might not hold a romantic love for Luke any longer, but she couldn't imagine the world without him and his bright smile.

"A friend of his crashed his car. Luke went out to help him. The car exploded. Luke shielded his friend's body with his own." Joseph's eyes filled with tears. "His back was burned from the fire." He shuddered. "A piece of the car fell on him. His legs are shattered. His hips, too. They say he'll walk again, but only after he relearns how."

But he was alive, and that was the main thing.

Joseph squeezed her hand where it lay on his shoulder. "It's in God's hands now."

"When I told you I would pray for you, this wasn't exactly what I meant."

Luke's eyes cracked open just a bit, but enough to see the tears sparkling in Emily's deep blue eyes.

He smiled or at least one side of his mouth did. The other was too swollen to do anything but stay in place. He couldn't see it of course, but he could sure feel it.

Every nerve ending in his body was on fire, shooting sparks that could only be assuaged by the massive painkillers they had been giving him. The pills made him sleepy and jumbled his thoughts so he waited until he couldn't stand it any longer before finally giving in and taking them.

"Emily." His voice was like sandpaper on wool, rough and full of snags. From what he had been told, he was lucky to be alive, so he couldn't very well complain.

She sat down in the chair next to him.

"Where's Sissy?" he asked. She had been in the chair when he had fallen asleep, but now she was gone. Which was strange considering she hadn't left his side since he'd been admitted.

"Who's Sissy?"

The bathroom door squeaked open, then clicked back closed. "I am."

"Sissy," he rasped. His throat was so dry. They said it was from the medication, but he knew the fire had sucked the moisture right out of him. "Drink."

She had been such a *gut* nurse to him and now was no exception. She moved to his bedside and held the straw while he wet his throat.

"This is my friend, Emily." His lids were getting heavy, so heavy he couldn't keep them open.

"Hi, Emily. I'm Sissy, Luke's girlfriend."

He smiled and drifted back to sleep.

Emily sat in the waiting room next to Elam, her thoughts as topsy-turvy as a crazy quilt pattern. Joseph had come by to tell them that he would be moving into the city until Luke recovered. No one blamed him. Luke was going to need constant care over the next few months.

The doctor said Luke was stable and should be able to be moved out of Intensive Care once they knew they held the infections at bay.

The racetrack was covering the hospital bills and all of the rehabilitation that Luke would need.

Emily was glad that Luke had met some *gut Englisch* people to help him through. Ben Smith had gone in to see Luke and give his regards, then the three of them — Emily, Elam, and Ben — would head back to Wells Landing. All should be well in the world, but it wasn't.

She could feel the tension in Elam and feared the worst for the two of them. They had such a fragile bond, recently repaired and so very delicate. She would do nothing — *nothing* — to endanger it, and yet somehow she felt as if she had.

"I had to come. You know that, right?"

He stared at her as if he didn't speak the language.

"I mean, I'm Luke's friend. I'm the bishop's daughter."

She pushed to her feet and started pacing, hating her anxiousness, hating her squeaky shoes, hating that she had messed up once again.

"Emily, sit down."

"I can't," she cried, the day, the stress, and the worry getting the better of her.

"There's no need to cry. The doctors all say Luke will be fine, eventually. It's going to take a while to heal, but God was watching over him."

Emily stopped and turned to face him.

467

"What about us, Elam? Was God watching out for us?"

His brow puckered into a familiar frown. "What are you talking about?"

"I did it again." She collapsed into her seat, her energy draining away with her admission. "I messed up."

"What did you do again, Emily? What are you talking about?"

"I'm talking about you sitting over there all angry because I came to see Luke. I love him, but only as a friend."

"I know." Yet the frown remained.

"Then why are you mad at me?"

He shook his head as if clearing his thoughts. "I'm not mad at you."

Tears welled in her eyes. "But you are."

"I think I would know if I was mad."

"And would you tell me?"

"*Jah,* I made the promise to be open and honest with you."

"Then what's wrong?"

He sighed, his gaze darting around the austere waiting room. "This is where we came with *Dat,*" he said. His voice dropped low and somber. "I sat here so many days not knowing if he was going to live or die. Those are days I never want to live again."

"And being here is bringing it all back?"

"*Jah.*"

"And you knew when we left Wells Landing," she said. It was not a question.

"Jah."

"But you came anyway?"

"Of course."

"Why?"

"Because it meant so much to you to be here for Luke."

Tears tracked down her cheeks. "Elam, I don't know what to say."

He smiled. "Just tell me you love me."

She returned his grin. "You love me."

He chuckled and stood, pulling her to her feet as Ben shuffled back down the hallway toward them. "Close enough."

The ride back to Wells Landing was so very different from the ride to Tulsa. Ben Smith drove with Emily and Elam in the backseat, but the tension was gone from his shoulders.

As jealous as he had been of Emily's previous relationship with Luke, he could only wish the man well. To have him hurt and near dead for a time made Elam pray even harder for his recovery.

But it was even more than that. Seeing Emily and Luke in the same room together, him introducing his new *Englisch* girlfriend, all of these proved to Elam without any doubts that he held Emily's love for his own.

He couldn't be happier.

"I'll swing by and take Emily home first." Ben glanced in the mirror at the two of them.

"Just drop me at Emily's, too. I can get home from there." Elam gently squeezed Emily's fingers and resisted the urge to raise her hand to his lips and kiss each fingertip.

He hated that he worried her and that she'd thought he was angry. He had learned his lesson about jealousy and love. Now he wanted to spend the rest of his life proving his love to her day by day.

"Where is everyone?" Emily asked as Ben pulled the car into her drive.

"Probably at my house planning our wedding." Elam laughed.

Ben smiled at the two of them. "I thought maybe," he said, shaking Elam's hand and slapping him jovially on the back.

"Are you sure I can't pay you for taking us to Tulsa?" Elam asked.

Ben twirled his car keys around one finger. "I wouldn't hear of it."

Elam nodded as Ben headed back to his car. The Mennonite stopped and turned to face them once more. "Well, there is one thing."

"*Jah?*" Elam asked.

"Invite me to the wedding?"

"You got it."

Together they turned back toward the house. "Where do you think everyone is?"

"There's no telling," he said as Ben Smith drove away. "Let's get inside where it's warm."

The house was empty when they got inside. Elam couldn't say the fact didn't please him. He treasured any time he could find that left him alone with Emily.

She perched on the edge of the sofa as he hung their coats by the door.

"We're okay, *jah*?" She looked at her hands in her lap. Her fingers were intertwined and twisted together in her apron.

"Is something bothering you, Emily?" He sat down next to her, careful not to sit too close. It would be months before they could say their vows. There was a lot of courting to do between now and then.

"*Nay*. It's just . . ."

He hooked one finger beneath her chin, lifting her gaze to his. "What is on your mind, *mei liewe*?"

"Am I your love?" The words slipped from her lips, breathless and burning.

"Have we not already covered this?" he asked, confused by her frown of worry.

"*Jah*, it's just that . . . well . . ."

"We promised to be honest and true," he

471

said. "Say what's on your mind, Emily Jane."

"Uhum, why haven't you kissed me again? I mean since we worked things out."

He managed to suppress his laughter. Her eyes flashed such a serious light, he didn't want her to think he was making fun. "You want me to kiss you?"

"Well, *jah.*"

"And that will settle your mind about us?"

"It would help. I mean, you've told me that you love me, but I —"

"You want me to show you," Elam supplied.

"*Jah,* please," she whispered.

Elam smiled, then lowered his head and kissed the bishop's daughter.

EPILOGUE

Somehow Emily and Elam managed to wait until the last week of October to get married. It wasn't easy. Emily was so very ready to start her life with Elam, but he insisted they have time to court. He wanted her to have the experience of Sunday drives and picnics and all the other things girls enjoyed.

Secretly she thought he wanted to replace all her memories of Luke with memories of him. And in truth she was okay with that, too.

"I've never been to a purple Amish wedding before."

Emily whirled around at the sound of the familiar voice behind her. "Luke!"

She wanted to throw her arms around him, but he looked barely secure on his own two feet. Aluminum crutches were clamped to his wrists, but all in all, he was the same ol' Luke. If their presence was any indication, he hadn't completely remastered the

473

art of walking, but he was well on his way.

"You remember Sissy?"

Emily smiled at the pretty blonde standing to Luke's left. "How are you, Sissy?"

The young woman smiled. "Thank you for inviting us. It was a beautiful ceremony."

"Danki."

"Even if it was purple." Luke made a face.

"Technically," she said, "it is lilac."

Luke rolled his eyes good-naturedly. "Technically it is purple."

"What's wrong with purple?" Sissy asked, looking from one of them to the other.

"Lilac is not a normal color for Amish weddings," Luke explained.

"So what color are Amish weddings usually?" she asked.

"Blue," Luke answered.

"All of them?" Sissy's eyes grew wide.

"Jah," Emily said.

"She only got away with it because her dad is the bishop," Luke groused good-naturedly.

Emily stuck out her tongue at him, so grateful they could joke the way they used to. Even after all this time.

"But why purple?" Sissy asked. "Is that your favorite color?"

Emily smiled. "In a way, *jah.* But more importantly, Elam's *dat* has a thing for purple. I couldn't deny him this." She pointed to where James stood holding two-month-old Hollis Fitch.

Andrew and Caroline's new son had been named after her father, Hollis Hostetler, and immediately dubbed Holly by those around him. Emily wondered if the child would ever live down the name. That and the fact that his gown matched the lilac James had chosen for the ceremony. It was a *gut* thing the Amish were against photography. There would be no proof of this to show in the years to come.

"You look beautiful," Luke said, staring at Emily with wonder in his eyes. "Very happy."

"I am happy." She smiled at him. "What about you?"

He cast a quick look at Sissy. "Yeah," he said. "It's been slow, but Sissy's father has been good to me. I'm working a little in the garage. Fixing the cars and such. I don't think I'll be ready for the upcoming season, but the next one for sure."

"What about Justin?" Emily asked.

"He came by the other day to check on everyone. I don't think he'll ever come back to racing," Luke said. "His *dat* got him a job selling insurance."

She wasn't sure exactly what that meant,

but Justin's reluctance to drive again was understandable. After nearly being blown to pieces, it surprised Emily that Luke wanted to return to the fast-paced, dangerous world. Then again, Luke was a born driver: easygoing, adventurous, and cool under pressure. She was so very *froh* he had found happiness in the *Englisch* world.

"There you are." Elam came up behind her, standing close as he greeted their guests.

A few short months ago she would have worried about his reaction to finding her talking to Luke, but those days were a thing of the past. Today they had pledged their love and their lives together. They were secure and committed. Funny how God's will worked.

Luke nodded in greeting to Elam, not exactly a warm welcome, but not all-out hostile either. He turned to Sissy. "Are you ready to go meet everyone?"

She smiled. "Lead the way." She looked to Emily and Elam. "Thank you again. Congratulations." Then she and Luke disappeared into the crowd of well-wishers.

"Have you seen *Dat*?"

Emily pointed to where James cradled Holly Fitch in his arms.

"I think he's getting in some practice."

A flush started somewhere around her neck and worked its way to her hairline. "Are you talking about us?"

She knew Elam wanted a family. She did, too. It was something they had talked about many times in the last few months.

It tickled Emily that Elam blushed at the meaning behind her words as well.

"I mean *Mamm.*" He pointed to where Joy Riehl stood one hand on her midriff, the other resting at her side. A slight curve rounded a body that months ago had seemed thin and frail.

"I thought maybe she was just putting on a little weight. You know, after everything."

Elam smiled and shrugged. "I think it might be more than that. Just a hunch."

Emily's heart surged. What wonderful news! "You're not worried about him, are you?"

Elam shook his head. "He might not be the same as he was a couple of years ago, but he's still a *gut* man, a *gut* father."

James was kind and loving. He cared about his children and his wife. Emily was proud to be a part of such a *wunderbaar* family.

"Elam." Becky hurried over to where they stood, hooking her arm through her *bruder*'s before trying to tug him away. "You said you would talk to Billy Beiler today."

"I did?" He looked to Emily for confirmation. "Did I?"

"Better get it over with."

Everyone expected that soon Billy would ask Elam and James to be allowed to court Becky.

Mary, Becky, Aaron, and Billy had all joined the church at the end of the summer. Emily had a feeling a big wedding season was building for next year.

Elam shrugged and allowed his sister to lead him away.

"How does it feel to be married?" Caroline Fitch sidled up to Emily and slipped one arm around her waist.

"Oh, Caroline. I'm so very happy." She returned her friend's sideways hug.

"You look happy," Caroline said.

"And no one deserves that more." Lorie Kauffman came up on Emily's other side.

"You're next," Caroline joked.

But Lorie shook her head. "I don't know."

"Trouble with Jonah?" Emily asked.

But it was more than that. Lorie hadn't attended the baptism classes that had been held in the spring. It would be another two years before the next classes would be held. She couldn't join the church until then. Even though Jonah Miller, her on-again, off-again boyfriend had bent his knee that very summer.

"Let's not talk about such things today," Lorie pleaded. "Today is supposed to be a joyful day."

And it was.

Emily let her gaze wander around the room at all the familiar and happy faces. All their sisters were sprinkled throughout the room, easily recognizable in their distinctive lilac dresses. The twins with their shiny red hair, Norma and Johanna eating cake from the same plate, two forks, one slice. Becky looked both shy and knowing as she watched her brother and Billy Beiler talk. No doubt Elam was stunning him with talk of the new milking machine he'd purchased just last week. Bea stood next to Rose as she talked to William Brontranger. If Emily knew that look at all, a romance was budding between the two young teens. Susannah talked in her over-the-top, animated way while Mary scanned the crowd, no doubt looking for Aaron Miller. Emily would be surprised if Aaron didn't ask her father for permission to court Mary in the next couple of months.

Jonah, Andrew, and Luke stood together, all laughing and talking about subjects only *buwe* understood. Sissy stood close, a confused wrinkle across her brow, even as her lips continued to smile. James cooed at baby Holly while Joy looked on, a sweet smile on her lips.

And her husband. From across the room, Elam's clear green eyes met hers, and Emily felt his gaze, like a caress. She never knew it was possible to love someone as much as she loved Elam. Her steady and true husband. She was grateful, fortunate, and blessed that he was a part of her life.

His lips lifted at the corners in a smile full of promise and more. Emily smiled in return, thinking of the night ahead. Her first night as Elam's wife.

Jah, God's hand was indeed at work. And Emily was so glad He touched the lives of them all.

GLOSSARY OF AMISH TERMS

ach oh
Aemen Amen
allrecht all right
baremlich terrible
bu/buwe boy/boys
brechdich magnificent
bruder brother
danki thanks
Dat/dat Dad/dad
Deutsch Pennsylvania Dutch
dochder/dochdern daughter/daughters
dummle hurry
eck special place for the bride and groom at
  the corner of the wedding table
eldra parents
Englisch non-Amish person
fraa wife
frack dress
freind/freinden friend/friends
froh happy
geb acht be careful

geh go
Gern gschehne You're welcome
Goedemiddag Good afternoon (greeting)
grank sick
grossmammi grandmother
guck look
Guder mariye Good morning (greeting)
gut good
gut himmel good heavens
halt stop
haus house
hochmut pride
hungerich hungry
jah yes
kaffi coffee
kapp prayer covering, cap
katzfisch catfish
kinner children/grandchildren
kumm come
liebschdi dear child
mach schnell hurry up (make quickly)
maedel girl
Mamm/mamm Mom/mom
meidung shunning
middawk noon meal
mudder mother
nachtess supper
naerfich nervous
nay no
nix nothing

Onkle/onkle Uncle/uncle
Ordnung book of rules
riewe red beets
rumspringa running around time (at age sixteen)
schee pretty
shveshtah sister/sisters
sohn son
Vatter/vatter Father/father
Was iss letz? What's wrong?
wunderbaar wonderful

The employees of Thorndike Press hope you have enjoyed this Large Print book. All our Thorndike, Wheeler, and Kennebec Large Print titles are designed for easy reading, and all our books are made to last. Other Thorndike Press Large Print books are available at your library, through selected bookstores, or directly from us.

For information about titles, please call:
    (800) 223-1244

or visit our Web site at:
    http://gale.cengage.com/thorndike

To share your comments, please write:
    Publisher
    Thorndike Press
    10 Water St., Suite 310
    Waterville, ME 04901